SEEDS
OF
DOMINION
LEGACY OF DECEIT

SEEDS
OF
DOMINION
LEGACY OF DECEIT

QUINCY J. ALLEN

Eldros Legacy Press
P.O. Box 292
Englewood, Colorado 80151

Cover Art by:
Jake Caleb

Cover Design by:
Jake Caleb, Sean Olsen, Melissa Gay & Quincy J. Allen

Map Design by:
Sean Stallings

Ordering Information:

Quantity sales. Special discounts are available on quantity purchases by corporations, associations, and others. For details, contact us at the address above or via our website.

Seeds of Dominion / Quincy J. Allen — 1st ed.

ISBN: 978-1-959994-14-5

DEDICATION

First and foremost, this book is dedicated to my wife, Victoria,
without whom none of this would be possible.

It is also dedicated to the Eldros Legacy founders, the rest of the
Eldros Legacy team, and specifically, Todd Fahnestock, who
has been cobalt to my plutonium for some time now.

WHAT IS ELDROS LEGACY?

The Eldros Legacy is a multi-author, shared-world, mega-epic fantasy project managed by four Founders who share the vision of a new, expansive, epic fantasy world. In the coming years the Founders committed themselves to creating multiple storylines where they and many others will explore and write about a world once ruled by tyrannical giants.

The Founders are working on four different primary storylines on four different continents. Over the coming years, those four storylines will merge into a single meta story where fates of all races on Eldros will be decided.

In addition, a growing list of guest authors, short story writers, and other contributors will delve into virtually every corner of each continent. It's a grand design, and the Founders have high hopes that readers will delight in exploring every nook and cranny of the Eldros Legacy.

So, please join us and explore the world of Eldros and the epic tales that will be told by great story tellers, for Here There Be Giants!

We encourage you to follow us at www.eldroslegacy.com to keep up with everything going on. If you sign up there, you'll get our newsletter and announcements of new book releases. You can also follow up on FaceBook at facebook.com/groups/eldroslegacy.

Sincerely,

Todd, Marie, Mark, and Quincy
(The Founders)

THE CHRONICLER
SEEDS OF DOMINION

The man in the stocks had been there for longer than anyone could guess.

He stood on a rise before a valley that contained broken buildings, collapsed walls, and a single metal tower. The ancient city behind him had been abandoned in another age, but the man remained, bent over, gnarled hands and gray-haired head stuffed through the holes of his forever prison.

He was a storyteller, and since he'd first begun telling his tales a year ago, the crowds had thinned, but there was one who stayed. A young man with blond hair and a tanned face. He wore a cowl pulled low over his head to protect himself from the summer sun. No matter how many times the old man told the same story, the young man remained in rapt attention:

"Do you know the story of the Second War of the Giants…?" the old man asked for the thousandth time. "I have told you about Khyven the Unkillable, how he discovered his magic. I have told you about Lorelle and her alliance with the Dark. I have told you about Rhenn and her journey without end…

"But I have not told you about Rellen, the one who sacrificed himself at the ultimate moment of the war. Khyven the Unkillable was the sword of destiny in that final battle, but Rellen's cut was deepest.

"How do I know? Oh, I know, young man. I know because I was there.

"I was there the day the blood goddess Nissra was loosed upon Daemanon. I was there when Abissar the Defiler received the Seeds of Dominion. And I was there when the Guardian Rellen ascended to the heavens…

"The heir to the throne of Pelinon, Rellen chose to guard the kingdom with his sword and his magic instead. He did not seek power, only justice. Abissar the Defiler tried to bind Rellen in machinations. Nhevalos the Betrayer tried to steal Khyven's victory, but it was Rellen who turned the tables and saved his brother. And because he did, Eldros endured.

"I'm going to tell you his story, the true story of the Guardian Rellen who held the demon armies at bay...."

MAPS

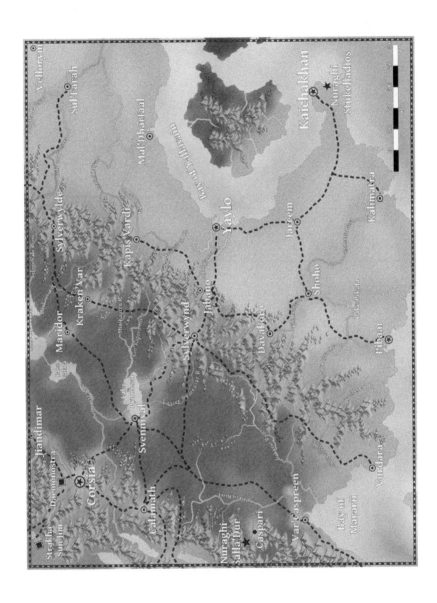

DEIHMANKOIOS

Thuroi Bakstadae'os

The Wyrm Lands

CH

Strakh

Strakha Ue

SOO KARI'MA
(Plains of The Dog Soldiers)

Strakha Kleema

Strakha Khar

Stra Ta

Strakha Suljim

Strakha Kamar

Strakha Vuul

RHO KARI'MA
(Hills of the Dog Soldiers)

Strakha Kekei

Cor

Calamath

Kemlasai

Var'Caspre

Miza Pala

The Paekkomere Ocean
(The Devil's Sea)

Rikasai

Vu

THE RIKARI
NATIONS

Tookarisai

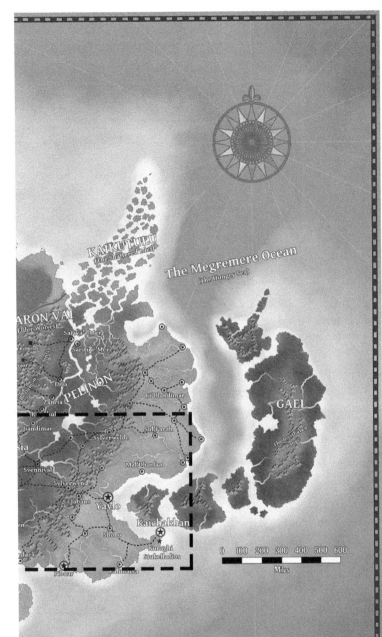

CHAPTER ONE

THE SUSPECT

Mygal's time was up. The clocktower rang twelve bells, each gong reminding him the murdered duke and his family remained unavenged. It had been six days. The Guardian's Conclave loomed, ready to judge Mygal's progress. His only suspect—handed to him by a cocky information broker he didn't trust.

"Are you sure he's going to show up?" he asked Tavyn. He eyed his informant as he sipped a tankard of dreadfully flat ale. He hated flat ale. He hated waiting even more. They'd been waiting two hours, and there was still no sign of the suspect. The Drunken Unger tavern was only half full—a mix of thugs and merchants—and none of them was the man Mygal wanted. He needed answers. He needed to stand before the king with more than empty hands and unsolved mysteries. He shifted his gaze to the informant he'd roped in two days earlier.

"I guarantee it," Tavyn replied. He was a lithe rogue of a man in his late twenties, with long, blond hair, a close-cut goatee, and keen, blue eyes that missed little. His leather jerkin and pants were a matching indigo, his light oilskin cloak the color of a stormy sea. He wore high, black boots and a matching black leather belt. The matching grips of a slim fencing dagger and a basket-hilted rapier poked up from his belt. The grips on both were worn from use, but well-maintained. "Like I said, my contact told me Dancer was bragging about burgling a noble, and neither the noble nor his family would ever miss anything again."

It fits, Mygal thought, but the more he sat here, the more something didn't feel right. He took another sip and traced a small, seemingly random pattern in a splash of ale on the table. The pattern, a sort of mnemonic device, helped him focus his mind. As he did, he reached out lightly with his ermajea, touching Tavyn's mind with what most people called Love Magic. Mygal was an accomplished erkurios, or "heartbender," in common parlance. It was one of the main reasons he'd been tasked for this mission. As he sifted delicately through Tavyn's emotions, he found only certainty with not even a glimmer of deceit. He did this sort of thing with all of the informants he worked with, which was one of the reasons he was still alive.

"That does narrow it down," Mygal replied, "but rumors are just rumors."

"You should trust me," Tavyn said with a mischievous grin. "Everyone else does."

"I don't trust *anyone*." Mygal met Tavyn's gaze with a raised eyebrow.

"Wisdom or cynicism?"

"Bit of both, actually." Mygal glanced at the front doors.

"He'll be here," Tavyn insisted. He took a swig from his own tankard and frowned. "He collects in this area on this night of the week, every week."

Mygal let out an impatient breath. "I hate to wait."

"Maybe you're in the wrong business."

"I like what I do. Waiting is just one of the few down-sides."

"Is the bounty high?"

"For killing a duke and his entire family?" Mygal put on the show of a greedy smile. "A thousand dakkaris, my friend. Assuming…"

"Assuming what?"

"That I get the right man—the killer will be compelled to truthfulness by the magistrates—and assuming this is the only thing he's responsible for. If there are other bounties on his head, then I get those too. It's not unheard of."

"What will you do with a thousand gold dakkaris?"

Mygal smiled again. "Answer only the questions I feel like answering."

"You planning on just grabbing him tonight and taking him in?"

"On your say-so alone?" Mygal raised an eyebrow. "It doesn't work that way. I need to follow him and see what evidence I can gather—*tangible* evidence. Search his quarters, maybe… see if he's got any of the duke's possessions, anything taken from the manor house."

Tavyn nodded. "I suppose that makes sense."

Mygal took another sip. "There are consequences—severe ones—when bounty hunters grab innocent people off the street and drag them in."

"He *is* part of a protection racket," Tavyn offered.

"Not my concern. The authorities only get involved—*I* only get involved—when there's a valid bounty or it involves the nobility. Protection rackets are part of the status quo."

"Charming."

"That's the world we live in."

"True enough." Tavyn looked at Mygal. "I guess I'd be out of a job too, if the king and magistrates looked too deep into the shadows of the city. There wouldn't be as much underworld information for me to broker."

"I don't know about that." Mygal shrugged. "Seems to me the underworld would just go deeper… you might even be able to charge more… less low-hanging fruit, so to speak."

"You talk like a merchant."

"My father was a merchant. Grains and stakka fruit, mostly."

Mygal considered his next question carefully. He wasn't sure he wanted to broach the subject, but Tavyn might be able to confirm some of the things he'd heard on the docks that afternoon. Finally, he decided it couldn't hurt.

"There's something I've been meaning to ask you," Mygal started slowly. "Maybe you've heard something. Maybe not. And it may or may not be part of this."

"What's that?"

"I've heard about two minor nobles here in the duchy... something about taxes being too stiff and demanding a change... Barons Umar and Gorven. Heard anything about them?"

"Not much," Tavyn replied evenly. Mygal didn't sense any deceit in the man, but that didn't necessarily mean there wasn't any. Even heartbenders could be fooled. "Why do you ask?"

"Well, if they were plotting sedition, the best place to foment it would be from the ducal seat. I've heard both of them would be considered to replace Duke Belvenim if he were to be removed." Mygal had made that part up, but he wasn't worried about being caught up on so tenuous a rumor... even one he started.

Tavyn looked thoughtful. "Those two? Their lands are to the south, right?"

Mygal nodded. "I checked. They were both far from here when the murders took place... although one or both of them could have hired people like Dancer to commit the crime. Do you think one of them could put a price on Duke Belvenim's head?"

"Have Dancer kill the duke and then play the odds that they got selected?"

"That's the theory," Mygal replied.

"Highly unlikely." Tavyn sounded confident. "I don't know much about those barons, but I know they have more bark than bite."

Mygal let out a long, thoughtful breath. "Killing nobles is a long-established tradition. People have been doing it since before Pelinon was even a kingdom. What I don't understand is why the duke and his entire family were killed the *way* they were…" He thoughtfully traced another circle in the puddle of ale on the table. "I mean, they were butchered. It would have taken one person a long time to kill an entire family like that. It would have to have been one at a time, and only a kurios could have subdued them… unless they were drugged. Odds are it was more than one person in the manor that night."

"Hey, more murderers means more bounties, yes?" Tavyn offered. "Especially if they're involved in sedition."

"True enough, but I'm not sure I want to tangle with an entire nest of traitors. I can't spend dakkaris if I'm face down in an alley somewhere."

Tavyn nodded. "You could just gather evidence and then turn the whole group over to a magistrate."

"And get just a percentage of the bounty?" Mygal shrugged. "I'm not a fan of that either… although, something is better than nothing, I suppose. What I can't figure—either way—is why not just kill the duke? Why slaughter the entire family?"

"Maybe someone just likes killing?" Tavyn offered.

"Maybe."

The barmaid, a pretty lass with delicate features and red curls down to her waist, stepped up to the table.

"Another round, milords?" She gave Tavyn a wink, as if she knew him, and then gave Mygal a friendly smile.

"Only if you're the one who brings them," Mygal said. He had to admit, she really was attractive. He reached out with his majea and discovered a hint of attraction toward him, enough that he figured he could probably arrange a tryst with her. He'd always had a good sense for such things. Only a few years earlier, he might have used his majea to increase his chances—just a little bump to up the attraction that was already there—but he'd left such abuses of his gift in the past where they belonged. He was a Guardian now and had vowed to set a much higher standard. Besides, tracking Dancer took priority.

She blushed and flashed him a lovely smile. "I promise it will be me."

"Then two more ales it is," Mygal replied. "Make sure the innkeeper puts a head on them."

Then, with a swirl of her dress, she was gone. Mygal glanced at Tavyn and found him watching her retreat, a knowing look in his eyes. It was a perfect opportunity for Mygal to test Tavyn.

"Ahh..." He put a grin on his face. "You've had her?"

Tavyn looked surprised. "A gentleman doesn't speak of such things." But there was a lascivious glint in his eye.

Mygal tapped gently into his majea and sent a filament into Tavyn's emotions. At first there was a hint of resistance, which surprised Mygal. Only heartbenders and certain individuals trained to control their emotions were capable of such things. A moment later, his tendril flowed into Tavyn's mind, and Mygal pushed ever so gently.

"I think gentleman is a strong word," he said, "and besides, she's a beauty."

He felt Tavyn's natural resistance. The informant truly didn't want to speak about it. Mygal pushed just a little harder, and the resistance gave way like the parting of a curtain.

"Well," Tavyn said with a sly grin, "I suppose the answer is yes." He got a fond look in his eyes. "It was a while back, but I'd definitely have to say we spent a long, agreeable night together."

Mygal nodded. He suddenly felt more comfortable with Tavyn. Having informants susceptible to his influences just made life... easier.

"He's here," Tavyn said, his eyes flicking toward the door. "That's Dancer."

Mygal didn't turn his head, but he assessed the young man that had just entered.

Dancer was around twenty, with a braid of silky, black hair down his back. He stood almost six feet tall and had a well-defined physique. He wore black leather pants tucked into leather boots laced up to his knees. His tunic was the color of blood. He had a black leather vest, a rapier at his hip, and a long dagger in a horizontal sheath across the back of his belt. He also wore a leather satchel over one shoulder and across his body, its strap strained with weight.

He walked up to the end of the bar, away from the other patrons, and waited for the barkeep to serve an ale to another patron.

Moments later, the barkeep reached beneath the bar and strode over to Dancer, who smiled in a friendly way. The two had a brief, hushed conversation, Dancer nodded, and the barkeep handed over a small leather bag with the telltale bump of coins within. Dancer opened it and scanned the contents. With a nod to the barkeep, he dropped the bag into his satchel.

"Protection money?" Mygal asked.

"Protection money," Tavyn echoed.

"Out in the open like that?"

"It's not like it's a secret around here."

The whole thing still bothered Mygal. Something felt out of place. "Why would local thugs, protection racket or not, slaughter a duke's family? They like secrecy, not blood splashed on walls. Such things beg the attention of the authorities."

"Maybe the duke was in on the racketeering? Made a false step somewhere. Corruption at the highest level here in Svennival?" Tavyn met Mygal's gaze. "Maybe he got greedy."

"This doesn't feel right. It feels like... I don't know what. It just doesn't make sense."

Dancer turned and headed for the door.

"I'm going to follow him," Mygal said as the front doors closed. He rose out of his chair. "Stay here."

"I really should go with you," Tavyn said. "What if he's not alone?"

"I told you," Mygal said, turning back. "I'm not planning on grabbing him. I'm going to *follow* him. I need more information, and I can do that better alone."

"Are you sure?" Tavyn said, rising out of his seat.

Mygal tapped into his majea again, sending a calming feeling into Tavyn's mind that he then tweaked to carry a feeling of passion for the barmaid.

"No, you should stay here and enjoy the evening." He reached into his vest and put a few silver coins on the table. "The rest of the night is on me. Maybe you can arrange for another meeting with that lovely lass." He spotted the barmaid headed in their direction. "Here she comes now."

Tavyn glanced at her and sat back down. "If you say so," he replied with a wicked smile.

Confident his majea had worked, Mygal walked out the front doors. The cobbled street, illuminated by magic lanterns, had little foot traffic at that time of night. He saw Dancer a block away, headed in the general direction of Svennival's riverfront area. He set off after his quarry.

Dancer went into three more establishments—a tavern, a blacksmith, and another inn. Each time, Mygal faded into the shadows and kept an eye on the front doors. For the next thirty minutes, they made their way through the darkened streets and finally to the wharf district, where the air was cooler and more humid. As they drew nearer, Mygal picked up the smell of fish and ship oil.

Dancer turned down a side street off the main thorough-fare. Mygal quickened his pace, running as silently as he could. When he reached the alley, he peeked around the corner to see Dancer turn left at a cross section set between the brick buildings of the riverfront. He made several more turns like that, moving deeper and deeper into the shadier part of the city. Mygal found himself in a wide labyrinth of waterfront warehouses and realized he'd lost his quarry. He took note of where he was, with the idea of putting on a disguise and coming back as a dockworker to start poking around.

Dancer had a satchel full of money, and if he was here, then he was going to deliver that money to the people he worked for. It meant the protection racket was based out of the riverfront. No great surprise, but it only gave Mygal an area to keep searching, not a location to spy on.

He let out a frustrated breath. With the Guardian's Conclave only eight days away—seven of those days would be traveling to the palace in Corsia—there was little chance of him breaking the case before then. The thought of standing in front of the king, empty-handed, made him cringe.

Looking around to make sure he was alone, he reached into a pouch at his waist and pulled out a slim sheet of vellum and a piece of charcoal. Using the brick wall beside him as a surface, he wrote a quick note:

"Have identified and am following suspect in duke's murder. Reports of sedition in Svennival as yet unconfirmed. Remote possibility the two may be related. Suspicion only. Nothing concrete."

He rolled up the note tightly and then focused his thoughts, placing his hand where the tattoo had been inscribed on his forearm only a few months earlier. Normally, the spell took several minutes when cast using the material component of a red feather. Doing it that way didn't tax his own majea at all. He was in a hurry, however, so he would have to draw upon his own energy. He tapped into his majea and whispered the incantation he'd been taught. Holding out his left hand, he made several motions in the air with his right.

As he combined the magic stored within the tattoo with his own, wisps of crimson swirled in the palm of his hand. The tattoo hidden beneath his tunic tingled. Within seconds, the wisps took on the outline of a small bird. He concentrated, willing the conjured avatar to take on solid form.

Within moments, a small red bird with a tall crest and black streaks on its wings stood in the palm of his hand, blinking at him. He held the rolled piece of vellum in front of the bird, and it gently clasped its beak around it.

"Now fly," Mygal said, lifting his hand.

The bird blinked once and then leapt into the air, rising into the darkness above with a flutter of small wings. Mygal watched it disappear and then turned, looking down the alley, wondering what he should do next. He contemplated searching for Dancer, but he saw little hope of finding the suspect.

Something shifted on the rooftops.

"Good, it's done," a grim voice called from above.

Mygal froze as three shadowy figures dropped from rooftops on either side of him. Another stepped into the alley from a darkened doorway twenty feet behind. They were all hooded, masked, and dressed in black. They also held swords.

Assassins!

Mygal's rapier and fighting dagger leapt into his hands. "You don't want to do this," he said, moving his head side-to-side, stretching his neck muscles out. He glanced at the furthest assassin, thinking that path might be his best way out. He wanted to escape, not fight four killers at the same time. As cocky as he was, he knew he was in trouble.

The furthest assassin stepped back a pace, as if he had no intention of fighting, but the three nearest him raised their weapons and came in.

Mygal tapped into his majea, deeply this time, and sent tendrils slashing out at the minds of all three. *Doubt*, he willed into their minds. Doubt caused hesitation, and he needed to reduce the number of blades coming at him simultaneously.

The first assassin halted in his tracks, probably because he already had doubt flowing thorough his thoughts. The other two, however, kept coming.

Mygal parried the second assassin's swing with his dagger and slashed at the third with his rapier. That assassin parried. Mygal side-stepped, putting the second assassin between himself and the third. He parried another swing from the second assassin and shoved up and out to create an opening. He stepped in close and drove his dagger to the hilt in the second assassin's chest. A shock ran up his arm as the blade pierced bone and heart.

The assassin grunted and sagged on Mygal's dagger arm.

Mygal jerked his blade free and kicked out, sending the dying assassin flying back toward the third as his blade clattered to the ground.

Mygal pushed hard with his majea, sending thoughts of fear into the third assassin's mind as the man dodged the body of the second assassin. He slashed three times in a wide X, driving the third assassin back and forcing him to parry each blow in rapid succession. Mygal felt the fear growing within the third assassin's mind, so he added to it. The man staggered back, holding up his weapons defensively, his eyes wide with fear.

The first assassin, who had succumbed to doubt, growled, "He's a blood-cursed heartbender!" His anger burned into the doubt as he charged.

Mygal poured even more doubt into the first assassin's thoughts, trying to overwhelm the anger. He could feel it taking root, but the assassin was so enraged, he was able to fend off Mygal's influences. Mygal parried a slash with his dagger and thrust with his rapier. The assassin blocked the thrust and riposted quickly. Mygal caught the riposte on his dagger, shoved the blade aside, dug deeply into his majea, and poured a torrent of fear into the man's thoughts. The first assassin screamed. Mygal slashed down on his sword arm, opening a deep gash through cloth and flesh. He felt his blade drag across bone.

The assassin's sword clattered on the cobblestones.

Mygal slashed again, drawing his blade deeply across the man's throat. A fountain of blood spurted into the air. The assassin gurgled, clutching at his neck as he staggered back. He slammed against the wall and slid down.

The third assassin regained his senses, but he looked at Mygal with doubt and fear filling his mind. He glanced at the two corpses on the ground, and then his eyes shifted to the figure still standing twenty feet away, watching the combat like a spectator at a gladiatorial arena.

"You don't think I'm going to let you get out of here now, do you?" Mygal snarled with a good deal of venom. He stepped in fast and slashed with his rapier. Simultaneously, he pressed hard with his majea, sending out another wave of fear.

The man's eyes went wide as he parried and struck back with a clumsy, almost haggard riposte.

Mygal slashed, parried, slashed, driving the attacker toward the stoic figure watching them both.

The man parried desperately.

Mygal continued setting him up with one calculated slash and thrust after another.

When they'd closed on the observer, Mygal parried hard with his rapier, stepped in, and drove the point of his dagger into the attacker's belly.

The man squealed in pain and dropped his sword.

Mygal bashed the hilt of his rapier into the man's temple. The assassin crashed into the wall and crumpled to the ground, unconscious. He'd question the assassin once he'd finished off the fourth.

He stepped toward the last assassin, sending out tendrils of fear to incapacitate the man. To his surprise, the tendrils crashed and splintered against a mind prepared for the attack—the mind of a heartbender just like him.

The masked figure chuckled and drew his weapons.

In a flash, Mygal found himself distracted, his emotions calling forth memories of the barmaid and then the bird he'd summoned. He shook his head, trying to clear his mind. He raised his weapons, attempting to steel his thoughts against the potent assault from an exceptionally strong heartbender. Violent emotional swings hammered into his mind—his anger turned to fear.

The last assassin stepped in, his weapon raised. He slashed. Mygal parried, dancing back as his mind went wild with a wash of mixed emotions. Distraction drew his eyes to the left and then the right, as if more attackers lurked in the shadows all around him.

Slash—parry—slash… he couldn't keep his thoughts focused.

He staggered as a blinding, sharp pain lanced into his belly. He cried out. His arms froze, mid-air. He glanced down to see the assassin's blade stuck through him halfway up its length. The assassin jerked the blade free and thrust again. Fiery pain flared in Mygal's shoulder this time, spreading out. He dropped his rapier as his arm fell limp. The assassin's blade protruded out his back.

"How—" Mygal started.

The assassin jerked the blade free. Mygal screamed. His mind became a maelstrom, emotions swirling toward a center of deepening agony. At the edge of his senses, he saw the glint of a rapier guard flash before his eyes. For a fleeting instant, he lamented not being able to make even one of the Guardian Conclaves. He wondered if his tenure as a Guardian would be the shortest in Pelinon history.

Steel crashed into his temple and darkness took him.

CHAPTER TWO

THE CONCLAVE

R ellen was in trouble, and he knew it. His thudding boots echoed off white slabs of marble, deliberately out of cadence with the armed and armored guards escorting him through the king's palace. The captain of the King's Corsairs strode two paces ahead, and four Corsairs marched close behind. Their presence reminded him that the palace was a prison, and with every step, he fought that sense of confinement, the shroud that squeezed him with every measured step of the king's troops.

He hated the gods-be-damned place, what it was, and what it meant to him.

Rellen looked down on his escort. They were tall, but not so tall as he, and every nuance of them was a reminder of what he'd turned away from. His close-cropped, brown hair set him apart from the long, braided queues worn by the king's soldiers and most men in Corsia. His black leather armor made a stark contrast to their gleaming silver plate mail. Rather than the standard issue bastard swords all Corsairs carried, Rellen wore a gleaming, silver falchion upon each hip—the matched blades of Baladon. And his brown, leather bandoleer—each loop and pouch another component for his use of symmajea or Line Magic—identified him as something other than just a soldier, something much more.

He was nothing like the Corsairs... not anymore.

The guards escorted him along the grand hallway, where several small groups of nobles conversed in low voices. At first, their eyes were drawn to the small, black dragonette perched upon Rellen's shoulder. Such creatures were rare in Pelinon and not known to bond with humans. The nobles looked surprised, intrigued, even impressed. Then they recognized the man carrying the small creature. When they did, they went silent. Their eyes filled with disdain, even contempt. They *all* knew him, and most resented him for, what many considered, a gross dereliction of duty.

Rellen wore their disdain like a badge of honor.

The dragonette shifted upon his shoulder. Feeling her discomfort, he petted her side to reassure her. The staring faces around them might have put her on edge, and despite the high ceilings of the grand hallway, he knew she didn't like enclosed spaces. Truth be told, he felt the same way.

It's all right, Xilly, he said in the voiceless manner with which they communicated.

I'm not worried, Xilly replied. *The guards seem to hate you, though. As do those others.* She turned her head toward a cluster of nobles and stared straight at them.

They believe I betrayed them, Rellen replied. *When in fact I served them. I serve them still.*

Served them how?

I'd have made a terrible king.

You were to be king?

Rellen pushed a surge of guilt aside, hoping she wouldn't pursue the subject. Even talking with Xilly about his past struck nerves, but she was sensitive enough to know when not to push. Instead, she nuzzled his neck to reassure him that she still loved him.

As they approached the last group of nobles, he spotted Chancellor Vrelleth, military adjutant to the king. The gray-haired veteran, with hard eyes and chiseled features, was an exceedingly capable officer who had served the Crown for decades. The old warrior still taught the use of arms at the academy and was rarely bested. Vrelleth had been Rellen's mentor once—and a friend of sorts—but Rellen's decision had worn that relationship down to little more than polite disdain. The chancellor now gave Rellen his customary look of barely veiled contempt. The loss was one of Rellen's deepest regrets, but even that had been for the best.

They exited the grand hall into the great, black-marbled throne room that had served Pelinon's kings for the past seven hundred years. Angling to the right, they moved around a tall wooden framework supporting Pelinon's battle standard. The banner was twenty feet tall and six feet wide, with a white, winged sword suspended amidst a royal blue background trimmed in gold. Behind the banner, hidden in the corner of the throne room, stood two more of the King's Corsairs.

They were an elite guard, always seen in their bright, silver plate mail, winged helms, and black bastard swords. The two before him stood at attention, blades point-down on the floor, their hands resting upon the cross guard.

Between them stood a heavy, iron door.

The captain stepped up to the door, pulled out a large, heavy key, and twisted it in the lock with a clank. Pulling the door open with a faint squeal of hinges, he stepped aside and faced Rellen with a look not dissimilar to Chancellor Vrelleth's.

"It's not appropriate to keep His Majesty waiting—even for *you*."

Rellen cocked his head to the side. "I can't thank you enough for reminding me of that, Captain Fenrith," he said smoothly. There was a time when he used the captain's first name. They had served together during several campaigns, but that was in the past, beyond a bridge that lay in ruin. Rellen regretted that loss too, but his choice had been the only one he could make. "Perhaps you could teach me how to wield a blade sometime?"

The captain stiffened and looked to Rellen's escort. "Make sure he makes it to the Guardian's Hall, and then return to your posts." He tossed the key to one of the guards. Without another word or even a backward glance, Captain Fenrith strode past Rellen, brushing up against him just enough to make his feelings clear.

Rellen didn't react, although he could have called the captain out for the insult. The truth was, it took genuine gall to make any sleight against the brother of the king. Rellen actually respected that.

With a faint smile, he strode into a long hallway. Bright glowstones suspended from the ceiling lit his way. His escort followed closely, and Rellen was unsurprised to hear them fall into step with his own cadence. They were trained to follow their leader, after all. He shook his head. He considered breaking his stride, but even he had to admit it would be petty.

The hall was twenty yards of smooth, gray stone, like the rest of the king's keep. At the end, bright sunshine filled the hall with afternoon light. Rellen suspected the architects had designed for just that effect.

He stepped out into a circular hall with a high ceiling that curved inward. Stone pillars ran along the perimeter, rising up to the vaulted ceiling forty feet above. Tall panes of magically strengthened glass rose from floor to ceiling along the far half of the chamber, following the contour of the structure. There were twenty windows, each eight feet wide and twenty feet tall. Between them, murals, rising nearly to the ceiling, depicted nineteen of Pelinon's greatest Guardians from their thirteen-hundred-year history.

In the middle of the room lay a round table of dark wood. It had been inlaid with golden versions of the winged sword that decorated Pelinon's battle standard. The largest of them pointed at the head of the table where King Saren III sat.

Thirteen lesser swords went around the table, each one pointing at a high-backed chair of dark, polished wood and deep blue velour.

Every other chair, save two, was occupied by a Guardian of Pelinon.

The king turned and gave Rellen an irritated glare. The king appeared to be a few years younger than Rellen, with hair a darker shade of brown. He was a little shorter, possessed of a slightly thinner build, though both of them had the family's strong, aquiline nose, firm cheekbones, and solid jaw. They also shared piercing eyes the color of a stormy sea. While Rellen wore his hair short, the king wore his hair in a long, braided ponytail, as was the custom with men in the capital city of Corsia.

The others around the table also turned toward Rellen. Some wore smiles—a few pained, even fewer genuine. The rest—the majority—gave him surly frowns. Each expression was precisely as he'd expected it to be.

Nothing has changed here, he thought.

Several expressions turned to fascination when they saw what was perched upon Rellen's shoulder.

"My Liege, King Saren," the nearest Corsair intoned, "I present Rellen of Corsia."

"That will be all," the king said with a dismissive wave. "Tell Captain Fenrith I wish to see him at sixteen bells."

"Yes, my Liege," the guard said. With that, he and his fellow Corsairs turned on their heels and marched out with that same steady beat of echoing boots.

The king eyed Rellen, a sour expression on his face. His eyes fixed upon Xilly for a moment, then returned to Rellen.

"You managed to be late again, Rellen," he grumbled.

"Apologies, Your Majesty," Rellen said with little apology in his voice. He tried not to smile.

Several of the others shifted in their seats, scowls deepening.

"This has been scheduled for six months." The king blew out a frustrated breath. "I swear, you're going to be late for your own funeral someday."

"If I can, I will," Rellen said with a grin, "*Sire*."

"Take your seat, *Guardian*," the king commanded, pointing to one of the two empty chairs.

Rellen gave an overly deep bow. Moving over to the sixth chair down from the king's right, he noted the thirteenth chair, that of the newest Guardian, was the one which stood empty. The king had replaced Voren—who had died three months earlier on a mission—with a young erkurios named Mygar or Mygeth... or *something*. He couldn't quite remember the name, but he'd been curious to see a new face at the table. Rellen wondered where the new Guardian was.

He took his seat and looked around the table. They were a diverse group—all human, save two. The first non-human, Jareth K'Ovall, was a tall, ominous-looking Kapros with deep purple fur, full black horns that curled back from his temples, and piercing red eyes. He was accomplished as both a warrior and a symkurios—a runecaster like Rellen. The Kapros fought with the curved sabers of his people and had a black leather bandoleer of vials, powders, and other casting paraphernalia. Jareth, a particularly surly member of his race, wasn't friendly with any of the Guardians, but he absolutely hated Rellen.

The other non-human was Boron Krakvaricht, a Delver born beneath the Sylverwylde Mountains. His short, stocky frame was clad in the partial plate mail of his kin. He had a fiery red beard, hazel eyes, and a shock of red hair flowing down his back that looked like an animal's unkempt mane. Boron was a weapons master—able to wield any weapon he got his hands on—and one of Rellen's favorite drinking buddies from way back. They weren't friends, but they still enjoyed a good tavern brawl when the opportunity presented itself.

Rellen looked to the king and caught Saleeria Beskovar—First Guardian of Pelinon—looking at him with her calculating, crystal blue eyes. Her blond hair, falling down the front of her left shoulder, was secured at her crown with a sapphire-encrusted clasp. Her gown, cut from the finest silk, was also sapphire with a deep neckline. She wore a sapphire pendant on a silver chain that highlighted her alabaster skin. She had the rare gift of being a clikurios—a Lore Magician—who could subtly manipulate events within her purview. Of all the kinds of magic, lore magic was the one Rellen understood the least, which was also why he had so much respect for her. She had served King Saren II for years before his death and now served King Saren III. She had held a seat at the Guardians' table longer than anyone else. Rellen knew her best. She was a good adviser and had provided much of the information the Guardians used to undertake their missions.

"Before we begin," Rellen said, "I wish to offer my deepest regrets to you, my Liege, and to this august body, for my tardiness. I humbly beg your forgiveness. I prostrate myself before your mercy." He bowed his head, his nose almost touching the table.

A muffled, feminine giggle escaped Kaila Mandivar on the far side of the table.

Rellen lifted his gaze slightly and caught the Tenth Guardian of Pelinon hastily covering her mouth. Her impish, dark eyes were filled with humor as she tried to control her laughter. She was a lithe, dark-skinned warrior from the south, and an erkurios with a talent for seducing both men and women. She was frequently sent to the various ducal and baronial keeps throughout Pelinon to glean information and keep tabs on the goings-on there. She wore the long Khavreem fighting daggers native to her people.

"Stop it, would you?" the king said, exasperated, but it seemed he too was trying to keep from laughing. "You just never quit, Rellen," he sighed.

Rellen met his brother's eyes. He would call him king in public, but in his heart, the king—Saren III—would also be his little brother, Stevar.

With the king joining in, a few others laughed out loud, while the rest rolled their eyes. The look on K'Ovall's goat-like face, however, was far from amused.

"Have you missed me?" he asked the king.

"Can we get down to business?" The king gave him an impatient look. "I have a busy afternoon."

Rellen held up his hands. "I really do apologize for being late, but there was an actual Life Stealer in Sabatar."

"I read your report," the king replied. "Your association was... short-lived, I take it?"

"Short-lived, Your Majesty."

"Good. I confess I'm actually more interested in your new association."

"Your Majesty?"

The king tipped his chin at Xilly. "She's remarkable."

"She is," Rellen said, glancing at the dragonette. He turned his gaze to the other Guardians. "I would like to introduce you all to Xilly." He stroked her neck briefly. "Xilly, these are the Guardians of Pelinon. We all serve my brother, King Saren III."

Bow your head, little one, Rellen said to her playfully. *You're in the presence of royalty.*

Apparently, I have been all along. Xilly bowed her head low, prompting a few gasps from around the table.

"She's quite intelligent," Rellen said.

Thank you. So are you. Xilly's voice rang in Rellen's thoughts.

"It's an honor to meet you, Xilly," the king said with a regal nod. "Now, if all the *distractions* are out of the way, let's get down to business." He looked around the table. "Rellen has, of course, missed all of your reports, but seeing as he didn't want my job, we'll forgo covering that ground at this time." He looked to Rellen. "For my brother's benefit, however, I will say again that Mygal Durintur, our absent thirteenth member, was nearly killed during an investigation in Svennival over a week ago. Injuries sustained during the course of that investigation prevent his attendance at the Conclave today, but he is recovering and should be able to resume his investigation soon. As he is new to the table and is clearly involved with something particularly dangerous, I would like one of you to mentor him." The king picked up a stack of vellum in front of him as Rellen cringed, dreading the notion of mentoring *anyone*. "More on that in a moment." The king laid out four neat piles. "I have four missions that require immediate attention. One of them requires a grypharri, which narrows down who gets it."

Rellen had been trained to ride the large beasts, and he loved flying. If he was assigned any of the new missions, he hoped he got that one.

"The first," the king continued, "is in Saritu'e'Mere, to the east. Bodies have been turning up drained of blood but otherwise unmolested. The local magistrates and constabulary suspect a zokurios is involved, as there have not been any wounds discovered on the bodies."

Rellen hated dealing with zokurioi—the ones that went bad, anyway. Most folk called them lifeweavers because they tended to help and heal. The Life *Stealer* he'd dealt with two weeks earlier, however, had been particularly nasty—determined to suck Rellen's life dry and enslave Xilly. He never did find out why.

"They have not been able to apprehend the killer yet," the king continued. "It's been four weeks. As a result, Duke Arrivar has asked for a Guardian to assist." The king looked to Kell Duranti, a pale human male with black hair and hazel eyes sitting in the fifth seat. "Kell, I'd like you to leave for Saritu'e'Mere as soon as we're done here. A ship is already waiting to take you down-river."

"Yes, my Liege," Kell replied with a nod of his head.

The king picked up the first stack of vellum and handed it to Saleeria, who handed it off. Each Guardian passed it along until Kell held it in his hands.

"Several villages surrounding the small town of Caspari," the king continued, "are suffering a plague of truly monstrous vellish. It appears a band of self-proclaimed heroes may be controlling the vellish and have set up some sort of extortion scheme along the southeastern edge of the Demon's Claw Mountain Range." The king got a sour expression on his face. "That bitch dynast of the Rikarri Nations has asked me to look into the situation, since these *heroes* are suspected to be living on our side of the border. As a means of keeping the dynast's Transport Guild happy, I agreed." He looked to a massive human warrior in blackened chainmail sitting in the sixth seat. "Grall, I need you to crush this one. A win here will give me a chit to play later when I need those Rikarri swine to haul something for me." The king handed off the next stack of vellum.

"I'll not disappoint, Sire," Grall replied. He bowed his head with a creak of armor.

"Next," the king said, "there are growing rumors of sedition within the ducal extended family of Mallorand to the southeast. This is the mission that requires a grypharri. It's a long ride to Ki-Ulandimar, but we need to quickly determine if the rumors are true and, if so, expose who is about to lose his, her, or their heads."

The king looked to Faleesh Namarre, causing Rellen to swear under his breath. He'd really wanted that assignment. Faleesh was a dark-skinned woman with a long nose, short, black hair, and keen, amber eyes that seemed to take in everything all at once. She was a deadly master of assassination and could be as cold-hearted as a stone in winter. They'd coupled once. Only once. When she realized Rellen had little use for emotional entanglements, she decided she had little use for him. He was particularly grateful she hadn't slipped a dagger into his ribs for her trouble.

"Faleesh," the king said, "this one is tailor-made for you. It is, allegedly, the nobility in Ki-Ulandimar who are involved. You shall go the ducal seat of Mallorand as an official ambassador of the Crown, sent with a gift of thanks to Duke Nassar for his service. Root out the traitors if they exist." The king's eyes turned hard. "Make a public example if the situation warrants." The king paused. "Or if you just feel like it."

"Yes, my Liege," she replied with a nod.

The king handed the next sheaf of vellum down.

"That leaves the last matter, and one that concerns me deeply. Duke Vladysh Belvenim of Svennival and his *entire family* were murdered. It may be related to sedition, although that isn't confirmed yet. I *will* say I believe Vladysh was incapable of sedition. While he and my late father rarely saw eye to eye, he was a devoted subject of the Crown. I knew the man, and he served my father and me loyally. If there is sedition involved, then I'll have to be doubly careful whom I install in his place. For now, Vladysh's nephew Corwyk will fill the role until I can make a final decision. He was the senior magistrate for the duchy, so I've made him duke regent until I either make it official or choose someone new at the Solstice." He looked to the dark-furred Kapron. "K'Ovall, I believe this one suits you best."

"My Liege," Saleeria said carefully, clearing her throat. "Please forgive the conceit, but I would like to respectfully suggest you assign this mission to Rellen."

The king turned surprised eyes to her.

Stiffening, Rellen choked back a curse and let out an irritated breath. The last thing he needed was to play wet-nurse to a new Guardian. What was Saleeria thinking? He'd wanted to meet the man, not babysit him. Rellen caught Jaquinn El Barad, the dark-skinned Second Guardian, giving him a stern look. Jaquinn was the only Guardian who could make Rellen feel admonished. He'd been Rellen's mentor when Rellen first joined the ranks of the Guardians, and he'd been a good teacher. Jaquinn was distant, calculating, and not prone to Rellen's appetites for taverns and drinking. However, they both looked at the role of Guardian with a certain gravitas. All of the Guardians were devoted servants of the king, but Jaquinn and Rellen took it much more personally. Of all the Guardians, Rellen respected Jaquinn the most.

"Oh?" The king ignored Rellen's sigh and kept his eyes fixed on Saleeria. "What is your reasoning?"

"I have gleaned information that the Nissra cult may be involved. If so, it could be the beginning of a move for the cult to take over Svennival. We have, as yet, not determined any overarching objective to the cults cropping up across the kingdom, although Rellen's recent experiences in Calamath suggest the possibility of a larger design. Since he has already faced the Nissra cult, he is, perhaps, the better choice." Her eyes shifted to Rellen and then down to where she knew a pendant lay hidden beneath his tunic. "The Eye of Tuluum might even lead him straight to the culprits."

Rellen started to say something about the Eye but held his tongue.

"Can you tell me where you got this information?" the king asked.

"One of my sources," Saleeria replied. She clasped her hands together and twisted a jeweled ring around her left pinky finger. It was a stunning diamond set into an intricate platinum setting crafted by a truly gifted artisan. "I would prefer not to reveal the individual, if Your Majesty will permit. As you know, Sire, an informant who is known to others can be compromised. Compromising the use of climajea—and the information which feeds it—can, and usually does, compromise the desired result."

"Of course, of course," the king replied. "I wouldn't presume to unduly influence your machinations. I've learned not to meddle."

"Thank you, my Liege."

"Rellen?" The king looked to his brother, a wary look on his face. "Thoughts?"

Rellen tried to keep the irritation out of his voice and was almost successful. "I'm not a nursemaid for new Guardians." He met his brother's gaze and realized he was now in dangerous waters, but he decided to stand his ground. "Perhaps Jareth would be a better choice." He offered, glancing at the big Kapron. Jareth's eyes burned as he stared straight at Rellen. "You know I prefer to work alone." Rellen insisted, turning his gaze back to the king.

The king's eyes hardened, and his lips pressed into a slim line.

In an instant, Rellen knew he'd pushed too far. He knew he wasn't going to win this one, no matter how much he hated the idea of mentoring a new Guardian. "But… I do serve the Crown, Your Majesty. And to be fair, the First Guardian does make a good point. The Nissrans are a scourge we should eradicate wherever we find them." He eyed his brother. "Anything to get me out of the palace." Rellen caught a few of the Guardians frown at that comment. He remained unapologetic, however.

"Are the Nissrans really that bad?" the king asked, ignoring Rellen's last comment.

"You haven't seen the bodies," Rellen replied grimly. "The Nissrans have an appetite for blood, just like their bitch-goddess. They mutilate with both pattern and purpose. If Duke Belvenim and his family were mutilated, it's possible the Nissrans did it. I'd have to see it for myself to say with any certainty."

"Mygal didn't mention any sort of pattern to the wounds in his reports," the king said. "This may be Nissrans. It may be sedition. I need to know which, who is involved, and how high up it might go."

"Well," Rellen said thoughtfully. "I can tell you it probably wasn't Corwyk, unless he's been possessed. I'd stake my reputation on that. I knew him at the magic academy, even raised a glass or three from time to time. The man I knew most certainly could not murder his uncle, nor, I would wager, could any of his family. Betrayal is hard to believe from a close-knit group like that, let alone the brutal murder of one of their own."

"It would seem Saleeria's recommendation is a well-reasoned one," Jareth K'Ovall spoke up with his deep, gravelly voice. He fixed steely eyes on Rellen. "Rellen has an existing relationship with one of the players *and* recent experience with the Nissrans." The corners of his goat-like mouth turned up. "It's also a *perfect* opportunity for him to take on the role of mentor. It's unfortunate Svennival is so hot and humid this time of year, but I'm sure the *Ninth* Guardian is more than up to the task of enduring that steam bath for the good of all.

And as Saleeria pointed out, the Eye of Tuluum might just guide him to his quarry."

You bastard, Rellen thought, although he couldn't argue with any of it. There was one thing he needed to mention, however. He cleared his throat.

"I should clarify one thing," he said carefully, "seeing as the Eye has become the subject of discussion amongst the rest of you." He glanced at his brother. "The Eye doesn't work in the manner suggested here." He reached into his tunic and pulled out the silver chain, letting the small, obsidian sphere dangle before them all. "I don't know how or why, but the Eye of Tuluum seems to lead me to answers only when I don't quite know the question. When I do, it ignores me. It seems to have an agenda of its own, and I doubt the duke's murder factors into that."

"Curious." Saleeria eyed the obsidian gem. "I'd love to examine it, if you would permit."

The Eye should stay with us, Xilly said, and there was a sense of urgency to her thoughts.

Don't worry, Rellen replied.

"Maybe later," Rellen said to Saleeria. "The next time I'm in the capital, perhaps." He glanced at the king. "I should add that I have an old comrade in Svennival. She likely has her finger on the pulse of the underworld there."

"Even more reason for you to go," K'Ovall said, a satisfied gleam in his eye.

Rellen locked eyes with the big Kapron and gave him a bored expression.

"Then it's decided." The king stared at his brother. "Rellen, you will find Corwyk and Mygal at the ducal keep in Svennival." He let out a long breath. "And you'll likely find Mygal there as well, chasing housemaids, no doubt, despite his injuries. Give Corwyk my regards and my deepest condolences for his family's sacrifice."

"Yes, my Liege," Rellen replied flatly, keeping his irritation buried.

The king nodded as he handed down the stack of vellum, which quickly made its way into Rellen's hands.

"Then, if you all will excuse me," the king said, "I have other matters to attend to. Those of you not leaving immediately are welcome to stay and enjoy the rest of the Conclave. We shall meet tomorrow in the banquet hall at noon, and we can relax then. I'm sure you all have more stories to share." He stood up.

The twelve Guardians rose to their feet and placed their right fists over their hearts in salute.

"Rellen, I'd like to see you in my quarters. Around eight bells?"

"I'll be there," Rellen replied.

"Good. Then I take my leave of you all. For the Honor of Pelinon," he said.

"For the Honor of Pelinon," they replied in unison.

King Saren III turned and strode through a door on the far side. When he was gone, Kell Duranti, Grall Akkrond, and Faleesh Namarre marched away, vanishing down the hallway. The rest of the Guardians broke up into several small groups, falling easily into the conversation of old friends. Unsurprisingly, none approached Rellen, so he moved over to where Saleeria was speaking with Jaquinn El Barad.

The Second Guardian was a tall, muscular man with ebony skin and a guarded countenance. He was a gekurios—a stoneburner—as well as a master with the scimitar he carried across his back. He wore the flowing gray and green robes indicative of the people who lived in the Duchy of Nikostohr far to the south.

"… four suspects, and the vizier is one of them," Jaquinn said in a hushed voice. "There's something off about him. I can't quite put my finger on it, but I intend to return to Kaichakahn and figure it out."

"Keep me informed," Saleeria said. "When do you plan on leaving?"

"I leave the day after tomorrow. I'll catch a river boat in Svennival. It will be faster that way."

Saleeria nodded.

"If I can interrupt," Rellen said gently, "I'd like to speak with Saleeria before I leave."

"Of course," Jaquinn replied with a slight bow. "I have other matters to deal with here in the palace. Perhaps we'll be able to catch up in Svennival, if the timing works out," he said to Rellen.

"Perhaps." Rellen nodded. "I'll be leaving in the morning."

"Here's to hoping, then," Jaquinn said with a slim smile. "Saleeria," he added, giving her a respectful bow. With that, he turned and walked away.

"What may I do for you, Rellen?" she asked, looking as composed as ever. Her eyes flicked to Xilly, whose attention was focused squarely upon Saleeria.

"I was wondering if, through all your contacts, you had any other information about the Nissrans—and I mean *anywhere*. My guts tell me something more than blood-soaked zealotry is going on with them. Maybe the murders in Calamath were isolated incidents, but maybe not. This thing in Svennival has me worried."

"Your reports indicated they were going after the baron's son in Calamath." She gave him a calculating look. "You think they may be trying to do the same thing elsewhere?"

"We can't ignore the possibility."

"I agree." Saleeria twisted the small ring about her finger again, a thoughtful expression upon her face. Rellen finally got a good look at the thing, and on one side he could just make out a small symbol that he recognized. It was the signature mark of Ionar Tomai, a renowned jeweler in Corsia who used his gemajea—his Land Magic—to craft magnificent and supremely intricate jewelry.

It must have cost her a small fortune, Rellen thought.

"Rellen, I have heard only rumors," she said carefully. Saleeria, more than anyone Rellen had ever known, chose her words with the greatest attention to detail and accuracy. "The murders in Svennival may very well be the result of sedition.

They could also be nothing more than random killings undertaken by a sick or greedy mind. Neither of those excludes the Nissran cult, and if that is the case, it *might* be part of a larger effort on their part." She seemed to consider the variables. "However, based upon your reports, I see no reason to assign greater import to these events at this time." She let out a slow, thoughtful breath. "I would council you to remain open to all possibilities."

"I'm a believer in the axiom," Rellen said.

"Your father used it often," Saleeria replied with a fond expression on her face.

"Thank you for your insight." Rellen bowed his head. "And thank you for recommending me for this mission."

"Of course," she replied. "Each to our talents."

"How is the king doing?" Rellen asked. "Things seem to be running well."

"He wears the crown well. He's taken up the mantle you cast aside like he was born to it and done so with a vigor that has taken many by surprise."

"I never doubted he could handle it," Rellen said. He gave her a long, thoughtful look. "You know better than most; he was always going to make a far better king than I."

"Tell yourself that if you must," she said, a serious, almost concerned, look upon her face. "You would have been an effective king... despite your wanderlust. I know it, even if you do not."

Rellen got a pained expression on his face. He had fond memories of a father who had taught from childhood that one day he would be king. When the moment came, Rellen turned his back on it and walked away. He wondered if Saleeria approved or condemned his decision. He really couldn't tell which.

"I can still hear him shouting," Rellen said. "Driving me to be better, know more, learn more." He locked gazes with her. "Does Stevar resent that I dumped the crown into his lap?" A pang of guilt and worry coursed through Rellen's heart. He wasn't sure he wanted to know the answer, but he was never one to avoid pain when it was necessary. "He's never said anything... never even suggested it, but... Well, he's the only family I have left."

Saleeria gently placed her hand upon Rellen's arm, and her touch—her caring—seemed genuine.

"You have nothing to fear, Rellen Falcoria. The king always speaks fondly of you. I believe he understood your decision better than any, perhaps even better than you yourself."

"Thank you," he said. "That means a lot."

She caught an impatient look from Boron Krakvaricht. "Will you excuse me, Rellen?"

"Of course," Rellen said. He turned and gave Boron a friendly nod, who returned it in kind. "I best get back to the stable and check on my horse. The stable boys seemed a little... inexperienced."

"Give Shaddeth some oats for me," Saleeria said.

"I will." Rellen turned away, but she caught his arm.

"Oh, and Rellen?"

"Yes?"

"You'll make a good mentor too," she said with compassion and encouragement.

He rolled his eyes, gave her a patient nod, and walked off.

CHAPTER THREE

SALEERIA'S SECRET

Saleeria unlocked the door to her study and closed it behind her. She spoke a single word and the lock clicked into place, making it virtually impregnable. She hadn't created the magic that secured the door, but she was the only one who could open or close it.

Her study had no windows and only the one door. The stone walls, like the iron door, were heavily magicked against entry and eavesdropping. Glowstones—three-inch spheres of white quartz—sat upon shelves in all four corners of the room, illuminating the space completely in cool, white light. Floor-to-ceiling shelves filled completely with tomes of every size and color lined the walls. Some were ancient, some were not. Many were not in the native language of Pelinon, but she could—and had—read them all, nonetheless.

She uttered a command, and the glowstones dimmed by half. She let out a long breath, relieved by the seclusion this one room afforded her. She crossed the room slowly, almost tentatively, moving past a well-used divan on one side and two sitting chairs and a low table on the other. Moving around a desk cluttered with books, vellum sheets, and maps, she settled into the large, leather-clad chair that had seen decades of wear. It was from this very spot she continued to further her studies and understanding of not only the machinations of Pelinon politics, but the world as a whole.

Her mentor in the Order of Readers had taught her well, and if she continued her studies, she might one day take his seat on the Reader Council, once he was elevated to the level of High Master, of course. But that day might never come, as Talliah Essoch had been High Master for six decades and didn't appear to be slowing down. However, should it come to pass, Saleeria would do everything in her power to be the only choice for the seat of Vice Master on the Council of Readers.

She leaned back in her chair and gently slipped the filigreed, diamond ring from her pinky finger. She held it before her eyes, twisting it this way and that to catch the light. The magic contained within was not inconsequential, and she continued to wonder where her mentor had acquired it. In all her studies, she'd never heard of anything that could communicate over great distances, save for the Thella stones utilized by the king's kurioi—his magicians—to communicate with the dukes of the kingdom. Nor was she aware of any similar artifact or relic that allowed a single person, even a kurios, to do so at all. The Thella stones required several powerful kurioi to channel their magic. The ring did not.

She focused her will upon the interior of the diamond, felt her way into the profound magics contained within, and sent out a single thought, just as she'd been shown. Moments later, a faint glow emanated from within the heart of the diamond. She closed her eyes and opened the connection.

Milord, she called.

I hear you. She heard his voice in her thoughts, as if he were speaking to her from across the desk. *What has transpired?*

I was able to convince the king that Rellen should be the one sent to Svennival. The brothers agreed Rellen is ideally suited, considering his experiences with the Nissran cult. Rellen leaves tomorrow, probably by horseback, so it will take some time for him to arrive. Were you aware there may be sedition brewing in Svennival?

Of course, he replied. *I have not put much stock in what are likely to be mere rumors or the grumblings of petty nobles who take their lives of ease for granted.*

And you are certain the Nissrans are involved? she asked.

Reasonably so, he said, but his words carried a great deal of certainty.

How did you learn of this?

Why do you persist in asking questions to which you already know the answer?

She felt a pang of embarrassment and let out a frustrated breath. She was not one to enjoy feeling the tip of her own sword. *A different question, then.*

Ask, he replied.

Saleeria knew better than most what a cult of the blood-goddess Nissra was capable of. The king shared all reports coming in from the cities throughout Pelinon, particularly those from the other Guardians. More and more of them over the past six months included references to Nissra and her followers. Those reports dripped with the blood of innocent victims butchered and branded by Nissran fanaticism. What's more, the cultists had all been killed or committed suicide before they could be captured and questioned.

Is there significant danger for Rellen?

Is this a manifestation of some deep-seated affection for that drifter? he asked. Saleeria suspected her master had woven webs of ermajea around Rellen as king, not Rellen as merely a Guardian. If that were the case, Rellen's decision to abdicate would have undone years of effort. *You must learn to be totally objective in all matters. Involvement clouds one's judgment and influences the outcome in ways one cannot foresee.*

I understand, she replied. *There is no affection, merely respect for a noble Guardian and a genuine asset to Pelinon. Nothing more. You need not worry on that front.*

Then be certain to maintain your dispassion, he warned. *A failure at this stage would jeopardize your standing with me and risk any hopes of advancement.*

I will not fail.

As to your question, you know the answer to that as well... Yes, there is most certainly danger, but there is danger in all things, particularly in those matters where the Guardians choose to involve themselves. However, it is unlikely Rellen will encounter anything he cannot handle. He is a most capable young man, as is his brother. I've had my eye on them both for a very long time—even nudged here and there from time to time.

That statement caught Saleeria's ear. She hadn't known with certainty that her mentor influenced King Saren II's sons at all... But of course he did. She did it herself as a matter of course. Like her, her mentor influenced and protected Pelinon. The sons of the previous king would have factored heavily into those manipulations.

Bear in mind, her mentor continued, *he also has his new pet, and that creature gives him considerable advantage, I suspect.*

You know of that too? She immediately chided herself for asking another obvious question.

Her mentor did not reply.

Is there anything else you require of me in this matter? she asked.

Not at this time. Rellen's journey lies before him... the outcome, as yet, uncertain. Continue on the path before you. Stay aware. Keep me informed. Grow stronger and wiser, and one day you shall take my place. The High Master cannot remain so forever, and while I shall miss her, I would be disingenuous to deny that I look forward to replacing her. You have done well, Saleeria.

Thank you, milord. I will reach out to you again in seven days.

I shall be here.

Saleeria lifted her focus away from the crystal and broke the connection.

The glow around the ring faded.

Unbeknown to both of them, a demon severed its own connection and smiled from within a distant, cold darkness.

Chapter Four

BROTHERS

How long will it take you to get there?" the king asked. He sat at a large table in the center of the war room, his chair leaned back and his feet up on the edge of the table. A decanter of whisky was within easy reach, as well as a large platter of bread, meats, and cheeses from across the kingdom. Xilly sat on the other side of the platter from the king, chewing on a thick slice of roasted koodoo buck and making occasional chirping sounds to express her delight.

Across the room, Rellen stood before a wall-sized map of Pelinon and some of the surrounding lands. He tossed back a shot of hundred-year-old whisky bottled by Delver spirit masters in the Duchy of Draksymsur. He and his brother had broken out the expensive bottle to celebrate seeing one another after almost a year of Rellen's travels. It was tradition.

He traced his finger along the jagged red line of the Great Wall, running along the top of the map from the northeast down at a steep angle west. The Wyrm Lands lay north of that. Little was known about the vast region, save that the

occasional dragon, sphinx, grypharri, and even dragonette—
among other flying creatures—found their way over the wall
into more southern climes. Then came the wide swath of the
Kari'Ma lands, whose tribes fiercely protected the massive
stretch of rolling grasslands and river valleys. Beneath that lay
the Demonspine Mountain range.

The northeastern mountains held the land of Charon Vai
and the Wolf Lords who ruled it. Southeast of that lay two
duchies: Islia'Stavahr—primarily occupied by Jareth K'Ovall's
people, the Kapron—and Strakhavahr, where the now extinct
Strakhanni warriors of legend had instilled great strength and
battle prowess in their descendants. The mountains and those
who populated them made a nearly impregnable line of
defense against the Kari'Ma.

It had been a long time since Rellen had even seen the
lands of the Kari'Ma.

He stuck his finger upon Corsia and ran it down a dotted
line marking the stretch of the King's Highway that led straight
to the river port city of Svennival. He glanced over his shoulder.

"I can meet—Mygal, was it?—in about six or seven days,
assuming I leave in the morning and the rains don't delay me."
He turned and took in what had once been their father's war
room... and was now Stevar's. He wondered if he would ever
get used to that.

Banners covered the other three walls, mixed in with a
smattering of weapons from across the kingdom. A great
fireplace filled the center of the far wall, but it hadn't been used
since the last time the kingdom found itself in an active war.
Rellen and his brother had come here often as boys to escape
chores, studies, and every other responsibility inevitably piled
upon the shoulders of princes. In the war room, above any
other place in the palace, the two had always been just brothers,
not lords, not princes, and certainly not future kings.

"Good," Stevar replied. "That should give Mygal time to
heal up completely." He wore a loose-fitting tunic of crimson
and black leather pants tucked into high, leather boots. He'd

undone his braid, and his dark brown hair flowed out like a lion's mane. He pushed the decanter of whisky closer to his older brother. "And you're dry."

Rellen looked at his glass and smiled. "We can't have that, can we?"

"No," Stevar said. "We can't." He eyed his older brother, and his expression turned serious. "You crossed a line today, you know that, right?"

Rellen stiffened for a moment, meeting his brothers' gaze, and then let out a slow breath. "The bit about mentoring Mygal?" he offered.

Stevar nodded slowly, an expectant look on his face.

"Yeah... I'm sorry about that." Rellen set his glass on the table. "It caught me by surprise is all. You know I don't like working with others, and being a mentor is even worse."

"I know," Stevar said. "I also don't care, and it's about time you did it. It comes with that tattoo, and you know it."

"You sound like Father," Rellen said, and gave his younger brother a faint smile.

"That's because I'm speaking as king."

"I know," Rellen replied. "I give you my word, I won't cross that line again."

"Good," Stevar said. "By the way, Svennival's Manifestation Festival starts next week, so you should get a good show, if you can take the time. There are several bloodlines there that have always produced remarkable talent with the magical arts."

"I remember Father speaking of it." Rellen was grateful for the change of subject. His brother—no, the *king*—was letting him off the hook, but he needed to make sure he was never on it again. "Here's to hoping I can." He poured himself another shot.

"Something tells me you won't," Stevar said, a concerned look on his face.

"You're worried about it, aren't you?" Rellen asked. His brother's posture was relaxed, but he knew Stevar well enough to know those eyes.

"Svennival?" His brother let out a long breath. "Yes, but not just because one of my dukes has been murdered. That would be trouble enough. There's a lot going on, all across Pelinon. I go to bed wondering if its more than I'll be able to handle."

"Tell me," Rellen said in the same manner he used when they were young and his brother was anxious about their father's ever-weighty expectations.

Stevar put his feet on the floor and sat up straight. He stared into his brother's eyes for several moments. He'd recognized Rellen's tone too, and they fell into an old cadence.

"Well," Stevar started, his eyes shifting to something far off, "at a glance, one might think the kingdom is running along smoothly—high times, even." He shook his head. "In the Conclave, I mentioned the possibility of sedition in Mallorand, right?"

Rellen nodded.

"That's one of *four*, but Mallorand is the only one we had knowledge we could act on. The others are just rumors—solid rumors, but no names, no places—just that something is festering. I'll be honest, I'm more than a little worried about the possibility of sedition to the east, west, *and* south. There's also been an increase of Kari'Ma raids along the northeastern half of the Strakha line. They've hit villages around several keeps, including Strakha Havaari and Strakha Kleemar. Lightweight stuff, so far, but it feels like they're probing our defenses again. Do you remember Galphoreth?"

"The Wolf Lord emissary?" Rellen asked. Galphoreth had been Charon Vai's emissary to Pelinon for over a decade, and one did not forget a Charonos. He stood seven feet tall, had deep black fur, and like the rest of his kin, had a muscled body topped by a wolf-like head. Galphoreth wore clothing as a matter of etiquette, but the Charonos rarely wore garments or armor, preferring only leather harnesses to hold tools and weapons when they needed them. Pelinon had maintained a truce with the fearsome race for over two hundred years. By treaty, they held the northeastern passes against Kari'Ma raids into Pelinon. In exchange, the Pelinon traded metals and other goods. "How could I forget him?

"He came to me last week and said the Soo Kari'Ma may be looking to break the truce and declare war. They're seeking an alliance of some sort with the Wolf Lord High Council. I don't have to tell you how bad that could be for Pelinon. Galphoreth assures me the council has no intention of allying themselves with the Kari'Ma, but I had to send more troops into those mountains, as has the Kapron Duke Syditios K'Dural. We've reinforced the entire line."

"I had no idea."

"No reason you should," Stevar said easily. "I also have trade negotiations coming up with the Rikarri Nations—those Guild bastards are talking about increasing rates for both cargo and passengers. I could deal with one on passengers—the nobility would absorb the bulk of that cost. But cargo?" Stevar shook his head. "The royal coffers would take a significant hit, and I have to be prepared for the possibility of a war on several fronts." He looked at Rellen. "That's why I sent Grall out to Caspari. I know he can get the job done, and I need all the leverage I can get to deal with that Elwhari'Ma dynast. I swear, she is a real a ball-breaker." Stevar closed his eyes for a moment and let out a long breath. "Bah!" He downed a shot of whisky and reached for the decanter. "But enough about matters of state." He poured himself another drink.

Rellen stared at his little brother for several heartbeats, and then a sad smile turned up the corners of his mouth. A wash of memories flowed over him—of Stevar, their father... and their mother.

"What is it?" Stevar asked, looking confused. "What's wrong?"

"Wrong?" Rellen fought the emotions raging within him and shook his head. "Nothing... Everything." He met his brother's questioning eyes. "It just hit me really hard that you're not my little brother anymore. You are my king, and it suits you. Father would be so very proud... *little brother.*" He let out a long, pained breath. "You are a far, far better king than I ever could have been."

Stevar smiled. "I don't know about that. In fact, most of the time, when I'm faced with really hard decisions, I ask myself one of two questions."

"Like what?"

"Well, if it's something to do with money or politics, I ask, 'What would Father do?' And if it has to do with conflict, the question is always, 'What would Rellen do?'" He tossed back his whisky.

Rellen stared into his glass. "I don't know what to say." As the words passed his lips, the swell of guilt and shame he'd been holding back crashed into him, carried on a storm of memory he'd kept buried for a very long time. His shoulder's slumped, as if the air had been let out of him.

"Nothing to say," Stevar soothed. "We are who we were meant to be, and I wouldn't have it any other way. Never forget, Father would be proud of you too, Rellen... of all you've accomplished as a soldier, kurios, and Guardian. You are one of Pelinon's greatest assets. You know that, don't you?"

Rellen just stood there, frozen, reliving old pain.

"Rellen?" Stevar asked, suddenly worried.

Rellen shook his head, trying to clear the vision of his mother's dead body floating in a bathtub. "I'm just good at getting into trouble..." he finally said. He lifted his gaze and stared at Stevar, a haunted look upon his face. "... and running out on the people who depend upon me. You know that better than anyone alive." There was something he needed to say—something he should have said a long time ago.

"What is it?" Stevar asked. "What's wrong?"

Rellen was silent for several moments, and with each heartbeat, his guilt and shame bubbled up in his breast.

"I need to apologize," he said softly.

Stevar looked perplexed. "For what?"

Rellen looked around the room, but he was really looking at the palace that surrounded them both… a place that had filled him with dread for decades.

"For sticking you with… all of this." He motioned to the walls and beyond. "I know you think we're doing what we were meant to, but when the time came, I ran out on Pelinon, on Father's wishes, on you… and for the *second* time."

"Second—"

"The throne," Rellen said, cutting him off, "and *Mother.*"

Stevar's eyes went wide, and he got a pained look on his face. "We swore we'd never talk about that."

"I think it's time we did," he said. "If I'm going to apologize for one, I have to apologize for both. When I abdicated the throne, I told you it was because I thought I could serve the kingdom better out there. That was only part of it." He swallowed hard. "I was scared." He expected his brother to be surprised, to interrupt him, do something or say something. Stevar just stared, a patient, compassionate look on his face. "Scared I'd let Pelinon down like I let her down."

Stevar's tone was even. "That wasn't your fault."

"Yes, it was." Rellen met his brother's gaze. "Father left her in my care—*mine*. He charged me with making sure nothing happened to her while he fought another war. You were there. You *know*. All I had to do was stand outside a door and listen. Instead, I told you to do it and went off to play games."

"There wasn't anything to hear. I told you that the day she died. She never made a sound."

"You were just a kid," Rellen snapped.

"So were *you*," Stevar barked back, and there was iron in his voice. "Her seizures… that gods-be-damned curse… there was nothing either of us could have done. Either way, Father *never* should have left it up to us."

"But he did," Rellen said, "and I'm the reason she's dead."

Stevar searched his brother's face. "I was seven, and you were eleven. You'd been standing outside that door every night for two months. Not once did Mother have a seizure while she bathed." He raised an eyebrow. "Is any of that not true?"

"It doesn't matter."

"I think…" Stevar's voice trailed off as a hard expression filled his features. "No—I *know* it does." He let out a frustrated breath. "It makes all the difference, Rellen."

Again, Rellen saw the shadow of his father in his brother's expression. He looked around the room. He didn't—*couldn't*—admit his brother was right. That was the reason he hated coming back to the palace. It brought up too many old ghosts, old guilt, old pain.

He motioned toward the map behind him. "You know, out there, my life boils down to clarity of purpose. Out there, I can right wrongs by spell and sword. I hunt the wicked. This palace… it was Father's cage. I left because I couldn't let it be mine. This cage made him helpless. The only time he ever really made a difference himself was when he left it. And, of course, when he did, Mother died."

"What are you talking about now?"

"How helpless a king can be."

Stevar gave him a strange look. "I'm not helpless—"

"Yes," Rellen said. "You are."

"Rellen," his brother said, stiffening, "I command armies. There isn't much I couldn't achieve if I wished it."

"You give orders, Stevar. You know when and how to give them, but you don't actually *do* anything. Don't get me wrong. We needed a good king, and in you we got one, but you need people like your generals, your dukes, your *Guardians*. We do what needs to be done in your name."

"I think I see what you're saying, at least a little… but I have no idea why."

"I failed Mother when she was made my responsibility. I knew I'd fail Pelinon if it was left in my care. The only skin I have to worry about anymore is my own. If I'd become king, the whole of Pelinon would have depended upon me. *Me*."

"I guess so, but—"

"That's why I didn't—*don't* want to be a mentor to anyone. If I do, they'll depend upon me, too. I'm sorry about Mother. I'm sorry about abdicating. I'm sorry about everything I've piled upon your shoulders."

Stevar's face turned more compassionate than Rellen had ever seen. He rose out of his chair and wrapped his arms around his older brother. Rellen hugged him back, fighting back tears that rarely saw the light of day.

"You can be so thick sometimes," Stevar said, squeezing his brother. He let go, stepped back, and stared into Rellen's bewildered eyes. "Neither of us could ever be anything but who and what we are."

Rellen's tears came. "But—"

"Rellen," Stevar said seriously, "you didn't abandon Mother, me, or Pelinon. At every turn, at every step in your life, you got stronger, more capable, and you did it to serve Pelinon in the best way you could. You've always been there for me, protecting me—fighting for me. *You still are.*" He clapped his brother on the shoulder. "What sort of brother—what sort of king would I be if I didn't understand you better than you understand yourself?" Stevar shook his head and gave Rellen a warm smile. "You have nothing to be ashamed of, although, I suspect these feelings will be with you for a long time." Stevar's expression once again reminded Rellen of their father's wisdom. "Someday you'll understand how easy it was for me to take up this one burden. Then, maybe, you'll be able to forgive yourself." He grabbed the bottle of whisky and poured himself another drink. He looked to Rellen's glass expectantly. Rellen held it up and Stevar filled it. "You're right about one thing, though."

"What's that?"

"I do need my generals, dukes, and Guardians to get anything done, and that includes you." Stevar stared at his brother for several heartbeats. "You're such an asshole sometimes," he finally said with a smile.

Rellen let out a relieved breath. His brother had known exactly what to say. "I'll drink to that," Rellen said, raising his glass in a toast. Stevar raised his own, and they tipped their glasses back.

Stevar placed his on the table and looked at his brother. "It's getting late. Be sure to check in with Corwyk as soon as you arrive in the city."

"I will."

"And promise me you'll be careful down there." Stevar looked genuinely worried. "Those Nissran bastards are out of their minds, and they don't take prisoners."

"Hey, you know what a cautious fellow I am."

"That's what worries me." Stevar turned to leave but turned back again. "Oh, and one more thing."

"What's that?"

"Mygal Durintur... I had no trepidations about selecting him to replace Voren. I know you and Voren were close, so I hope it won't be a problem."

Rellen nodded. "Thanks. I'm alright about it though. I don't really have any friends... well, it's a short list. Voren was who he was, and he wouldn't want us to dwell."

"You're not wrong," Stevar said. "As to Mygal Durintur, you need to be his mentor whether you like it or not. That being the case, he's rather full of himself. It's not undeserved. He's good at what he does, which is why I chose him. He's the perfect infiltrator, but he sometimes uses his majea to play with people's heads. Nothing serious, just mischievous. He kind of reminds me of you a not-too-long time ago. He's young, but he's proven himself to be quite capable. Get to know him. Let him get to know you before you... school him. Promise? It's not babysitting. It's mentoring, and you benefited from the same thing when I made you a Guardian."

"I will. I promise."

"Good. Then let's call it a night. You have to head out in the morning, and I have to deal with a list of problems a mile long before the sun sets tomorrow night."

"You've got a deal," Rellen said, and grabbed the decanter one more time.

CHAPTER FIVE
SVENNIVAL

Rellen pulled back the hood of his cloak as Shaddeth's great hooves clopped down a stretch of the King's Highway that cut through the heart of Svennival and continued south. It connected all the ducal seats in Pelinon. Unlike any other road in the kingdom, the King's Highway was three carriage-widths across and made of sturdy, timeless, pale gray stones that seemed impervious to the passage of time.

He'd pushed the black stallion on their journey south from Corsia, but Shaddeth's muscled frame was tireless. The sun was just coming up, burning away clouds that had drizzled all night long. He'd been on the road for several hours already, having risen from a restless night in the damp forests north of the city. He hadn't tried to keep a fire, although that was nothing new.

The whole of Pelinon was subject to rains throughout most of the year, in drips and downpours. As a soldier, he'd come to terms with riding—and sleeping—in the rain long ago. He was pleased, however. He'd made the journey from the palace in only six days rather than seven.

He felt movement beneath his cloak at the back of his saddle. Xilly crawled out from where she'd been sleeping, climbed up onto his saddle horn, and stretched out her body along Shaddeth's black-maned neck. She yawned with a mouth of tiny teeth. She took a few moments to look around and then turned toward Rellen.

Time to eat? She sent the drowsy but insistent thought.

Rellen reached into a pouch at his waist and pulled out a thick piece of jerky.

Here, he said, offering it too her. *Chew on that.*

She snatched it out of his hands with a snap of her small jaws and then drew back, clutching the jerky in her claws as she gnawed on the tough, seasoned meat with a good deal of enthusiasm.

Yum! Xilly's delight came through loud and clear.

"And there's more where that came from," Rellen assured her.

When the edge of town came into sight, he pulled on the reins and brought Shaddeth to a halt. "Time to report in," he said out loud. He pulled out a small sheet of vellum and a piece of charcoal from one of his pouches.

Tell the king I said hello, Xilly said, lifting her head from the jerky.

"I will," Rellen replied out loud and began writing.

> *"Arrived in Svennival, damp but safe. Will meet*
> *with Corwyk and hopefully Mygal today. Will keep*
> *you appraised of progress. Also, Xilly says hello."*

He pulled a black feather from a pouch on his bandoleer and stuck the quill through Shaddeth's mane. Closing his eyes, he tapped lightly into his majea, feeling the energy swell within his breast. He made several motions with both of his hands as he uttered the familiar incantation. The tattoo on his shoulder tingled. Energy flowed down through his hands to coalesce in the space before him. He poured that magical energy into the feather, causing it to glow an unearthly blue. He spoke the incantation again, focusing his will. When he finished, the feather glowed white. In a flash, it was consumed by dark swirls that twisted about, forming into the shape of a bird. Within moments the swirls solidified and transformed into a living crow. The bird, perched upon Shaddeth's head, turned toward him and blinked several times.

Rellen rolled up the small piece of vellum and let the bird bite down upon it. The crow leapt from its perch and flew off. It adjusted its course and headed northwest, quickly rising above the trees as it disappeared into a patch of fog.

With that out of the way, Rellen shook Shaddeth's reins and continued into the city. The streets of Svennival were mostly empty. One and two-story buildings slid past, as a morning fog ebbed and flowed around him. He passed a portly man guiding a donkey that pulled a cart full of milk cans. A baker stepped out the front doors of her bakery, shaking out a small carpet. Occasionally, Rellen passed doors and windows that held the distinct shape of a Kuriositarri wreath. Each one, set out during the Manifestation Festival or Kuriositar, indicated someone inside, usually around the age of puberty, had manifested their majea and would be participating in the festival.

It was one of Rellen's favorite holidays: three days set aside for young, burgeoning kurioi to show off their powers and, hopefully, get picked up by a tradesman or artisan looking for an apprentice. The festival, celebrated by most of the people of Pelinon, involved mostly teenagers, but there were younger kurioi—some much younger—as well as older youths with as many as twenty-one seasons behind them. After that, if one's majea hadn't manifested, it usually wasn't going to. Only about one in ten humans ever manifested, and of those, only a handful possessed it in any meaningful way. The rest were capable of simple tricks and tasks, like lighting fires, controlling insects, or shaping metal. Few outside the nobility ever made it to a magic academy, but those of exceptional talent and little means were sometimes given scholarships.

He guided Shaddeth through the center of Svennival, taking in the wide ribbons and wreathes that decorated the city square. His brother had been right. It looked as if Svennival went all out for the Manifestation Festival.

Rellen continued through the city, taking in the feel of it. Every city had a different combination of sights, smells, and sounds, and it had been years since he'd been here. As he continued, foot traffic picked up, forcing him to navigate around one carriage or wagon after another. He rode past the main docks, where two large sailing ships and an oar-driven barge were tethered at the far end of the pier. Several hundred yards out on the lake, another sailing vessel approached. Its sails were furled, but two heavy ropes stretched out away from her bow. The water along both ropes churned and rippled out of cadence with the waves, as a clan of Bhirtas'Vuoda—water goblins—towed the ship in. It was how many of their race earned their living near port cities.

The docks disappeared from view, and within minutes, Rellen found himself in front of the ducal keep. It was a tall, blocky structure of gray stone, with a ten-foot wall and six towers arranged around the central part of the main building. More festival banners decorated the outer walls. The iron portcullis was open, and no soldiers manned the walls. He guided Shaddeth to a hitching post outside a stone livery beside the keep.

Nobody came out to tend his horse, but that wasn't unusual.

He swung his leg over Shaddeth's withers and set his boots upon the ground. Xilly leapt off the saddle and landed on his shoulder, coiling her tail around his neck to steady herself. Something made him pull out the Eye of Tuluum. The black sphere dangled on the chain before his eyes. He expected it to either do nothing or point in a random direction. To his surprise, the jewel leaned forward, away from his body, and straight toward the main doors of the keep. He scratched his head, confused. Normally, when he knew where he was going, the artifact didn't do anything. There was no indication of why it was guiding him inside, although even that was an assumption. It might just as well be pointing toward something five hundred miles away.

"There's no telling what this thing will do, eh, Shaddeth?" he said, patting the horse's neck. "Well," he added, slipping it beneath his tunic, "it doesn't matter. I know where I'm going for a change."

He lashed Shaddeth's reins around the hitching post and took a quick inventory of his gear. His spell books were still secured upon Shaddeth's withers, along with his saddlebags, bedroll, and oilskin shelter. He drew upon his majea, uttered a brief incantation, and felt a faint surge of energy flow from his outstretched palm to surround Shaddeth. The protection spell would send a severe shock into anyone who touched his belongings. He knew Shaddeth would stomp anyone who tried to steal something, but he'd learned long ago to be thorough.

"Let's go meet Corwyk and the Thirteenth Guardian," Rellen said, looking at Xilly. He remembered his brother's warning about Mygal's propensity for magic mischief. He pulled a small crystal from a pouch at his belt. Holding it firmly between his fingers, he made a quick gesture and muttered a short incantation not too dissimilar from the one he'd just cast. A soft white glow momentarily encompassed his body. He felt a tingle across his entire body that quickly subsided. He knew the spell would remain effective for several hours in case Mygal decided to play with him.

Rellen strode up the wide, stone steps of the keep, grabbed one of the large, iron knockers, and banged it against the door twice. Moments later, he heard a heavy bar lifted away. The wide, double doors swung inward, revealing five bored-looking guards in the ducal livery of red and blue. They wore chain mail and steel cap helms. Longswords were strapped to their hips.

"State your business," the one in the center said with only a bit of grit. He wore a lieutenant's insignia on his collar. His eyes flicked to Xilly, widened slightly in surprise, and then focused on Rellen.

"I'm Rellen of Corsia. I'm here to—"

"See Lord Corwyk and his guest," the lieutenant finished for him. "We weren't expecting you until tomorrow."

"I made good time."

The lieutenant turned to the sergeant beside him. "Might as well keep the doors open for today's business," he said. "If that beggar, Thomar, comes around looking for table scraps again, toss him out the front gate on his ear."

"Yes, Lieutenant," a grizzled, old-timer with a salt-and-pepper beard and stern eyes replied. "And with pleasure."

The lieutenant turned back to Rellen. "Follow me. I'll take you to them."

"Thank you, Lieutenant," Rellen replied.

The lieutenant turned crisply on his heel and marched off with Rellen in tow. They crossed a grand entry hall, with several banners draped down the walls, a large painting of what Rellen assumed was Duke Belvenim and his family, and an assortment of arms and armor. Wide staircases curved up each side of the hall, meeting at a large balcony on the back side, with hallways stretching to the left and right. The wall beyond the landing was a series of glass doors and windows.

The lieutenant took the right-hand stairs, and as they climbed them, Rellen heard the distinct, metallic clicking of fencing blades clashing together. Beyond the glass was a wide patio of sorts with a low stone railing, a view of the lake, and a stretch of marsh grass in between.

On the patio, a young man with an athletic build fenced with an attractive woman wearing the ducal red and blue. Her hair was tied up, and she handled the light rapier with remarkable skill. The young man wore a loose-fitting tunic of white, baggy slacks, and had a long mane of black hair that danced in the light breeze as they fenced. Rellen could just make out bandages around his left shoulder beneath his tunic. A decanter of juice sat on a nearby table, along with a half-full glass of juice and a plate of yellow stakka fruit.

They seemed to be only sparring, perhaps even stretching the man's injured muscles out a bit.

As Rellen and the lieutenant reached the top of the stairs, a tall man roughly Rellen's age appeared from the hallway on the right. He had angular features, intelligent hazel eyes, and wore a fine, tailored suit of indigo that fit his slim frame perfectly. He carried himself with confidence, but there was something in his stride that belied a more-than-capable readiness for conflict.

"Rellen Falcoria!" Corwyk shouted with a smile. "It's been what? Twelve years? It's good to see you, old friend." He stepped up and grabbed Rellen's extended forearm in a warrior's grasp.

"Far too long, to be sure," Rellen said. "It's good to see you, too, Corwyk."

Corwyk turned to the lieutenant. "That will be all, Fantyn. Thank you."

"Yes, sir," the lieutenant said. He gave a crisp salute and marched back down the stairs.

Corwyk's eyes turned to Xilly. "And what do we have here?" He cocked his head to the side, examining her at a safe distance. "I'd heard of dragonettes, but I've never seen one, and certainly not as a companion of any kind." He raised his hand and then hesitated. "Does it bite?"

"Only when *she's* hungry, which is most of the time, I'm afraid." Rellen scratched her side, eliciting a soft cooing sound. Corwyk reached out, and Xilly extended her neck, sniffing his offered hand. She licked it once, and he scratched the back of her neck, drawing out more cooing from her.

"Is she intelligent?"

"Very," Rellen replied. "Remarkably so, in fact. Allow me to introduce Xilly. Xilly, this is Corwyk Belvenim, Duke Regent of Svennival," he added as gently as possible. He knew Corwyk well enough to know that the new title would be a reminder of *why* he had that title.

Corwyk stiffened, drawing his hand back quickly. A pall of pain and anger filled his features as he turned his eyes to the floor and gritted his teeth.

"I was very sorry to hear about your uncle and his family," Rellen offered, placing a hand on Corwyk's shoulder.

"Thank you," Corwyk replied softly. "I'll never forget the sight of them." He clenched a fist. "They were *butchered*." He lifted his eyes slowly, and they were haunted by something Rellen knew his old friend would never be able to unsee. "I suppose you have questions."

"I do," Rellen said gently, "but I thought it might be easier to question Mygal. He saw the aftermath too, yes?"

"Yes."

"Then I'll grill him, not you." Rellen glanced out the windows where the two fencers still went at each other. "Is that him?" He tried to keep the irritation out of his voice. He'd told his brother he'd do his best as a mentor, but he still resented it.

Corwyk turned and nodded. "Yes. A rather agreeable fellow, I must say." Corwyk turned back to Rellen. "He seems a bit young to hold the post he does." As duke regent, Corwyk knew Rellen and Mygal were Guardians, but it was customary to not mention such things in public, unless there was a good reason to do so.

"Or maybe we're just getting old," Rellen offered.

"That too."

"Who's that with him?" Rellen asked, watching the woman with an appreciative eye. Her sword play was as fluid as water and lightning fast.

"Lieutenant Savarre," Corwyk said. "She's been assigned as my personal bodyguard.

"She seems quite capable with that thing."

"You have no idea," Corwyk replied. "She got assigned because she's the best in the keep with edged weapons."

Rellen placed a hand on Corwyk's arm. "Before we go out there, I want to ask you something unrelated to what's going on here in Svennival."

"What's that?"

"When you left university, you joined the staff under the old Duke of Mallorand, didn't you?"

"That's right," Corwyk replied, a curious expression on his face.

"Do you still keep in contact with people there?"

"My sister is an aide to the court," Corwyk replied. "Why?"

Rellen hesitated for a moment, not certain he should broach the subject. If Corwyk was involved in sedition here in Svennival somehow, Rellen could be showing his hand. He decided to trust his instincts in the man he'd known at university.

"I was wondering if you'd heard anything of late... maybe grumblings from the nobles there?"

"I got a letter from my sister just last week. She works closely with Duke Arrivar. From her letters over the past few months, everything seems to be running smoothly, although she did mention Arrivar is at least a little unpopular with the old guard, but that's to be expected. He is, apparently, quite popular with the younger barons." Corwyk looked thoughtful for a moment. "I wouldn't be surprised if Arrivar stirs up trouble for the old guard to either get them in line or drive them out, but that's a long way from sedition. Why do you ask?"

"Just curious... something I'd heard recently. It's most likely nothing for anyone to be concerned about. Duchy politics are the same all over, eh?" Rellen hoped Corwyk's sister wasn't somehow involved. With Faleesh Namarre investigating, she would follow the king's orders to the letter and likely kill everyone involved.

"Isn't that the truth," Corwyk said, letting out a long, weary breath.

"Come on," Rellen said, nodding towards Mygal. "I want to find out what the king sees in this fellow."

With Corwyk leading the way, they walked out onto the patio to find Mygal still fencing with Lieutenant Savarre. The woman noticed Corwyk and Rellen approaching and stepped back, holding up her hand. Mygal froze mid-thrust and looked over his shoulder. He turned back to the woman, raising his rapier in salute, and she returned the gesture.

"Nicely done," the woman said. "I think you're recovering nicely."

"Thank you, Veraiya."

"Don't you two ever quit?" Corwyk called out.

"No," she replied matter-of-factly.

"And I needed to get back in shape as quickly as possible," Mygal added, laying the rapier on the table. He then faced Rellen. "Rellen Falcoria, I presume?"

"That's right." Rellen held out his hand, and they exchanged a handshake that bordered on unnecessarily firm. Rellen gave more than he got. "Mygal... Durintur? Did I say that correctly?"

"Perfectly." Mygal flashed Rellen a friendly smile. "I'm honored."

"No trouble at all, especially considering our mutual friends."

Mygal's eyes lit up at that, as if the acknowledgement as a Guardian was somehow profound to him.

"And this is Veraiya Savarre," Corwyk nodded to her, "Captain of the Ducal Guard and Master at Arms."

"It's a pleasure to meet you," Rellen said, bowing slightly. "I must say, your bladework—both of you—is commendable."

The lieutenant nodded her thanks.

"Again, I'm honored," Mygal said, and as he said it, Rellen felt the tingle of Mygal's ermajea brush against his protection spell. It was like a cobweb sliding over his arm. If he hadn't cast his protection spell, he'd have never felt it.

So it begins, Rellen thought.

He locked eyes with the younger Guardian, a bland expression upon his face. For a fleeting moment, he felt Mygal's ermajea press harder, ever so slightly. Rellen gave the young man a superior smile and raised an eyebrow. Mygal's jovial smile wavered for a flickering instant, and his eyes went just a hint wider. The tingle of magic jerked away.

Rellen gave the faintest of satisfied nods. If he was going to be Mygal's mentor, he had to put him in his place from the outset. "Shall we get down to business?" He motioned for everyone to sit down.

Mygal swallowed once and straightened his back. "Yes, I think that would be best."

"Good," Rellen replied.

"I won't be able to join you," Veraiya said. She looked at Mygal and then Corwyk. "Besides, there's nothing I know about the murders that either Corwyk or Mygal don't."

"Very well," Rellen replied, glancing at her. "It was a pleasure meeting you."

"The pleasure was mine." She gave a stiff bow, and as she strode away, the three men sat down at the table.

Rellen never took his eyes off Mygal, pleased with the younger Guardian's discomfort. It was a perfect way to begin. He caught Corwyk glance at him out of the corner of his eye, the obvious question there.

Rellen scratched his cheek twice, using an old court signal to wave Corwyk off.

Called Crysvardish, the sign was part of an exceptionally subtle sign language known to members of the high court. Involving simple gestures and the accoutrements of noble settings. Rellen had learned it as a boy, and he was reasonably confident Mygal didn't know it—and wouldn't catch the sign, even if he did.

Rellen plucked a grape from the platter on the table and held it up for Xilly, who took it eagerly and dug in.

"So," Rellen said smoothly, staring straight at Mygal, "I suppose my first question is, did the murders take place here or someplace else?"

Mygal glanced at Corwyk with a trace of discomfort, but then he looked back to Rellen. "It all happened at the duke's manor house about a mile from here on the lake. They were all... butchered... in their beds."

"Did you get to see the bodies before they were taken away?"

Mygal got a haunted look in his eyes. "Yes. I was here purely by chance, but when the alarm went up, I informed

Corwyk who I was. He was gracious enough to let me begin my own investigation in tandem with the constables assigned to find the killer or killers. Whoever did it also set fire to a small cottage behind the manor house, leaving only a pile of ash and a few burned timbers."

That caught Rellen's attention. "Nothing else was burned?"

"No," Mygal replied.

Rellen tucked that fact away. "Did you notice anything odd in how the family was killed? Were there any patterns to their wounds?"

"None that I could tell," Mygal replied. He closed his eyes and shivered once. "I've never seen anything so brutal, and I grew up in the Beskiar District in Corsia."

Rellen nodded. As a prince in Corsia, he knew Beskiar well, although he'd spent very little time there. That district was where most of the organized crime took place in the capital city. Plenty of patrols roamed the area, always had, but the king's constables only dug deep when innocents were killed. Beskiar was the one place in Corsia where criminal activity was at least marginally tolerated, mostly because it kept it from spreading to other parts of the city.

"Could you tell what sort of weapon or weapons were used?"

Mygal was thoughtful for a moment. "From what I saw, at least three different blades were used... a dagger on the daughter, a different dagger on the son, a longer blade on the duke's wife, and an ax to kill the duke."

"What was your conclusion, then?" Rellen asked.

"Based on the weapons, I suspect no less than two—probably three, perhaps more—killers were in the house that night. As near as I could tell, they were all murdered in their sleep. There was no sign of a struggle."

"I'd guessed as much, but you've just confirmed it." Rellen eyed Mygal. "And if they didn't put up a fight, how was that accomplished?"

Mygal got a knowing look on his face, obviously aware Rellen was testing him, but he didn't seem to resent it.

"The two most likely scenarios are that they were either drugged—probably during a meal they shared—or a lifeweaver of some skill put them to sleep to do whatever he—or she—wanted."

Rellen nodded at that last part. Despite Mygal's attempt at playing with Rellen's emotions, he was growing at least a small measure of respect for the young Guardian. He appeared to be thoughtful, didn't take anything for granted, and the comment about it being a man *or* a woman showed he assumed nothing.

"Let me ask you another question, then," Rellen said. "I've heard rumblings of possible sedition here in the duchy. Could these murders have anything to do with something like that?" He cast a sidelong glance at Corwyk to see how his old classmate reacted to the mention of sedition.

Corwyk looked surprised, but far from guilty.

When Rellen returned his gaze to Mygal, the young Guardian had an impressed look on his face.

"I don't *think* so, but I have to tell you both that it's a possibility. During my investigation, I did hear rumors of at least two minor barons, Umar and Gorven, who were, perhaps, disgruntled enough to act on it. Something about taxes being too stiff and demanding a change."

"That's the first I've heard of it," Corwyk said, sitting upright, an annoyed look on his face. "I'll look into that immediately."

Rellen placed his hand on Corwyk's arm. "I'd ask that you do nothing, at least not yet."

"But Rellen—" Corwyk started.

"For now," Rellen soothed, "it's just rumors." He looked to Mygal. "Is that correct?"

"It is," Mygal assured Corwyk. "I also know both of the barons were far from here when the murders took place. That doesn't mean they didn't hire someone, but I just don't see them doing it."

Rellen nodded, and then he looked to his friend. "There's something I want to ask, but I don't want you to read too much into it. It's just part of my investigation."

"Go ahead," Corwyk replied, a wary look on his face.

"There was no love lost between your uncle and my father. I mean, their feud was an old one. Is it possible the duke got caught up with something, and when he wasn't willing to go far enough, his associates had him killed so they could take his place?"

"I didn't know about that," Mygal said.

"No reason you should," Rellen assured him, and then he locked eyes with Corwyk, who looked almost offended.

"Rellen," Corwyk said a bit stiffly, "I'll admit, there was some bad blood. Whatever it was, goes way back and had to do with matters Vladysh never shared with me. But sedition? Whatever conflict existed between them died with your father. What's more, my uncle was *always* a proud servant of the Crown. And my uncle never had a bad thing to say about Saren III. The idea of Vladysh being involved in any sort of plot against the Crown, then or now, seems totally out of character and pointless in the extreme. He'd have opposed such a thing. I'm certain of it."

"Maybe that's why he was killed," Rellen mused.

"Do you really think that's possible?" Corwyk asked.

"I honestly don't know, but I intend to find out." Rellen was reasonably confident neither Corwyk nor Vladysh were involved in sedition. He didn't have any proof, but he'd developed a good sense for reading people over the years. There would be little benefit for a duchy so close to the capital to revolt. Such things were more likely in the far reaches of a kingdom and rarely at its heart.

"Then, there's one last thing before Mygal and I set off to dig deeper into the investigation."

"What's that?" Corwyk asked.

"Tell your constables and magistrates to keep an eye out for Nissran cultists."

"The Nissrans," Corwyk and Mygal blurted together.

Rellen nodded. "There have been reports across the kingdom, and I scorched a nest of them in Calamath only a few months ago. They tried to possess the baron's son, and they almost succeeded."

"Gods save us," Corwyk said. "The last thing we need here are those vermin spreading their filth."

"Agreed," Rellen replied. "Keep an eye out, and watch yourself. If they're here, they may come after you. You're in a perfect position to serve their purposes."

"Don't worry. With Veraiya's help, we'll crush any Nissran that pokes its head up."

"Good," Rellen replied. "The method of the duke's murder does suggest the possibility of them trying to infiltrate Svennival, but from what Mygal described, I'm inclined to think that isn't the case. The bodies I found in Calamath all had a specific mark cut into their foreheads, although that was part of the ceremony to possess the baron's son. The Nissrans crave blood, so we can't discount them as the culprits, but without that mark, I don't think they're trying to possess anyone here." The number of possibilities was giving Rellen fits. "Bah!" He shook his head. "Maybe I'm just stuck in a rut. You deal with those bastards once, and you start seeing them everywhere."

"I can see how you might," Mygal said.

What confused Rellen the most was that neither Mygal nor Corwyk knew of anything concrete regarding either the Nissrans or sedition, yet Saleeria had made a point of it as a possibility.

"Alright, so there may not be a Nissran cult here, and there doesn't seem to be sedition, yet the duke and his family are dead." He looked to Mygal. "Have you discovered anything concrete?"

"I'm embarrassed to say I haven't." He let out a frustrated breath. "I was following a local thug involved in a protection racket. I'd been told he bragged about stealing from the duke and mentioned that the encounter had been a final one."

Rellen raised an eyebrow.

"I know," Mygal assured him, "it's tenuous at best, but it's all I'd uncovered. I was attacked while I was following him. I can't say for certain, but I suspect it's likely that whoever skewered me was involved in the murders. I know what happened, and I have a suspicion of who, but I have no idea why."

"Something's bothering me," Rellen said. "If this was just some random, brutal murder of an entire family, even just to steal their property, then why attack you after the fact? Murderers who kill for money usually fade into the woodwork until the heat is off, or they move on. Something doesn't fit here. Murderers who kill for sport would have struck again by now, unless the individual or individuals are slow starters. Is it possible the duke was involved with some shady characters we don't know about?"

"I suppose that's possible," Corwyk offered. "The duke—all dukes for that matter—have to occasionally deal with seedier sorts in order to keep a duchy running. Even the king does it." He glanced at Mygal. "The Beskiar District in Corsia is proof. In Svennival, it's the Black Wyrm Clan. Although, I can't imagine my uncle getting in deep enough with them to warrant something like this."

"That makes sense," Rellen said. "But it's always a matter of degrees, and from time to time, things can get out of hand—and quickly."

"I think that's the path we should be pursuing," Mygal chimed in. "Not Nissrans. Not sedition. The city's underbelly is a bit more sullied than I would have thought. I was just starting to scratch the surface. I do know someone who might be able to help us on that front. I was working with him before I was attacked."

"It's agreed then," Rellen said. "You and I will dig deeper in that direction and see what we can turn up." He turned to Corwyk. "I need a favor."

"Name it."

"I need you to track down a woman by the name of Miranda Torai. She'll mostly likely be on the bounty hunter rolls for the duchy. It's important I meet with her as soon as possible." The king had said Mygal was good, but Rellen didn't like going into a fight with an untested blade.

"A bounty hunter?" Corwyk frowned.

"Much more than a bounty hunter. She'll be useful. I promise." He gave Corwyk a reassuring smile. "So, where can we stay? We need to be closer to where the gutters have more blood in them."

"The Drunken Unger," Mygal said without hesitation. "It's just at the edge of the red district and where I first saw my only suspect, Dancer."

"I know where it is," Corwyk replied a bit too quickly.

Rellen and Mygal looked at him with mischievous, accusing eyes.

"It's not what you think," Corwyk replied a bit sheepishly. "I've just had a few meals there."

"Sure, sure," Rellen said.

"The food *is* pretty good," Mygal offered.

"Then let's get moving, if you're up to it," he asked, looking at Mygal. "I want to go to the duke's manor first, then we can head for the Drunken Unger."

"I'm ready to go. I just need to remove this bandage and change clothes." He looked at Corwyk. "Thank you for your hospitality."

"Of course," Corwyk said. "We all serve the king."

CHAPTER SIX

SCENE OF THE CRIME

Beneath a partly cloudy sky and a canopy of old trees, the two Guardians rode side-by-side through the streets of Svennival, headed for the duke's manor house. They were a picture of opposites. Rellen, in his dark leather armor and heavy cloak, rode a giant warhorse. With matched falchions and potent magics, he looked ready to ride straight into battle. The dragonette on his shoulder only added to his mystique.

Mygal, on the other hand, rode a lesser steed of mixed breeding and a mottled hide. He wore a light tunic of deep green, with a high collar and ruffled cuffs. His pants were dark gray leather, as were the gloves that came up to his forearms. Where Rellen was ominous, Mygal was roguish, and in both cases, the look suited the man.

"You're not upset, are you?" Mygal asked, glancing at Rellen.

"For what?" Rellen knew the answer, but he wanted to draw this out.

"For trying to influence you back at the keep." Mygal sounded apologetic but not quite embarrassed.

At least he's honest, Rellen thought. *I'll give him that.* "Is that what happened?" he said, the side of his mouth crimping up.

"You know it is."

Rellen stayed silent for several heartbeats, just long enough to make his point.

"No," he finally said. "I'm not angry." He cast a sidelong glance in Mygal's direction. "There's something you need to know."

"What's that?"

"I'm not just here to help with the investigation."

"Oh?" Mygal got a worried look on his face. "The king isn't relieving me, is he?"

"No," Rellen said, "nothing like that. He has every confidence in you, but as of now, I'm officially your mentor."

"Mentor?" Mygal looked disappointed.

"That's right, and as long as I'm being honest, I resent the assignment." He met Mygal's gaze. "That has *nothing whatsoever* to do with you."

Mygal's disappointment turned to discomfort. "So, you're here under duress."

"Technically? Yes." Rellen got a thoughtful look on his face. "You'll never know the details, so you'll never understand my motives. I do resent getting saddled with being a mentor. Having said that, I don't mind mentoring *you*. I give you my word, I'm going to do my best to teach you what I know, just like the Second Guardian, Jaquinn El Barad did with me. I do this because it's my duty. I do it for the king and for Pelinon. I do it so that, as a Guardian, you are as capable and competent as I can make you. Understand?"

"I think I do."

"Good," Rellen said. "Then let me say one last thing about you using your ermajea on me back at the keep. "Pull that stunt again, and we're going to have more than words. We understand one another?"

"We do." Mygal went silent for a few moments. "Just so you know, it's sort of a habit, you know?" He pressed his lips together. "Instinctual is the best word for it."

Rellen nodded. He'd known a number of erkurioi over the years, and many of them used their magic the same way other people breathed.

"If I may offer a suggestion—and for now it's just that—consider easing back with it when you first meet people. Only use it when you need to. In our line of work, it's sometimes best not to show your hand, especially when it comes to majea. It's about control."

"I see your point." Mygal's eyes slipped down to Rellen's chest. "You're a runecaster, so what about your bandoleer?" he asked. "Doesn't that show your hand?"

Rellen nodded. *The kid is sharp.*

"It does." Rellen patted the vials and pouches running across his chest. "I take it off when it's appropriate, but it fits the bounty hunter motif most of the time. And if I didn't need it, I wouldn't wear it. *You* have a choice." It was Rellen's turn to go quiet for a few moments. "I'm beginning to see in you what the king does, by the way."

"Oh?" Mygal let a satisfied smile cross his face.

"You've got a keen mind, your sword work is more than respectable from what I saw, and you've got natural charisma, with or without the heartbending."

"Thank you." Mygal got a humble look upon his face. "That actually means a lot to me." He went silent, but it looked like there was something he wanted to say.

"Go ahead and spit it out," Rellen offered. "I may be your mentor for the time being, but we can't have secrets. Always speak your mind with me. Do that, and we'll get along fine."

"You're the first Guardian I've met so far. When the king offered to make me one, he said I would replace a man named Voren... and he was your friend."

"Friend is a strong word, but Voren's passing meant something to me," Rellen replied.

"I'm sorry, then," Mygal offered. "Losing comrades is never easy."

He's compassionate too, Rellen thought. *I'm beginning to like him, damn it.* He pushed that thought away like it was poison.

"It's dangerous to have friends in our line of work. Voren died doing what he loved." Rellen remembered all the good times he'd had working and fighting side-by-side with Voren. He knew he would miss him, but he'd already buried those feeling in a dark hole in his mind. It didn't pay to get emotionally involved with Guardians—or anyone else, for that matter, which is why he'd stopped doing it. "The truth is, I'll probably go the same way one of these days. You too, for that matter, and the rest of the Guardians... except maybe Saleeria." He turned and locked eyes with Mygal. "Guardians rarely die of natural causes... although I met one recently who probably will, so it's at least possible."

"As long as I go out fighting on the right side, I won't complain."

"That's the spirit," Rellen said.

"Thank you." Mygal stood up in his saddle and leaned forward to look around the bend in the cobblestone road. "It's just up ahead, there on the left."

As the road curved around a large, manicured hedge, a fine manor house came into view. It was a bastion of pale gray stone atop a low rise, with columns in front of the main structure and wide windows facing outward on the wings to either side. A red cobblestone drive curved up from the main road, passed under an outstretched overhang, and curved back to the main road again. A wide carriage house stood off to the side a short distance, with two gilded blue carriages parked inside. Rellen spotted movement inside a big bay window of the west wing. He pointed it out to Mygal as they guided their horses up the drive.

"That's their butler," Mygal said. "Stiff fellow and wasn't all that prone to sharing. I couldn't tell if it was me or he was still shaken up about the murders."

"You questioned the entire staff?"

"As best I could," Mygal replied. "The butler, cooks, and housekeepers, all of whom had been in their quarters in the attached dormitory behind the east wing on the opposite side of the manor. It's well away from the family's quarters but wasn't necessarily out of earshot. They claim to have heard nothing, and I got no sense that wasn't the case. If what they told me is true, then none of them knew anything until they heard the cottage in the back burning."

They stopped in front of the main doors and dismounted.

"Stay here, Shaddeth," Rellen said, not seeing any place to secure the reins. "Will your horse stay put?"

"Usually," Mygal replied. "Although Sheila sometimes has a mind of her own," he added, patting her neck fondly.

"Here," Rellen said, holding out his hand. "Let me have her reins."

Mygal handed them over, and Rellen lashed them around Shaddeth's saddle horn. "That'll keep her here, and he'll stomp anyone who messes with our gear."

"He's that well trained?" Mygal said, sounding impressed.

"And then some." Rellen patted Shaddeth on the neck. "I've never ridden a finer steed."

Rellen led them up the front steps and knocked on the door.

Moments later, the door swung open, revealing a thin, older gentleman with a naturally dour look.

"May I help you?" he offered automatically, and then his eyes fixed on Mygal. "Oh, it's you." He clearly wasn't happy to see Mygal, but there was no animosity in his features.

"Good morning, Renton," Mygal said. "My associate and I would like to continue our investigation. You've left everything just as it was, like I requested?"

"Of course, sir," the butler replied. "We would never do anything to impede your efforts. We are as eager to see the miscreants brought to justice as anyone."

"Has the entire staff remained here?" Rellen asked.

"None of us have been dismissed yet, sir. The Belvenim extended family still grieves and has, as yet, not decided what to do with this property or the staff."

"I see," Rellen said. "May we come in, then?"

"Of course, sir," Renton said, opening the door wide and motioning for them to enter. "Is there anything I can do to assist you?"

"No, thank you," Rellen said. "Please go about your business as if we're not here."

"Certainly, sir," Renton replied. Without another word, he turned and walked off, disappearing down a long hallway that cut through the middle of the house.

The interior was just as Rellen had expected. There was a large foyer with a curved staircase going up on either side of a long hallway that probably led to a kitchen and dining area. A large sitting room with a fireplace lay off to the left, and a study lined with books was off to the right. An assortment of artwork, vases, and statues filled the interior, and everything was of the finest quality.

"Walk me through it," Rellen said, turning to Mygal. "From the outside in."

Mygal nodded and stepped into the foyer. "For starters, the place was—allegedly—warded. All windows and doors, from what the staff told me."

"Who cast them?"

"The duke's wife. An accomplished runecaster, like you. Apparently, she and the duke adventured together when they were younger. It was how they met. Renton said there were potent and long-lasting wards on all windows and doors that she refreshed regularly."

"Was the duke a kurios?" Rellen asked.

"No, and neither were the children. Only the mother."

Rellen nodded.

"Any sign that the murderers broke in somehow?"

"None that I could tell," Mygal replied. "Any kurioi good enough to put them all to sleep and kill them might have little difficulty negating the wards, though."

"They'd have to know they were there, and at least a hint of what sort of magic," Rellen said. "To do it quickly, anyway."

"Really?" Mygal asked, a thoughtful look upon his face. "I don't know much of anything about runecasting."

"I do," Rellen said confidently. "If you assume I'm right, then what should we deduce from it?"

"That they had inside information, or it *was* one or more of the staff."

"It's possible," Rellen said. His eyes flicked around the interior, taking in every detail. "And nothing was missing or moved when the staff woke up?"

"Not down here," Mygal replied. "A few items were stolen from upstairs where the murders took place, but all of this was untouched."

Rellen gave Mygal an expectant, questioning glance.

"I thought it odd as well," Mygal said. "There's plenty down here worth stealing, and whomever did this left it all in place."

"So…"

"So, it was more about the killing, and less about the stealing."

"That would seem to be the case." Rellen looked up the stairs. "Show me where it happened."

Mygal nodded and then moved up the right-hand stairs with Rellen close behind.

"I don't know the order of the murders," Mygal said, looking back over his shoulder. "There's was no way for me to tell, based on what's up there, but I'm not sure it's all that important."

"You're probably right, but I never assume anything is fact until I have proof." Rellen looked down at the hardwood stairs and noted an occasional drop of dried blood along the way. Many had been scuffed and scraped by people walking up and down, but from the looks of those that were unmarred, they'd hit the polished wood as someone was coming down the stairs. *It makes sense*, he thought.

Mygal nodded as they reached the top of the stairs and turned right. There was even more blood on the landing, and the traces he saw were also consistent with a killer or killers coming out of the bedrooms and down the stairs.

"Hold up," Rellen said, kneeling down. He leaned over and looked at the droplets that had fallen along both sides of the staircases.

"What?" Mygal said, turning back.

Rellen scanned the landing between the stairs. There were no blood droplets.

"We definitely have more than one killer," he said, looking up at Mygal.

"I guessed that, but how can you be certain?"

Rellen stood up. "Take a look," he said, pointing at the landing. "Those droplets come out of that side and go down those stairs. These droplets come out of this side and go down these stairs. If it were one person, they would have had to cross here. I'm also thinking they wiped off the weapons and themselves, at least somewhat, after each murder, otherwise there would be a lot more blood around here."

"They did," Mygal said, sounding impressed, "and I see what you mean about the landing."

"Whose bedroom is back there?" Rellen asked, nodding toward where Mygal was going.

"The duke and his wife, Esselyn," Mygal said. "I figured I'd show you that one first."

"Good."

Mygal turned and walked down a long hallway. There were closed doors on either side. At the end of the hall, a tall, wooden door stood open. From where Rellen was, he could already see blood streaks on the floor and furniture.

They made their way into a large, well-appointed bedroom with a tall, four-poster bed surrounded by drapes that had been pulled back. Dried blood streaks and spatter were literally everywhere: bedclothes, drapes, walls, ceiling, and large pools of it on either side of the bed. The exposed down mattress had been completely soaked in blood. Rellen immediately understood why Corwyk and Mygal had gone pale at the memory of the scene.

Mygal pointed to the right-hand side of the bed. "They found the duke there, and he'd been hacked to pieces. His arm and the lower part of his leg were on the floor. His head had been severed, and his chest was a gory patchwork of ax strikes. It looked to me like rage."

"That does sound a little like the Nissrans, but you said there were no sigils or symbols upon his body?"

"Not that I could tell." He pointed to the other side. "The wife was hacked upon with a longer weapon... a sword of some kind, although I couldn't tell what. It *might* have been a straight blade rather than curved. I just don't know." He turned around and pointed to an open jewelry box on a nearby dresser. It was empty. "They cleaned that out, and the butler told me a small chest full of gold and jewels had been mostly emptied, but not completely."

"Not completely?" Rellen asked, astonished.

"No. The bottom of it was covered with gold coins... old ones, apparently."

Rellen was thoughtful for a moment.

"They took what they could easily carry and went for gems and jewelry before coins." He looked around the room. There were silver-handled brushes on a vanity in the corner, a pair of crossed swords on the far wall, and an unopened, gold-embossed gentleman's box on the other dresser. Rellen walked over, opened the box, and peered inside. Within was an assortment of silver cravat pins, two gold cloak pins, and a few rings of precious metal. They'd left the duke's lesser jewelry behind. "This was an execution," he said almost to himself.

"That was my assessment."

Rellen stepped up to where the duke had been killed and kneeled down over the dried pool of blood. He pulled a small glass vial from a pouch at his waist and drew a short dagger from within his right bracer. It was a spell dagger used in conjunction with his majea. The blade was simple, with a wide, drop point; the pommel was a quartz sphere. There were runes inscribed into the silver hilt. He scraped up some of the dried blood and placed it in the vial before jamming a small cork in the end. He then closed his eyes and focused his majea. He whispered an incantation and then used the tip of the dagger to etch a "V" into the glass.

"What are you doing?" Mygal asked.

"Collecting a bit of their essence," Rellen replied.

"What for?"

"I'll show you later." He moved around the bed and did the same thing with the wife's blood, carving an "E" into the glass vial. Rellen turned around. "Show me the rest."

Mygal nodded and strode out of the room. They crossed the landing and went down the hall. There was another study lined with bookshelves at the far end. A wide desk sat in the middle, with a quill and ink on top, but nothing else. Mygal stopped at the first door on the left, which also stood open.

Rellen followed him in and found a scene similar to the last one. It was a young man's room, by the look of it. There was a large oak bed in the center, with a dresser in one corner and a fencing dummy in the other. The dummy had a suit of leather armor over it, and a well-crafted longsword leaned against the wall beside it. Blood streaks and spatter lined the walls and ceiling above and around the bed. There was also a large pool of dried blood on the floor on one side of the bed. The mattress and bedclothes had a large stain of blood, from almost the top to about where the victim's knees would have been.

"The son was killed here?" he asked.

Mygal nodded. "Stabbed repeatedly in the chest. I counted at least seventeen wounds from a fairly wide and double-edged dagger."

"And nothing was taken? I see they left the sword, and it looks to be of good quality."

"Nothing at all."

Rellen kneeled down beside the bed and collected some of the son's blood. "What was his name?" he asked.

"Stolan."

Rellen etched an "S" into the glass vial and rose to his feet. He nodded toward the door.

Mygal strode out, walked down the hall to the last door on the right, and stepped in.

Rellen followed to find a young woman's room. A dresser and vanity in light-colored wood stood off to the right, and the bed, made from the same thing, was on the left. The bedclothes were a pale green and trimmed with lace. However, there was almost no blood to be found. He could only see two lines of it on the mattress, outlining what would have been the daughter's torso. He looked at Mygal with a questioning look.

"Why didn't you mention this room was different from the others?"

"What do you mean?" Mygal looked around. "Granted, there's not as much blood in here, but that's easy to explain. The daughter had only been stabbed once—a single thrust into her heart."

Rellen cocked his head to the side. *You still have much to learn*, he thought. "Whoever killed her, knew her," he said, like a teacher to a pupil.

"How do you know?"

"Because she was killed but not butchered." He looked at the bed. "Think about it. With all the rage we found in the other rooms, this one is virtually untouched. The murderer ended her life with a single stroke, and I'm pretty sure that life had been important to him or her... although I'm leaning toward *him* now."

Mygal looked around the room and stared at the bed for several moments. Finally, he nodded slowly.

"I see what you're saying, although it's possible the killer's arm just got tired." Mygal gave him a weak but humorous smile.

"Maybe," Rellen said. "Something to always keep in mind is observing what *isn't* there as much as what is."

"You're really good at this," Mygal said, clearly meaning it.

"It's a knack... and I've had some very good teachers over the years." He let out a long breath. "Now for the tricky one." He stepped up to the bed, drew out another vial, and tried scraping blood off the bedclothes. He struggled with it at first but finally found a patch thick enough for him to collect what he needed. "What was her name?"

"Jacinda."

Rellen uttered the incantation and etched a "J" into the glass.

He looked around the room, a thoughtful expression on his face. "I haven't seen anything that suggests the Nissrans, at least not conclusively. If the daughter had been killed like the others... maybe it would make sense. Nissrans love blood as sacrifice. But without hers, the scene is incomplete. I also don't see anything here that suggests sedition. In that case, either just the duke would have been killed, or all of them would have been dispatched simply and cleanly."

"You're reaching a little there," Mygal said. "If the duke was involved and they wanted to get rid of him, there's nothing saying they couldn't butcher him and the others in the process."

Rellen nodded. "You're not wrong. It just doesn't feel right. If it is sedition, then we're missing a big piece of the puzzle. Having come here, I have to wonder if it's more along the lines of the duke being made an example of. Corwyk mentioned the Black Wyrm Clan, and their reach extends from Corsia all the way south to the coast, in one form or another." He looked around the room again. "The more I think about it, the more this feels like a madman who didn't like this family in particular." He shook his head. "Meh... it could still be any one of those."

He looked at Mygal. "Show me the burned cottage," he said.

Mygal nodded and walked out of the room. They made their way down the stairs, through the hallway to the back of the house, and passed a large kitchen where a sturdy, older woman of considerable girth pounded out a slab of pork. She paid them no heed, and they continued out through a conservatory full of mostly blooming plants.

Once they were outside, the property opened up onto a large, manicured lawn and garden. The servant's quarters were off to the left, stretching away from the house. Thirty yards away lay the remains of what had been a small cottage or guest quarters of some kind. The stone foundation was mostly intact, but there was nothing left of the walls or roof, save for a few charred timbers.

Rellen and Mygal circled around the remains of the ruined building as Rellen inspected the ground closely—both the ash and the area surrounding it. He spotted the remains of a few trinkets in the ash, as well as a few pieces of mostly burned furniture, but there was nothing that caught his eye. Whatever had been inside was gone with the rest of the building.

"Do you want to dig through it?" Mygal asked.

"No, or at least not yet." Rellen looked out at the lake a dozen yards away and then faced Mygal. "I have a better idea of what to do with this, but we'll have to tackle it tomorrow. It will take all day and most of my majea." He turned back toward the manor house. "Let's get to the inn. I want to stow my things before we head back out."

"Out?" Mygal looked perplexed, looking up at the evening sky. "It'll be dark soon. Where are we going tonight?"

"You'll see. Everything in its time."

"You know, for someone who didn't want to be a mentor, you do seem to be getting into the role."

Rellen gave him a wicked smile.

CHAPTER SEVEN
THE DRUNKEN UNGER

T he streets of Svennival bustled, with throngs of citizens moving along the main thoroughfares a testament to the success of the river port city. Afternoon rainfall, common throughout much of Pelinon in late summer and early fall, came down in a mist rather than a downpour, but even a cloudburst wouldn't keep most Pelinese indoors.

Rellen shrugged into his cloak, careful not to dislodge Xilly from her normal spot when things got wet. She was tucked in beneath his cloak, curled up on the back of Shaddeth's saddle. They passed the dock area, rife with shoremen, laborers, and a few more unseemly types who gathered near the entrances of alleys for the most part.

"Down that way is where they got me," Mygal called over his shoulder, pointing down an alley that went off toward the wharf area.

Rellen glanced in that direction, and a question slammed into him. He gave Shaddeth a bump and caught up with

Mygal. "There's something that's bothering me, and it didn't occur to me until you mentioned the alley."

"What's that?" Mygal glanced behind him.

"Why didn't they kill you?" Rellen shook his head, irritated with himself for not thinking about it sooner. "I was so focused on the duke's murder, I missed the obvious question. Why are you still alive?"

Mygal's head spun around. "Would you rather they'd killed me?"

"No, no, no," Rellen said, holding up a hand. He let out a patient breath. "You misunderstand. I know you got stabbed in the belly and the shoulder. The question is, why didn't they just finish the job by slitting your throat?" He locked eyes with Mygal. "What *exactly* happened back there?"

Mygal told him, and as the story unfolded, Rellen got more and more confused.

"So, the fourth one stayed out of the fight until you'd already killed the other three?"

"That's right."

"And *then* he turned out to be a potent heartbender who wounded you badly, knocked you out, and then... what? Went to get help? What happened after that?"

"Well, I *was* unconscious," Mygal said defensively. "I woke up in the ducal keep three days later. I always assumed someone found me and got the authorities. Corwyk said that city guards brought me in, and his staff nursed me back to health. We always just assumed Dancer's associates wanted me out of the way."

"I'll ask again," Rellen said slowly. "Why not kill you?"

"Maybe they didn't want another murder hung around their necks?" Mygal didn't sound even close to certain.

"There's no appreciable difference between murdering five people rather than four," Rellen observed.

"Maybe they weren't willing to kill a Guardian?" Mygal looked thoughtful. "They seemed to know about the Guardians' Avatars."

"That bothers me too," Rellen said. "It suggests there's a leak somewhere, but there's no way to tell if it's here, in Svennival, or back in Corsia, although I'd lean toward here."

"You know, I'm not saying I think you're wrong, but it could just be as simple as someone coming down the alley because of all the fighting, shouting, and screaming. Maybe that last assassin needed to cut out quick and figured I wouldn't make it."

"I suppose that's possible," Rellen agreed, but the whole thing bothered him. They continued on in silence, and Rellen kept kicking around all the possibilities, trying to see which scenario might fit the events best. It was a game he played with himself, but no matter what he tried, he was left with the obvious truth. Cutting a man's throat takes only a moment. He finally pushed the notion aside. It would either resolve itself later or it wouldn't.

They came upon a large, nicely maintained, two-story inn. Above the polished, oaken double doors hung a simple sign that read, *The Drunken Unger*. There were wide windows on either side of the entrance, and just past that was the entrance to an attached livery where an actual unger, wearing simple garments of loose-fitting cotton, swept hay into the street. As they guided their mounts toward the open doors, a pang of something like anger laced with disgust and regret crept into Rellen's heart.

Ungers were a bipedal species of creature native to the lands between the Demonspine Mountains and the Sylverwylde range to the south. Halfway between a man and an animal, they usually had gray or bluish skin, wide, doe-like eyes, and brutish forms topped by flattened heads and thick brows. Long tusks stuck out from their lower jaws, and they had flat, root-mashing teeth that were normally the color of grass or corn. They were smart enough to perform simple tasks, but their intelligence was rudimentary at best—more like smart dogs than stupid people. There were still places in Pelinon where they were used, abused, and killed as slave labor... sometimes just for sport. The practice had been outlawed by Rellen's grandfather as one of his final decrees, and Rellen had actually killed an Unger slaver or three in his travels—on principle alone—and he'd done so without an ounce of regret.

"I'm going to do something about that," Rellen said under his breath as the unger stepped aside to let them into the livery.

"It's not what you think," Mygal said, "although I agree with why you said it."

"What do you mean?" Rellen asked as he stopped in front of an empty stall. "Come on out, Xilly," he said quietly, lifting the edge of his cloak. Xilly crawled out and up Rellen's chest to take a perch on his shoulder.

"I asked the innkeeper about him when I first found this place. I was as angry as you are. Willyck over there," he nodded toward the unger, "He's a part of their family. You could even call him adopted. That's why the magistrates haven't done anything about it. He helps around the inn, sleeps upstairs with the rest of the family, and eats at the same table." Mygal got a compassionate grin on his face. "He seems happy, healthy, and loved." He got a strange look on his face. "I wish I'd had it half that good when I was a kid."

Rellen didn't miss the import of that statement, but it didn't require a response. Instead, he eyed the unger, who had gone back to sweeping out the livery. "Stranger things have happened, I suppose." He got down off Shaddeth and led him backwards into the stall. "Leave them saddled, we won't be long," Rellen called out.

"Right," Mygal replied as the unger and dragonette started making sounds at one another.

Xilly leapt off Rellen's shoulder and fluttered to a rafter directly above Willyck. The unger looked up and then made a strange cooing sound.

Xilly chirped back.

Can it speak? Rellen shot the thought at Xilly.

Not really, she replied. *We're just playing.*

Rellen attended to his gear. He removed the bundle of oilskin-wrapped spell books from the saddle and set them aside. He hung his bedroll, shelter, and other gear on pegs against the back wall. Pulling a small iron rod from a pouch on his bandoleer, he concentrated for a moment, made a quick gesture with his hand, and spoke an incantation. The rod evaporated in a pale flash of light that surrounded his gear. The spell locked everything against the wall and would send a searing shock through anyone who touched it. His saddlebags went beside the books. He fetched a bucket of water and filled a bin nearby with a mix of hay and oats taken from bins at the back of the livery.

"We'll be back in a bit," he said to Shaddeth, patting the horse's neck.

With that, he hefted his bundle of books over one shoulder, his saddlebags over the other and stepped out of the stall to find Xilly sitting on Willyck's shoulder. He walked over, and Xilly fluttered back to his shoulder. Willyck made a strange huffing sound and then resumed sweeping.

I think that means goodbye, Xilly said.

"Goodbye, Willyck," Rellen said gently as he strode past with Mygal in tow.

The unger lifted its massive head, and Rellen would swear it smiled at him.

Rellen and Mygal stepped out of the livery and headed toward the front doors of the inn. Rellen glanced over his shoulder and found Willyck following them. Moments later, they strode into the tavern portion of the Drunken Unger.

It was well-lit by glowstones hanging from the ceiling. There were over a dozen tables, some in the middle and the rest along the walls. A long bar ran along the right-hand wall. A staircase bent around the far-left corner, going up to the second floor. Three of the tables were occupied by what looked to be merchants of some sort. A tavern maid moved amongst them, setting down or picking up tankards. Behind the bar stood a heavy-set, agreeable-looking fellow with bushy black hair, a thick mustache, and the burly forearms of someone who knew how to crack skulls when it was required of him. They moved inside, and Rellen saw Willyck step partway in through the doors and flash the barkeeper two fingers.

"Good afternoon, lads," the man called out with a hearty smile and thick accent as he ran a towel over the bar. His eyes flicked to the dragonette perched on Rellen's shoulder. His eyes went wide for a moment, but he quickly recovered his composure. "I'm Drumore Haddy, Esquire, if ye can believe it, owner of this establishment. Are ye here for food, drink, or mayhap a dry roof and a warm bed?"

"All of it, before the day is out," Rellen replied, setting his books on the floor.

"Excellent, and Willyck tells me ye both have steeds in the stable. Is that right?"

Rellen got an impressed look on his face and glanced over his shoulder, but Willyck was gone. Ungers were even smarter than he'd originally thought. Turning back, he said, "It is. A big, black warhorse."

"And I have the painted mare," Mygal added.

"It's an extra sepik a day fer each horse," the innkeeper said, "and two sepiks a night fer a room."

"Do you have any doubles?" Rellen asked. He sensed Mygal stiffen beside him. The young Guardian wasn't keen on sharing a room, apparently. He hoped Mygal had the good sense not to say anything in front of the innkeeper.

"Aye. It's still just two sepiks though. I do me best to make it easy on travelers where I can. Keeps 'em coming back when they come thru."

"We appreciate that," Rellen said.

"How long will ye be staying?"

"At least a few days, I suspect," Rellen said. He pulled a pouch from inside his cloak. "I'd like to pay for a week, if I can."

"No problem there," the innkeeper said enthusiastically. "Seven days at four sepiks is twenty-eight fer the week."

Rellen extracted two gold dakkaris and held them out. Twenty-five silver sepiks were equal to one gold dakkari. His brother's face, stamped into the coin, glinted in the light, causing a surge of guilt and shame to course through his heart. He fought to keep his expression blank as he relived his mother's death and the conversation with his brother. "Hang on to the rest as a deposit, will you?" he said evenly. "In case we have to stay longer."

"I'll be happy to," Drumore said, holding one of the coins up to the light. "Ahh... Gods bless the king, especially when his face is so golden." Drumore paused for a moment, still holding the coin up and looking at Rellen's face. His eyes flicked back and forth. "Oi... did ye know ye look a lot like the king?"

Rellen winced. It wasn't the first time he'd heard the question, and it always carried a lot of memory. Mygal cast him a sidelong glance, his expression turning somewhat worried.

"I get that every now and again. I was born in Corsia... a lot of the men there have similar features."

"Aye," Drumore said. "'Tis the same in these parts. Folks look like their neighbors. 'Tis the way of things I suppose."

"Indeed, it is," Rellen said, wanting to change the subject. "Now, about that room? I suspect there's a key around here somewhere."

"Aye," Drumore said, slipping both dakkaris into his apron. He reached beneath the bar and pulled out a thick, iron key. "Top o' the stairs, third door on the right, above the stables." He eyed both of them as he handed the key to Rellen. "Men like you, I suspect, like to know if something's going on in the livery, yeah?"

"We do," Mygal said.

"And could you send up some food," Rellen said. "I'm starving, and I suspect you are too," he added, looking at Mygal.

Mygal nodded.

"Aye," Drumore said. "The house specialty is what we call a Bag-o-Cats. 'Tis battered and fried catfish, caught fresh daily.

'Tis spicy, sweet, and savory all at once, and the best ye'll find in all of Svennival. Me wife, Estelle, has more secrets in the kitchen than she does in the bedroom, which is sayin' something I don't mind tellin' ye." Drumore gave a wink and chuckled heartily. Rellen and Mygal chuckled right along with him. "It'll be a sepik fer both together."

Rellen looked to Mygal, who nodded again.

"We'll take them." He reached into his pouch and handed over a tarnished silver sepik with the image of his father on one side... without a pang of memory. "And thank you."

"No trouble at all," Drumore replied and then headed off toward a pair of doors at the rear that, Rellen assumed, led to the kitchen.

"Let's see what this room is like," Rellen said, stepping away from the bar. He caught a sour expression on Mygal's face but said nothing. He knew the room arrangement was bothering him, and he suspected why. Mygal hadn't said anything yet, so he wondered if the young Guardian would bring it up or have the good sense to stay silent while they were in public.

They crossed the tavern, climbed the stairs, and headed down the hall. Mygal stepped in close and whispered, "Why are we getting only one room? If it's the cost, I have my own money."

"It's got nothing to do with coin," Rellen said softly, stopping in front of their door. "We have no idea how the next two days are going to go. If we get jumped in the middle of the night, I want us in the same room." He eyed Mygal, and a strange fear came over him as he imagined Mygal getting ambushed. He wasn't going to let that happen. "Frankly, you should feel the same way," he scolded. "We need to have each other's backs while we're working together, and it's all too easy to get murdered when you're on your own." He eyed Mygal. "That assassin in the alley is a perfect example."

"Hey, I beat three of them, and I was working on my own for years before I became a Guardian," Mygal shot back as Rellen turned the key and pushed the door open.

"So had I," Rellen said, stepping in. "And I still do, most of the time." There were two narrow beds and an armoire on the left, two sitting chairs and a small table on the right, and a small fireplace with a low mantle just past that. He slipped the key into his belt as Xilly leapt from his shoulder and alighted upon the far bed. "But let me tell you something, it was only a few months ago in Calamath when I almost got killed in my room. I wish I'd had help then, because I barely got out of that mess in one piece."

"I get that, but I'd still—" Mygal started as he stepped inside.

"Look," Rellen cut him off and closed the door. "Mentoring aside, I'm the Ninth Guardian, and you're the Thirteenth. That means we do this my way." He set his books and saddlebags on a small table by the fireplace. "You understand that, right?" He put just an edge of iron in his voice.

Mygal's mouth snapped closed. They both knew the hierarchy of the Guardians and what went with it. It was drilled into all of them, starting with the king just after their initiation ceremony, and it was a law respected by all. Failure to do so had severe consequences.

Mygal's ire faded quickly, and he looked duly admonished.

"Listen," Rellen said softly. "This isn't like that game you played at breakfast. Most of the other Guardians would have let that slide too—except the Kapron, Jareth K'Ovall. He doesn't have any sense of humor at all. You've got to defer to the experience of your seniors. Always. I'd do it too, if Eight were here. Alright?"

"I understand," Mygal replied, sounding genuinely apologetic. "I'm just not used to working with others."

"Believe me, I get that." He had a patient look upon his face. "Why do you think I accepted the duties of a Guardian? We normally *do* work alone."

"Thanks for spelling it out for me," Mygal said. "This is going to take some getting used to, but I know you have a lot to teach me."

"We're always learning," Rellen said. "We stop when we die."

"My uncle used to say the same thing."

"He must have been a wise man."

"He was."

"Look, there's something I wanted to... emphasize." Rellen let out a patient breath.

"What's that?" Mygal said, looking uncomfortable.

"When you first saw me and tried to influence me..."

"I said that was habit, not intent."

"That may be the case, and from what little I could tell, you've got a real talent for it, if you don't *abuse* it. I won't tell you how to do your job, but you *need* to consider not opening with it. I meant it when I said keep it to yourself unless you absolutely need it. If nobody knows what you are, then they can't prepare for it later, when your life depends upon surprise. Understand?"

Mygal nodded, and it looked like his cheeks had flushed slightly. "Perfectly."

"Good, then it's in the past," Rellen said. "I'll tell you, I'm beginning to like you. We may even become comrades, although that's unlikely. On the other hand, you may just end up hating the sight of me. You wouldn't be the first Guardian to feel that way."

"The Guardians aren't all chummy?"

"Gods, no," Rellen said with a chuckle. "Our oath to the king holds us together, not our feelings for one another. That oath, however, means we do this job whether we like each other or not. Most of the Guardians get along fairly well, and there are a few who are the true comrades. Voren, the Guardian you replaced, he and I were at least sort of like that. On the other hand, there are a few personalities that clash like fire and fuel oil. Spend enough time at a Conclave, and you'll quickly discover that I don't get along well with Faleesh Namarre... and yes, we slept together. The Kapron, Jareth K'Ovall, thinks I'm a dilettante at best but won't say it to my face. Grall Akkrond and

Zaphreem Yskyndiar don't have much use for each other, either. In fact, if we weren't all Guardians, some of us might just try to kill each other when nobody was looking. But we *are* Guardians. Our oath to the king trumps all. Never forget that."

"I won't. I swore it to him, and I'll swear it to you."

"No need," Rellen said, holding up his hand. "Your oath to the king is more than enough. Now..." Rellen looked around the room. "We'll sleep here, and if you'll step aside, I'll make it so we can sleep more soundly than we otherwise might."

"Wards?" Mygal asked, sitting on the nearest bed.

"Wards," Rellen said.

"Whatever you need," Mygal said, meaning it.

"Just shut up for a bit and stay out of the way."

Mygal snapped his mouth closed and stepped back to sit on the nearest bed.

Rellen faced the window first. The sun was about to drop below the horizon, casting long shadows across Svennival. The stables were just below a wood-shingled roof outside the window. If someone were to climb onto it, they'd be able to come right in.

He reached into a pouch at his waist and pulled out a small piece of quartz. Holding it tightly in a closed fist, he summoned his majea. Feeling the power surge slightly, he whispered an incantation, funneling that energy into the crystal. Heat pressed against his palm and fingers as he repeated the incantation over and over again. With his other hand, he ran his index finger over the glass in a very specific pattern, tracing out one symbol after another as majea flowed into the transparent surface. A very faint glow began to emanate from the glass. When he completed the incantation, he opened his palm. The small crystal glowed brightly, as if it were a piece of red-hot iron just taken from a blacksmith's furnace.

He drew in a long, deep breath, and the glowing crystal levitated out of his palm, hovering there as it rotated slowly. Rellen blew upon it, as if he were blowing out a candle. The crystal shot straight into the windowpane. When it struck, there was a crack, as if the glass were breaking, but instead, the red-hot crystal expanded in the blink of an eye, covering the entire surface of the window.

Rellen drew in a long breath and then let it out slowly.

"What did you just do?" Mygal asked.

"Let's just say it's much stronger than it was," Rellen replied. "A war hammer couldn't break that now." He turned toward the door.

"How long will it last?"

"A few days, at least," Rellen said, glancing at Mygal. "Now hush. I have one more." He wanted to keep people out, but he also needed to reserve his majea for the evening's activities. That part was going to take a lot out of him.

Drawing in a deep breath, he pulled a steel vial covered with runes from his bandoleer and took out the stopper. Taking the room key from his belt, he uttered a simple cleansing incantation and poured several drops of thick, white liquid from the vial onto the key. The fluid spread out across the metal, covering the entire surface, and wherever it touched, tiny wisps of smoke rose. In moments, the entire key had been purified. The white dissipated in a cloud of steam.

Rellen inserted the key into the door and focused his majea once again as he carefully formed the syllables of a very different spell. Once formed, he held the magic suspended in his thoughts. He could feel it, twisting and turning, waiting to be released. He spoke another incantation, focusing his thoughts upon the door itself, drawing a series of symbols in the air. As he traced each symbol, one on top of the other, a thin line of amber light flowed out from his fingertip, suspending each arcane symbol a few inches from the door in one bizarre jumble of light. Finally, he drew a large X over the entire pattern and gently pushed the floating image against the door, where it stuck, suspended against the dark wood. "Come place your hand on the door, and don't touch the rune," he said to Mygal without looking. "Quickly."

Mygal stood up and moved over. He placed his hand upon the right side of the door, just above the handle. Rellen placed his own on the left side and then uttered a single word to release the magic.

The runic symbol upon the door flashed bright orange. A tingle of electricity shot through both their hands. Mygal jerked his hand back in surprise as the rune faded out of sight.

"There," Rellen said, "now only you and I can open that door. Someone would have to break it down to get in." He turned to Mygal. "You'll still need the key. When you want to open it, place your hand on the door where that rune is and turn the key."

"I've never seen Line Magic actually used," Mygal said, "at least, not like that."

"I think it's the most versatile of them, but I'm biased. Although… what I do is a little different from what other runecasters can do. It's always been a special talent."

"I take it you're formally trained?"

"The academy in Corsia."

"Of course," Mygal said, and there was just a hint of jealousy in his voice. "What's next?"

Just then, there came a knock on the door.

"Your food, sir," a woman's voice called out.

Rellen turned, placed his hand in the upper-center portion of the door, and turned the key. He opened the door, revealing a short, plump woman with a stupendous bosom and rosy cheeks. She was lovely, had a brilliant smile, and her eyes glinted. She held two pewter platters, each topped with a lump of something wrapped in several layers of cheese cloth.

"Two Bag-o-Cats, I believe," she said in the same accent as Drumore.

"Thank you," Rellen said, taking the platters. The aroma was mouth-watering.

"Just holler if ye need anything else." The woman gave him a wink, turned, and walked down the hall with the pleasant jiggle of a plump backside.

Rellen turned, platters in hand, and closed the door with his foot.

"First," he said with a smile as the smell of the fried catfish began to fill the room, "we eat."

Yes, eat! Xilly blurted from the mantle.

"Then what?" Mygal asked as Rellen placed the two platters on the small table.

Rellen moved over to his saddlebags and opened one of them. "Well, now that it's finally dark, we can go see what's what?" He pulled out a small, silver figurine, tossed it into the air, and caught it deftly.

"Are you going to tell me where we're going?"

"The cemetery," Rellen said simply.

"What? Why?"

"Because sometimes the dead *can* speak, and you can hear them better at night."

Chapter Eight

TRUTH AND CONSEQUENCES

The dark streets of Svennival, illuminated by glowstones set atop wrought iron posts, looked ominous in a fog that blanketed the city. Figures floated in and out of the fog as Rellen and Mygal made their way toward the edge of the city. The few pedestrians about were obviously not the upper crust of Svennival. Such people either had the means or good sense to stay in on such a night.

That isn't to say those about were necessarily criminals, but in a port city like Svennival—and this close to the docks—the odds were good that dirty work was afoot. As the two Guardians headed toward the cemetery where nobility was interred, Rellen kept his eyes open and a hand on one of his falchions. It wasn't far from the duke's manor, a quarter mile or so, and it lay both inland and well outside the city proper.

When the last glowstone fell behind them and the darkness folded in, Rellen considered creating some light of his own but decided against it. There was a half-moon directly above, illuminating the fog just enough to see the cobblestones, and he really didn't want to draw any attention. He still suspected that whoever attacked Mygal had an agenda deeper than just wounding someone following Dancer. If he was right, then it was possible they were still watching Mygal and, therefore, Rellen. If they did know Mygal was a Guardian, then they could easily assume Rellen was too. That might work in their favor, however. The Crown had spent centuries building up the reputation that Guardians were not to be trifled with, and there were few, even in the more rural areas, who didn't know it.

"Are we really going to talk to the dead tonight?" Mygal asked, "or was that just a metaphor?" There was a hint of frustration in his voice. "I thought that was supposed to be impossible."

"Talk to them?" Rellen asked with a wry grin. "No... although impossible is a relative notion for runecasters." His expression grew more serious. "This is more like dragging a lodestone through sand to see what gets picked up."

"So, why are we doing it at night?"

"Because what I'm going to do works better after the sun goes down," Rellen replied.

"More symmajea?"

"More symmajea," Rellen replied, unwilling to say anything further. He might be Mygal's mentor, but he wasn't going to explain everything either.

Mygal stiffened, gave Rellen a sour look, and then turned forward in his saddle.

They finally entered the cemetery. As they turned through the wide archway of old, mossy stone, Rellen thought he heard something in the street far behind them. He turned in his saddle, forcing Xilly to flutter her wings and adjust her position on his shoulder, but he couldn't see through the fog, and he didn't hear anything else.

"I heard it too," Mygal whispered.

Xilly, watch our backs?

Yes, she replied. She leapt off his shoulder, dropped several feet to gain momentum, and spread her wings. As silent as an owl, she flapped slowly and gained altitude, rising above Rellen's head before disappearing into the darkness and fog.

And check the rear first.

I heard it, Xilly replied, and she was gone.

Rellen spurred Shaddeth gently and entered the cemetery. On the left was a pair of small, stone buildings—probably the gravedigger's sheds—and between those, a casket wagon used to haul the dead to their respective graves.

"Where did you get her?" Mygal asked quietly.

"At the Bear Claw Tavern in a village with no name," Rellen replied, "but that's another story. Maybe I'll tell you someday."

Mygal shrugged and let out a weary breath. "They're over this way."

"You'll be able to find their graves in the dark?" Rellen asked.

"Of course," Mygal said, sounding a little offended.

They rode a short distance along a small stone path running through the countless graves and mausoleums. Most were large and elaborate, reflecting the wealth of those interred there. However, there were a few smaller, simpler headstones here and there.

"Right up there," Mygal said, nodding toward a large tree. As they drew near, Rellen could make out four freshly dug graves. The largest headstone, a tall monolith of alabaster, had a simple inscription:

~ Duke Vladysh Belvenim ~
Proud Servant, Devoted Husband, and Loving Father
Born: Wynmoanne 24, 1664 ~ Died Rispmoanne 16, 1713

The headstone of Duchess Esselyn Belvenim, set beside her husband's, was a simple slab of alabaster. She'd been two years younger than the duke. Her headstone bore the mark of Corsia's magic academy, with an accent sigil indicating she was a symkurios like Rellen. The other two headstones, also of alabaster, were slightly smaller. The son, Stolan, had been twenty-three, and the daughter, Jacinda, was eighteen at the time of her murder. Flowers had been placed on each, but there appeared to be more placed beside Stolan's headstone than Jacinda's. That struck Rellen as peculiar. Normally, it was the other way around.

The four graves, rectangular patches of dark earth with small sprouts of grass poking up, were laid out in a row beneath a large, beautiful tree with wide branches and what would be a good deal of shade during the day.

Rellen wondered if he would be buried, or if his body would simply be lost in the wilds while on another mission. He gave much better odds to the latter. He cast a sidelong glance at Mygal, and another pang of guilt washed through him. He'd do everything he could to make sure Mygal didn't die on his watch. He dismounted and stepped up to the foot of all four graves.

"Let's get to work," he said. He pulled the small, silver figurine from a pocket within his cloak and kneeled before the graves. Reaching into another pouch, he held out the four vials of dried blood he'd taken from the murder scene. "Would you place these on their respective headstones?" he asked holding them out. "And from here on out, don't say a word until I say you can."

Mygal nodded, got off his horse, and took the vials, placing them at the base of each headstone.

Meanwhile, Rellen placed the figurine in the grass at the foot of the graves, between mother and son. The figurine was a depiction of Kalistar, the goddess of knowledge in the Zaliphur pantheon. The image of that particular goddess didn't hold any special meaning for Rellen, not specifically, anyway. He'd needed a solid mass of silver about that size for spells like this, and he'd seen it in a bazaar during his last year at the academy. He didn't personally offer devotions to Kalistar, but he figured it couldn't hurt to have such a talisman in her image. As a rule, he liked to hedge his bets.

He picked through the soil of each grave and pulled out a single, small stone as spherical as he could find. He placed one at the foot of each grave and then focused his majea, summoning a good deal of energy to begin forming a rather complicated spell. With the energy suspended in his thoughts, he began the lengthy binding incantation, using the names of the four victims as anchors to the spell. He repeated it over and over, dribbling out measures of his majea and spreading it out across the talisman, the four stones, and the vials that rested upon the base of each headstone.

He lost track of time.

Eventually, the small talisman of Kalistar glowed with a pale, blue luminescence. A gossamer thread of light stretched slowly out from it, reaching toward the stone at the foot of the duke's grave. It connected, the stone glowed faintly, and then the filament reached out toward the vial. When it connected, the vial began to glow. A thread of energy reached down from the headstone and disappeared into the freshly dug soil. Deep in the back of Rellen's mind, he felt his spell make a final connection with the corpse below. With that in place, Rellen continued the incantation, pouring more and more of his majea into the spell as the stone at the foot of the wife's grave began to glow.

He continued repeating the incantation again and again, until there was a connection from the talisman to each corpse buried beneath him. When the final connection was made, he closed his eyes and let out a long breath. The spell took a good deal of concentration, and its cost in majea was quite high. He took a moment to examine his work. The objects involved glowed brightly, and the thin filaments connecting them were solid and unwavering. He nodded once with satisfaction.

They would hold.

He pulled out several small pieces of vellum and a piece of charcoal. On the first, he inscribed the words "Black Wyrm Clan" and included a very rough depiction of their mark—a black dragon's claw. He'd dealt with them before, and all members had such a device tattooed upon their bodies. On the next, he wrote out the words "Seditionists." The next got

"Family Nemesis," then "Thieves," and on the last piece of vellum, he wrote "Nissrans." On that one, he included the mark of Nissra, a circle with two curves in the middle forming a V shape topped by a half circle.

Rellen summoned his majea once again, building up the energy as he spoke a similar incantation and laid out each piece of vellum between himself and the stones. He closed his eyes, stretching out with his majea, running his mind along the filaments connected to each murder victim. He raised his hands before him and began the somatic portion of the spell. In his mind, he stroked each filament, almost as a musician strokes the strings of an instrument, getting a feel for the people who had once lived and breathed. He opened his eyes and focused on the five pieces of vellum. Above each, a small mote of light appeared, growing in intensity as he repeated the incantation over and over again. He drew energy from the filaments and channeled them into the motes. As the spell built to a crescendo, he uttered a final release command and clapped his hands together.

Each mote of light shot down into the vellum beneath it with a burst of light. In a flash, a series of faint glowing filaments shot out from three pieces of vellum. Nissra connected to all four stones, as did the Black Wyrm Clan. The note that said "family nemesis" connected to father, mother, and son, but not the daughter.

Letting out a long, exhausted breath, Rellen stared at the filaments before him. His stomach sank. He'd actually been hoping the Nissrans weren't involved. He was confused by the mixed message though. It seemed clear that the Nissrans were, somehow, working with the Black Wyrm Clan, and they'd employed an individual or individuals who held a personal grudge against the family, except the daughter.

He looked up at Mygal, a worried expression on his face. "We have a problem," he said. Mygal looked like he wanted to say something, but he held his tongue. "You can talk now."

"So, that magic will just tell you who did it?" Mygal asked, dumbfounded and impressed all at once. "Why not just write in names of people in the city and see which one killed the family?"

"If only it were that easy," Rellen replied. "First off, I'd need to know the name *and* have a part of them. But even if I had both, this spell only allows me to narrow things down. If I were to put in the butler's name as well as the maid's and even yours, you'd all be connected to varying degrees, just not necessarily with either the Nissrans or the Clan. Also, because you were attacked by at least one or more of those who committed the murder, you'd have a connection to both. With a spell like this, it's best to keep things a bit less specific. It's more like a compass, not an X on a map. It can point you in the right direction, but it usually won't tell you where you need to go." He suspected it was similar to how the Eye of Tuluum worked: direction but not location, although it wasn't quite the same.

"Let me see if I can give you an example. Imagine someone has been possessed by Nissra. Using this spell, I could write their name, and this would connect them to the murder. However, that just connects their body to the crime, not their intent or even that they were under the influence of another. If I jump to conclusions, I could easily persecute the wrong person or ignore the actual murderer. This acts like an arrow, or another bread crumb, but it doesn't tell me who, what, where, or even why. It just says, go look over there."

"Isn't that how that necklace of yours works? The Eye of whatever?"

"Tuluum," Rellen replied. He shook his head and let out a frustrated breath. "So, you know about that...?"

"I think all of the Guardians do," Mygal replied a bit uneasily. "The king considers it a potential resource all of us could call upon. At least, that's what he told me."

Rellen realized he'd have to talk to his brother. He didn't want everyone knowing about the Eye. It was a potent tool, but he really knew very little about it, other than he'd used it to guide him on his Guardian patrols. The less shared with others, the better, as far as he was concerned.

"Well, the Eye works differently. If I have a name or a place or a thing already in mind, it doesn't do anything, or it muddies the waters. If I don't have any of that, it leads me in a direction, but that's about it. I'm still trying to figure the thing out. I honestly don't know if it's leading me for my sake or its own. It does, however, generally lead me into trouble, which is what Guardians look for, so it's worked out so far. Here, let me show you." He reached into his tunic and pulled out the Eye, holding it before him. He expected it to do nothing, but again, just like in front of the ducal keep, the Eye leaned away from him, only this time, it leaned toward the piece of vellum with the Nissran mark upon it. Rellen stretched out his hand and moved it back and forth. The Eye of Tuluum seemed to be focused on the mark of Nissra. "Well, I'll be damned," he said.

"So, what does it mean?"

"I have no idea. I doubt it has anything to do with these murders—but who knows? Frankly, I trust the spell I just cast more than I trust the Eye at this point. Having said that, it does seem to have some sort of affinity for the Nissrans... or someone in the cult. It led me to Calamath, where I faced the cult. But it also led me to a tavern in the middle of nowhere and almost got me killed—without a Nissran in sight. That's where I met Xilly. I don't know... I wish I knew more about this thing."

"Well, either way, it seems that the clues and that little trinket of yours are leading you in the same direction."

"I suppose, but I wouldn't connect the two quite yet." He slipped the artifact back beneath his tunic.

"Where'd you get it?" Mygal asked.

"The Eye? In a nuraghi a while back, but that's another story too."

"You've been inside a nuraghi? I thought they were forbidden."

"Two, actually." Rellen quashed a very different pang of guilt that swelled in his breast as those words crossed his lips—just like it always did. The pang and the lie were old habits, because he'd actually been to three nuraghi. The one he never talked about was when he was much younger, and he was sworn to secrecy about what had happened there. It was where he'd picked up the matching falchions of Baladon sheathed on his hips. Some very bad things had happened at that first nuraghi. He'd never spoken about those events, not even with his brother and father.

Rellen scratched his cheek, a thoughtful expression on his face. "Being forbidden is more for the common good than anything else," he continued. "From everything I've learned, most of them are very dangerous, with strange creatures, deadly magics, and ancient artifacts that can kill you with a touch. The first time I went into one was a long time ago, and it's not something I like to talk about. The other was last year in the Duchy of Volikhari. It was mostly ruins. I was after a band of brigands who had been using it as a base of operations for raids up and down the coast. There was nothing special about that place other than it was very old and in ruins."

"And you just found that thing?" Mygal asked, dubiously.

"Well…" Rellen said slowly, "Let's say I had an accident that led to a labyrinth. I found this along the way." He patted his chest.

Several humans creeping up on you. Black cloaks and masks. Xilly's warning blared in Rellen's mind.

Rellen instinctively slid his hand around the grip of a falchion.

"What is it?" Mygal asked.

"Shh…" Rellen whispered. "Don't react, but we're not alone." His eyes darted toward the entrance of the cemetery. "There are humans sneaking up on us. Dressed like the ones that got you."

"What do you want to do?" Mygal asked. "Get out of here or fight? Your call."

"We fight," Rellen whispered as he rose to his feet.

He pulled a small crystal from a pouch on his belt. The half dozen crystals contained within each pouch held complex runes he'd inscribed upon them, storing a great deal of his majea within each. He closed his fist around the crystal, made a quick gesture, and muttered a three-word incantation. A faint, white glow momentarily encompassed his body. He felt a tingle that quickly subsided. The spell would remain in place for several hours, at least.

How many? Rellen sent the query into Xilly's mind.

Seven. One does not have a blade. Came the immediate reply.

Rellen peered into the darkness and could hear movement a short distance off. There was still a fair amount of patchy fog, and through the gaps, he spotted the movement of several figures in black moving from one headstone or crypt to another.

"There's seven of them," he said, turning to Mygal. Mygal's eyes had rolled back in his head, and he was breathing deeply, with deliberately long breaths in and then out. For a moment Rellen worried something was wrong with the young Guardian, but Mygal's features returned to normal.

"I'm ready." Mygal drew his rapier and fighting dagger in one smooth pull. He cocked his head sideways, one way and then the other, loosening his neck muscles. He bounced up and down a few times and took a few quick swipes with his blades.

Rellen drew a silver-hilted falchion in his right hand and jerked a small vial from his bandoleer in the other.

"Stick together," he said, "and when you hear my first incantation, leap back and close your eyes."

Mygal nodded and they strode forward into the fog.

They made it about twenty feet when three shadowy figures leapt out from between two crypts.

Rellen barked out a one-word incantation and threw the vial straight at the nearest of the three assailants as he leapt back with his eyes closed. An explosive crack, coupled with a bright flash, filled the cemetery. The concussion drove both Rellen and Mygal back a half step. Two pained screams filled the night. Mygal staggered back. Rellen, however, dashed forward.

The assailant Rellen had hit with the vial lay upon the ground. His leather vest and cloak had been burned and blown apart, as was much of the flesh beneath. His ribs were exposed, and his charred, lifeless face held a surprised expression. One of the other assailants had been blown to the right, toppling over a headstone, while another had slammed into a crypt on the left.

Rellen leapt at the one on the right as the man was regaining his feet. The assassin raised his eyes, a stunned expression filling his features. He got his longsword up just as Rellen's falchion came down. The clash of steel rang out. Rellen kicked the man's elbow as hard as he could, sending the longsword flying, and stepped in, driving his blade into the man's ribs. The assassin screamed in agony. Rellen twisted hard with a grinding of blade on bone and yanked the weapon free. He smashed a gloved fist into the wounded assassin's face, driving him into the ground. He turned at the sound of steel on steel.

Mygal had engaged the other man, whose face was a mask of terror. He cried out in fear as Mygal sent three calculated strikes against the assassin's ragged defenses. With each blow, Mygal seemed to open up the assassin's guard a little bit more. Mygal reversed the swing of his rapier above his head and smashed the assassin's blade aside, leaving his body wide open. Mygal stepped in and drove the point of his dagger into the assassin's throat, eliciting a gurgling sound as he crumpled to the ground.

Get down! Xilly's thought was frantic.

A crossbow *thwanged* as Rellen dropped instinctively to the ground. A bolt swooshed through the air where he'd been standing and clattered off of stone somewhere in the darkness. Rellen turned toward where it had come from. A dozen yards off, he saw a dark figure disappear behind a tree.

Rellen rose to his feet quickly. It would take time for the assassin to cock and reload the small handheld crossbow. The weapons could be fired with one hand and were much more easy to conceal than a regular crossbow. Rellen scanned the fog for any sign of movement and pulled a vial of green liquid from his belt. He realized it was his last and muttered a curse at how hard it was to find yallaho berries this far from the coast. He spoke an incantation and threw the vial as hard as he could at the base of the tree. The vial shattered. Magic flared as the contents erupted into an expanding cloud of thickening green smoke that quickly enveloped an area ten feet across. A horrendous coughing fit came from behind the tree. Rellen sucked in a breath, drew his other falchion, and dashed forward.

The sound of steel on steel rose behind him—Mygal had engaged another assassin.

Rellen ran into the green miasma only to find the assassin had moved away from the tree. He was still coughing, but his weapon was out, and he'd been joined by the last of the assassins. That left only the one Xilly said hadn't been armed.

Rellen drove into both assassins, slashing at the one coughing as he parried the thrust of the other. The coughing one got a block up in time, exactly as Rellen had hoped. In one motion, Rellen drove the blade he'd parried with into the shoulder of the coughing assassin and twisted around, putting the now wounded assassin between Rellen and the other one. The wounded assassin tried to bring his sword down, but Rellen blocked with his arm, smashed his forehead into the assassin's nose, and stepped back, kicking him in the chest. The wounded assassin flew back into his companion. Rellen came in hard, driving a blade into the assassin's belly as the other tried to get around and swing.

Rellen parried the attack as he jerked his blade free and sent out a sideways kick into the knees of the wounded assassin. The assassin dropped with the crack of cartilage, screaming out in pain.

Rellen now faced only one assassin, but he wondered where the caster was.

The assassin before him narrowed his eyes. They flickered to the side, looking at something, and then he attacked. Rellen raised his blade to block, knowing that something was about to come in from behind. He could only hope it was the caster, and the caster was going to use a spell of some kind.

As steel met steel, Rellen felt a tingle of magical energy lash up his back. The protection spell around him surged with pale light as it absorbed the caster's attack. He didn't have much time. Rellen drove in hard, slashing with his other blade. The assassin parried with quick reflexes. Rellen swung again and again as tingles of energy, one after the other, lanced across his back, each one dissipating against his protection spell, but growing in intensity as his spell was consumed.

Slash—parry—slash. He hammered against the assassin's defenses with ruthless efficiency. With each blow, he opened those defenses just a little more—but he was running out of time. *Where's Mygal?* He thought frantically.

He drove a thrust at the assassin's belly. The assassin parried, his sword going wide. Rellen twisted and brought his falchion in from the side in a low arc. It sliced deeply into the assassin's blade arm, drawing a scream of pain. Rellen twisted again, bending his elbow and driving his other blade through the assassin's belly and up into his rib cage. The assassin gave a wet, sickly grunt.

Searing pain coursed across Rellen's shoulder, as if a red-hot blade had cut through his flesh. He screamed out and turned. Standing a dozen paces off was a tall, slim figure in black. The man made a slashing motion with his hand, and a pale scythe of ruby light lanced out and struck Rellen in the chest. Fiery, blinding pain scorched across his chest where the scythe had struck him. Rellen had seen the spell before. He now faced a zokurios who could inflict wounds at a distance. It was a rare talent for a lifeweaver, but a useful one in the right hands.

Rellen fell to his knees as the caster prepared to send another agonizing scythe into Rellen's body.

Through a haze of pain, Rellen drew upon his own majea, but it wasn't going to be in time. The zokurios slashed with his hand. The scythe lanced out and struck Rellen again in the chest. He screamed as pain flared across his body.

One more of those, and the pain would drive consciousness from him.

As the lifeweaver raised his hand for a final slash, a glint of silver flashed through the fog. A fighting dagger appeared in the zokurios' belly. He cried out in agony and clutched at the weapon buried to the hilt in his gut.

Rellen drew upon his majea once again, raised his falchion, and uttered a brief incantation as he sketched a symbol in the air with the sword tip. In a flash of motion, the zokurios' clothing came alive. His cloak slithered up and wrapped itself around the caster's head and then his shoulders. His belt came free, slithered down his legs like a snake, and coiled about them. With muffled shouts, the zokurios slowly toppled to the ground.

"Don't kill him!" Rellen shouted.

Mygal appeared from behind a tree and dashed up to where Rellen kneeled upon the grass.

"Are you alright?" Mygal asked, kneeling beside Rellen.

Rellen let out a pained breath as the fire dancing across his torso faded. He shifted left and right, wincing with the pain.

"I think so," Rellen said. He didn't feel blood running beneath his armor and clothes, but the muscles beneath felt like they'd been hit with smithy hammers. He was certain his back and chest would be covered with bruises by morning. "He could cause pain, but not serious injury... at least not at that range. I've seen powerful zokurioi who could take an arm off at fifteen paces."

Mygal's eyes went wide. "I don't ever want to meet one of them."

"Fortunately for me, she was on my side."

"Lemme guess," Mygal said, helping Rellen to his feet. "Another long story."

Rellen nodded. "Now, let's go see if we can get some answers. Don't let him touch you, and if he tries to do anything, bash his brains in." He blew out a frustrated breath. "I hate dealing with lifeweavers."

They strode across the grass, stepping around a few headstones where the lifeweaver lay perfectly still.

"Is he playing dead?" Mygal asked, peering closely. "That belly wound shouldn't have killed him, not for hours, if not days."

"I don't think he's playing," Rellen said slowly. As he stepped up, the memory of a room in Calamath in the dead of night flickered in his thoughts. One of the locals there, a minion of Nissra, had tried to kill him.

He kneeled beside the body, a blade at the ready, and carefully lifted the man's right hand. There, on his pinky finger, glinting in the night, was a small ring with a symbol on it that made Rellen's blood curdle. He carefully turned the ring and found the small needle that stuck out the side. There was a small mark of blood on the next finger in.

"Just like in Calamath." He let the zokurios' hand fall back onto his stomach. "These Nissran swine kill themselves rather than being captured."

"What do we do now?" Mygal said.

"We see if Dancer is among the dead," Rellen said. "If not, we find him next. Either way, we take this lot back to Corwyk and see if he can identify any of them. Nissrans travel in packs and hide in plain sight. I'll let the king know about this as well. He'll want to send a contingent of some kind, just like we did in Calamath." He turned his eyes to Mygal as Xilly fluttered out of the darkness and landed on his shoulder. He gave her a grateful pat. "We do know one thing, though."

"What's that?"

"Apparently, they were watching you... and now me. Whatever this is, I think it's pretty bad."

"Wait a minute," Mygal said. "This one was a lifeweaver, right?"

"Definitely."

"None of the others were kurioi."

"I think that's a safe bet. They certainly could have done something during the fight other than swing those blades, if that were the case."

"The one who got me last week was a heartbender, and a powerful one at that." He gave Rellen a worried look.

Rellen nodded his head. "So, we're after Dancer and an unknown erkurios." He grunted, straining against a wave of fatigue, and got to his feet. "We'll have to be more cautious from here on out."

"You got that right."

"On the bright side, at least we know we're sniffing around the right tree." He glanced back across the cemetery to where he'd seen the coffin wagon and let out a long, weary breath. "Help me put these bastards in that wagon back there. I don't have anything left."

CHAPTER NINE
THE COST OF MAJEA

Rellen fought off a yawn, hoping he wouldn't fall asleep right there on the driver's seat of the wagon. Wincing with pain from the bruises crisscrossing his body, he gave the reins a gentle shake. He wanted to keep Shaddeth moving through the fog, and it hadn't been easy. "Sorry about the harness, boy," he called out as a yawn finally won the battle. Shaddeth turned his head, his heavy feet clopping along the cobblestones, and gave Rellen a dirty look. He snorted once and turned his head forward with an annoyed shake of his mane.

"You'll have to find him a stakka fruit or two when we're done," Mygal said with a chuckle. He rode beside Shaddeth, keeping pace as they made their way to the ducal keep. The streets were empty, and the pale moonlight had made the patchy fog shimmer like sliver.

"I suspect a single stakka won't be enough apology for this particular indignity," Rellen said. "I'm sure I'll be paying for this for days." He yawned again, trying to push away the fatigue that plagued him. The connection spell he'd cast on the four murder victims had been tiring enough, but that coupled with the fight and the punishment he'd received from the caster left him wanting nothing but a heavy meal and a week's worth of sleep. He pulled a thick piece of jerky from a pouch at his belt and bit off a hunk. He thought about giving some to Xilly, asleep on the wagon bench beside him, but realized he needed the food a lot more than she did. Majea always took a toll. Food and sleep was the only cure.

As they moved through the fog, the smell of the lake seeped into their nostrils. Warehouses and the occasional, darkened, shop front slipped by. They hadn't even passed any of the lamp posts that illuminated most of the city yet.

"We're near the wharf district," Mygal said. "Have you given any thought to how we'll proceed in the morning?"

"To be honest, I'm too tired to think of anything but the bed waiting for me." He popped another piece of jerky in his mouth. "We'll cross that bridge when I can think straight."

Three shadowy figures brandishing swords dashed out from an alley and halted a few yards in front of Shaddeth.

"Hold!" the one in the middle shouted, holding up his hand. He was a big man, with grizzled salt-and-pepper hair and a thick beard. He wore brown leathers and a black cloak with the hood pulled back. His companions, both black-haired lads in their late teens, were shorter, skinny, and their clothing bordered on tattered.

Shaddeth reared back, snorting angrily as he beat the air with his hooves.

"Easy, Shaddeth!" Rellen shouted, pulling back on the reins. The big horse calmed, his massive front hooves slamming onto the cobblestones with a double *crack!*

"Gallantyr's bones!" Mygal barked. "Are you out of your minds?"

"Not at all," the big man said, eyeing Shaddeth warily. "I'm afraid there's a toll to be paid tonight on this particular stretch of cobblestones." He eyed Mygal and then Rellen. "We'll take whatever money and weapons you have…" his eyes shifted to the wagon… "or that fine horse and the wagon it's pulling. Your choice."

"You really don't want to do this," Mygal said. "You have no idea what you're getting into."

"Oh, I think we do," the big man said. "I like our odds with three on two—" His eyes drifted towards the rear of the wagon. "But five on two puts you in a very bad place."

The wagon shifted slightly, and Rellen turned to find two more men climbing up into the bed of the wagon with battered longswords held at the ready. One had dark hair and skin, with a burly frame wrapped in tattered, grimy clothing. The other was pale, with blond hair falling out from the hood of a dark green cloak. His garments weren't tattered, but they weren't clean by any means.

"Behind us!" Rellen shouted, drawing a falchion. A shock of pain flared across his shoulder, and he realized he was in no shape to fight one, let alone two men, but he couldn't let them take the reins. Xilly's head jerked up from the driver's bench. *Xilly, stay down!* Rellen urged.

Mygal leapt from his saddle and hit the ground with his weapons in his hands as Rellen jerked an explosive vial from his bandoleer. Rellen tapped into his majea to utter the brief incantation and discovered he couldn't summon enough. Panic filled him as the two brigands stood up on the back of the wagon, swords held at the ready.

"No need for you to die too," the burly one said as Mygal engaged the brigands at the front with a ring of steel on steel. "Hand over that sword, and you might just live through this night." He stepped forward onto the tarp covering the bodies, and his weight shifted sideways. "Hey—!" He toppled sideways over the side as one of the men at the front screamed in fear. Mygal had put the fear of gods into someone.

"What the—" another brigand said, looking down at the bed of the wagon. "What do you have—?"

Drawing deeply on his reserves, Rellen surged up from the bench, pulled his other falchion, and leapt straight at him, pushing off from the wagon bench and sailing over the bodies. The brigand lifted his eyes just as Rellen's boots caught him in the chest. The man *whoofed* and sailed backward over the rear of the wagon.

Movement to the right caught Rellen's eye. He turned, leading with a falchion, and barely managed to block a slash from the brigand who'd gone over the side. Rellen's bruised body screamed in protest.

The brigand came around to the back of the wagon and swung again. Rellen countered, their swords clashing together, and the vibration sent a shock all the way up into Rellen's shoulder. He thrust with his other blade, aiming for the brigand's head, but the brigand stepped back out of reach just as the burly one rose to his feet from the cobblestones a few yards behind the wagon.

Jump down! Xilly's urgent call filled Rellen's mind as she flashed by him. She sailed straight into the face of the blond, slashing with her claws. The man screamed and flailed as she passed by his head.

Without thinking, Rellen dropped to the ground, going down into a crouch as the blond continued to scream in pain. As Rellen came up, he saw that Xilly had managed to rake her claws across one of his eyes, destroying it.

With a heave, Rellen drove a falchion up into the brigand's belly and twisted, impaling him clean through. Fiery pain lanced across Rellen's shoulders, and he cried out as the brigand grunted and dropped his weapon, his eyes going wide. Pushing through the pain, Rellen shoved the brigand's body between him and the burly one charging forward.

Rellen stepped back as the brigand stepped around the falling body of his comrade and took a swing at Rellen's head. Rellen parried the blade, sending a painful shock up his arm and stepped back again. Another of Mygal's opponents screamed—this time in pain—as the brigand came on with a flurry of blows. Rellen parried each one, wincing with each impact as he backed his way along the wagon. He had an idea, and it might just get him out of this mess.

Another pained scream echoed down the streets.

Rellen struggled to block every blow as he backed up along Shaddeth's dark body. The burly brigand followed, hacking down with one brutally powerful swing after another. They passed Shaddeth by a few feet. Rellen heard swordplay behind him, a dozen yards off, but it seemed that Mygal was engaged with only one brigand.

Perfect, Rellen thought, and turned in front of Shaddeth, drawing the brigand towards him.

Rellen parried again and then sent a quick feint at the brigand's head.

The brigand halted in his tracks, blocking a swing that never came.

"Shaddeth, attack!" Rellen shouted.

The fully trained warhorse reared up on his hind legs with a fearsome whinny and swiped through the air with his front hooves, striking the brigand not once, but twice, in the head with a dull, wet, cracking sound.

The brigand staggered and fell sideways, his skull split open.

Another scream echoed down the streets. Rellen turned to see Mygal pulling his sword out of the throat of the last brigand. The others lay all around, stains of blood on their clothing and across the cobblestones.

Mygal turned towards Rellen then glanced at the burly brigand lying in the street.

"That horse of yours really is well trained, and you look like you're dead on your feet."

Rellen could only nod. He sheathed his falchions and then let out a long, exhausted breath.

"Come on," he said wearily, "let's throw these bastards up in the wagon too."

"Corwyk's going to lose his mind when he sees what we've brought him."

"Any sane person would," Rellen replied, and then another, mighty yawn took him.

"Sorry about the mess," Rellen said, looking a bit sheepish as he pulled the tarp out of the back of the wagon.

"Kalistar have mercy!" Corwyk blurted, his eyes going wide. He stood there a few moments in a deep purple robe and slippers, staring at the blood-covered bodies piled up in the back of the wagon. He looked horrified, disgusted, and dismayed all at once. Finally, he turned to Rellen, his face filled with disbelief. "Is it always like this for you?"

"Not always," Rellen replied a bit defensively.

In the courtyard of the ducal keep, Rellen, Mygal, and Corwyk had gathered around the back of the wagon while a half dozen guards held torches aloft along the sideboards. Xilly, of course, lay curled up again on the driver's bench, snoring softly, as if nothing had happened.

"How many are in there?" Corwyk started counting feet.

"Seven assassins from the cemetery, including a zokurios—I'm hoping you can figure out who they are—and five brigands from near the wharf district. I can tell you those first seven are Nissrans. They all bore the ring, and the caster used it to kill himself rather than be captured."

"Selestina help us," Corwyk said.

"The others…" Rellen shrugged. "I think they're just local riffraff stupid enough to pick the wrong fight. Mygal here proved himself most capable, I must say."

"You're unbelievable," Corwyk groaned.

"Any luck finding Miranda?" Rellen asked, wanting to change the subject.

"Not yet." Corwyk pulled his eyes away from the bodies. "But that may take a day or three, assuming your bounty hunter is here at all."

"Fair enough." Rellen got a thoughtful look on his face. "I need you to do me another favor."

"You don't ask much, do you?"

"Not at all." Rellen gave him a patronizing smile. "This one may be easy, though."

"What is it?"

"Can you find out if Jacinda had a boyfriend?"

"Boyfriend?" Mygal asked. "Why would—?"

"It's a hunch," Rellen said. "The flowers on her grave have been bothering me."

"She did," Corwyk said. "And I can get you his name." Corwyk scratched the back of his neck thoughtfully. "My uncle often spoke of the young man—and not favorably."

"We'll check with the butler tomorrow," Rellen offered.

"I know he was from the Sylvemar family." Corwyk looked more certain. "The patron is a minor noble—a merchant I believe—but with considerable means. I've never met him, though. My uncle used to say the Sylvemar boy was going to be the death of him. The family is involved in the shipping business, handling goods over both land and water but not air. I got the sense Lord Sylvemar avoided politics for the nightmare they are. They pay their taxes and, as far as I know, have stayed completely off the ducal shit list. I'll have Veraiya's agents do some asking around about the son though." He eyed Rellen. "You want me to have him arrested?"

Rellen looked to Mygal. "What do you think?" His estimation of the young Guardian had gone up considerably after the day's events.

"I could argue it either way," Mygal replied thoughtfully. "Assuming they could even find him. It might be better if we got to him first. We could then follow him and see who he leads us to."

"I suspect we could interrogate him in custody," Rellen said, "but there are no guarantees we'd ask the right question, and if he's involved in Nissra cult, he might just suicide on us. Observe only for now?"

Mygal nodded his head.

Rellen turned to Corwyk. "Have your people find him, if they can, but don't make contact. Just let us know who and where he is. We'll take it from there, assuming we don't find him first."

"Oh," Mygal said, "and if your people see us following him, tell them to hold off."

Rellen gave Mygal an appreciative eye.

Corwyk nodded. "I'll see what we can do, and I'll send a runner to the Drunken Unger if we learn anything."

Rellen stretched his still sore muscles and yawned. "Then let's go get some sleep. I'm absolutely exhausted, and tomorrow will be a long, tiring day... for me, anyway. You," he said, glancing at Mygal with a smile, "get a bit of rest and relaxation tomorrow. Bring a book."

CHAPTER TEN

FROM THE ASHES

Rellen knocked three times on the manor door, his muscles still stiff and sore. His wounds had turned into long, dark bruises, and his muscles ached down to the bone. After sleeping the sleep of the dead for nine hours and gorging himself on a massive breakfast that had the innkeeper shaking his head, Rellen felt almost like his old self. He'd need it for the day ahead of him.

The sun was shining, for a change, casting long, early morning shadows through the canopy of trees. Birdsongs filled the air, and something furry chittered at Rellen and Mygal from high branches, hidden as it threw small nuts at them. One of them bounced across the front steps and rebounded off Rellen's boot.

He leaned out and looked up, but he couldn't see anything.

"Cheeky little bugger," he said, prompting a chuckle from Mygal.

Moments later, the door swung open, revealing the thin, gray-haired butler.

"Good morning, Renton," Rellen said easily.

Renton raised an eyebrow, his features remaining stoic. "Good morning, gentlemen. How may I help you today?"

"We had a few more questions for you or someone else on the staff who might know a little about the relationships the family had with outsiders," Mygal said.

"After that," Rellen cut in, "I'd like to spend a good portion of the day out back to work with the remains of the cottage. Would that be alright with you?"

"Gentlemen," Renton said, speaking as if he were explaining something very simple, "Lord Corwyk commanded me to afford you both every courtesy and assist you in whatever manner you required. I am at your service and, truthfully, hope you will be able to capture or kill the perpetrators of this horrific tragedy." A spark of anger flickered in his aged eyes. "Furthermore, although you may not have deduced it, I was a willing and very happy servant of the duke and his family for decades. They treated me like a member of their noble house when protocol didn't require it of them. It was the same for the rest of those who served them. It is my sincerest desire that the murderers are *executed in the most painful manner possible.*" Renton's features filled with rage as he said the last, and then he regained his composure. "And *soon.*"

Rellen and Mygal both raised their eyes at that. They hadn't expected such an answer from the stoic old man.

Renton opened the door wide and motioned for them to enter. "Please come in."

They stepped into the foyer as Renton closed the door behind them.

"Renton," Mygal said, "you said you felt like a member of the family. Does that mean you were privy to at least some of their more private affairs?"

"Indeed, sir," Renton replied. "While the duke and his family did not include me in all things, I certainly knew more than most. The duke even confided in me from time to time when wrestling with the turmoil that can come from both marriage and fatherhood."

Rellen didn't show it, but he'd been hoping that was the case. It was rare for Pelinese nobility to be that familiar and forthcoming with the staff.

"What can you tell me about the relationships the duke's children had?" Mygal asked. "Was there anything unusual?"

"Stolan," Renton replied with a thin veil over his sadness, "may he rest forever in the loving embrace of Selestina, from whom all life flows—" He bowed his head for a moment and then looked up at Rellen "—he was involved with a lovely young woman of good breeding. I believe there was even some discussion of marriage, although it had not gone past that point."

Renton got an uncomfortable, almost distasteful look upon his face. "Jacinda, on the other hand, possessed extremely poor taste and judgment. She chose to consort with a dreadful young cretin and continued, despite the protests of her father, in a rather embarrassing association of the worst kind. The young man she involved herself with, although born of a noble house, was little more than a common criminal." Renton seemed to be working himself up into a bit of a rage. "That bastard, figuratively speaking, had even been disowned by his father, Baron Dukatt Sylvemar. How he earned his keep after that, I'm sure I don't wish to even fathom a guess. I do know the young lady did things with him she ought not. The duke said the young guttersnipe had taken the young lady to a number of rather unseemly taverns and other establishments along the wharf, and with some regularity."

"Does the wretch have a name?" Rellen asked.

"I believe his given name was Riven, but under this roof, the only name he used was—" he sneered "—Dancer." Mygal and Rellen stared at each other as Renton regained his composure and straightened his coat with a frustrated jerk. "I'm afraid that's all I know. The duke was much more involved with the cur, and I did my best to avoid the subject at all costs. If you ask me, he had to be involved in their ghastly murders."

"What did he look like?" Mygal asked.

Renton drew in a deep breath and let it out slowly, a thoughtful expression on his face. "I only saw him on a handful of occasions, and that was some time ago. As I recall, he was around twenty, with long black hair he always wore in a braid. He was slightly shorter than I, and rather muscular. I also remember seeing him in black and red more often than not. That, and he was generally armed like a criminal—" He glanced at Rellen's and Mygal's weapons "—no offense."

"None taken," Rellen said with a half-smile.

"Dancer gave no appearance of a young nobleman and possessed all the dignity and poise of a common thug."

"Thank you, Renton," Rellen said. "That was a missing piece of the puzzle."

"Do you believe the swine was involved in the murders?" Renton asked, and fire burned in his eyes.

"At least peripherally," Rellen said carefully, "although it is quite possible he was here that night." He wanted to be careful. He didn't want the old codger going after Dancer, whether he was wrong or right. At Renton's age, he'd mean well, but he'd likely get himself killed. Rellen placed his hand on Renton's shoulder, and he stared into his eyes with as much iron as he could muster. "Trust me when I say, should we become certain of his involvement, we'll do something about it."

"Thank you, sir," Renton replied. "May Selestina watch over you and keep you safe."

Rellen nodded. "I did have a couple more questions."

"Proceed, sir."

"The cottage in the back, what was it for? Who used it?"

"That structure was the duke's private study. He kept mementos of his youth—and that of the lady. It was also the only place milady permitted him to smoke his pipe. As I mentioned to Mygal, they were rather ardent adventurers when they were younger. The duke had been a rather capable swordsman and his wife an exceptionally competent runecaster.

The two of them traveled with a group who had been involved with clearing out a nearby nuraghi. The duke at the time gave them all medals for their heroism. Apparently, a den of murderous beasts had taken up in the ruins and had been raiding nearby villages, farms, and fishing camps. That was some distance to the east, on the other side of the lake, along the river."

"I didn't know that about him," Rellen mused.

"No reason you should sir," Renton said. "No offense, but I doubt you and the duke traveled in the same circles."

"You're not wrong," Rellen said. "It just never occurred to me that adventurers sometimes become dukes too."

"Indeed, sir. In my youth, I was quite the pugilist... although you wouldn't know it to look at me."

"No kidding?" Mygal said with a grin.

Renton's chin rose a bit. "No kidding, sir," he replied with a good deal of pride. "Often a local favorite in some of the... shall we say... less organized prize fights."

"Renton," Rellen said, clapping the butler on the shoulder, "I knew I liked you for a reason." He looked to Mygal. "Now we really do have to get back there, but thank you for all your help."

"It was indeed my pleasure, sir. Shall I escort you?"

"No, thank you. We can take it from here."

"As you wish." Renton gave a slight bow. "Please don't hesitate if you require anything... food, drink... what have you. The household and its staff are at your disposal."

"You have our thanks," Mygal said.

Renton nodded his head and then moved off into the next room.

Out of the corner of his eye, Rellen caught the old butler strike a pose and throw a few punches. With a soft chuckle, Rellen led Mygal down the hall, through the arboretum, and out the back where the ruins of the duke's study awaited them.

Nothing had changed. The ash still lay all about, with charred timbers sticking up in a few places. Buried in the ash were the burned up remains of furniture and other items one might find in a study. Nothing was salvageable, as far as Rellen could tell, but only by digging through it would they be able to find any metal or stone objects that might have survived the blaze. He had a better idea, however.

Rellen walked two full circles around the perimeter, looking for the perfect spot. He finally found a level area, three yards from the edge of the ash, between the ruined cottage and the house. A small, flat stone stuck out of the grass. It would make a perfect surface for what he was about to do.

Go hunting, little one, he said to Xilly. *This will take quite a while.*

I'll keep an eye out too, she replied as she fluttered off. *You'll be vulnerable.*

Rellen smiled as she disappeared up into the trees. When she was gone, he let his eyes flow over the grassy area. He glanced at Mygal as he started unbuckling a bracer.

"You really don't have to stick around for this," he said. "It's going to take four or five hours for me to cast this spell, although, once it's done, it's pretty impressive."

"I wouldn't miss it," Mygal said. "Seeing a well-trained runecaster in action is not something regular folks get to enjoy." Mygal looked serious for a moment. "Besides, after listening to Renton this morning, I want to get these killers even more. I can be very patient." He glanced at the manor house. "I didn't know there was a nuraghi in these parts."

Rellen unbuckled his other bracer. "You'd be surprised at how many there are. Now that you're running Guardian patrols and getting into trouble, the odds are you'll make your way into one every now and again." Rellen turned serious. "Just be careful with the cursed things. Sometimes they are just piles of old stone. Other times..." He shook his head. "There's evil in there from ancient times."

"Do *you* know who built them?" Mygal asked. "Where I grew up, they're just legends... evil places to be avoided."

He knew what Mygal was implying. Rellen had grown up in the palace, so he might know more.

"Actually, no, I don't." Rellen unbuckled his greaves. "There was little taught about them either at university or the magic academy—although a little more there. And neither my father nor any of his advisers ever talked about the history of nuraghi. I'm certain they didn't know, either. All we ever dealt with was when something bad happened around them."

"And you've been in two of them?"

"That's right." He pushed away the old memory of children screaming.

"I can't wait to see one."

"You may not always feel that way." Rellen let out a long breath to calm himself. "Now, step back a bit and let me get to work."

Mygal nodded and stepped back a few paces, a curious look upon his face.

Dropping his chest piece on the grass, Rellen stepped over to the ash, picked up a handful, and moved back to the small, flat stone. He sat down cross-legged in front of the stone, facing the ruins. Opening a pouch on his waist, he pulled out the short stub of a candle, with only an inch of it remaining and a nub of a wick. He carefully placed the candle upon the stone, making sure it was completely level.

He closed his eyes, drew in a deep breath, and let it out slowly, tapping gently into his majea. The spell was a test of both endurance and concentration, and one of the most difficult he'd ever learned.

He placed his free hand on top of the candle and uttered a quick incantation. When he pulled his hand away, a small, burning flame danced atop the wick. Drawing from his majea again, he began a new incantation—one of rebuilding. He pulled deeply, steadily, channeling majea from his outstretched hand into the candle. As he did, tiny wisps of energy flowed from his hand, curling through the air and into the candle. The entire world became that small, flickering flame as the wisps were drawn into it. The lengthy incantation flowed in a whisper from his lips almost unbidden, and as he spoke it, the flame slowed and finally stopped moving. Tendrils of white light wrapped around the flame, and it froze in space, motionless, as if it had been painted by a master.

With his other hand, Rellen poured a tiny stream of ash into the flame. The wisps of light curled around the falling ash, coiling around it into a thin line. He began the litany once again, focusing all of his concentration upon the flame as it consumed the ash. His majea seeped into candle and flame as the ash was consumed. Suddenly, the flame began to move again, but now it seemed to be flickering backward. A swirl of light flowed around both candle and flame. Removing his hand, Rellen poured more of his majea into the spell, repeating the litany over and over again, and as he did, the swirls of light increased. The candle began to grow before his eyes.

He repeated the incantation again, now focusing his attention upon the ruins of the cottage. He wove a connection between the cottage and the candle. Wisps of the white light multiplied and streaked over to the ruins of the cottage, flowing around and through it. When the bond was complete, he drew more deeply upon his majea, pouring that energy into both the candle and the ruins, channeling it through the wisps of light. He continued repeating the incantation, and each time, the swirls of light flowing around the cottage grew. Time passed, although he couldn't say how much. Bit by bit, the cottage reformed, just as the candle had. The candle was now several inches in height, and as Rellen poured more majea into the spell, the cottage took shape, as if it were burning in reverse.

The wisps were a faint tornado around the ruins now, and as they swirled, the walls rose from the ash a little at a time, rising, taking on their original form. They changed from charred black to a pale tan. The roof returned. The interior reshaped itself, and objects that had fallen from the walls rose up to take their place on the walls or furniture where they had originally been.

The litany continued until, finally, the candle was fully reformed and the flame went out.

Rellen let out a long, exhausted breath. The spell had taken most of his majea, and he would need another hearty meal and a full night's rest to restore his strength again. He placed his hand on top of the candle, uttered the incantation, and removed his hand to reveal a new flame.

The cottage was a single-story structure of pale tan and blue trim, with a high-pitch roof of wooden shingles. A chimney poked up to Rellen's right, and there was a small, wooden bench outside the structure on the left. The front door faced him, with windows on either side. Through the door, he could see a wide, bay window on the far side, facing the lake.

He slowly got to his feet, letting out a faint groan as his bruises gave protest once again. He turned to find Mygal a short distance off, sitting against a tree with a look of awe upon his face. Xilly was asleep in his lap.

"That was… astounding," Mygal said. "I've seen a lot of magic, but I've never seen anything like that," he added as Xilly leapt from his lap and fluttered over to Rellen's shoulder.

"It's an exceptionally difficult spell to learn, and the most taxing one I know," Rellen said, scratching the dragonette beneath her chin. "We're eating heavy again tonight."

Mygal nodded in understanding. "Is that real?" he asked, nodding toward the cottage.

"No," Rellen replied. "It's something in between real and illusion." He pointed to the candle, which was burning down much more quickly than a regular candle would. "We have about a quarter of an hour. When the candle burns out, the cottage will return to ash, just the way it was." Rellen shook his head to clear his fatigue. "Let's get inside." He walked over to the front door, opened it, and went inside.

The interior, exactly as it had been a moment before the fire started, was just as Rellen expected from an old, retired adventurer. The floor was a rich, dark wood, with the blue, furred hide of a bear-sized beast Rellen didn't recognize covering the center. A desk filled the left-hand side of the room, with a high-backed chair covered in red leather on the far side and a wide window beyond. Two large sitting chairs faced the bay window, with a low table between them and a large ashtray upon it. A pipe sat in the tray, and there was a small box of tobacco beside it. Beneath the bay window was a low, narrow table upon which a set of crystal decanters sat, each full of a different liquid, with two tumblers beside them. There was a small table in front of the fireplace, and several maps rolled out on it, one atop the other.

A few old, but well-maintained, blades hung on the walls. The cat-like head of a particularly large vellish hung on one side of the fireplace and a terrifying, blue-furred monstrosity on the other. It had a short, curved snout, sharp tusks jutting up from its lower jaw, and a mouth full of long, pointed teeth. A ridge of darker blue fur ran over its head, and it had wide, leather wattles sticking out from its neck, lined with sharp spikes that radiated out. Rellen figured the head had once been attached to the rug in the middle of the room. He wondered if this was one of the creatures the young duke had slain to earn Svennival's respect, as Renton had described. There were a few smaller objects, including a golden human skull, upon the mantle, but something else caught Rellen's eye.

He and Mygal both moved toward the fireplace. Mygal stopped at the table and placed his finger on the exposed map where someone, presumably the duke, had circled an area well east of Svennival, across the lake, and along the river. There was nothing indicated on the map, but someone had written the word "*Py'ellios.*"

"I wonder if that's the nuraghi Renton spoke of," Mygal asked.

"It may very well be." Rellen reached into a pouch and pulled out a small sheet of vellum and a piece of charcoal. "Sketch that area of the map and write down that word." He turned back toward the area over the fireplace.

There was a wooden plaque directly above the mantle. The darkened portion held the outline of a wide-bladed longsword. The hilt had been wide and curled at the ends, and the pommel was two downward facing curls that came to fairly sharp points. Rellen had to wonder if whoever had burned the building had taken the weapon as a trophy or for some other purpose.

To the right, was another outline, this time in the paint. It was circular, like a ring about ten inches across, with cutouts along the inner edge. The shape reminded him of a cog, but with the gears on the inside. These gears, however, were irregular in both width and depth. He pulled out another piece of vellum and drew a quick, rough sketch. He turned and looked around the study. Crossing the room, he moved behind the desk and was surprised to find nothing disturbed.

"They didn't search the room," Rellen said.

"What?" Mygal replied, lifting his eyes from one of the other maps.

"They didn't search the desk, or if they did, they pushed the drawers back in."

He looked to where the sword and ring had been.

"They came here for one or both of those," he said, pointing to the mantle. "They knew what they were after, and they razed the place when they were through... probably to keep anyone from figuring it out."

"How can you be sure?"

"Sure?" Rellen replied. "I'm not sure, but that's the only thing that fits." He nodded toward the bay window. "They left other weapons behind, and a few of those are worth a dakkari or three. What burglar leaves such things behind, especially when they're easy to grab and carry?" He stared at Mygal. "The house was pretty much the same, and now I'm thinking the murders were ancillary to what they did here." He shook his head. "I don't know. This whole thing is bizarre." A tiny mote of ash floated down before his eyes. "We better get out of here. It's about to come apart."

They moved quickly out of the cottage. Rellen glanced at the candle to find that virtually all of the wax was gone and the flame sputtering. The wick, with nothing left to hold it up, fell over, and the flame went out with a tiny puff of smoke.

Rellen turned as the entire cottage turned to ash and collapsed into a swirling pile. Within moments, the ruins returned to exactly how they'd found them.

Mygal watched the last bits of ash settle to the ground, an awed look upon his face, and then turned to Rellen.

"So, they *might* have taken a sword and whatever that ring was," Mygal said. "What do we do now?"

"I think we have to track down Dancer, now more than ever." He glanced at the sun and realized it was almost dusk. "But first, I need to get some food in me and recuperate. I'll also send a message to the king, updating him on all this, particularly that sedition was *not* a motive for the murders. Maybe we can go over all this and put something together. I feel like we're missing a piece… several of them, actually."

CHAPTER ELEVEN
A MATTER OF TRUST

H ow do we track Dancer down quickly?" Rellen asked
then shoved a forkful of scrambled eggs into his
mouth. The din of a dozen other patrons filled the
Drunken Unger tavern. Rellen had eaten like a horse the night
before and fallen into another deep, dreamless slumber. He'd
awakened feeling refreshed but still famished.

Xilly sat on the table, just within reach of his plate, getting
dirty looks from some of the patrons. Rellen ignored them.
Her head darted out, and she chomped down on a chunk of
his scrambled eggs.

"I have an idea there," Mygal replied. He sipped his juice,
eying Xilly with an amused smile on his face. "I see no reason
why Tavyn couldn't at least point us in the right direction."

"Tavyn Daggerayne?" Rellen asked. "The report the king
gave me indicated Tavyn was the one who put you on
Dancer's trail to begin with." He raised a dubious eyebrow. "Is
there more to that story?"

"No," Mygal replied. "That's how it happened."

"Can you trust him?" Rellen wasn't comfortable with the idea, and he was at least a little worried that a Guardian, even a new one, would so readily suggest someone like Tavyn, considering what had happened. "How do you know he wasn't the one who set you up?"

"Well," Mygal said slowly. "I honestly have to say I don't know." He got a thoughtful look on his face. "I went over the whole thing in my head again and again, while I was recovering." He finally shook his head and locked eyes with Rellen. "What you don't know is that I tested him a few times while we were together, sifting through his emotions as lightly as I could, and never sensed any deceit or betrayal." He took another sip of juice, staring off into space as he tried to formulate his words. "Those emotions have a certain smell to them… or maybe it's taste. It's hard to explain." He looked to Rellen again. "He's nothing more or less than an information broker, as near as I can tell. It wouldn't be good for him to get *involved* in anyone's business. The only way he gets paid is by being *aware* of everyone's business. Don't misunderstand, I trust him about as much as I trust any of my contacts… that is, not at all. I do, however, trust my instincts, and my majea. I believe Tavyn can still help us solve this mystery. You can take that or leave it. You're the one in charge."

Rellen eyed Mygal for several seconds. He kept it off his face, but once again, his respect for the young Guardian went up a pip or two. Rellen frequently followed his own instincts. He usually got it right—sometimes not. He always owned the mistakes and didn't make them again. He was growing more convinced Mygal had that same skill, but only time would tell.

Rellen finally nodded. "Information brokers are the same all over, aren't they?"

"They are, and I've been dealing with them since I was eleven." Mygal tossed a small corner of toast over near Xilly. Her head darted out, and she chomped it. "The real question is, what do you want to do with Dancer once we find him?"

"Still follow him," Rellen said firmly. "We don't know nearly enough to just grab him, and we know there was more than one person involved. If we're lucky, he'll lead us to the nest, assuming he was involved. I'm pretty certain he's the one who killed Jacinda, and under orders from the Nissrans. If I'm right, he *had* to, but he didn't want to. Just a hunch, but it stands up."

"I figured I'd find you here," a friendly voice called from the open front doors.

Rellen and Mygal looked up to find a young, roguish-looking man approaching them.

"Tavyn," Mygal called out. "Come join us. We were just talking about you."

"I can imagine," Tavyn replied with an overtly friendly smile. "Nothing good, I hope. I'm an incorrigible philanderer."

By the look of him, Rellen suspected Tavyn wasn't joking about being a philanderer and that he was *very* good at it. He wore a leather jerkin and pants of indigo, cut close and clean, with high, loose leather gloves of the same color. He looked young, but there was a confidence and wariness in his eyes that belied a hard-earned street sense. Rellen noted the leather grips of his weapons were well worn from frequent use.

Tavyn's companion was a heavily muscular woman, almost as tall as Rellen and obviously a warrior. He knew her well. She was a zokurios who could harm or heal quite effectively. She wore burgundy, brown, and tan leather that precisely followed her form. A silver saber with an intricately carved hilt and pommel stuck out of a burgundy scabbard at her hip. She had close-cropped hair of deep red, and her emerald green eyes glittered when she recognized Rellen, although she said nothing as they stepped up to the table.

"I'm glad to see you're up and about," Tavyn said, "Who's your friend?" He gave Rellen a cursory once-over.

"This is Rellen... another bounty hunter," Mygal replied. "He came to help me track down Dancer." His eyes shifted to the woman, and he gave her an appreciative look. "And who are you?"

"Miranda Torai," Rellen said, staring into her eyes. She gave him just the hint of a smile and nodded her head to

Mygal. Mygal and Tavyn turned surprised faces to Rellen. "We served in the military together a while back. It's good to see you, old friend."

"It's good to be seen," she replied. Her voice was low, inherently sultry, but that was a fact he knew she'd mostly resented throughout her adult life.

"I *am* wondering how the two of you ended up here together," Rellen said, glancing at Tavyn and back again.

"The duke regent put out the word that Miranda needed to be connected with Mygal here, so I went looking and found what I was after… as usual."

Rellen rose out of his chair and stepped over to Miranda. They wrapped each other in a great bear-hug, slapping each other on the backs a few times. "I missed you," she whispered in his ear.

"The feeling is mutual," Rellen said as they moved apart. Of all the people in the world, he trusted her as much as he trusted his brother. He caught Mygal and Tavyn staring at him with wide eyes and suggestive expressions upon their faces.

"It's not what you think," Rellen said to Mygal. "We served together… saved each other's lives more than once." She nodded. "I always felt safe when she had my back. That's why I asked Corwyk to find her. Knowing what I know now, I'm glad I did."

He scratched his eyebrow, cheek, and chin with different fingers. It was a sign language they'd both learned as military scouts, much like the Crysvardish he'd used with Corwyk. The military version was much more succinct, used only to convey critical messages covertly. The message said, *Explain later.*

She replied with an almost imperceptible nod.

Rellen looked around the room. "Come, we have business to discuss."

He stood up, wincing with muscle aches, and grabbed his plate. He urged Xilly to climb up onto his shoulder.

"Hey, Drumore," Rellen called out to the innkeeper.

"Aye?"

"Is it alright if we take a couple of these chairs up to the room?"

"Aye!" he replied. "Just bring 'em back down when yer done."

Rellen nodded his thanks.

"Mygal, Tavyn, would you grab those chairs?"

"Sure," Mygal said, standing up.

The four of them quickly made their way upstairs, with Rellen continuing to shovel food into his mouth as they did.

Once they were in the room, they all sat around the small table in front of the fireplace and settled in, with Rellen groaning as he sat down.

"Busy night?" Miranda asked. "You look beat."

"You have no idea." He stretched out his shoulders. "Miranda, are you interested in helping out an old friend?"

"You know you don't need to ask," she replied. "That was always the deal."

Xilly crawled down Rellen's arm and took a few steps toward Miranda. She stretched her neck out, sniffing lightly, and immediately made a soft thrumming sound.

"I think Xilly likes you," Rellen said, a surprised look on his face. "She normally doesn't take to people this quickly."

"Hello, Xilly," Miranda said, holding out her hand. "I see you have excellent taste."

The little dragonette gave Miranda's knuckles a sniff and a lick, then gave a sharp cooing sound.

"So, Tavyn," Rellen said, shifting his focus, "you should know straightaway that I'm a cautious sort. I like to let people know where I stand up front. I know her." He nodded to Miranda. "I know him." He pointed a thumb at Mygal. "And I know her." He stroked Xilly. "I trust them." He locked eyes with the informant. "I don't know you." He wanted to come on strong to watch Tavyn's reaction.

"I can tell you," Mygal chimed in, looking at Rellen, "it was Corwyk who recommended him to me, and he did put us on the right trail."

"There's no reason you should trust me," Tavyn said easily staring straight at Rellen. Even that told Rellen something about the man. "You just met me, and to be honest, considering the sequence of events and how it ended," he glanced at Mygal, "you have even less reason to trust me than if you knew nothing about me."

"Oh?" Rellen said, feigning surprise.

"Come, now," Tavyn said, raising an eyebrow. "We both know you're not surprised. If you were, you never would have survived this long. I appreciate honesty as much as you do. It's so hard to find in my line of work." He leaned back in his chair, looking a bit more comfortable. "By now, Mygal will have told you that two days after meeting me, and just hours after I aimed him at Dancer, he ended up bleeding and unconscious in an alley." He gave Rellen an expectant smile. "I wouldn't trust me either. Only a fool would."

Rellen never took his eyes off Tavyn as he picked up a piece of bacon and popped it in his mouth. He chewed, eyeing Tavyn thoughtfully. "Fair enough," he said evenly.

"For what it's worth," Tavyn continued, "I'm no threat to you or your pursuit of Dancer. I'm assuming you're still after him, yes? I've heard nothing on the streets about his apprehension or demise—not that I necessarily would have, especially if he's dived into a Vuoda hole."

Rellen placed the mug back on the table. "We are." He wasn't quite sure what to make of Tavyn's reply. On one hand, it was the perfect response. On the other, Rellen had to wonder if Tavyn's answer was too perfect. Rellen suspected much, but Tavyn was probably the shortest path to Dancer. He'd have to play along for now and see what happened.

"I can tell you, Rellen," Miranda chimed in, "I've seen Tavyn around. I've never worked with him, but as far as I know, he's always played fair, or at least as fair as you can in this business."

"That's good to know," Rellen said, turning to her. She gave him a faint, reassuring nod. He returned his gaze to Tavyn. "And it works in your favor."

"Tavyn," Mygal said, "you helped track Dancer down before. We'd like you to do it again, and as discreetly as possible."

"What I'm hearing is, you want him now more than ever." Tavyn got an almost larcenous look in his eyes.

Rellen had seen that look on the faces of more informants than he wanted to think about. The response actually made him feel better. In that moment, he had at least a slightly better idea of who and what he was dealing with.

"That's right," he said. "But don't get greedy."

"Wouldn't think of it," Tavyn said with an easy smile, "but I do believe I may be able to help you." He leaned forward with a very down-to-business look on his face. "I've brokered information for the duke more than once over the past few years, and he was never disappointed. I can do the same for you, but as Mygal knows, I don't work for free."

"That goes without saying," Rellen replied.

"Good." Tavyn leaned back in his chair once again, a comfortable look on his face, as if he felt like he was in the coachman's seat. Rellen wanted him to feel that way. Comfort often breeds mistakes. "There isn't much I miss in Svennival. It's how I've earned my living since I was fifteen, and business has been pretty good. You need at least a little reassurance. To show that I'm on your side, and as a sign of good faith, I think you should track down the murdered daughter's boyfriend."

Tavyn doesn't know we figured that part out, Rellen thought. In that moment, he grew at least a bit more certain Tavyn hadn't been involved in either Mygal's attack or the murders. That didn't mean he wasn't involved in any plots of sedition though.

"Why should we do that?" Rellen asked, testing him.

Tavyn smiled. "The first one is free, but not the second."

"I suppose that's how the world turns," Rellen said, letting out a patient breath. "But your generosity isn't worth anything."

"Oh?" Tavyn asked.

"Dancer *was* the daughter's boyfriend."

Tavyn looked disappointed.

"We also know Dancer was born Riven Sylvemar, so you don't get to sell that one either," Rellen said. He eyed Tavyn. "You should know that we've uncovered a great deal in the past day and a half, so let's cut to the chase. What would a couple of direct answers to a couple of direct questions cost me?"

"Generally, ten sepiks apiece," Tavyn smiled and then leaned forward once again. "But I have a better idea. If you're after killers in Svennival, then you could end up having to go all over the city, chasing down gods-know-who. Hire me on for fifteen sepiks a day, plus two sepiks for every useful introduction I make or lead I provide along the way." He raised his eyebrows, encouragingly. "I think you'll find it money well spent. Bonuses are always appreciated, by the way."

"Hire you?" Rellen asked, a bit dubious, although part of him thought the idea had merit. "I'll be honest, I'm torn between cutting you loose as soon as possible or keeping a close eye on you until this is over." He narrowed his eyes. "We still don't know if you're involved in all this, although I'm leaning away from that. You know we're looking, which gives you information to sell to the person or people we're looking for." Rellen leaned in a little closer. "You haven't done that already, have you?"

"I wouldn't be here if I had," Tavyn replied easily. "Nobody's asked me about you nor whoever might be hunting the killers, and I haven't gone looking to sell. I figured I'd be able to shake you down for a few more sepiks, considering Dancer is still at large." He gave Rellen a confident smile. "And let's be honest, bounty hunters generally have deeper pockets than the people they go after. You're the better bet."

"Fair enough," Rellen replied. "You should know that this may take a while."

"The longer the better. I get paid no matter what, and there are more dangerous places to be than in the company of three such as you."

Rellen nodded. The more he thought about it, the more he wanted Tavyn close at hand. And the truth was, even with Miranda, Tavyn's knowledge of the underworld in Svennival would be an asset.

"If you take the King's Credit," he said, "you have yourself a deal."

"King's Credit?" Tavyn replied, raising an eyebrow. "You don't look like a king's man to me. You do, however, look like a bounty hunter."

"Thank you," Rellen replied. "Looks can be deceiving, and can't a man be both? Regardless, do we have a deal? Before you answer, you need to know that if you agree, the dance changes. The stakes go up, and the consequences for betrayal become more than severe." Rellen made the warning as ironclad as he could.

Tavyn's eyes narrowed, and he took on a wary posture. "Alright…" he said slowly. "If you can prove you're a king's man. I generally don't run tabs. Coin only. And the consequences for betrayal in my business are *always* severe."

"I figured as much," Rellen replied, "but I'm about to trust you with something that not many are aware of." Mygal gave him a curious look. "There's something else," Rellen said. "And if you back out now, you'll be in a jailer's cell before the end of the day."

"Hold on," Tavyn said, holding up his hands. "I'm not about to commit to something without knowing what it is."

"Then let me sweeten the pot. I'll pay you a dakkari a day, not fifteen sepiks, and for every week in this particular harness, you'll get an additional five dakkaris. You'll work for me until we track down those who murdered the duke's family or I release you. Not sooner."

Tavyn looked stunned. "You certainly know how to negotiate." He cocked his head to the side thoughtfully. "I'm still not comfortable making a bargain when I don't know all the risks and commitments."

"You'll understand shortly, if you agree. I can assure you that there's no risk to you whatsoever unless you sell us out. In fact, if this works out, it's likely there will be more such work in the future, not only with me, but with my associates." Rellen smiled. "This would be the one secret you would always have to keep. It would be profitable for you to do so, and *lethal* if you didn't." He locked eyes with Tavyn. "What's it going to be?"

He watched Tavyn's conflict—the doubt, the greed, and even the fear. Rellen was confident the young man would cave in, and if it went south, the consequences for Rellen were minimal. Svennival was not part of his regular patrol route, so it would be unlikely to affect him in the future.

"Alright," Tavyn finally said. "I agree, but I'm trusting you." He gave Mygal a sidelong glance.

"Good," Rellen replied. "What's your full name—and I mean your given name."

"Tavyn Daggerayne."

Rellen turned and opened one of the saddlebags sitting on the floor beside him. He took out a small roll of parchment and a fine-pointed stick of charcoal. Unrolling the parchment, he tapped into his majea and channeled a small portion of it as he drew three very specific sigils at the top of the parchment. The first was his personal sigil, known to the king and the other Guardians. The second was a binding rune that would hold the magic in place. The third was a second binding rune that would connect Tavyn to the spell Rellen was about to cast. Then he wrote out the following contract, directing more majea into the script:

> *Tavyn Daggerayne is hereby conscripted into temporary service under a Guardian of Pelinon. He shall earn one dakkari a day plus two per meaningful introduction or lead during the investigation into the murder of Baron Vladysh Belvenim and his family. So long as he is conscripted, at the end of each week, he shall earn an additional five dakkaris. He may collect in part or full at any time, upon termination of this contract, or the event of my death, whichever comes first, and from any King's Assayer's Office.*

As he wrote, he felt Mygal stiffen beside him. Guardians were generally disinclined to reveal who they were without good cause. Rellen turned the parchment around so Tavyn could read it, and then he summoned his majea once again, focusing on the tattoo on his shoulder.

"A Guardian," Tavyn said, his eyes going wide. "I had no idea…" There was a wary sense of awe in his voice.

Rellen's eyes flicked to Miranda. She hadn't known what he'd become after he'd abdicated the throne. To her credit, her face was immobile, but he caught a glint of… was that satisfaction in her eyes? Happiness? He could tell she had taken some delight in the discovery. It was an exceptionally short list of people who hadn't condemned Rellen for his decision. Miranda was at the top of it.

"That's right," Rellen said, returning his gaze to Tavyn.

"But how do I know you're really a Guardian? I won't be able to collect until after at least the first day has passed, and I don't plan on helping you until I'm satisfied."

"I'm about to show you," Rellen said. "If you know about the Guardians, then a man in your position probably knows about their avatars." He eyed Tavyn. "I'm trusting you now, and if you betray that trust, I'll kill you outright." There was a deadly sincerity in his voice. "Now shut up. I need to concentrate."

Tavyn's mouth snapped closed.

Rellen closed his eyes and whispered the incantation, holding out his left hand. Within moments, a crow stood in his hand, blinking at him.

Rellen placed the bird on his shoulder and stared at Tavyn, an expectant look on his face. "Believe me now?" he said.

"I've heard of the Guardians' Avatars," Tavyn said. "I never thought I'd see one." He eyed Rellen. "I'll want to hit the assayer's office tomorrow, just to be sure, but as far as I'm concerned, we've got a bargain."

"I expected no less," Rellen replied. "Let's bind the agreement, then, shall we?"

Tavyn nodded once, pushed the parchment to the center of the table, and held out his hand. Such contracts were common in Pelinon and considered both personally binding and enforceable by magistrates.

Rellen drew the slim spell-dagger once again from within his bracer, its silver blade and heavily inscribed runes glinting. He gripped Tavyn's hand and pricked the index finger. He allowed three droplets of blood to fall upon the bottom of the parchment, and then he released Tavyn's hand.

"Roll up your sleeve and lay your arm on the table."

Tavyn did.

Rellen then held his own index finger over the parchment and pricked it. Three droplets of blood fell, landing just below Tavyn's.

Sliding the dagger back into his bracer, Rellen focused his majea upon the parchment and uttered a long incantation that included his name, Tavyn's, and King Saren III.

He released the magic into the parchment. Red filaments of light swirled up from the droplets of blood in tiny twisters that spun with increasing speed. Rellen formed his mind around the swirls of crimson and willed them onto Tavyn's arm. They darted out, and as they touched flesh, they swirled and danced in a very specific pattern. Moments later, a tattoo appeared on Tavyn's arm.

It included Rellen's personal rune and smaller symbols for days and weeks. As time passed, the numbers would increase, and they would be removed or altered anytime Tavyn showed up at an assayer's office to receive his payment. The tattoo would last until the terms of the contract were met and then evaporate in puff of smoke.

"It's done," Rellen said. "You work for me now." He rolled up the parchment and placed it in the crow's beak. Standing, he moved to the window and opened it. "Fly," he commanded.

The crow flew out the open window and fluttered out of sight.

"Show that tattoo in any assayer's office, and they'll make good on our bargain. You can collect accrued payments along the way, if you like, or get it all when we're through."

"That'll be fine," Tavyn said, pulling his arm back and examining the new tattoo. He looked pleased with the result.

"Now," Rellen said, "where do we go from here. How do we track down Dancer?"

"We contact the Black Wyrm Clan." Tavyn leaned back in his chair, a confident look on his face.

"Burning Giant's balls," Rellen muttered. "I hate dealing with the Wyrm."

Miranda got a mischievous grin, "They're not so bad, once you get to know them." She turned to Tavyn. "Who in the Clan?"

"Rickavyn Dennilish," Tavyn replied quickly.

"That makes things a little easier," Miranda said. "I've worked with him before."

"Excellent," Rellen said. "That's two more sepiks for you. Do you both have horses?"

"Just outside," Miranda said.

"Then, let's get going."

They rose from their seats and the others started making their way out. Rellen picked up his saddlebags and threw them over his shoulder. Xilly fluttered up to rest on his other shoulder.

Watch Tavyn, Rellen said. *We may have a bargain, but I still don't trust him.*

Understood, she replied, turning her head to stare at Tavyn's back.

CHAPTER TWELVE

DIVIDED LOYALTIES

Tavyn had carefully maneuvered his gray gelding back a bit, as the four of them rode through the streets of Svennival, headed for the wharf district. Rellen and Miranda were in the lead, side-by-side, focused on catching up on old times. He paid them no mind. Mygal seemed intent on listening to the other two, like a puppy follows a master. There was at least a little hero worship going on there, which made sense now that he knew Rellen was a Guardian too. That revelation had shaken Tavyn a bit, but only for a moment. The game was still the same, and if he could deceive one Guardian, he had little doubt he could deceive two.

Everything was going just as his employer had predicted, although he was a bit annoyed the man hadn't mentioned they were drawing in a second Guardian. He could see—now that the plan had been executed—why it worked. But why his employer wanted Rellen in Svennival was a complete mystery. Either way, with two Guardians, he would have to be doubly careful.

Placing his hands on the saddle horn, one atop the other, he focused his will upon the bracelet around his left wrist. It was a slim band of dark metal, decorated with an intricate, leafy vine pattern etched into its surface and a simple onyx stone secured by a platinum setting. There was a small symbol on either side, near the clasp, but he didn't recognize it. Where it came from didn't matter. What the thing was capable of did.

He reached out and focused his will upon the black stone. He felt his way into the remarkable magics contained within, and sent out the query, just as the old man had shown him. He closed his eyes and opened the connection.

Milord, he called.

I hear you. Have you joined them?

Bound by a blood contract with the Guardian, Rellen. You never mentioned a second Guardian was involved.

There was a momentary hesitation.

I did not because you didn't need to know and, ultimately, it doesn't matter, his employer said. *So long as you are travelling with them, then my needs are met and you will be paid… twice, it would seem.*

Tavyn sensed his employer's amusement. He'd realized early on that his ermajea worked through the artifact, and it had surprised him. He was exceedingly grateful for it, though. He'd sensed a hint of deceit from his employer on several occasions, which gave him a sense of comfort. Most of the people he worked for lied to him.

Do they suspect anything? his employer asked.

I don't think so, Tavyn replied. *Rellen never would have joined in the contract. He would have just killed or arrested me.*

Don't assume anything with that one. He is clever, cagey, and unpredictable.

Tavyn sensed a hint of frustration in his employer's voice. It was clear the man knew Rellen personally. Tavyn didn't know what he'd gotten himself into, but the coin was going to be a considerable sum when all was said and done.

Another has joined us, Tavyn said. *A woman named Miranda Torai. She and Rellen served in the military together, and they seem very close.*

A warrior?

Yes.

It is a surprise, but a welcome one. His employer was silent for a few heartbeats. *That should prove to be useful. It should put Rellen at ease and increases the likelihood of his success.*

What do you want me to do now?

Keep up your end of Rellen's bargain. Help them find what they seek. Keep me appraised as you have. Aside from that, I have no more requirements of you for the time being. Report again in three days.

I will.

The connection was broken.

Tavyn said a quick prayer that he wouldn't, someday, have to kill Mygal. He was, after all, a kindred spirit. He'd do it of course, if there was enough money in it, but that was just business. The real trick would be not getting caught or killed, and the odds against him were now three to one if something went wrong.

He would just have to make sure nothing did.

CHAPTER THIRTEEN
THE BLACK WYRM CLAN

And that's how I ended up a Guardian," Rellen said to Miranda as the four of them entered the river front district. "I've been doing it ever since." They rode through a warren of two-story warehouses separated by oyster-shell streets. The smells of grain and fish and fruit was heavy on the air, overlaying a foundation of marsh and decay found in any river or lakefront area. Bright sunshine had pushed away at least some of the humidity, and there wasn't a cloud in the azure sky.

Miranda eyed Rellen for several seconds, and the corner of her mouth crimped up. "It seems you traded the prison of the throne room for the yoke of a Guardian. I always knew it wasn't the responsibilities of a king that you feared."

"I finally told Saren the real reason I left," Rellen said.

Miranda's eyebrow went up. "How did he take it?"

"He said he already knew I hated being responsible for the kingdom, and he understood about... the rest. He said I had nothing to be ashamed of."

"He's obviously smarter than you are," she said, chuckling.

"That's true," Rellen said.

"It must have been a relief for you? Cathartic, even."

Rellen gave her a sidelong glance. "Maybe."

"You needed it," she offered firmly. "Keeping things like that bottled up don't do anyone any good." She eyed him, a suspicious look in her emerald eyes. "I bet he said you were actually one of the bravest people he's ever known."

Rellen nodded.

"Someday you'll figure it out," she said. "You have one of the sharpest minds *I've* ever known, but Gallantyr save me, you can be thick."

Rellen started laughing.

"What?" Miranda asked.

"Saren said exactly the same thing," Rellen shook his head.

"We know all too well, Rellen of Corsia," Miranda turned and stared ahead toward a nearby warehouse. "That's where we're headed." She nodded in that direction.

"What can you tell me about this Rickavyn Dennilish?" he asked. "I feel like I'm going in at least a little blind, and I hate that feeling."

"He's a captain in the Black Wyrm Clan. Everything you see around us, and for quite a distance, is under his control."

"Do you trust him?"

"I trust him as much as I trust anyone in the Clan."

Rellen raised a suspicious eyebrow.

"Don't misunderstand me," she said. "The Clan, for all its criminal activities, has a code, and they not only follow it, they enforce it amongst themselves with an iron hand. If Rickavyn gives you his word, you can count on the fact that he'll keep it. But he's a slippery one. If there's wiggle room in the agreement and it's in his best interest, he'll take as much as he can get."

"That's good to know." Rellen eyed the building looming before them. "At least all we're looking for is information."

"If he has it, it's for sale," Miranda said. "So long as it doesn't break the code, *everything* is for sale." As they neared, she peered inside the wide-open warehouse doors. "That's him there," she said, nodding. "The fellow with the broad hat and black and red clothing."

Rellen spotted him, standing a few yards inside the warehouse, talking to a smaller man with gray hair who was reviewing a long sheet of parchment. There were at least a dozen dock workers spread throughout a warehouse filled to the ceiling with crates. They were moving them around or taking inventory and seemed disinterested in anything but whatever task was in front of them.

Rickavyn reminded Rellen of a tall Delver—as wide as he was high—and he looked like he could rip the legs off a bull with his bare hands. He had no neck to speak of. His sleeves were rolled up over burly forearms, and the dark tattoo of a black dragon made a stark contrast along his left forearm, with a thick, white knife scar running through the middle. His knuckles were rough and lumpy, and his nose had clearly been broken more than once.

The four of them rode up to the warehouse doors and stopped just outside. Rickavyn turned and spotted them, a slim smile spreading across his face. He said something to the older man, who then scurried off, rolling up the parchment.

"My, my, my," Rickavyn said, thrumming stiff fingers together in front of him. "Hello, Miranda. Tavyn." He nodded to them both and then let his eyes flow over both Rellen and Mygal. They hovered on Xilly for several seconds, and he got a very interested look on his face. "As I live and breathe, I never thought I'd see the two of you together. Who is that with you?"

"Ricki," Miranda said, "This is Rellen, and that's Mygal. They're *friends*."

"I understand," Rickavyn replied with a knowing nod. His eyes flowed over them all one more time. "You are a motley bunch. I think I smell an opportunity." The smile he gave them was exactly how Rellen imagined a wolf would smile at a lamb if it could manage the feat.

"Possibly," Rellen replied. "Can we talk a bit more privately?"

"Of course," Rickavyn replied easily. He peered outside the warehouse. There was nobody around, so he called over his shoulder, "Killyn, close these doors, would you?" A young man with dark hair set down the crate he'd been carrying and jogged over.

"Yes, sir." Killyn quickly closed the doors behind the Black Wyrm Captain.

"Now what is it I can do for a group like you?" He eyed Rellen. "And keep in mind, nothing is free," he added, glancing at Xilly again.

"I have no doubt." Rellen pulled a small coin purse from his belt, jerked it free, and tossed it over. Rickavyn caught it and felt the weight. The purse had twenty dakkaris inside, and Rellen had no doubt Rickavyn knew how many coins were in it just from the weight and the sound. "We're looking for someone, and we've heard that he might work for you," Rellen said.

"If you're here to collect a bounty on one of my people, we may have a problem," Rickavyn warned. "We don't sell each other out." He looked at Miranda. "Right, Miranda?"

"We're aware of that," she replied easily. "It may not come to that, and this all could affect your business too. It might just be in your best interest to help us."

"Oh, really?" Rickavyn replied, his eyebrow going up. "You have my attention, if nothing else."

"We're looking for someone who we believe might have been involved in murdering Duke Belvenim," Rellen said flatly. "So, yes, this involves a bounty, but I suspect you'd be the last to have wanted the duke killed." Rellen watched Rickavyn's expression closely. The captain's face remained immobile, but Rellen spotted a slight clenching of jaw. "It was my understanding you and the duke maintained a variety of arrangements—just like every other city where the Wyrm does business. Now you have to make new arrangements with whomever replaces him, and that's bad for business. You never know what they're going to want in return, eh?"

"It's possible," Rickavyn said smoothly. "And you say it may have been someone under my employ?"

"That's the rumor, although, at this point, I'm fairly confident it's more fact than fiction."

"Does this person have a name?"

"They call him Dancer, also known as Riven Sylvemar."

Rickavyn sneered, as if someone had handed him a sack of dog turds, and there was no mistaking the anger in his eyes. "I know him," he said slowly, "but he doesn't work for me."

"Oh?" Rellen asked.

"I should have said, he doesn't work for me anymore."

Rellen nodded slowly. "Is this a fairly recent thing?"

"It is." Rickavyn opened the purse and glanced inside. "Dancer disappeared a few days ago, along with one of my lieutenants who owed me a substantial amount of money, I might add. He'd sort of taken Dancer under his wing, although I never understood why."

"A Black Wyrm lieutenant ran out on you?" Miranda asked, her eyes wide in disbelief.

"Aye," Rickavyn replied. "His name is Javyk Sukari." He fixed his gaze on Miranda. "And I'd very much like to see him again." He turned to Rellen. "Here's the thing. Javyk is not actually one of mine. He's based out of Kaichakahn to the south and had been doing some work for me. At first, he was fine, but for the past few weeks, he was acting a bit strangely. Not focused on the job." Rickavyn paused. "His behavior seemed to get even more odd around the time the duke and his family were killed."

"So, you don't know where either of them are?" Rellen asked.

"Like I said, they've gone to ground. I'm sure they know what I'll do to them when I find them, but if they were involved in the duke's murder, then it's not the only reason."

"Any ideas on how to find them?"

"Yes, actually," Rickavyn replied, with a hungry light in his eyes. "As it turns out, men matching their descriptions purchased passage for two in a posh coach with a caravan that's headed south toward Sylverwynd. I just found out, and I was about to register a bounty for Javyk with the Hunter's Guild." He eyed Miranda again. "You interested in the job? If the four of you are going after Dancer anyway, you can kill two crows with one arrow. The job pays two hundred dakkaris for Javyk's head—same terms as last time. I'd file the official bounty with the Guild as soon as we're done here—and put your name on it."

"Done," Miranda replied. "What does Javyk look like?"

"He's hard to miss," Rickavyn said. "Thin fellow with sunken eyes, long, dark hair, and an almost sickly pallor. He stands a little under six feet tall and wears only a long knife on his hip... no other weapons."

"Excellent," Rellen replied. "When did the caravan depart?"

"Two days ago."

"We've got some catching up to do."

"If you ask me," Rickavyn said, "he probably isn't staying in Sylverwynd."

"Oh?" Rellen replied.

"Like I said, he was based out of Kaichakahn. If he's going anywhere, he's headed back home." The captain got a thoughtful look on his face. "And there's something else that was a little odd."

"What's that?" Rellen asked.

"I can't be sure, but I always got the sense he was taking orders from someone outside the Clan. That's about when he started acting strangely."

"Everyone knows that's a good way to get dead," Miranda said.

"True, but it's usually not enough to warrant a bounty. Most of my people earn their gold from more than one source. If it doesn't conflict with our business, we turn a blind eye. It's the debt and the betrayal that put a price on his head."

"Is there anything else you can think of that would help Miranda collect that bounty?" Rellen asked.

"The answer is no, but I'd say you've got your money's worth, wouldn't you?"

"Indeed."

"Then I'll take my leave," Rickavyn said. He turned away and then turned back. "Oh, and I almost forgot." He eyed Xilly again. "What would you take for the dragonette? I know at least a dozen people who would pay a hefty price for it."

Xilly's head perked up, and she hissed angrily.

"She's not for sale at any price," Rellen replied easily. "Have a good day, Rickavyn."

"Good luck," the captain called out with a chuckle, and then he turned and moved off toward the warehouse doors.

They'd only gone a short distance when Rellen pulled on the reins and turned Shaddeth around. Everyone fell in around him, and he let his eyes pass over each of his companions. "If we're going to join the caravan, we'll need a plan. Dancer might recognize Tavyn, and four people just joining a caravan might draw more attention than we want. Any ideas?"

"I have one," Miranda said, "but some of you may not like it." The smile on her face was mischievous as she reached into her saddlebags and pulled out two sets of iron shackles.

CHAPTER FOURTEEN

A PERILOUS ROAD

"A re you sure we have to ride the whole way with them on?" Tavyn asked, eying the shackles distastefully.

Rellen was pleased with Tavyn's disguise. He'd dyed his hair brown and paid a local zokurios who specialized in altering appearances. The goatee was gone, and he now had a thick mustache and heavy sideburns. He'd also braided his hair back into a long queue he'd wrapped around his neck. He had an eye patch over his left eye and had changed into rough-looking, gray garments and a black cloak that spoke of someone who had little means and didn't care. The lifeweaver had also darkened his skin somewhat, so he looked like he'd come from the southern parts of Pelinon where the sun shone more often. Rellen hadn't even recognized him at first.

Mygal's transformation was even more dramatic. He'd shaved his head completely. The lifeweaver had forced his beard to grow out into a thick, bushy thing that added at least ten years to his appearance. She had also darkened his scalp, so it matched the rest of his skin. He now wore leathers of deep green, had a matching, leather cap, and a dark gray cloak.

"You can release yourself any time, like we already told you," Miranda said over the rain, and there was no missing the amusement in her voice. She secured them around Mygal's wrists. He too looked a bit uncomfortable but hadn't argued when Miranda had explained her plan. "Besides, I'm betting it's not the first time you've worn shackles."

Rellen got an impatient look on his face. "You know perfectly well we can't have anyone see you riding without them."

Tavyn made a show of looking up and down the empty, rain-soaked cobblestone path. "Who's going to see?"

"What do you care?" Rellen asked. "You're getting paid."

"I didn't factor in wearing shackles for the foreseeable future. If I had known, I probably would have held out for more coin."

"Just shut up and hold your hands out," Rellen said.

"Yes, sir," Tavyn grumbled and raised them.

"Thank you," Rellen said. He pulled the cuff of Tavyn's right glove down and secured the first shackle. It would lock into place, but a quick jerk would release it. He then pulled back the cuff of Tavyn's left glove, exposing a bracelet. It was simple band of dark metal with a leafy vine pattern etched into its surface. A large but simple onyx was set into a thick ring of platinum. It was an exquisite piece of craftsmanship, and as he secured the shackle just above it, he noticed the signature mark of Ionar Tomai on either side, near the clasp. "Nice bracelet," he said, "where'd you get it?"

"This?" Tavyn held up his wrist and looked at it. "From my father," he said a bit fondly. "I always admired it, so when he passed, he bequeathed it to me."

"I hope the shackles don't scratch it up."

"I'm not worried. It's supposed to be heavily enchanted, although I never found out how."

The response seemed a little odd—maybe even a little hurried—but Rellen couldn't quite put his finger on what bothered him about it. He shook his head and focused on the task at hand.

"Now the weapons," he said. "Miranda, you take Mygal's. I'll carry Tavyn's."

"I'm not happy about that either," Tavyn said.

"Like Miranda said, if anything comes at us, you drop those shackles, and we'll get them to you in a hurry. Don't worry."

Tavyn let out a long breath but said nothing.

Rellen looked them over and gave a satisfied nod. "Let's get moving," he said. "Daylight is burning, and we have a long way to go."

They set off, this time two-by-two, with Miranda beside him and their "prisoners" a short distance behind.

As the rain came down and filled the air with its drone of water on stone, horse, and rider, Rellen glanced at Miranda. In a softer voice, he said, "I figure he'll complain the whole way about the shackles, but I think you came up with a good strategy."

"Thank you," Miranda replied.

"There's something I want to get clear, though."

"And that is?"

"This whole thing involves the Black Wyrm Clan and the Nissrans. And now it seems someone else may be driving it. I'm fairly certain that it all has to do with whatever they took from the duke. There's a lot more going on here than just murdering nobility. As a Guardian, I need knowledge right now, more than just roping in Javyk Sukari so you can collect a bounty. I need to find out why they killed the duke, what they took, and why they took it. That's more important than anything else, alright?"

"Don't worry," Miranda said. "While we're out here, I work for you, and I won't forget that, not even for two hundred dakkaris. A blind man could see this is a pretty deep Vuoda hole you're into."

"I think I'd rather dig into the holes of an entire clan of Bhirtas'Vuoda, neck deep in river muck and fighting them every step of the way. Angry water goblins are nothing compared to the Nissrans, and at least I'd know what I was dealing with."

She looked at him thoughtfully. "Are they really that bad?"

"Crazed, blood-thirsty butchers is the only way to describe them, and I've only dealt with them once. My brother says that nests of them are popping up all over."

"What are they after?"

"We have no idea. It's been a hundred years since the Nissrans have been more than a nuisance. Usually, it's just small groups here and there that get wiped out pretty quickly. This feels different. Bigger and maybe more organized. It seemed clear the ones I dealt with in Calamath wanted to replace the baron with one of their own."

"That doesn't bode well," Miranda said.

"No, it doesn't." Rellen shook his head. "And if they're trying the same thing in other places, it means they have a much larger plan than just gutting people and drinking their blood."

Miranda was silent for a while. "And you think Dancer and maybe this Javyk fellow are involved with the Nissrans."

"That seems to be the case."

"Then you need to infiltrate them the way they tried to infiltrate Calamath, and I think I know a way."

"How?" Rellen asked. He had some ideas on what they would do once they caught up with the caravan, but he wanted her input. Miranda could be fiendishly devious when she wanted to be.

"Well, travelling as bounty hunters with our prisoners in shackles gives us a good cover story. We're delivering them someplace to the south, and we can be vague about it, but that's not enough to get you in with Javyk and Dancer."

"How do we do it then?" Rellen asked.

"We travel as a married bounty hunter team—one that fights a lot."

Rellen gave her a confused look. "How will that help?"

"When we join the caravan, we link in near Javyk and Dancer. If we fight, loud and nasty for everyone to hear, then you'll have a reason to storm off. It seems to me that men like to commiserate over shrewish wives, whether you're married or not. It's in your blood." She gave him a patient smile that only a woman could fully understand.

Rellen nodded his head. "That's good. If the two of us are at odds, I may be able to create an opportunity to embed myself with them. I'd have to play it by ear—maybe even open the door to joining the Nissrans or even betraying you for the money. After all, who doesn't like a little extra coin?"

❦ ❦ ❦

The sun had reappeared, peeking out from thick, swollen clouds that lazily trundled by overhead. Xilly now reclined against Shaddeth's neck, her haunches perched against the saddle horn. There was only about thirty minutes of daylight left, but the rain had, thankfully, stopped. They'd passed a wide, open field beside the highway where the caravan had stopped several nights earlier. It was probably about ten miles ahead of them by now.

Rellen eyed the edge of the forest up ahead and spotted another open area, much smaller than the first. Such rest areas were normal along the King's Highway, providing a relatively safe camp site for travelers to bed down for the night. It was generally unwise to camp in the thick forests that lined most of the King's Highway. The forest gave predators easy cover, and any buffer was better than none between travelers and the edge of the trees. The most common hunters were vellish. They were easily the deadliest predator in the forest. Usually likened to cats because of the shape of their bodies and heads, it was a loose comparison at best, and only if one imagined a four-hundred-pound cat stepping out of the absolute worst, hellish nightmare possible.

Adults were usually about twelve feet long from nose to tail, with six fiercely clawed paws, a mouth full of sharp, bone-crushing teeth, and a prehensile tail barbed with a venomous stinger. They usually hunted in twos and threes, coming in at their prey from multiple angles. The worst part was that they had a strange hypnotic power. If a vellish could stare into its prey's eyes, even for a few heartbeats, it caused the prey to freeze or even fall over. Once that happened, one of their companions came in for the kill from the side or the rear.

"We'll camp up there," Rellen said, pointing toward the clearing. On a whim, he pulled out the Eye of Tuluum and held it before him, wondering what it might do. It leaned forward and to the left, pointing southeast at a steep angle. He glanced in that direction, peering into the forest. "What's out there, you little bastard?" he said softly.

"What did you say?" Miranda said, turning his way.

"Oh, nothing," Rellen replied, slipping the Eye beneath his tunic. "Just playing around, actually."

"What was that?"

"It's called the Eye of Tuluum. It's an artifact of some kind. I've been using it to guide me toward trouble on my Guardian patrols, but to be honest, the thing is a mystery to me."

"How long have you had it?"

"A few months. I found it in a nuraghi, actually."

"You should be careful with that thing, then. Good rarely comes from a nuraghi."

"Oh, I don't know," Rellen patted the hilts of his falchions. "I got these in a nuraghi. They've served me well for years."

"True enough, but I wouldn't set foot in a nuraghi if you paid me."

Rellen grinned. "I bet you would if there was enough coin in it."

Miranda tried not to smile and failed. "You're probably right."

They reached the clearing and led their horses off the cobblestone road. The grass was wet, the ground soft. They quickly dismounted and found a wide, flat area devoid of rocks.

Rellen said, "You two tend to the horses, and we'll go try and find at least partially dry wood for a fire."

Tavyn and Mygal nodded, releasing their shackles so they could work more easily. Rellen and Miranda each drew a blade and set off for the trees. They entered the forest, searching for any deadfall they could use for a fire.

"Go hunting, little one," Rellen said, turning to Xilly.

I'll stay close by, she replied as she leapt from his shoulder and flapped off into the forest.

"She's remarkable," Miranda said.

"She really is." Rellen stepped over a log too large to be useful. "Do me a favor. Keep an eye on Tavyn, would you?"

"Of course." Miranda gave him a look like he was stating the obvious. "You know I keep an eye on anyone I've just met. What do *you* want me to look for?"

"I can't put my finger on it. Maybe it's just nerves after the whole Calamath Nissra thing." He turned and faced her, a serious look on his face. "And if you start to think I'm getting paranoid, say so. Alright?"

"As if I wouldn't," she said, her head cocked to the side.

"I knew I could count on you. That's why I asked Corwyk to track you down." Then it hit him. "I think I know what's been bothering me."

"What's that?"

"Coincidence."

"What do you mean? Not that I believe in them."

"Exactly." The more Rellen thought about it, the more it made sense. "Of all the people in Svennival who could have tracked you down, and I'm talking overnight, it was the one person who had led Mygal to Dancer."

"I see what you mean," she said. She looked thoughtful for a bit as they continued their search. "I could argue it either way." She turned to face him. "Sure, it's a coincidence, but while I've never worked with Tavyn, I know of him. As far as I know, he is what he seems to be—an information broker. He was in the right place at the right time, and he'd already been working with Mygal. I like Mygal by the way. He's quiet. Friendly."

Rellen chuckled. "Don't be surprised if he makes a pass at you—and keep your guard up. He's an erkurios."

"You know nothing like that would work with me—at least not with a man."

"I know that, but he doesn't." Rellen picked up a chunk of solid-looking wood a couple feet long and thick enough to burn for a while. "And if he does try, don't kill him. I've actually started to like him…" he let his voice trail off.

"You're not letting someone in past that iron-clad guard of yours, are you?" She had a curious look in her eye. "I thought you'd sworn you'd never do that again."

"I did." Rellen paused. "I think he'll make a decent Guardian with a little time and seasoning. I'm mentoring him."

"It sounds like you *are* letting someone in," she said.

"Maybe I've grown older."

"Maybe," she said a bit dubiously.

"Alright," Rellen said, sensing she was calling him on it. "Maybe that conversation I had with Stevar hit me harder than I thought—for the better."

"You've always been too guarded," she said. "I bet you can count your friends, and I mean real ones, on one hand. The rest are just people you like to drink with."

She knew him well. Not as well as his brother, but well enough. He knew she was right. What she didn't know was that the only two people he truly trusted was her and his brother. Rellen let out a long breath.

"Maybe you're right."

"Maybe." She gave him a wink. "Let's get back to it. I want to be sitting in front of a fire before it gets too dark. The vellish in this area get pretty big, although they tend to avoid the highway."

"Right," Rellen said, and went looking for more wood.

❦   ❦   ❦

A fire crackled and popped, the damp wood releasing a good deal of white smoke and steam as it burned. Rellen and

Mygal both sent brief reports to the king, and then they sat down to dinner. Their meal consisted of hard tack and jerky, which went down quickly and with a good deal of water. All the while, Tavyn and Mygal traded stories of what it was like growing up in the underbelly of one of Pelinon's larger cities.

It became almost a contest between the two of them: who could come up with the most ridiculous or brutal story? Who was the most dangerous criminal they'd ever seen and the most corrupt constable? Rellen listened with keen interest.

He'd heard stories like them before. Many of the people he'd served with in the military came from the rougher or less-fortunate places across the kingdom. As he listened, that same old feeling hit him… a feeling of guilt, even helplessness. He'd served with those people… bled with them, and watched far too many die. Early on, as an officer, he'd done his best to protect them. As the deaths stacked up, he'd put in a formal request to join the scouts. On his own, he didn't have to carry the burden of keeping them alive or the guilt when he couldn't.

Eventually, the clouds gave way enough to expose large swaths of starry sky. The stories dissipated with them, and an easy silence settled around the campfire. It wasn't long before Mygal reached into his saddlebags and broke out a wooden flute. Without a care in the world, he began playing a tawdry tavern song, and as the notes flowed out into the forest, Tavyn began to sing along. A few verses in, even Miranda began singing along, a smile upon her face.

His three companions ran through a few more drinking songs, and then Mygal started in on a ballad Rellen had never heard before. It was soft and soothing, and as the music flowed over them, Xilly fluttered in out of the darkness and landed on the ground beside him. Her belly looked like she'd eaten her fill. She yawned, crawled into his lap, and curled up. Rellen stroked her back a few times, letting his fingers run over the bony ridge that ran from the crest of her head, down along her back, and over her tail.

"Where did you get her?" Miranda asked.

"A place you never heard of," Rellen said. "Between Calamath and Sabatar." He glanced down at Xilly. "And she wasn't the only remarkable thing about that very unremarkable village."

"What do you mean?"

"I met an actual Strakhanni—the old warriors of legend out of the mountains. I couldn't believe my eyes."

Miranda gave him a dubious look. "You're joking."

"I'm not. I saw the tattoos and what they could do. He fought a wall of brigands, and as he did, the tattoos lifted off his body and fought with him."

"They were supposed to have died out a hundred years ago."

"He was the last one, apparently," Rellen said. "In the end, he faced the entire gang and released the magic in those tattoos all at once. It consumed him and them." Rellen scratched beneath Xilly's chin. "Xilly was originally bonded to him, but she's been with me ever since."

"When was that?"

"About a month and a half ago, but I feel like she's been with me forever."

Xilly jerked up and went rigid, her tail straight out and her back arched as she sniffed the air.

Rellen! Her urgent call shook his mind. *Vellish!*

"Everyone up!" Rellen shouted as he rolled to his feet. He came up with a falchion in his hand. Xilly leapt away and flapped up into the darkness.

"What is it?" Miranda said, yanking the filigreed silver saber from its sheath.

Mygal and Tavyn both jumped up and drew their weapons.

"We're being stalked," Rellen said. "Xilly says there's vellish out there." He peered out into the darkness that lay beyond the edge of the weak campfire light. He could just make out the rumps of all four horses, but they seemed to be standing completely still. "The horses are paralyzed, otherwise

Shaddeth would have done something by now." Something padded across the grass to his left, away from the road. "Backs to the campfire!" he shouted. "Keep your eyes focused on the stinger." He reached for one of his poison gas vials and cursed. He'd used the last one in the cemetery. He peered into the darkness, trying to see the monsters that now stalked them. A shadowy shape slipped past, just at the edge of the firelight.

"I sense eight of them out there," Miranda said.

"Eight?" Rellen blurted glancing over his shoulder. She had her eyes closed and her hand stretched out, away from the fire.

"Make that nine…" she said.

"Nine?" Mygal said, disbelief filling his voice. "They never hunt in packs that big."

The heavy footfalls of padded feet came at them from Rellen's right, somewhere in front of Tavyn.

"Watch out!" Miranda shouted.

Rellen turned as she made a slashing motion with her left hand. The shadowy shape of a large vellish rose out of the darkness, its jaws wide, front claws extended. Tavyn raised his blade as a scythe of ruby light flashed out from Miranda's hand and struck the vellish in the shoulder.

The vellish howled in pain, twisting mid-air to get away from the gash that had just appeared on its shoulder. Tavyn side-stepped. His blade flashed out and down as the wounded vellish passed by, slicing through the middle of its tail. The beast roared out, landing beside the fire. Rellen stepped in and drove his falchion through the beast's face. It went limp as he jerked his blade free.

"I'm going to brighten things up," Rellen shouted. "Keep your eyes turned away from the fire, and whatever you do, don't look straight at it."

Everyone shifted as Rellen grabbed a vial from his bandoleer. This one was metal, with a simple inscription on it. He uttered the last part of an incantation he'd cast weeks earlier and dropped the vial into the embers of the fire, releasing the majea contained within. He turned away to face the darkness.

The vial heated in the blink of an eye. A moment later, there was a hissing flare as the ingot of metal within the vile ignited with a flash. Bright, white light seared into the darkness for another thirty feet around them. Their own shadows stretched out along the grass amidst the brightness of that artificial dawn.

Vellish roars of pain filled the night.

Rellen realized they were surrounded. Not only that, but all four horses remained stock still in the darkness twenty feet away. There were vellish on either side of the horses, but they still didn't move. It was as if the big predators knew where the real threat was.

Impossible, Rellen thought. *Vellish aren't that smart.*

Seven vellish crouched low in a circle around them, only twenty-five feet away. Their snarling heads were turned away from the light as their barbed tails thrashed in the air. The eighth vellish, a truly massive one, was back another fifteen feet, the forest at its back. Rellen had hoped the light would scare them all off. Instead, four of the smaller ones charged in despite the light, howling their fury.

"Don't look into their eyes," Miranda called out.

Rellen charged forward as he drew his second falchion. He closed the distance in a heartbeat. The vellish's barbed tail darted in like a spear thrust. He parried hard, knocking the venomous barb aside only a foot from his chest as he stepped in again.

He heard the others engage, but he couldn't worry about them now. He would have to hope everyone survived. Another vellish shrieked out in pain.

The vellish lifted the front part of its body and slashed with one of its claws, barely missing Rellen's leg. He sidestepped back as the tail came in again. The tail passed by, and he swung up with his off hand. He caught the tail just right and gouged out a chunk of flesh. Several more pained, vellish shrieks filled the night behind him.

The vellish howled and slashed again with a claw. He parried, caught the paw with an edge, and drew more blood. The vellish snarled, crouched, and leapt straight at him.

Rellen dropped beneath it and drove a falchion straight into its chest. It shrieked, slashing with its claws. One caught him on the arm, gouging deep furrows into his left bracer and pauldron. The vellish's momentum carried it past him, ripping the falchion from Rellen's left hand. He rose, swinging hard with the other, and cleaved the vellish's tail from its body, just above its rump.

In that moment, Rellen saw Miranda had already killed one vellish. Its body lay beside the fire, a telltale gash halfway through its neck, with dark blood seeping out onto the grass. Tavyn, dripping blood from his left arm, raised his rapier above a vellish that had his dagger sticking out of its shoulder. The barb of its tail was also missing. Mygal stood stock still, staring at the two vellish that had come at him. His rapier was in one hand, but he held his dagger out, almost as if he was motioning for the beasts to halt. They looked frozen in place. It was as if Mygal was controlling them, holding them at bay, but that wasn't possible for an erkurios. Erkurioi affected emotions, and animals didn't have emotions complex enough for an erkurios to latch onto.

Rellen turned back as the other, larger vellish stalked toward him warily. Its tail twitched back and forth, the barb aimed at Rellen's face. For a moment, he considered retrieving his other falchion, but there wasn't time.

The vellish surged forward and drove its tail straight at him. Rellen dodged to the side, parrying, and stepped forward. The barb came in again. He parried, pushing it aside to scrape along his pauldron. He stepped forward, forcing the vellish back. He prepared himself for the next attack. He would have to be quick if this was going to succeed.

The vellish shifted left. Rellen followed, moving into a low crouch as he kept it straight in front of him. The vellish snarled. Its tail rose and stiffened. *Now*, Rellen thought. He shifted his elbow inward, judging the angle of the attack he knew was coming.

The tail darted in. Rellen dropped, laying out flat as he leapt forward. The barbed tail scraped across the back of his leather chest plate as he drove his blade straight into the vellish's chest with all of his weight and momentum behind the thrust. His arm and shoulder shuddered with the impact, but he held firm. The vellish let out a strange, low, guttural sound as he drove its body back. Its mouth opened and closed several times, its tongue lolling. It shuddered violently, coughed up a splash of blood onto Rellen's arm and face, then dropped straight down, pawing weakly at him.

Burning pain flared out from the back of Rellen's left thigh and began to spread across his flesh.

He struggled to roll over in the grass and discovered the vellish's barb stuck in the back of his leg, still pumping venom into his body. He tried to call out but found that he couldn't move his jaw. His tongue felt heavy in his mouth.

Rellen closed his eyes and prepared to fight death on its own turf.

Through a strange, hissing fog, Rellen heard an ear-splitting, vellish roar that filled the night, coming from somewhere in the darkness. The staccato grunts of three more vellish followed, and then padded feet ran off through the grass. He heard a flutter of wings from far away, and then he thought he felt something licking his face.

You're hurt, Xilly said. Her voice drifted into his thoughts through a fog.

I have to go now, he said. *Miranda is a good person—you can bond with her...*

"Rellen!" a voice called out.

Rellen couldn't tell who had said it. It seemed to have come from far away, as if it had been called out over a wide mountain valley. He wondered what the fuss was all about. He just wanted to get some sleep. The grass was comfortable, and he was so very tired. It seemed odd that his ass hurt as much as it did, but that wouldn't matter for too much longer.

Don't leave me, a faint thought crept into Rellen's mind. It seemed familiar somehow. *It's too soon.*

The fog swallowed him whole, and darkness closed in.

CHAPTER FIFTEEN

THE CARAVAN

Rellen opened his eyes to a sky streaked with orange and pink and wondered if his head was going to come apart. He heard birds singing somewhere, and there was a weight on his chest. He looked down slightly to find Xilly curled up there, her head tucked beneath a wing, breathing slow and steady. She stirred, lifted her head, and stared at him for a moment, her eyes blinking slowly.

You need to be more careful, she said.

Rellen drew in a breath and let it out slowly. Some of the pain in his skull went with it. His left butt cheek tingled, reminding him of the fight. The pain that had been there before the vellish's poison knocked him out, however, was gone. He shifted a bit. There was an ache, but no pain.

You're right, he replied. *Can you get off me? I need to pee.*

Xilly hopped off his chest, landing in the grass beside him. Rellen sat up, fighting off a slight wave of dizziness.

"You're up," Miranda sat by the campfire, roasting a piece of meat on the end of a stick. The smell of it struck him, and his stomach rumbled. Her eyes had a trace of worry, but not much. "Hungry?" She held the roasted meat out to him. "It's stringy, but vellish actually tastes pretty good."

"You think so?" Rellen replied, surprised by her opinion of roasted vellish. "And yes, I do, but let me piss first."

She nodded.

Rellen got to his feet with a groan. The bodies of five remarkably large vellish, all of them missing their venomous barbs, lay a dozen yards off. One had been partially butchered. The voice of one of Rellen's old commanding officers floated up in his memory. *"On the road, you eat what is available, and are thankful for it."*

"It's good to see you up," Mygal called out. He and Tavyn were securing their saddles to the mounts. "How do you feel?"

"Groggy. Sore." Rellen walked off a short distance and watered the already wet grass. He turned and walked back to the campfire, and as he did, Xilly fluttered up onto his shoulder.

Miranda held out the meat.

Rellen grabbed it between two fingers, grimaced, and took a hearty bite. He then held it still for Xilly to do the same.

"I hate vellish," he said as he chewed. "But this isn't the first time I've eaten it, and probably won't be the last, either."

But it's delicious! Xilly blurted in his thoughts.

"You don't have to eat it," Miranda said.

"Not what I meant," Rellen said. "It tastes great. I just hate *fighting* vellish." He swallowed. "And I've never heard of them attacking in such numbers before."

"Did you notice they subdued the horses before coming after us?" Miranda said. "I've never heard of them doing that either."

"It was strange," Rellen said, glancing at the mounts. He shook his head. "Normally, they would have worked their way from the outside in, using those tails." He locked eyes with Miranda. "They sneaked up on us, like they were soldiers. If it hadn't been for Xilly, they probably would have gotten us all before we even knew what was happening." He shook his head. "That's just what the world needs—smart vellish."

"How could such a thing even exist?" Mygal said, stepping up.

Rellen let out a frustrated breath. "Well, I've heard stories, coming mostly from well south of the Sylverwylde Mountains, of strange beasts appearing in the jungles out of nowhere. Things nobody has ever seen before. Maybe these came from the same place and managed to make it this far?" He looked at Miranda. "You got a better idea?"

"Most of that comes out of Nikostohr, Faign, and Aradeen, but those are just stories, and that's six hundred miles from here." She shook her head. "Assuming the stories aren't just a load of donkey shit, it's a long way... although vellish do roam all across Pelinon." She shrugged. "Who knows?"

"There's something else you should know," Mygal said ominously.

"What?" Rellen asked.

"I could sense their emotions. Even control them, at least a little. I was able to hold two off while the rest of you fought, and I could feel the anger, in a calculating sort of way, from the big one that didn't engage us."

"I didn't think an erkurios could control animals. I know some zokurioi can, but not a heartbender."

"Some, but not all," Miranda added.

"I saw that," Tavyn chimed in. "It was almost as if the big one controlled them."

"Like I said," Rellen looked to the tree line, "that's just what the world needs... smart vellish." He shook his head. "Let's get out of here, shall we?"

"Agreed," Miranda said.

"Are you strong enough to travel?" Miranda asked, looking at Rellen's backside.

"Not much choice, but you tell me. You're the one who saved me."

"Well," Miranda said, walking over. "I was able to use the life force of that last vellish, the one that got you, and purge the poison as well as close up the wound, which wasn't that bad."

"Thanks for that," he said, giving her a warm smile."

"It's the real reason you wanted me around," she replied.

"Maybe." He glanced at Tavyn. "I take it you did something similar to his arm? I saw him get wounded."

"I used a kara root I found nearby, but his wounds were superficial." She gave Rellen a cautious look. "You'll be weak for at least a day."

"I'll keep that in mind," he replied, rolling up his bedroll. "But the faster we get going, the sooner we'll catch up to the caravan. Then we shouldn't have to worry about getting attacked by any more vellish."

"You hope," Mygal said a bit gloomily.

"On the bright side," Tavyn said, climbing up into his saddle, "I got the venom from six tails, so that's something." He patted his saddlebags with a satisfied smile.

"What do you do with that?" Mygal asked.

"Reduce it down over a low heat. It becomes a paste and makes a great poison for my blades."

"I'll keep that in mind," Rellen said. "Let's get those shackles back on you." The frown on Tavyn's face was accentuated by a rolling sound of thunder that echoed in from the west.

⬠　⬠　⬠

The next two days were more of the same, just without vellish trying to kill them. They rode all day in the rain. At night, they dried themselves out beside a fire, Rellen and Mygal sent reports to the king, and everyone slept restlessly when they weren't on watch. It was a long, plodding ride, and Rellen continued to push them as hard as he thought the lesser horses could take.

On the afternoon of the third day, one thankfully without rain, they came around a wide bend in the King's Highway that curved around a low hill, one of many that sculpted the landscape. They entered a long straightaway and spotted the tail end of the caravan already in a shallow valley about half a mile ahead.

Someone blew two quick blasts on a signaling horn that echoed down the road. It was an alert to the King's Teamsters that someone was approaching the caravan.

"Check my hair," Tavyn said, turning toward Mygal.

Mygal leaned over and looked closely at Tavyn's face. "You look fine." He examined Tavyn's crown. "You may have to dye the roots in a day or two, though."

"I have more in my saddlebags," Tavyn said. "I can do that any time I like."

"Check those shackles," Rellen called out from ahead of them. "And I want the two of you in between Miranda and I." He looked at Miranda. "Take up the rear, would you?"

She nodded and pulled back on the reins to let Mygal and Tavyn pass by.

Xilly, Rellen said, *can you pace us from the forest while we're on this journey? Word of you might have gotten back to Dancer or even this Javyk fellow. If they see you, they might guess who I am, and we can't have that.*

Yes, she replied, but he could hear the disappointment.

You're sure you can keep up?

Of course! Her disappointment changed to indignation.

Alright, little one. I'm sorry about this, but it's necessary. Just keep up with us and keep an eye out for trouble.

I promise. I won't be far.

He scratched behind her head. *Thank you, Xilly.*

She flew off, rising quickly up into the trees.

Rellen increased their pace somewhat, and within an hour, they'd caught up with a heavily laden wagon at the rear of the caravan. A teamster sat on the back, his legs dangling and a horn hanging from a rope over his shoulder. He had on the blue vest, white tunic, and blue and white striped trousers of the King's Teamsters. He also held a nocked bow, and his eyes never left them. As they approached, three more of the King's Teamsters appeared on horseback, a big fellow with bushy black hair, flanked by two smaller fellows. The big one held up his hand, causing the other two to pull up short. He kept coming, though, his dark eyes fixed on Rellen.

Over the centuries, the kings of Pelinon had employed retired and injured veterans to lead and protect the commerce and citizens that kept Pelinon running. There were posted rates in every town and city along the highway for those who traveled on foot, on horseback, or rode in wagons and carriages. Travelers purchased "legs" of a journey, indicating where they intended to break away from the caravan.

"Hail," the big man said, turning his horse around and coming up beside Rellen so they could keep pace a dozen yards behind the last wagon. He was truly huge, probably four inches taller than Rellen, with broad shoulders, thick arms, and meaty fists. Rellen felt sorry for the horse he rode. "State your business, if you please."

"Are you the Head Teamster?" Rellen asked.

"Aye," the man replied. "Collyn Pearce, at your service. But it's Master Pearce, to the likes of you bounty hunters, and I better warn you, the caravan is at capacity with the number of teamsters I have."

"Now, that's a problem," Rellen said, suddenly worried they'd be turned away. "My partner and I would very much like to join the caravan. We've got two bounties here that we need to deliver south."

"That may be your problem, but it's not mine. I have my orders. I'm afraid I just don't have the manpower—we're stretched thin as it is." He eyed Rellen and the riders with him. "You can follow, but the law states you have to keep your distance… at least a quarter mile, and we won't help you if you get into trouble."

"You've got to be kidding me," Mygal groaned in a particularly loud voice. Everyone turned their heads at him, surprised looks on their faces. Rellen's eyes flicked to Miranda, worried everything was about to be undone. Mygal grabbed his reins, making a point of jingling the chains of his shackles.

"Master… Pearce, was it?" He gave his horse a light kick and moved her over a bit closer.

"Aye," the teamster replied, looking warily at Mygal.

"You've got to let us join the caravan." Mygal moved his horse even closer.

"And why would that be?" The teamster glanced at Rellen, a disbelieving look on his face.

"Because I'd rather ride in the safety of the caravan and end up in prison than suffer one more day alone with these two imbeciles."

Everyone's eyes went wide.

"Watch your mouth, you cur," Rellen barked, but he gave Mygal the faintest nod to encourage him.

"I won't," Mygal shot back. "These two beat us every morning, we haven't eaten in two days, and they almost got us killed a few nights ago, ripped to pieces by a pack of vellish!" He glared at Rellen. "Anything would be better than what we've suffered so far. As far as I'm concerned, my safest bet is to be mixed in with a caravan. They're less likely to beat us, anyway, and we won't have to worry about our guts being eaten in the dead of night by the next hungry beast to catch our scent."

Rellen glared at Mygal. "You'll—"

"I'll what?" He glared back haughtily. "You can't do anything worse to me than you've already done. The bounty says *alive*. Remember? I'm no good to you dead."

Master Pearce cocked his head sideways, his eyes flitting over them all. They rested for a moment on the blood that stained the sleeve of Tavyn's tunic, and then he looked more closely. Everyone had blood on their clothes, and the gouges on Rellen's bracer and pauldron could only come from one thing.

"Is it true?" He stared at Rellen. "Ambushed by a pack of vellish?"

"It is," Rellen said. "One almost killed me with its venom, but my wife was able to pull me back from the brink." He glared at Mygal once again, but he was impressed with the young man. It had been a bold play. He wasn't sure if it was a subtle casting of ermajea or if Mygal was just that good of a liar. He suspected it was probably both, and he now had a much better idea of why the king had selected him to be the Thirteenth Guardian. Mygal thought fast on his feet and had skills to back it up. Looking back at the teamster, he asked, "How far are you going?"

"All the way to Yaylo," Master Pearce said, a stern but wavering look in his eyes. "Supper every night is part of the deal, if you didn't know. If there are leftovers, you can grab them from the mess wagon in the morning, but plan on only one meal a day. Water will also be available."

Rellen didn't know where Javyk and Dancer were headed. If they left the caravan at Sylverwynd, Rellen could simply follow. The teamster probably wouldn't even notice. If Rellen's quarry went past Yaylo, he'd just have to figure something out.

"That'll work for us," he replied.

"And where are you headed?" the teamster asked.

"We'd rather not say, Master Pearce, but we'll pay to get to Yaylo, if that's alright with you... just to make things easy. I believe that's four mounted travelers at ten sepiks each to get to Sylverwynd. Jabono is five more, and Yaylo would be another ten. That's a hundred sepiks to join the caravan." Rellen reached into his cloak and pulled out a coin purse.

"So, you know the routes?"

"Not my first caravan," Rellen said, handing over four golden dakkaris.

"You do seem a tad bit familiar to me." Master Pearce slipped the coins into an inner pocket of his vest.

"It's possible. I've covered a lot of Pelinon over the years." He glanced at Mygal and Tavyn and then met the teamster's gaze. "Oh, and there's one other thing. They don't know where we're taking them, and I'd like to keep it that way." Rellen tossed the teamster another dakkari. "We're willing to pay a little extra for our privacy until we get where we're going. Will that work for you?"

"Done." The coin disappeared into one of the teamster's vest pockets. He looked up the road ahead of them. "You'll want to get around these wagons and join the travelers in the middle. Just slip in between some of the others, there's plenty of room." He peered down the road for several heartbeats. "But you better hurry. We're coming up on the next way station. We'll be stopping there and setting up our camp."

"Understood," Rellen said. He looked to the others. "Let's get moving." He stared at Mygal again. "And that'll be enough of your mouth, if you know what's good for you." He slapped Mygal's arm with the back of his hand.

Master Pearce gave a satisfied nod, turned his horse, and galloped off toward the head of the caravan.

Rellen led the four of them past a line of fifteen heavily loaded wagons. After every fourth one, they also passed a pair of mounted teamsters with longswords, lances, and crossbows strapped to their saddles.

The travelers in the caravan were a mix of men on foot, riders, a few dozen wagons with mostly families in them, and a dozen fine-looking, enclosed carriages in the line, all mixed together. Rellen drifted out a bit, moving off to the side of the highway to get a better angle on the passengers. He passed the tail end of the line, moving forward at an easy pace, and surreptitiously glanced into each carriage. He'd made it to the middle of the group when he came upon one that seemed to be keeping a somewhat larger gap between itself and the others. The riders ahead and behind it were just a bit farther away than the others in the caravan had been.

He thought it peculiar, so he slowed his pace. One of the men inside caught his eye. He was a thin fellow, gaunt even, with pale skin and deep-set eyes so heavily shadowed that they looked almost like the eyes of a bare skull that had been set atop a black tunic with a high collar. His hair was pulled back, tied at the back of his head. Rellen couldn't tell how tall he was, but everything else matched the description Rickavyn had given them.

He casually looked back to the others and then slowly drifted back into the line, taking a spot directly behind the gaunt man's carriage. The others settled in, doing their best to look like nothing more than bored bounty hunters and anxious prisoners.

Rellen leaned over to Mygal. "Excellent work back there," he said, keeping his face impassive.

The corner of Mygal's mouth turned up a fraction of an inch, but he didn't say anything.

"Ermajea, or just gall?" Rellen asked.

Mygal let out a satisfied breath. "Both."

An hour later, with the sun hanging low in the sky, the caravan turned off the King's Highway into a wide field that had been cut into the forest. When the central wagon came to a stop in the center of the field, several of the teamsters hustled to the back and started breaking out what Rellen recognized as a military-style field kitchen. The riders, wagons, and carriages spread out, only roughly directed by Master Pearce and a handful of teamsters who had taken up a position around the mess wagon. The grass was uneven and cut deeply in places, making the wagons and carriages jounce heavily as they passed over them.

Other teamsters spread out across the field in pairs on horseback. When they reached the tree line, they dismounted and disappeared into the forest to scout the area, leaving the horses tethered to nearby trees.

The size of the caravan, now that he could see it spread out, was larger than most of the others he'd traveled with. It forced some travelers to set their camps up against the edge of the trees, which was a little out of the ordinary. Normally, the teamsters wanted a wide buffer between the forest and the travelers, but there just wasn't room. The driver of the carriage they'd followed steered his four-horse team to a spot at the back of the field, up against the trees. He quite deliberately put as much space as he could between his carriage and the other camp sites.

Rellen followed suit, picking a spot about twenty feet away, also against the forest, beneath a massive tree whose limbs stretched out over the field a fair distance. It was close enough to the carriage to be useful but not enough to arouse suspicion.

"We'll set up here," he said to the others, getting off Shaddeth.

He stretched his legs, back, and arms, scanning the forest for any sign of his winged companion.

Xilly, he thought. *Are you nearby?*

Look up.

He did. It took him a few moments, but eventually he spotted a black shadow perched on the branch above. She stretched out her wings slightly and then pulled them back in, disappearing into the foliage.

Good girl, Rellen thought. *Keep an eye out. When this is all over, I'll get you the biggest feast of whatever you want for a week straight.*

I'm not starving, but I find your terms acceptable, she replied with a good deal of enthusiasm.

Rellen still marveled at how much like a… well… a person she was. To him, Xilly was the same as Miranda—a *person* he could count on, and he'd had no difficulty letting her in past his guard. It had felt perfectly natural.

He started unbuckling Shaddeth's saddle when the door to the carriage opened. A young man, around twenty, with a long, black, braided ponytail down his back stepped out. He was about six feet tall, with a well-defined physique. He had on black leather pants, knee-high black leather boots, and a tunic the color of blood. He had a rapier on his hip and a long dagger in a horizontal sheath across the back of his belt.

Rellen glanced at Mygal and Tavyn, motioning slightly for them to look with a question in his eyes. They both cast sidelong glances in that direction and then nodded. The young man stepped down to the ground and held the door open. With his back to them, it looked like he had something circular hidden beneath his shirt, secured somehow across his lower back. As they watched, the man Rellen had seen before stepped down out of the carriage and stretched his lean, pallid frame out.

"Thank you, Dancer," Javyk said with a nod of his head. He turned to the driver, a bony old man with a crooked nose and a wispy ring of white hair surrounding a sun-weathered patch of liver-spotted scalp. "Mr. Bawth, see to the horses and get a campfire going. Riven and I are going to stretch our legs before they serve supper."

"Yes, Master Sukari," the old man said with a bow.

With that, Javyk and Dancer strolled off, caught up in a whispered conversation.

Rellen turned to the others. "We'll get the horses tended to and set up camp as quickly as possible. I want to be done before they get back, if we can."

⬠ ⬠ ⬠

A fire crackled before them. There was the hushed drone of travelers talking around enough campfires to push the darkness all the way to the edge of the trees. Thunder echoed distantly, coupled with subdued flashes illuminating high clouds to the east. The sky above, however, was a blanket of stars.

Miranda had chained Mygal and Tavyn together with a good deal of show and even some shouting and insults, drawing the attention of several campsites nearby, including Javyk and Dancer. The last slab of vellish meat, cut into four thick hunks, roasted over the fire, tended by Miranda.

"So, what happens next?" Tavyn asked quietly, running his fingers absentmindedly over his expensive bracelet.

"Next, I go see what I can see," Rellen replied. *Xilly, meet me about twenty or thirty feet into the trees.* He looked for her in the foliage above.

I'll find you, she replied.

He thought he caught movement up above, but he couldn't be sure.

"But to do that," Rellen then said, glancing at Miranda, "we need to have a fight."

"What?" Tavyn said, looking perplexed. Neither Rellen nor Miranda had told them about this part of the plan. They wanted the reactions of their companions to be genuine.

"Are you out of your Nissra-loving mind?" Rellen shouted, jumping to his feet. He glared at Miranda. "I didn't sign up for that! Once we get their bounties, I'm gone."

"Fine then," Miranda barked back. "Take your money and go! You've been wanting to run out on me for months."

"Longer than that, my love. If I didn't need a partner to do this job—"

"Stings, doesn't it?" Miranda said in a sickly sweet tone. "You'd be lost without me."

"Bah!" Rellen shouted, waving a dismissive hand at her. He glanced around and was happy to have achieved the desired result. The travelers around them, despite the spacing, were all looking in their direction, including Javyk and Dancer. Rellen made a point of meeting Javyk's gaze and rolling his eyes in Miranda's direction. "I'm going for a walk," he shouted, and then he marched off straight toward the forest. "I swear, you're the most infuriating, life-wrecking, woman I've ever known."

"Nobody else would have you," Miranda shouted back. "I hope something eats you, you bloody fool!"

"It would be better than living with you," Rellen shouted from a short distance into the forest.

"Trouble in paradise?" Mygal asked and his delight seemed genuine.

Miranda shook her head and glared at the trees. "I've been married to that stubborn son of a Giant's whore for ten years. He'll calm down soon enough and come crawling back. Sometimes I don't know why I stay married to him."

"Maybe you could just let us slit his throat for you. Call it payment for letting us go."

"Think of the headaches it would save you?" Tavyn chimed in.

Miranda kicked Mygal's leg. "Shut your mouths. Both of you. When I want your opinion, I'll beat it out of you. Now go to sleep or I'll just brain you both and eat the bounty." She glanced up and caught Javyk staring straight at her.

"What are you looking at," she called out.

He quickly turned away, and Miranda went back to roasting the vellish.

CHAPTER SIXTEEN

RECONNOITER

*K**eep an eye out for vellish or anything else that might rip my throat out, would you?* Rellen asked as Xilly fluttered down to his shoulder. She coiled her tail around his neck and licked his ear.

I will, she replied and immediately started scanning the forest.

The sounds of the forest closed in, with the chirps, shrieks, and calls of all manner of animal and insect.

The campfire light dimmed quickly, so Rellen pulled out a small glowstone from within his cloak and spoke the word that would activate it. A pale, white glow sprang forth, casting the forest in the equivalent of bright moonlight. When he'd gone about a hundred yards, with thick boles rising into a dense canopy that blotted out the stars, he came upon a small rivulet cutting its way through the forest. There was a narrow gap in the canopy, revealing a starry sky, unfettered by the campfire light. Rellen deactivated the glowstone with a word and took a moment to just stare up at the stars.

The night sky was one of his favorite sights. Since his childhood, a starry sky filled him with awe and a profound appreciation for how lucky he was to lead the life he did. Most people rarely left the safety of their towns and villages… rarely left the safety of light and the small bastions of civilization they shielded themselves with. He thrived out in the open. It was where he felt most comfortable.

Tearing his eyes away from the stars, he pulled a small crystal from the pouch on his belt—he was now down to five—and a blob of wool from another. Focusing his majea into the crystal, he spoke the incantation, and a faint flash of pale light formed around his body and dissipated.

Next, he rolled the blob of wool between his fingers, summoned another small amount of his majea, and poured it into the material until the wool had elongated into a long rod that went rigid as the spell filled it. Within moments, the rod of wool took on a pale, bluish glow. Finally, he used the rod to inscribe a series of sigils upon his chest, the tip leaving a faint trace of light on the cuirass of his leather armor. Laying down several runes in quick succession, he uttered another incantation. With the final word, the woolen rod evaporated as the runes flashed and disappeared. As they did, the sounds of the forest dimmed slightly, as if they were passing through a thin shroud.

Satisfied the spell had worked, he reached out and plucked a small, leaf-covered strand from a nearby vine. Again, he focused his majea and tied the vine into three small, loose knots, uttering the first half of the incantation with each loop. He uttered the second half of the incantation as he placed the knotted vine into the collar of his armor. With the final word, the vine flashed with a pale green light and began to grow, expanding and coiling around his chest, arms, legs, and head. Within a few heartbeats, the vines covered him, or at least appeared to do so. His majea dealt with symbols and manifestations rather than living things, but the illusion would serve his purposes.

The first spell would protect him from any magic attacks, the second would keep anyone from hearing him moving through the forest, and the third would keep prying eyes from seeing him. He was ready.

I'm heading back, he said to Xilly. *You'll have to be my eyes for a bit. Guide me to the back of Javyk's camp, will you?*

I will.

Navigating through the dark forest was trickier than Rellen had thought it would be. He stumbled over several thick roots as he went, but the silencing spell kept his thudding footfalls and muttered curses from passing beyond the shroud of the spell. Xilly guided him around tree trunks. After a few minutes, the faint glow of campfire light filtered through the trees, and he could make out Javyk's carriage.

He cautiously moved up to the edge of the forest to find Javyk and Dancer sitting quietly in front of their campfire a few yards from the carriage. The old driver, Mr. Bawth, sat on the grass, leaned up against one of the carriage's wheels. He held a tankard in one hand and chewed on a thick piece of jerky, as he occasionally looked out into the darkness of the forest.

Rellen moved slowly through the trees, looking for the perfect spot. *There,* he thought. At the base of a large tree, there was a line of shrubs and vines growing thick around the bole. Rellen crouched down and took a position beside them, his camouflage blending perfectly with the foliage and shadows around him.

He glanced to his left, where Mygal, Miranda, and Tavyn sat around their own campfire, chewing on roasted vellish. They weren't talking, and Miranda's eyes seemed focused on the forest behind Javyk's carriage. Her eyes passed over the spot where Rellen was hiding, but they didn't pause or even slow down as she scanned the tree line. Rellen focused his attention back on his quarry.

Javyk and Dancer spoke in low voices, and Rellen could just make out what they were saying.

"…know how far we are from Sylverwynd?" Dancer asked.

"The cooks said we'd be there in six days." Javyk prodded the low campfire with a long stick, sending a small column of embers into the air. "I'll be happy to be done with this dreadful carriage."

"It is a bit uncomfortable, but even discomfort brings us closer to the source."

Javyk turned appreciative eyes to Dancer. "You truly have embraced the master."

"Happily so," Dancer replied. "But I'm also excited to see Sylverwynd. I've never been out of Svennival before. My father wouldn't have it."

"A whole new world is opening up to you." Javyk glanced at Mr. Bawth. "Excuse me, will you?"

He rose to his feet, headed for the trees, and seemed to be looking straight into Rellen's eyes. Rellen's heartbeat quickened. Rellen prepared to bolt, hoping that if he did, Javyk would be disinclined to follow him. He sucked in a breath and held it.

Close your eyes and don't move, little one! he urged. He felt her tuck her head under his chin, hidden partially by his camouflage. Closer and closer Javyk drew, and with each step, Rellen feared he'd been discovered.

Javyk stopped only a few paces away and scanned the area. Rellen placed a hand on one of his falchions and prepared for a fight. The last thing he wanted was combat this close to the camp, and certainly not with Javyk. He needed information, not a corpse, and revealing himself as a Guardian to the teamsters would be problematic.

A moment later, Javyk took several paces into the trees and turned toward a large bole. There was a rustling of cloth, and then the sound of water falling on tree bark.

Rellen let out the breath he'd been holding, staying as motionless as possible.

When the sound of falling water stopped, Rellen heard Javyk muttering an incantation of some kind. Again, he tensed, his heart suddenly pounding in his chest. If Javyk had somehow detected him, he might try and surprise Rellen. They knew there was an erkurios involved. One had attacked Mygal, and the odds were that a zokurios was involved too. Was Javyk either one of them?

Moments later, Javyk turned and walked away from the trees, paying Rellen no attention whatsoever.

Rellen let out another breath as he watched Javyk casually walk back toward the campfire. Javyk got to within about ten feet of the old driver and made a gentle slashing motion which he tried to make look natural. There was no manifestation of the magic that Rellen could see, but an instant later, Mr. Bawth sagged slightly, his head drooping upon his chest. He started snoring.

That's how he made the duke's family sleep through it all, Rellen thought.

Dancer glanced at the now snoring driver and then up at Javyk, who quickly took his place again by the campfire.

"Alright," Javyk said, "we can talk a bit more freely, but keep your voice low. An explosion couldn't wake Bawth. Those bounty hunters and their captives, however, are closer than I would prefer." He eyed them carefully for a moment and then nodded. "Even that may prove to be useful in the days ahead."

"Yes, milord," Dancer replied.

"How are the blisters? Are you settling into the pain?"

"I am, and happily so. I believe they have gotten much worse during today's ride. The agony is exquisite, but I fear my flesh may be coming apart. Each jounce of the carriage seemed to press the artifact deeper into my spine."

Javyk raised a questioning eyebrow, as a teacher questioning the dedication of a student.

"Don't get me wrong, milord," Dancer said, holding up his hands. "I'm willing to suffer any pain… any injury, but I wanted you to know in case it might cause you difficulties later on."

"A prudent concern." Javyk's questioning look turned to one of approval. "You continue to impress me. I believe you will go far in our master's designs."

"Thank you, milord," Dancer replied, and the way he said it sent a shiver up Rellen's spine. Dancer's voice had been devoted to the point of what Rellen could only describe as madness—a hunger without end.

"Now come here and let me take a look at you."

"What of the artifact?"

Javyk looked around at the campsites nearby. Nobody seemed interested in what was going on. "Caravan travelers are rarely interested in the goings-on of others. They gave little or no heed to the marital dispute of our neighbors. Even if someone were to see it, they wouldn't know what they were looking at, and couriers carrying things beneath their garments is almost as common on the King's Highway as horses. Now, pull it out and hold it away from me."

Dancer rose to his feet and extracted the artifact from beneath the back of his shirt. It was a ring of jade-green metal about ten inches across with irregular cutouts along the inside like gears. The object looked to be about an inch thick and the outer portion was roughly two inches wide, with runes running around the perimeter. It was too far away for Rellen to get a good look at the runes. But he immediately recognized the artifact's shape from the outline he'd seen on the wall of the duke's cottage.

A thrill of excitement passed through him. *That's what they'd been after*, Rellen thought. At least his little scouting mission had solved one mystery. Now all he had to do was figure out what the thing was and why they'd gone to so much trouble to get it. He wished Saleeria was with him. Her knowledge of lore and artifacts was unlike any other.

Holding the ring in front of his crotch, Dancer stepped up to Javyk and turned around. Javyk carefully lifted Dancer's shirt, exposing a leather harness and pouch that draped down Dancer's back. Javyk pulled the pouch aside, exposing a blistered circle of angry, red flesh.

Rellen cringed. He knew what had caused it. He'd only seen that sort of wound a couple times before, but there was no mistaking the burns of Mavric iron exposure.

Mavric iron, in its pure form, was generally deadly to all living things. The only exception Rellen knew of were the Delvers, a race of small, stocky people who generally lived beneath the mountains or in the Duchy of Draksymsur in the center of Pelinon. Many Delver weapons were forged with Mavric iron blended into the metals because it was a natural magic enhancer of astonishing potency. The Delvers needed kurioi to then imbue their weapons with majea—they couldn't practice magic themselves—but their weapons were renowned.

Rellen's own falchions, the matched blades of Baladon, had been forged with some Mavric in them, but not enough to be harmful. The magic contained within them was simple and straightforward. They were appreciably lighter than falchions of similar size, ever sharp, and capable of cutting through even heavy plate or wyvern scale if there was enough force behind the blow.

However, most of the casters Rellen had seen use Mavric iron generally died young of consumption and other ailments. Only a very few were able to utilize the stuff and not shorten their lives significantly, and they were all zokurioi.

The last thing in the world Rellen wanted to deal with, however, was an artifact made of enough Mavric iron to cause the burns Dancer had on his back. Such objects were ancient and dangerous. Dancer had no idea what he held, or he wouldn't be holding the artifact so close to his nether regions. Rellen had learned at the academy that Mavric iron and pitchblende could also keep a person from having children. He suspected Javyk, however, knew exactly what was happening.

Javyk tsked several times, inspecting Dancer's burns closely. He gently pressed his finger into the swollen, blistered tissue, causing Dancer to hiss in pain.

"Pain is worship," Javyk said.

"I rejoice in it, milord," Dancer said.

Wretched Nissrans, Rellen thought. Part of him wanted to just go over and execute them on the spot. He'd be within his rights to do so. He had no doubts now that both Dancer and Javyk had been responsible for the murders. There had been others, to be sure, but he also suspected the men he and Mygal faced in the cemetery had been there as well. Fortunately, they were all dead, and while Corwyk identified them, the king would have already sent a detachment to track down and wipe out any Nissrans that might be left in Svennival.

Javyk let out a long, thoughtful breath. "Once we get to Sylverwynd, our contacts there can get us something to secure the artifact. I had no idea it would do this to you." Rellen doubted that. "We still have a long way to go to get it to my master. Still, we can't have you falling apart before we get there, can we?"

"I will endure whatever is required of me," Dancer said.

"Your sacrifice will be rewarded," Javyk said. He then lifted his head toward the trees above and raised his hand up toward the foliage. He closed his eyes, his hand swaying back and forth slightly. A few heartbeats later, there was movement along one of the branches that stretched over Javyk's carriage. Something small and furry leapt from the branch and landed upon the carriage with a faint thud and clatter of tiny claws.

It was a jack glider, a small mammal with long ears, large eyes, a rudder-like tail, and a membrane that stretched between its front and rear legs. They were nocturnal creatures that fed on insects. The creature paused at the edge of the carriage.

"Come on..." Javyk said in a gentle, almost sickly sweet tone. "Come to me." He held out his hand, and the tiny animal leapt with a faint squeak, landing in the palm of his hand.

"That's it, little one," Javyk said in a soft, cooing voice. "You have what I need for my friend here." He seemed to stare into its eyes for several moments, and then the jack glider went limp in his hand, its sides rising and falling slowly.

Rellen dreaded what he knew was about to happen. Miranda had done something similar with his own wounds, but she'd used the already dying vellish. Javyk was the sort who would use any living creature he could get his wretched hands on.

Javyk calmly placed his hand upon Dancer's burned flesh, and a strange, wholly malevolent smile crossed his face. He seemed to delight in what he was doing as he closed his hand around the jack glider. A faint, ruby glow emanated from its body. He concentrated for several moments in silence, and as he did, the jack glider started to shrivel. It made only one pitiable squeak and then went silent as Javyk ripped its life from its body and passed into Dancer's wounded flesh.

Dancer's injury glowed faintly with the ruby light from the glider. After several more moments, the jack glider was a completely desiccated, lifeless husk. Javyk pulled his hand away, and the light emanating from Dancer's back faded. The blisters were gone, and the skin, while still red, was neither swollen nor flaking.

"There," Javyk said, lowering Dancer's shirt. "It's not healed, but it's markedly better. I can do the same each night as needed until we reach Sylverwynd." He threw the shriveled corpse of the jack glider toward the trees. It landed only a few feet from where Rellen hid.

Rellen let out a slow, angry breath. He wanted to kill Javyk more than ever, but he couldn't. The bastard had mentioned a master, and Rellen knew he would have to track that person down to know exactly what was going on. He was also worried about Javyk's capabilities. Only a zokurios of considerable ability could do what he just did.

"Thank you, milord," Dancer said, letting out a relieved sigh. "The pain has abated."

"This is but one of my gifts and is, in no small part, why I was selected for this particular mission. Keeping you alive is critical, for our lord wishes to thank you in person. We can't have you falling ill along the way?"

"Where are we headed, anyway?" Dancer asked, turning around. "Surely you can tell me now. Svennival is well behind us."

"Oh, I suppose you've earned the right to know at least some of the details. We're meeting with members of the Sylverwynd Circle. After that, we shall travel through Jabono to Yaylo. There we will deliver the artifact to my master. Serve him well, and some small part of Pelinon could be yours. Perhaps even Vladysh's duchy someday. Our master might delight in the irony of it."

Javyk got a thoughtful almost concerned look upon his face. He rose to his feet and stared into Dancer's eyes. He then held his open palm out a few inches from Dancer's face and closed his eyes for a few seconds. When he opened them again, he looked somewhat concerned. "How do you feel?"

"I feel much better. Perhaps a little weak, but I'm more than willing and able to continue carrying the artifact. Some rest should help."

"Your enthusiasm and resolve are commendable," Javyk said. "However, I believe you're not quite in top fighting form. That's not your fault. I'll see if I can't hire some additional protection prior to our meeting in Svennival. One cannot be too careful, and the Circle in Sylverwynd has forces working against them who may choose to involve themselves in our dealings."

"I'm strong enough to fight, if needed, milord," Dancer assured him.

"I understand, but I'm not one to leave anything to chance."

Rellen caught Javyk glance over at his own camp. Miranda was sharpening her blade with the steady *whisk* of stone on steel. Rellen smiled. He saw an opportunity, and it looked as if Javyk might actually meet him halfway. Letting out a slow breath, he rose up slowly and backed away from the edge of the trees. With Xilly guiding him again, he moved deeper into the forest and then angled back toward his own encampment. When neared the edge of the forest, he went down into a crouch.

Back into the trees, Xilly, he said.

I'll watch that dark one closely, Xilly said, and there was no missing the anger and disgust in her words. *He enjoyed killing that jack glider. Took satisfaction from it.*

I know, Rellen said as she fluttered up into the trees. *His time will come.*

He waited another fifteen minutes or so for the spells to wear off. When the vines evaporated before his eyes and the sounds of the wildlife grew sharp in his ears, he activated his glowstone and walked out of the forest, deactivating it when he cleared the trees.

"So, you didn't get eaten after all," Miranda said with disappointment thick in her voice.

"Apparently not."

"Have you calmed down?" Miranda asked.

"Enough to eat, anyway," Rellen replied as he strode up to the campfire.

Miranda held out the stick with the last hunk of vellish on it. "Here. It's cold, but that's your fault, not mine."

"You never quit, do you?" Rellen said, jerking the meat away.

"Never."

Rellen took an angry bite and sat down in front of the fire with his back turned toward Javyk and Dancer. He eyed his companions. Tavyn and Mygal hadn't moved, both of them reclining against their saddles, with their cloaks over them in case it rained during the night. Miranda gave him just the hint of an expectant look.

"Things just got a bit more complicated, but there's good news too," Rellen said, and then he related everything he'd seen and heard. When he was done, he stared into the fire for a few moments as an idea started to solidify in his thoughts. "We're following these bastards all the way to Yaylo. Your bounty will have to wait for a while."

"I assumed as much," she said, but her disappointment was clear.

Mygal did his best not to look disappointed that they were travelling even further south. Rellen got the sense that he wanted to resolve this all as quickly as possible. No doubt to impress the king with a big success story. Tavyn, on the other hand, didn't look disappointed at all, which surprised him. Rellen would have thought that an information broker in Svennival would lament being away from that which earned him his living. Instead, Tavyn looked almost eager. Still, Tavyn knew he was getting paid a pretty tidy sum each day for just being there. It was easy money, and coin rarely just came into one's hands. Rellen pushed his suspicions aside, but he couldn't keep from thinking there was a lot more to Tavyn than met the eye.

"There's one other thing," Rellen said quietly. "As of now, you're Maybor," he looked at Tavyn, "and you're Tygeth."

"Why the new names?" Tavyn asked. "Do you have something specific in mind?"

"I might," Rellen said. "If the opportunity presents itself, I plan to join Javyk's journey to Yaylo, and take the rest of you with me. He'll be looking for a swinging blade or two in Sylverwynd, and I expect to be one of them."

Now the game would be patience.

CHAPTER SEVENTEEN

THE VALUE OF PATIENCE

With rain pouring down almost nonstop, the next four days passed without incident. Rellen didn't risk another reconnoiter. He didn't need to. He'd gotten what he wanted, and like a good hunter, he'd wait to move another step closer in plain sight of his prey. Rellen and Miranda kept up their regularly scheduled pissing matches. The other travelers had even started to anticipate them, even Javyk and Dancer. Like clockwork, Javyk would then put Mr. Bawth to sleep and heal Dancer's back. It was hard to tell, but even at that distance, it seemed to Rellen that the wound looked just a little worse after each of Javyk's ministrations. Rellen suspected the zokurios was fighting a losing battle.

From time to time, they got a glimpse of the Sylverwylde Mountains rising slowly above the tree line and dominating the horizon. On the morning of the fifth day, the rain stopped, and the forest opened up. The mountains were a high, jagged line from left to right. Straight ahead lay Sylverwynd, a rugged-looking city almost as large as Svennival.

It lay at the base of a relatively straight and very deep mountain pass that followed a wide river flowing out of the mountains.

The original walled keep of Sylverwynd, a sturdy-looking structure with lines distinctly not Pelinese, was set into a high hillside, surrounded by the rest of a very large city.

Delvers had built the fortress at the behest of Pelinon's king six hundred years earlier, and throughout the city were clusters of stone buildings and towers done in the same style.

Those were the warren-like enclaves where Delvers thrived and generally isolated themselves from the predominantly human populace. They'd been built as high as four and even five stories, and the human homes and shops flowed out from them. They traded and sometimes worked with humans, but they didn't mingle with them.

Although Sylverwynd wasn't a ducal seat, it sat upon the largest trade crossroads along the entire Sylverwylde range. The city spread out as if it had tumbled out of the mountain pass like a landslide. A faint but persistent pall of smoke floated above the city, borne of the countless wood-and-coal-burning forges that made up a good portion of the city's industry.

Mountains meant gems, minerals, and ores. Those meant forges, and forges meant all manner of trade goods derived from them. Sylverwynd was renowned for everything from exceptional jewelry to some of the best weapons and armor available anywhere.

A quarter mile from the edge of Sylverwynd, the caravan turned down a wide road of irregularly shaped, dark gray cobblestones that were clearly not part of the King's Highway. They led to a site along the river where caravans could gather without overwhelming the city. Several inns, taverns, and shops made up a small village outside the city. Stretching out from the central village were rows of vendor wagons, carts, and tents, arranged like the spokes of a wheel extending out, where travelers could purchase just about anything they wanted.

At least four other caravans had camped in the enclave. The teamsters led the caravan to an open field up against the river, and the caravan spread out, with those at the head of the line taking up positions right along the riverbank. Once again, Rellen led his group to a site beside Javyk and Dancer's carriage. The driver had barely set the parking brake when the carriage door opened, and Dancer got out. He held the door for Javyk, who stepped onto the ground and immediately turned up to the driver.

"Set up camp, Mr. Bawth," Javyk ordered. "Dancer and I need to go see about engaging a few capable bodies. We'll return when we can."

It was precisely what Rellen had been waiting for. He had to act quickly.

"I'm telling you," Rellen snapped, glaring at Miranda, "I'm headed into the village for supplies. I'm almost out of components for my spells, and this is the first place we've come across where I can get them." He hoped Miranda would respond without looking surprised.

"It's just like you," she barked back, "take off when there's hard work to be done."

"If I can't cast my spells, we can't do our jobs, now can we?" Rellen said, getting off Shaddeth. "You know it's the best advantage we have."

"Go and be damned," Miranda snapped, waving a dismissive hand. "I swear, you're the laziest layabout I've ever known."

Javyk and Dancer walked past. This time, Rellen looked directly at Javyk, shook his head, and rolled his eyes. "You wouldn't believe what I have to put up with," he said.

Javyk gave Rellen a pained nod but said nothing, continuing on his way with Dancer in tow.

As Miranda barked orders at Tavyn and Mygal—using the assumed names of Tygeth and Maybor—Rellen glanced up at the sky. High above, looking like any other bird, was a small black, winged shape.

Can you hear me, little one?

I can. Xilly did a quick loop in the air.

Do you see Javyk and Dancer?

Yes, they just walked off.

I'm going to follow them, but at a distance. I don't want them to see me yet. Can you guide me if I lose them?

Of course. She adjusted her path through the sky and followed along in the same direction Javyk and Dancer had gone.

Rellen loosened the straps of Shaddeth's saddle, to ease the strain, and then grabbed his saddlebags, flopping them over one shoulder. He fully intended to get at least some of the spell components he would need, especially the yallaho berries. He gave Miranda a parting glance and flashed the military sign for "thank you."

She smiled, nodded, and then signed the words "good luck."

With that, Rellen turned and set off toward the center of the enclave, weaving his way through the travelers and teamsters mulling about the area as the caravan started setting up camp.

The area bustled with activity, but he managed to catch glimpses of Javyk and Dancer as they made their way. Rellen had a good idea of where they were going, and before long, his suspicions were proved out.

Javyk made his way straight toward a two-story, wooden building with a plaque hanging over the door. The plaque bore the mark of the Bounty Hunters Guild, crossed swords with a dragon skull above them. Inside, one could register bounties or search the boards for bounties that had been duly registered. Some were from private parties, some from the authorities, but there were always at least a few jobs listed in a caravan village.

Out front were three rows of tables with wooden benches. Javyk sat down at the nearest one, with Dancer taking a position beside him. The etiquette was straightforward. Anyone who looked to employ bounty hunters or bodyguards on short notice could wait there. Eventually, those looking for work would come by and ask what the job was. It was a simple arrangement and consistent throughout most of Pelinon.

Rellen approached the table on his way to an apothecary he'd spotted a half dozen doors down from the Hunter's Guild. Just then, a burly man with a bald head and light leather armor sat down across from Javyk. He had a longsword belted to his hip, and he leaned a sturdy, steel-banded buckler against the bench.

Rellen caught Javyk's eye and nodded in recognition.

Javyk immediately recognized Rellen and nodded back. "Please come see me when you're done with your errand, would you?"

"Certainly," Rellen replied nonchalantly and moved on. His instincts had been right.

◆ ◆ ◆

When Rellen's saddlebags and pouches were full of the supplies and spell components he needed, including a half dozen vials of mashed yallaho berries, he left the apothecary and made his way back toward the Hunter's Guild. As he wove his way through the wide avenue, he passed an aging bard plucking away at a stringed instrument and singing a dirge-like tune that was oddly pleasing to the ear. As a gentleman in fine-looking clothing passed by, he dropped a coin into a small, metal cup hooked into the bard's belt.

Rellen moved quickly up the avenue and found Javyk and Dancer still sitting at the table, thankfully alone. Javyk motioned for Rellen to join them.

He walked up to them, an expectant look on his face. Now that he got a good look at Javyk, he realized the man's pallor was even more profound than it had appeared at a distance. His flesh was sickly, but there was a resilient strength to his posture, as if his body contained a strength that shouldn't be there. His sunken eyes had dark circles around them but held a fierce strength that came through like candles in the dark.

Dancer, on the other hand, had a somewhat healthier pallor, but he looked to be the weaker of the two. His shoulders slumped slightly, and he was obviously fatigued. There was a sheen of perspiration on his brow, and his breathing came in unnaturally short breaths. It was clear Javyk's attempts at healing were losing the battle.

"What can I do for you?" Rellen asked warily.

"It's Rellen, isn't it?" Javyk asked. There was something almost disquieting about his tone of voice. He was the epitome of politeness and poise, as if he'd been raised amongst the nobility to automatically treat everyone with kindness and grace—to their faces. Rellen recognized the mark of a manipulator immediately. He'd been raised surrounded by men and women just like that.

"How do you know my name?" Rellen asked, his eyes going hard.

"Forgive me," Javyk said, holding up a calming hand, "but your... wife, is it...?" He looked apologetic, even compassionate. "Her voice carries. I don't mean to pry or be insulting, but she does seem like a... difficult woman."

"She's got a tongue like a razor blade," Rellen said bitterly, shaking his head. "Sometimes I think I should have killed that bitch years ago, not married her."

"So I gathered. Love, like hate, can be a fickle taskmaster, can't it?"

"That's the truth," Rellen replied, softening his posture slightly. He wanted to draw the man in.

"Please, join us," Javyk said softly.

"Why would I want to do that?"

"Because I have a proposition for you, one that is likely to be profitable for you—with or without your wife—and might even lead to more coin down the road."

"Everyone says they have a profitable proposition, but do you have the coin to make good on it?"

"A fair question," Javyk replied. He reached into the folds of his dark robe and drew out a rather thick coin purse. He reached in and pulled out a few dakkaris. "I'll most certainly be able to compensate you adequately. What I require is, in fact, a very simple matter."

"What do you need done?"

"Before I go into that, I do have a rather indelicate question I need answered first."

"And that is?" Rellen added a hint of boredom to his answer.

"Well, what I require may involve matters at least somewhat outside the boundaries of the law."

"I'm not going to murder anyone for you, if that's what you're after," Rellen said bluntly. "I doubt you have *that* kind of money, despite the fancy carriage."

"Oh, no," Javyk said easily. "Nothing like that. However, it might require you to injure or kill one or more persons in defense of myself and my associate here." He eyed Rellen. "Would you have any problems with a situation like that?"

"You're talking about a straightforward bodyguard job." He raised a confident eyebrow. "It wouldn't be my first one, so, no, I'd have no problems killing the other guy to protect my employer." He locked eyes with Javyk and sat down. "Let me put it another way. I've killed more men and women than I can count. Most of them were legal as a duly authorized bounty hunter in the Kingdom of Pelinon. The others all had it coming and were armed when I killed them. If I think it's a justifiable killing, I'll even stick around for the constables. If I don't, then I'll disappear faster than you can say magistrate, and you'll never see me again. You'd be paying me to protect you... not go to jail or a gallows for you. Does that make you feel better?"

"Indeed, it does," Javyk almost purred.

"For the right price, I might be able to help you out, but you need to know that I'm pulling out in the morning. Headed south. If you need protecting between now and then, I can help you... especially if it gets me away from my wife for *any* period of time."

Rellen paused, glancing at the bard who was coming up the street, his music floating over the conversation. He turned back to Javyk. "Turn me over to the authorities," he said in a suddenly dangerous tone, "and I *will* kill you. You'll never see me coming. The same applies if I think you just dropped me into a meat grinder. I'm not fodder for any man, not even a king."

"I think we understand one another," Javyk said, nodding, and then he motioned for the bard to come over.

"So, what would I be up against?"

"I can give you at least a rough idea of what you might run into, but I cannot make any guarantees. I don't even know if we *will* face opposition, let alone what its composition might be. I can only say that I am employing several individuals such as yourself merely to ensure that a transaction takes place and we are not injured in the process." He paused and held up his finger. "Excuse me for a moment, would you? I've always loved this song." He motioned for the bard to come closer.

As the bard approached, Javyk reached into an inner pocket of his robes and pulled out a coin. He tried to cover it, but Rellen's quick eyes spotted a strip of vellum wrapped around it.

The bard stepped up, shifting his hip out as he played a rather lively tune, making the metal cup more accessible. Javyk dropped the coin in as he met the eyes of the bard, who gave Javyk a jovial nod of thanks and then moved on. Javyk quickly turned back to Rellen, an innocent look on his face. But Rellen had not missed the exchange. He guessed Javyk had just sent a message to the people he intended to meet.

"So, what are we actually talking about?" Rellen asked. "I mean the whos and whats?"

"Without divulging any details you don't need to know, the plan is to meet some of my associates inside Sylverwynd this afternoon. There will be an exchange of several objects. We will then leave. It's all very simple."

"And if it gets complicated?" Rellen asked drily.

"In that event, I would expect you to stop anyone from interfering with my transaction or from taking my property—at all costs. What will it cost me to engage you for the afternoon?"

"Fifteen dakkaris, five now and ten after."

Javyk raised an eyebrow, a dubious look upon his face. "That much? One of the individuals I engaged only asked for three dakkaris before and five after."

"Then he's either a fool or fighting way out of his weight class." Rellen leaned back, a thoughtful look on his face. "I'll tell you what. If things stay simple, I'll take three now and eight after. If it gets *complicated*, it's back to five and ten. I don't come cheap, and you'll definitely want me on your side."

"That's a rather bold boast," Javyk said.

"I put up only when I know I can back it up. Do we have a deal?"

"I believe we do." Javyk gave Rellen a thoughtful look as Rellen got up. "I like how you do business. I'll tell you what. If things do get complicated and we escape with our lives and my property, there's an additional five dakkaris in it for you."

"I won't argue with you." Rellen looked suspicious. "But why the generosity?"

"Because I like working with professionals. When I find good people, I make it easy for them to come back for more when I need them."

Rellen nodded his head appreciatively. "Not a bad practice."

"I won't keep you any longer, but before we part company, I'd ask you to give some thought to your future between now and this afternoon."

"I'm always thinking about my future."

"If this works out, it may lead to more work, not only for you, but perhaps even your partner. We too," Javyk nodded to Dancer, "are headed south."

"Let's play that by ear," Rellen said. "It all depends on how this afternoon goes."

"A wise precaution. Then let's conclude our business." He reached into the coin purse and handed over three gleaming dakkaris.

"When do we leave?" Rellen asked, slipping the coins into his cloak.

"Meet here in two hours. We'll go into town together."

"I'll be here."

He got up and strode away to tell Miranda and the others what had happened. As he moved through the crowd, he glanced up at the small, black form that circled lazily above him.

I'll need you to keep an eye out, he said to Xilly.

I believe you will, she replied, a bit of worry coming through.

It'll be fine, Rellen assured her.

...Her silence spoke volumes.

Chapter Eighteen
SECRET MEETING

Rellen followed several paces behind the others as they moved deeper into the city of Sylverwynd. Javyk had made a point of telling Rellen and the other two bodyguards that they would know where they were headed when they got there, and that was the end of the discussion.

Dancer now carried a long bundle wrapped in black cloth and tied with light rope. That, and he looked both paler and weaker than he had before. The shape of the bundle suggested it was a sword of some kind, and Rellen had to wonder if it was the one stolen from the Duke Belvenim's study.

Ahead of Rellen and to the right, was the same burly, bald-headed thug he'd seen Javyk talking to initially. His name was Bodrugar, and Rellen had taken an instant disliking to the bruiser. Bodrugar had added a steel helm to the light leather armor, as well as thick bracers covered with iron spikes. He clutched the battered longsword in his one hand and strapped the steel-banded buckler to his other. Rellen had him pegged as a fairly low-rent thug and barely worth the money Javyk was paying him.

The other bodyguard called himself Sallintyr, and he had a much more professional feel about him. He wore light leather armor of red and gray that was similar to Rellen's. He carried himself like someone who had been a professional soldier at one time or another. He had a heavy saber on his right hip and a thick, long, drop-point knife strapped to his left. He turned his head left and right as they moved through the street, scanning for threats.

Javyk led them through a smithing district where smoke filled the air and hammers rang on steel. The streets were full of a wide variety of pedestrians, and unlike in Svennival, many of them weren't human. That included Delvers, a few Bhirtas'Vuoda and quite a few Kapren—cousins of the Kapron. Where the Kapron resembled mountain sheep, with their thick horns spiraling back around their temples, the Kapren tended to be a bit shorter, with dual-spiraling horns rising above their heads and goat-like features.

As Javyk turned them down a wide avenue that led straight down a slight hill toward the river, they passed a massive dewkalve in a wooden docking cradle over a hundred feet long. The gigantic dewkalve hooted once and shifted slightly, causing the timbers to creak. The creatures were the means by which the Elwhari'Ma Transport Guild maintained its monopoly on hauling cargoes and travelers across the central part of Pelinon. At a hundred feet long, it was capable of carrying tons of materiel and passengers. Its sleek, bluish-white body was covered with something like fish scales, although they were the size of shields and larger. It glistened with an iridescent pattern of light, and its elongated head supported a massive set of jaws. Their tails were long, almost shark-like, which they used to propel themselves forward through the air, supported by gaseous bladders inside their bodies.

The dewkalve was tended by a dozen or more of the feathered Elwhari'Ma who wrangled the great, cargo-carrying beasts. The Elwhari'Ma were a tall, graceful, and generally ill-tempered bird-like race, with long beaks, cold, blinking eyes, and a heavy covering of feathers that could be any color of the rainbow. They frequently adorned themselves with expensive jewelry and were prone to elaborate headdresses made from other Elwhari'Ma they'd defeated in the ritualistic fighting arenas where their species settled feuds.

Javyk led them into a warehouse district where a number of piers stretched out into the wide river. Some of them were large enough to hold rows of smaller warehouses, and the entire area was busy with activity as cargo moved in and out of Sylverwynd. They wove their way through the warren of warehouses and came upon one of the larger piers, where six tall warehouses stretched away from them. They were all painted a dull gray, and along the tops, just below the roof lines, were small windows, some of which were propped open.

The pier itself seemed strangely devoid of activity. At the edge of the dock, where the pier connected to the wharf, there were two large, gruff-looking brutes with stern faces. They had the look of men paid to keep people away.

Javyk stopped, held up his hand to get his entourage to stop, and glanced over his shoulder. "Stay here for a moment."

He walked up to one of the brutes. He leaned in and whispered something. The big man nodded once, almost respectfully, whispered something back, and then made a slight motion for Javyk to move on.

Javyk turned. "We're going into the third one down. My associates should already be there. Do not say anything. Keep an eye out for anyone showing undue interest in us as we move along the pier, and stay sharp throughout the entire exchange. If all goes well, we will depart without incident, and you will all get paid." He eyed all three of them. "Now keep close."

Rellen glanced up and spotted where Xilly circled in a wide pattern high above them.

When I go in, see if there's a way to get inside without being seen. If not, then just stay out of sight.

I will, she replied.

Javyk strode up to the third warehouse where the main doors were closed and blocked by several rows of wooden crates. He approached a nearby door and opened it as if he'd lived there his entire life. As they entered, Rellen found himself in a well-lit warehouse full of more crates stacked high enough to almost reach the ceiling. Spiderwebs suggested most of the crates hadn't been touched or moved for quite a while.

A wash of bright sunlight emanated from the back side of the structure, and Rellen assumed that the main doors on the water side had been slid open. There was a strange scent upon the air mixed in with the smells of wood and fish, reminding him of burning coal. It was faint, barely perceptible, but he knew he wasn't imagining it.

Javyk turned down a narrow gap between the warehouse wall and the crates, moving quickly forward. They'd gone about twenty feet when the gap opened up into a wide area free of crates. A half dozen individuals wearing red hoods to conceal their faces stood on the far side.

The leader had a silver pendant Rellen recognized immediately. It was the symbol of Nissra.

Rellen tensed, his hand sliding to one of his falchions. He worried that he and the other bodyguards had been led into the warehouse for some perverted sacrifice to the bitch-goddess of blood.

I'm in, Xilly's voice echoed in his head. He scanned the rafters above but couldn't see her. *Far corner, in the shadows.*

Rellen peered more deeply and could just make out the curve of her body, hidden behind a thick beam supporting the ceiling. *I see you,* he said.

There's something odd, she warned. *I smell musk... and coal or something... unlike anything I've ever encountered. It shouldn't be here.*

Rellen's eyes darted around the warehouse, looking for any sign of trouble. *I smell it too.* There were a number of recessed areas along the walls of crates that surrounded them where someone could hide, but he didn't see anything that was cause for alarm.

"Greetings, my brothers," Javyk said reverently. He then uttered a phrase in a language Rellen had never heard before.

The six hooded figures repeated the phrase together in unison, as if they were praying. Rellen had no doubt the phrase was in celebration of Nissra. He fought the urge to curse her name out loud.

"Do you have what I asked for?" Javyk asked.

There was something in the way he said it that caught Rellen's ear. It was as a master speaking to a minion.

"It is here," the leader of the hooded figures said and pulled out a black leather satchel. It looked somewhat rigid, as if hardened plates lined the interior. It was just big enough to fit the artifact Dancer still carried.

"Excellent," Javyk said. He turned to the young man beside him. "Dancer, please hand that over and take the satchel."

Without a word, Dancer stumbled over and gave the sword-shaped bundle to the leader.

"In the proper hands, that should serve our cause well," Javyk said. "Be certain this gift is not squandered," he added, and there was no missing the warning tone.

"We hear and we serve," the leader said with a nod of his head. In exchange, he gave the heavy satchel to Dancer. If Rellen had to guess, he would say the thing had to weigh at least fifteen pounds.

"As it is commanded," Javyk responded to the cult devotion. "Test it." He gestured to the bundle, a beneficent smile on his face.

The leader untied and unwrapped the bundle, pulling out a longsword in an intricately patterned blue, leather sheath. The shape of the guard and pommel gave it away. The sword from the duke's study. He drew the weapon out with a ring of fine steel, and the blade flashed in the light coming in from the doors behind him. He hefted it, feeling its weight, and then the blade of the weapon erupted into blue flames with a *whuff*. Fire danced along its length, like flames on water.

The two bodyguards beside Rellen gasped in surprise. Firebrands were rare weapons indeed, although not entirely unheard of. Rellen and a gekurios—a Land Magician—had once worked with a talented smith to create one for a general they'd served under, but that was long ago.

"I know precisely who to give this to," the leader said, sliding the blade back into its sheath. The flames were immediately extinguished.

"I trust your judgment," Javyk replied. "Now, I fear I must take my leave of you."

"We had hoped you could stay, take sacrifice with us, but we understand."

"Another time, perhaps," Javyk said politely. "Come, Dancer."

Dancer, whose eyes had never left the duke's sword, turned and walked back, the satchel held firmly in his hands.

"We'll attend to this when we return to the carriage," Javyk said softly. "It is lined with metal plates that should protect you. It will be a bit heavier, but it will keep you safe."

Dancer nodded and slipped the strap of the satchel over his shoulder.

Suddenly, a muffled but booming voice shouted the Delver word, "Attack!"

A half dozen crates around the warehouse exploded, sending wood and splinters in all directions. Six armed and armored Delvers, in the distinctive, heavily flanged and spiked black plate mail of their people, shouted battle-cries as they charged in.

As Rellen jerked his falchions free, he wondered if the others knew how much trouble they were in. Aside from trade, Delvers rarely interacted with humans and the other races, and it was an exceptionally rare event when they crossed swords. Facing Delver weapons and armor was bad enough, but they were also immune to magic and generally stronger than other species. In short, they were tough little bastards to kill. Rellen had only fought a Delver once. The encounter had almost cost him his life, and he still had a scar along his thigh to prove it.

Yes, they were in trouble, indeed... and Rellen would have to do this the hard way.

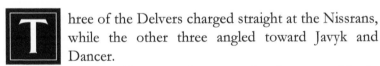

CHAPTER NINETEEN

THE KLYMRUKAAR

Three of the Delvers charged straight at the Nissrans, while the other three angled toward Javyk and Dancer.

"Protect the artifact!" Javyk screamed as he stepped back. There was no fear in his eyes, only anger. He uttered an incantation and slashed with his hand. A scythe of ruby light flashed out and passed through the nearest Delver's throat, but the short, stocky warrior didn't even slow down.

Dancer seemed frozen, staring at the three roaring Delvers coming straight at him. One wielded an axe, one a sword, and the other a massive war hammer.

To their credit, the other two bodyguards, Bodrugar and Sallintyr, leapt forward to engage the three Delvers headed for Javyk and Dancer.

For half a heartbeat, Rellen contemplated letting the Delvers have at the Nissrans. It was unlikely the Nissrans would survive the encounter, unless they were far better fighters than the nest Rellen had faced in Calamath. It would be fun to watch, but the fact remained that he needed Javyk to lead him to the bastard behind everything. Rellen surged forward, only a half step behind.

Bodrugar raised his buckler and took a mighty blow from the Delver's war hammer with a clang of metal on metal. The man was huge, but the blow halted him in his tracks and staggered him sideways.

Sallintyr engaged the Delver wielding the axe, forcing his opponent to come up short with a flurry of fast slashes that put the Delver on the defensive. The Delver with the sword raised his weapon, ready to cleave Dancer's skull, but Rellen stepped in and blocked, catching the Delver's blade with a crystalline ring of steel on steel. The blow vibrated up to Rellen's shoulder, and his hand stung from the impact.

"Get out of here," Rellen shouted over his shoulder and shoved Dancer back with an elbow. He pushed the Delver's blade aside several inches—not an easy thing to do—and sent a thrust angling in at the Delver's exposed face. The Delver shifted his head to the right, stepped back, and came straight at Rellen with two quick slashes that Rellen was barely able to parry. The Delver was fast, skilled, and could put a lot of muscle behind every swing.

Rellen found himself on the defensive.

Another scythe of ruby light flashed out and hit the Delver in front of Rellen directly in the face.

The Delver smiled, and as he did, Rellen noticed a familiar sigil etched into the neck ring of the Delver's plate mail. It was a strange, demonic skull in the center, with horns rising above and below, with harsh eyes and the narrow slits of a skull-like nose. The whole thing was transfixed upon an upright, Delver blade.

These Delver are allies of the king! Rellen thought in a panic.

It was the symbol of the Klymrukaar. Rellen knew very little about them, save that the kings of Pelinon had maintained some sort of alliance with them for centuries. His father had mentioned them on a few occasions, remarking that he trusted them implicitly. Rellen had vague recollections of one of them showing up at the castle from time to time when he was in his teens.

He suddenly felt very, very trapped, caught between enemies that were friends, and friends that were enemies. He hesitated for a fraction of a heartbeat. The Delver didn't miss the opportunity. His blade flashed in again and again. It was all Rellen could do to parry each blow with his falchions, one high and one low. Even more frustrating was that the Delver was good enough to direct his attacks so any riposte or counterthrust would hit only plate mail.

The leader of the Nissrans fought using the duke's firebrand, and he clearly knew how to wield it. One of the other Nissrans, however, turned and raced through the wide-open doors. Another Nissran screamed out in pain and went down, impaled on a Delver blade.

At the same time, a mighty crash of heavy metal slamming against wood and steel filled the warehouse. Bodrugar grunted as his buckler gave way, splintering into shattered wood and twisted steel bands. He staggered sideways and crashed into Rellen, who barely managed to leap back and avoid a sharp thrust that filled the air where his stomach had been a moment ago.

Bodrugar roared out his fury as the Delver raised the hammer once again for a killing blow. The big man surged forward, grabbing the haft of the Delver's war hammer with his wounded arm and thrust with his sword. The blade skittered off the Delver's chest plate and slid past. The Delver clamped his arm down, pinning the blade in place.

Sallintyr's blade was a blur, darting left and right. He'd already drawn blood from several shallow wounds along the Delver's hands and face, but they were far from injuries that would slow the Delver down.

Rellen fell back even further, parrying every blow from his opponent's dancing blade. He was setting up a counterstrike, learning the pattern and pace of his opponent's combinations.

Sallintyr slashed again. The Delver caught Sallintyr's saber in the blade-catching-curve of his axe and twisted hard with powerful hands. The blade got hung up for only a moment, but it was enough. The Delver stepped in and punched Sallintyr in the crotch. Sallintyr doubled over, grunting in pain. The Delver brought the pommel of the axe up and caught Sallintyr squarely on the chin. The tall warrior's mouth exploded with blood and teeth as his head snapped up and back. He toppled onto his back and lay motionless, his face a ruin.

Bodrugar released his sword and punched the Delver, staggering him back. He leapt forward, tackled the Delver, and they went down in a tangle of swinging fists and pounding knees.

Another Nissran screamed and died.

Rellen blocked, parried, and smashed the Delver's blade to the side. The Delver countered, but Rellen blocked again, opening up the Delver's right-hand guard. He'd made his opening and put everything he had into a swing aimed at the Delver's sword arm. He hoped that a blade of Baladon was harder than Delver plate mail.

The Delver shifted sideways to get away from the blow. Rellen's strike hit home with a ring of steel. He felt his blade bite deep. The Delver howled in pain. Rellen jerked his blade free. Blood poured down the black metal. Rellen swung his other blade. The Delver's parry, slowed by the gash in his arm, didn't come in time. Rellen caught him in the elbow, cutting another gash into his opponent's flesh. He wanted to disable, but not kill. His third swing caught the flat of the Delver's blade with a splitting ring of steel. He struck the blade from the Delver's hands, and it clattered to the floor, sliding up against where Bodrugar and his opponent thrashed on the ground, their meaty hands wrapped around each other's throats.

Rellen raised a falchion, drawing the Delver's arms up in a defensive block. Rellen drove a hard kick into the Delver's chest. It felt like he'd kicked a tree, but the Delver was driven back, stumbled over a body, and went down.

The six Nissrans had been whittled down to two, and they were caught in a desperate fight against the two remaining Delvers on that side. The Nissran leader, still wielding the firebrand, had resorted to panicked slashes back and forth, as he and the other Nissran backed toward the open doors and a drop-off to the water below.

One of the Delvers shifted around, blocking their path. The Nissran leader turned to defend from two directions, and as he did, a Delver slashed his blade deep into the leader's thigh. He screamed out, distracting the other Nissran. The other Delver stepped in and drove his blade into the Nissran's belly. The Delver facing the leader now severed the leader's arm at the elbow. The flames went out and the blade, along with part of the leader's arm, tumbled to the floor. The Delver's backswing took the leader's head off, silencing his cries as both head and body toppled over with gruesome thuds.

"Fall back," Javyk shouted at the top of his lungs.

Rellen turned to find Javyk motioning for Rellen to follow, so he did, moving backwards, with his guard up. He backed into the narrow corridor of crates that led to the door they'd come in through. Heavy boot steps echoed across the warehouse floor, just out of sight. There were two or even three Delvers coming after them, and Rellen knew he'd never be able to hold them off. His magic wouldn't work against them directly, and they could just run through his poison gas spell and be right back on top of him. He caught sight of some thick cobwebs lining the crates, and an idea popped into his head. He needed to stop them but make it look like he'd tried to kill them while still getting Javyk to leave. The bastard might want Rellen to kill the Delvers outright if they were subdued.

He knew what he had to do.

Run! Xilly's voice rang in Rellen's thoughts. *They're coming!*

Rellen ignored her. He set a falchion on the crate beside him and grabbed a mass of cobwebs in his left hand. He uttered a quick incantation, drawing a symbol in the air with the cobwebs.

Three Delvers came around the corner in a tight line, their weapons raised.

Rellen uttered the last word of the spell and threw the cobwebs straight at them. The white, sticky mass streaked away, expanding quickly. It hit the center Delver and exploded outward, sending thick cords of spiderweb to entangle the Delvers as webs stuck to the walls and crates on either side. All three Delvers came to an abrupt halt and started thrashing to get free.

Rellen grabbed a vial of the yallaho mash from his bandoleer and uttered another incantation. With the last word, he threw the vial at the floor between himself and the trapped Delvers. He could have thrown it at their feet, but he didn't want them to die of the poison, either.

He glanced over his shoulder as the poison gas cloud started expanding.

"Run!" he shouted at Javyk, who was standing in the doorway. "The poison will expand and kill us all!"

Javyk disappeared through the doorway. Rellen, grabbed his falchion from the crate, turned, and ran. He reached the doorway, and at the last moment, he stopped. Turning, he gave the Delvers a salute.

While the other two Delvers continued to struggle within the webs, the one in the center gave Rellen a strange, almost appreciative look, as if he realized Rellen hadn't wanted to kill them. At that, Rellen turned and dashed through the doorway, leaving the Delvers to extract themselves. The webbing he'd created would last only a few minutes, at best, but he suspected they'd be able to cut their way out faster than that.

Get on out of here, Xilly, Rellen said.

You're not hurt?

No. But keep watch. We're not out of this yet.

As he exited the warehouse, he saw Dancer at the end of the pier, satchel clutched in his hands and a frightened look upon his face. Javyk was running for all he was worth in that direction. The bodies of the two Nissran guards lay on the pier with crossbow bolts sticking out of their throats.

Javyk reached Dancer and motioned for the frightened and weak young man to get moving. Rellen pounded after them, and they ran up the avenue a block, passing between several warehouses, where they quickly encountered a mass of foot traffic. As they did, they slowed their pace, gasping for breath and trying to look casual.

They drew quite a few glances at first, but the further they got from the river, the more normal they looked. They'd gone a few more blocks when Javyk came to a stop, still gasping for air.

"Hold on a moment," he said, wheezing, "it doesn't look like they're following us, and I need to catch my breath." He bent over, his hands on his thighs. He glanced up and looked at Rellen. "Thank you," he said sincerely. "They would have gotten us all had it not been for you."

"Probably," Rellen said. "We all got lucky though." He watched Javyk for several seconds as the man continued to draw in deep, sucking breaths. "Who were those Delvers? They don't normally get involved in human affairs."

"I don't know," Javyk replied, clearly bewildered and obviously shaken. He motioned for them to get moving again, and they set off up the hill toward the center of Sylverwynd. "I was told that there might be others interested in what my young friend here carries, but nothing more. But why didn't my zomajea work on them? It was as if they were immune somehow."

"You've never fought Delvers before, have you?"

"No." Javyk stiffened a little, obviously not accustomed to someone asking him what he didn't know.

"And I take it you didn't go to one of the magic academies?"

Javyk stiffened even further, looking offended. "No," he said, "I'm self-taught. Most people couldn't even—"

"That explains it then," Rellen replied smoothly, not wanting to get into some pointless debate about Javyk's past and achievements. "Delvers *are* immune... at least, to magic cast directly on them. On the other hand," Rellen added with a bit of relief, "they can't use it directly either."

Javyk deflated somewhat, an astonished look on his face. "I didn't know."

"Most people don't," Rellen said, "and there's little reason for them to even think about it. Like I said, it's practically unheard of for Delvers to involve themselves in human affairs, aside from trading goods with us."

"How do you know all this?" Javyk asked, and there was no missing the suspicion in his voice.

"Magic academy," Rellen replied easily. "I'm formally trained. That, and years running up and down the King's Highway. I can count on one hand the number of times I saw a Delver fraternizing with a human. If there isn't a deal to be made that they can profit from, they're just not interested— not with humans, anyway." He pondered this new mystery. He couldn't fathom why Delvers, let alone the mysterious Klymrukaar, would be after Javyk and the artifact Dancer carried. It didn't make any sense.

Javyk eyed him, a calculating look in his eyes. "I want to ask you something."

"Go ahead."

"You didn't seem to react when you saw those people in red robes."

"No," Rellen replied flatly. "Should I have?"

Javyk hesitated for a moment. "There are some who are not comfortable with those overtly devoted to their deity. Do you know who I, and those others, follow?"

Rellen put a bored expression on his face. "What I know is that I really don't care. I've traveled across much of Pelinon and beyond. I've seen devotees of damn near every pantheon in the heavens. A lot of them lived and died, healed and harmed in the name of one god or another. It didn't seem to make much difference either way, in the end. They all end up in the same dirt. The one thing I do know is that I have no use for any of it. I won't ever tell a man how to pray. I also won't bend a knee to someone else's god." He eyed Javyk with a bit of mettle in his eyes. "Does that answer your question?"

"It does... and I'd like to engage your services further."

"You think they'll come after you again?" Rellen asked, glancing toward the river.

"I honestly don't know, but I intend to be as prepared as possible if they do. You survived, and you managed to get us out of there, despite their resistance to magic."

Rellen kept the satisfied smile off his face. This was exactly what he'd been hoping for. But he had to play hard to get.

"Considering we just faced six Delvers, I'm disinclined to take the job without at least a little help, and someone not only more skilled than those two back there, but someone I trust. I'd want my wife to be part of the deal."

"I thought you hated her?" Javyk replied, looking perplexed.

"I do." He gave Javyk a wry grin. "She and I might not get along most of the time, but when it comes to business— especially the business of money and fighting—there's nobody I'd rather have backing me up. We get twenty dakkaris a day for escort duty and an extra twenty each per engagement with an enemy. That's not negotiable."

"I suspect we can come to an arrangement," Javyk replied, "but before I agree, what about your bounties?"

"I still want to take them in. It's a substantial bounty, although they're not wanted for murder or anything. It's actually a pity."

"What?" Javyk asked, looking a bit surprised.

"They owe somebody money... quite a bit of it, actually." The seed of an idea popped into Rellen's head, but it would be a tricky sell. "Under different circumstances, I'd actually suggest you hire them too."

"You're joking," Javyk blurted.

"No." Rellen let out a thoughtful breath. "I've known them for a while. That's actually how I got close enough to capture them. They're good in a fight and fairly dependable."

"If that's the case, why is there a bounty on them?"

"Honestly, that whole thing was more personal than anything else. I'd rather not go into the details, but let's just say that the fellow they were working for might have deliberately left out some details of the job he hired them to do, and they almost got killed because of it. Turns out, he knew it was going to go south. They decided to... ahhh... take the initiative and exact their own bonus."

"Then why are you taking them in?"

"Because they're valid bounties, and business is business."

"Your loyalty is commendable," Javyk said drily.

"I'm loyal to coin," Rellen said. "It begins and ends there. I get paid to do what's agreed upon. Nothing more. Nothing less. I've never broken a contract or betrayed the person paying me, although I will say, if I'd been in their shoes, I might have done something similar."

Javyk raised an eyebrow. "Oh really? Should I be worried I'll get the same treatment?"

"So long as you pay me and you don't set me up for slaughter, we'll get along just fine, as I've already told you. Will we be working for you or whomever you work for?"

"You'll be working for me. I'll be paying you to protect me and young Dancer here, as well as something he's carrying, but who I work for is none of your concern. Prove yourself, and who knows what the future might hold, however."

"I just like to know who I'm working for," Rellen said, and he put a bit of iron in his voice. "That way, I know where to go if I don't get paid or I get dropped into a sausage grinder."

"You don't have to worry about that from me," Javyk said.

"Fair enough." Rellen shrugged. "We don't care too much where it comes from. How far are you headed?"

Javyk hesitated for a moment… obviously calculating how much to tell Rellen. "Yaylo, actually."

"That'll work," Rellen said, and the seed of his idea had sprouted into something more substantial. "The bounties were put out in Jabono, so we'll collect there. My wife and I will be able to escort you unencumbered all the way to Yaylo, although we'll have to attend to a few things in Jabono."

"How long?" Javyk asked.

"Not more than a few hours," Rellen replied. "Although I wouldn't be too worried. It's highly unlikely anyone, *especially* Delvers, would come after you in Jabono or the caravan enclave. Too many teamsters and other travelers about."

"I see your point," Javyk replied. "In that case, let us return to the enclave. I need to tend to young Dancer here, and I'm sure you have some talking to do with your wife."

"You have no idea," Rellen said.

"Assuming she agrees, I'll expect you to ride with us in the morning, and your employment will resume then. I'll pay you at the end of each day. Agreed?"

"Agreed," Rellen said, and they shook on it.

Javyk started to turn away but halted. "Oh! I almost forgot." He reached into his robes and pulled out a fairly heavy coin purse. "Here's the agreed-upon ten, the bonus five I promised, as well as the five and eight I would have paid the other two."

"Now that is downright generous of you," Rellen said. "But you have me wondering why?"

"Because you'll tell your wife, and it will influence her. It will also give you incentive to argue in my favor should she still be reticent." Javyk gave Rellen a sly grin.

"Well played," Rellen said.

"Then let's get going," Javyk said.

As they made their way back to the caravan, Rellen fought to keep the smile off his face. Things could not have gone better—aside from almost getting killed.

CHAPTER TWENTY

INTRIGUE AND DECEIT

We got out of there as soon as I locked down those last three Delvers," Rellen said, shaking his head. "We almost didn't make it." He glanced at Miranda, and she looked as perplexed as he felt by the situation.

The four of them sat close around their campfire as a cool wind blew over them from out of the mountains. They were all eating bowls of a savory and particularly tasty stew Miranda had fetched from the caravan cooks. The sun had gone down, and half a moon hung bright in a cloudless night sky. Xilly had managed to fly in over the river and alight in a nearby tree. Javyk and Dancer had left a short while earlier, probably having a meal themselves.

"What in Kalistar's name would Delvers want with those two?" Miranda asked.

"I have no doubt it's that artifact, and maybe even the sword they delivered," Rellen replied. "The Delvers got the sword, although I have no idea what happened to the other Nissrans or those two bodyguards, although they're probably dead. Dancer still has the artifact. What I did find peculiar is that Javyk didn't seem to care one way or the other about those other Nissrans. All he cared about was the artifact. We all need to keep in mind that he'll have no problem throwing us all to the wolves to protect it."

"Do you think the Delvers will come after them while they're with the caravan?"

"I doubt it, although I haven't told Javyk that."

"Why not?" Tavyn asked.

"It's too public. At least some good came of all this."

"What do you mean?" Mygal asked.

"Miranda and I will be working for Javyk as of tomorrow morning. Although we'll need to have another public fight about it tonight."

"What?" Miranda looked shocked.

"He was so impressed that he offered me a job as a bodyguard on their journey south to Yaylo. I told him I wouldn't do it without my wife." He gave her a wink.

"Oh, come on," Tavyn blurted. "You two have been fighting every night since we joined the caravan. Why would he agree to that?"

"It's simple, I told him there was nobody I trusted more in a fight, despite our arguments." Rellen glanced at Miranda. "I mentioned that she's all about the coin... that business was business... which is not too far off the mark."

She stuck her tongue out at him, and he winked again.

"And what about us?" Mygal said. "Your two bounties?"

"I told him I've known you both for a while, and this is just another bounty. Javyk is under the impression you two stole a good deal of money from someone who actually deserved to get robbed. A bounty was placed on your heads, and for Miranda and I, a bounty is a bounty. It's just business. I even suggested that under different circumstances, the two of you would make good additions to his bodyguards, if you weren't about to be delivered for the prices on your heads. He bought it."

"Not bad," Tavyn said, nodding slowly. "Not bad at all."

Rellen smiled. "I planted a seed, nothing more." He let out a long breath. "What I can't figure out is how to bring the two of you into the fold. It would be hard to explain if you're supposed to be in a jail cell or in the hands of some rich bastard with a grudge."

"What if we do a coin and carry?" Miranda asked.

"Coin and carry?" Rellen asked.

"I've never done it myself," Miranda said. The way she said it, however, made Rellen suspect she had. "But there are some bounty hunters who collect the bounty on their prisoners more than once, especially if the bounty can be paid in more than one city." She looked at Rellen. "I've even heard of hunters hiring their bounties after they break them out and even a few who trade off being the bounty that gets jailed. Their partners break them out again after, and the whole thing starts over... sometimes for even more coin."

"That might just work," Rellen said. "We'll have to get our stories straight, but we can work on it between here and Jabono."

"Jabono?" Miranda asked.

"That's right. Those two," Rellen nodded toward the carriage, "are headed for Yaylo, and I need to make a stop in Jabono. I figured, if we do anything, that would be the place to do it."

"I know a constable there. He owes me a couple of favors. His wife doesn't know about his mistresses." She smiled. "I suspect he'd be willing to falsify a report and post new bounties as a misdirect."

"That's all well and good, but what are you going to do about that artifact?" Mygal asked. "How do we figure out what it's for before Javyk has a chance to use it?" He glanced over at Javyk's carriage. "No matter what it is, it can't be for good."

"I agree, but for now, there's nothing we can do about it. I suspect we'll have to see it through to the end, although I don't know how. That's why I'm taking a detour at Jabono. I'm going to go see someone there and maybe get a few answers."

"Who?" Tavyn asked.

"There's a magic academy in Jabono, albeit a smaller one."

"What?" Mygal looked baffled. "You're planning on going in there to do some research?"

"Something like that," Rellen replied. "I have no intention of discussing the specifics. I need to know more, and I may be able to do that at the academy. My guts tell me that ring, or whatever, is the key to all of this, which means I have to learn everything about it that I can. All we know right now is that it came from the duke's study, it *might* have originally been found in a nuraghi, it's made of a good deal of Mavric iron, and that it's important to Javyk and, to a lesser extent, Dancer. For a while there, I was fairly certain it was going to kill the young bastard, no matter how many times Javyk healed the tissue. What they picked up today may just save his life, although I doubt it."

"What are we into?" Miranda asked, utterly perplexed.

"I don't know," Rellen replied. "The Vuoda hole just keeps going deeper, eh?" He eyed Miranda and then looked to Mygal and Tavyn. "Let's work on getting our stories straight and then get some sleep. I want us to speak as little as possible on the journey to Jabono, but we need to be prepared."

❦ ❦ ❦

Hours later, Rellen picked his way along the riverbank, avoiding the boulders and roots illuminated in the moonlight. He didn't need to go far, but he wanted to be far enough away from Javyk's carriage to do what he needed to. He'd gone about twenty yards, moving as silently as possible, when Xilly fluttered out of the darkness and landed on his shoulder.

Hello, little one, Rellen said. *I've missed having you around.*

Me too, Xilly replied. She coiled her tail around his neck and tucked her head under his chin. She quickly started making a soft thrumming sound. *Reporting in?*

I need to give Stevar an update… and ask him reach out to the Klymrukaar.

He moved another ten yards upriver, relieved his straining bladder, and then sat on a nearby rock. Pulling his cloak up around his body to form a tent of sorts, he removed his glowstone and spoke the incantation to activate it. Light bloomed inside his cloak, and he pulled a small piece of vellum from a belt pouch as well as a charcoal stick.

Nissrans in Sylverwynd. Send a detachment. Headed to Jabono. Miranda and I to be hired by target as bodyguards. Have plan to include "prisoners" as bodyguards. Must reach Yaylo to learn who target works for. Klymrukaar involved. Father dealt with them. Do you know more? If possible, send answer to Headmaster in Jabono. Arrive in three days.

Extinguishing the glowstone, he slipped it into a pocket within his cloak and pulled the cloak off his head. The air was cool, but not cold, and the sound of the river flowing by calmed his nerves, at least somewhat. That the Klymrukaar were involved really had him worried. He couldn't mention it to the others, not even Mygal, because his father had made it clear the Delver organization, whatever it was, preferred their secrecy and would kill to keep it. He rolled up the note and then summoned his avatar. When the small bird stood in his palm, he let it clamp down on the note and flutter off to the north.

He sat there for a few minutes, just going over everything in his head, wondering if he'd missed something. He didn't think he had.

Someone is coming, Xilly's urgent thought flared in his mind.

Rellen's hand went immediately to the grip of a falchion. *Which way?* Rellen strained to hear footfalls or anything else that would give away their position.

From the way we came, she replied. Rellen still didn't hear a thing. *He's quiet, I'll give him that,* Xilly said, sounding impressed. *Oh,* she added a moment later, *it's just Mygal.*

Rellen released the grip of his blade.

"I thought I'd find you down here," Mygal whispered as he appeared out of the darkness and stepped up beside Rellen. "I didn't hear you get up. Writing home?"

Rellen nodded, releasing his sword. "Just did. You?"

"I haven't since we left Svennival. I knew you were sending reports, and I told the king anything I said would duplicate that. No point in it, and there was some risk at being discovered."

"Agreed," Rellen said, rising to his feet. "What made you want to tonight? Anything in particular?"

"Not really. I figured it would be safe tonight, since those two are sleeping in the carriage rather than out in the open."

"The Delvers really shook Javyk." Rellen had gone over the whole thing in his mind again and again. "He said he was warned that he needed extra protection, but I'm convinced he had no idea Delvers were involved, which suggests one of two things."

"What?"

"That either the person he works for didn't know or didn't bother to tell him, and either answer just begs more questions."

"Why are Delvers such a big deal?"

Rellen let out a patient breath, remembering that he needed to be Mygal's mentor. "You just don't think about them, do you?"

"Delvers?"

"Yes."

"Well… no… I suppose I don't."

"Have you ever dealt with them? Had them involved in something you were doing, commit a crime, want information? Anything at all? Have you ever even just traded with them?"

Mygal went quiet for a moment. "No, actually. I can't say that I have."

"But you've seen them around, especially in Central Pelinon, right?"

"Yes."

"The Delvers are a curious people," Rellen said. "They keep to themselves. They don't share. They don't ask for anything. The only overlap there is between their society and ours are those points where trade takes place, and that's only because it is of use to them. They've never seemed to have much interest in humans as a whole."

"But they're part of Pelinon... they have a duchy right in the middle of the kingdom."

"That's true, but you won't find many humans living in the Duchy of Draksymsur. The caravans that pass through don't linger. Delvers have a funny way of letting you know you're not welcome."

"What about around here? Delvers have a huge presence."

"They do, but their business is their own, and they keep it that way. As we ride through the city tomorrow, keep an eye out for Delvers and whether or not any of them are chummy with humans or any of the other races you come across. The odds are, you won't see it, or if you do, it'll be once or maybe twice... That's all."

"Have you dealt with them?" Mygal asked.

"A few times in my life."

"And?"

"And that's all I'm going to say about it. Like I said, their business is their own." Rellen stepped away from the rock and motioned for Mygal to sit down. "Kept it warm for you," he said, smiling in the darkness.

Mygal sat down a bit stiffly as Rellen moved off. "Rellen?"

"Yes?"

"You have an awful lot of secrets."

"Yes." Rellen said unapologetically, "Yes, I do."

CHAPTER TWENTY-ONE
SERPENT IN THE GRASS

Tavyn had always been a light sleeper, so he heard Mygal loose his shackles and slip off into the darkness, presumably to catch up with Rellen, wherever he went. It was the best opportunity he'd had in a while to check in with his employer. He wasn't worried about Miranda. She snored like a sawmill and was obviously sound asleep. Tavyn had reported in every three days as instructed, usually when the others were asleep. The day's events, however, seemed worth an early report. Once Mygal left, Tavyn reached out and focused his will upon the large onyx set into the bracelet his employer had given him. He felt his way into the magics within and opened the connection.

Milord, he called.

There was a pause of a dozen heartbeats.

I hear you. The man's voice came immediately into Mygal's thoughts. *What do you have to report? I'm assuming there's a reason you're checking in a day early.*

There is. Rellen and Miranda have been hired as bodyguards by the Nissran Javyk, and once we get past Jabono, it is likely Mygal and I will join them under the guise of escaped bounties looking for work as bodyguards.

Why?

Rellen believes it's the best way to find out who Javyk is working for and what they want that artifact for.

Have you learned anything more about it? His employer had seemed keenly interested in the artifact's potential uses, from the first moment Tavyn had mentioned what Dancer carried.

Nothing about the artifact. It's still a mystery, apparently one for Javyk as well. It seems even he does not know what it's for. There is one thing though, and it's why I'm contacting you.

What is it?

Tavyn gently reached out with his ermajea, sending the lightest of tendrils across the connection. *Delvers are involved,* he said. He'd wanted to surprise his employer with that part, to gauge the man's reaction. He knew better than to ask what it was all about, but how people responded to such things told astute men like Tavyn a great deal.

Delvers? his employer replied. He seemed surprised, but only slightly so. Tavyn had expected his employer to be as shocked as Rellen had been, but this seemed little more than just a new and small detail in a very complex puzzle. *I hadn't expected that. Tell me exactly what happened.*

A small group of Delvers attacked the Nissrans today when Javyk went to meet them, and it seemed clear they were after both the sword and the artifact. Rellen believes they got the sword. The artifact is still with Dancer.

Now that is interesting, his employer said, and there was a long pause. *It would seem the Delvers know more than I'd hoped, although that isn't surprising. Did Rellen give any indication he knew who they were?*

No, Tavyn replied. *He seemed mystified by their involvement.*

He may not have recognized them.

Sir?

Never mind. Just keep doing what you've been doing. Play the part. Report. And if it looks like you'll be captured by those Delvers, make certain they don't find that bracelet. Dispose of it if you must, but only if there is no choice.

Why? Something like this must be worth a fortune.

It is. More than you could possibly imagine. If they find it on you, they will torture you to get to me, and neither of us wants that.

Tavyn swallowed hard. That was a bit more than he'd bargained for. *I'll keep that in mind,* he finally said.

You do that, and check in once you reach Jabono.

His employer broke the connection.

CHAPTER TWENTY-TWO

A PLAN BEARS FRUIT

T he caravan continued its long, uphill slog along a zigzagging stretch of the King's Highway that cut through the mountains between Sylverwynd and Jabono. Xilly paced them through old-growth pines that followed along on either side of the road. Rellen rode beside Javyk's carriage, while Miranda paced along ahead of the horses pulling it. They'd had their obligatory fight about being hired by Javyk the night before, and a fierce argument in the morning about securing Mygal and Tavyn's horses to the back of the carriage. Javyk had offered, Rellen had accepted, and Miranda had objected because she wanted control of the two, rather than having them just pulled along. Tavyn and Mygal's horses ended up being tied to the back of the carriage, their shackles secured to their saddles.

It all had gone exactly the way Rellen planned. He'd needed to create an opportunity for Javyk to feel comfortable conversing with him. With that riding arrangement—with everyone else just out of earshot, it was now inevitable.

"Rellen," Javyk called out, leaning his head slightly out the carriage window. "Could you come a bit closer? I wish to have a word."

"Of course." Rellen pulled lightly back on the reins and guided Shaddeth closer to the wheels. "What can I do for you?"

He took a quick glance at Dancer before focusing his attention on Javyk. The lad was huddled in the rear seat up against the far wall, asleep. He did not look well. His skin was almost as pale as Javyk's, but with a sickly pall that seemed decidedly unnatural.

"How long have you been a bounty hunter?" Javyk asked.

"Formally?" Rellen said, feigning surprise at the question. He'd been hoping Javyk was going to start a conversation. "For about six years... at least, that's when I joined the Guild."

"Do you enjoy it?" Javyk seemed to be genuinely interested in the answer.

Rellen was silent for a moment. "I *enjoy* good whisky. I *enjoy* hunting koodoo bucks in the mountains when the trees turn orange. I'm *good* at what I do, and I do what I'm good at to do what I enjoy."

"That seems very practical," Javyk replied. "As do you."

"Most bounty hunters are. We sort of have to be. Pragmatic. Unencumbered by compassion. Driven by coin. And, as a rule, unencumbered by extraneous relationships."

"Your wife being an exception?"

Rellen let out a long, weary breath. "Not really. That was pragmatism more than anything else. We discovered we work well together and *endure* each other to earn more coin."

"I don't suppose you're a religious or even spiritual man, considering all that."

Rellen chuckled bitterly. "I never had much use for the gods, like I told you before. My mother died screaming and coughing up blood with Selestina's name on her lips." Rellen's resentment for the gods was as genuine as the shining sun. His mother had been a devotee of Selestina. Prayers hadn't kept her from being cursed or dying in a bathtub. Neither had Rellen. Deep down, he blamed Selestina as much as he blamed himself. "They never did anything for me. I stopped when they planted my mother in the ground."

"There *are* some gods and demi-gods who answer prayers… for the truly faithful, anyway," Javyk said. "Although there is frequently a price."

"Are you saying my mother wasn't faithful enough?" Rellen replied with a bit of venom. "That Selestina rejected her because she didn't believe enough? Sacrifice enough?" Rellen let some of his genuine anger flow through.

"Not at all," Javyk said, holding up a calming hand. "I wouldn't ever presume." He looked thoughtful for a moment, as if he were searching for the right words to say. "What I am saying is that, with some of the gods, those truly devoted can overtly benefit from their faith… even their adoration."

"I'd believe it when I saw it," Rellen replied. "Are you one of them?"

"It's not something I like to talk about with just anyone," Javyk replied smoothly. "There are those who would… misunderstand… judge unfairly. Regardless, the answer would be meaningless to anyone other than myself and those who share my beliefs."

"Well then, who or what *do* you believe in?"

"I don't believe I'm quite ready to share that with you."

"Suit yourself," Rellen replied. He paused for a moment and then glanced at Javyk, looking as casual as he could muster. "Not that it's any of my business, but what was that whole trade thing about? I'm assuming that firebrand was payment or a reward for something."

Javyk stiffened suddenly, a suspicious look on his face. "Why do you want to know?"

"Seems a lot of trouble to go through just to deliver a simple sword, even a firebrand. And, let's be honest, the lot of you seemed to put a fair amount of ceremony into it. Only an idiot wouldn't assume it has to do with whatever faith it is you follow. If you don't want to answer, that's your business, but it'd be reckless of me to not ask about it. I do like to know at least a little something about who I'm working for."

Javyk let out a long breath. "While I'm not very comfortable with it, I suppose I can't fault you for the question." He looked thoughtful for a moment. "It's not a simple matter, but yes, that blade was a reward and possibly a means to an end."

"Was it more than just a firebrand?" Rellen asked. "Something special?"

"More than that?" Javyk replied. "I honestly don't know. I wasn't told, and I didn't ask." He looked thoughtful for a moment. "As for being special, only my employer and, I suspect, the one who receives it will know with any certainty."

"So, why did you have it?" Rellen asked as casually as he could. To ease Javyk's suspicious nature, he followed up with, "Let me guess? You borrowed it or something."

"No, nothing like that." Javyk managed a faint smile and seemed to have loosened up a bit. It meant Rellen was beginning to get inside the man's guard. "It was taken from someone in Sylverwynd a number of years ago. He only recently learned where it was, and I was sent to… *fetch* it… from Svennival."

"Must be valuable then."

"It's been my experience that objects the wealthy and powerful covet can vary quite a bit… and sometimes objects are merely tools meant to influence and manipulate." Javyk smiled. "A firebrand, for example. They are certainly impressive in battle, but they are not appreciably more dangerous as a weapon than a skilled warrior wielding a lesser blade. Their only real advantage is that they can start fires more easily and cause, perhaps, a bit more injury when slashing someone, although, they cauterize flesh, slowing or even preventing an opponent from bleeding out. I'm no warrior, but even I know that a few bleeding cuts can be the difference between victory and defeat. Considering the amount of energy it takes to create a blade like that, I would think they're hardly worth the expense and effort."

"You have a point there," Rellen said. Given a choice, he'd much rather have one of his falchions, hardened and sustained as they were, to a firebrand. "I've never been one to second-guess the whims of gods, nobles, or women."

"You are wise," Javyk said with a laugh.

"Can you tell me anything at all about what we might run into between here and Yaylo? If we're going to protect you, I'd like to know a little bit more about what we might come up against."

"I'm afraid I can't. I will tell you it's possible we'll run into more Delvers. If they're after the artifact, then I don't see why they'd stop. It could be brigands, mercenaries, or even bounty hunters. I don't how who is after it, let alone why. There are those who oppose my... employer. It is the nature of his endeavors. I will say this: his designs are far-reaching, and he holds an expanding sphere of influence. Serve him well, and you will be rewarded. I feel I must tell you, betrayal of any kind will be met with a most severe retaliation."

"That's the same all over," Rellen replied easily. "Every job is like that. As long as I get paid, I don't really care, and I like the idea of an open-ended association. So long as you have coin, I suspect I'll be available."

"I'm glad to hear you say that."

"I better go check on our prisoners. It's been a little too quiet back there, and I don't want any complications while we're on the road. Besides, the wife would chew me to pieces and spit out the bones if that happened."

"You make me glad I'm not married."

"There's good and bad, sir. Good and bad."

❁　❁　❁

At Rellen's suggestion, Mr. Bawth parked the carriage in the middle of the caravan once it had pulled over for the night. It was an easy sell to Javyk, the rationale being that in the middle of it, they were less likely to get attacked, especially by Delvers who might appear out of the darkness. Rellen also knew it would keep all conversation to a minimum. He didn't want anyone getting friendly. Friends got comfortable and comfort allowed people to make mistakes. If his next conversation with Javyk went well, then they'd be able to travel all the way to Yaylo with the man and meet his mysterious employer.

Xilly had taken up a spot at the edge of the encampment. She had curled up quickly and gone to sleep. Rellen knew she was starting to get fatigued, but there was nothing he could do about it.

Once the carriage brake had been set, Javyk and Dancer got out. Rellen and the others dismounted and began pulling their gear off the mounts, but Rellen kept his eye on Javyk.

"Go for a walk, Mr. Bawth," Javyk called out. "I have matters to discuss with these people, and it doesn't concern you."

"Of course, sir," the old man replied, nodding his head.

"Return in an hour so you can set up our camp."

Mr. Bawth nodded again and then strolled off. Although his back was turned to Javyk, Rellen caught the driver's relieved expression. Mr. Bawth apparently didn't care for Javyk's company.

Javyk motioned for Rellen and his companions to join him.

"I believe introductions are in order," Javyk said rather pointedly. "This is my... associate... Riven Sylvemar, although you may call him Dancer."

The lad looked weak, and Rellen thought he detected just a hint of a shiver flow across Dancer's body. He had to admit, the young murderer's discomfort gave him a certain amount of satisfaction—especially for what he'd done to Jacinda. Rellen had never inflicted a slow death on anyone, and he wasn't likely to, but he'd shed no tears over Dancer's continued suffering. It seemed poetic, and deep down, he hoped Javyk would go the same way.

"Of course," Rellen replied, stepping forward. "This is my wife, Miranda." Miranda gave a curt nod with a wary look on her face. Her eyes flicked to Rellen, and there was no missing the irritation there. They planned to maintain the tension, just dial back the arguments.

"Madam," Javyk said rather formally. "I'm pleased you are willing to engage in this new arrangement."

"Willing is a good word. I'm here for the coin, but we always keep up our end of the bargain." She eyed Javyk and then Dancer. "Keep up yours, and we'll get along well enough."

"Of that, you can rest assured." His eyes turned to the "prisoners."

Rellen pointed at the still-disguised Tavyn. "That is Tygeth Kurm, and the fellow beside him is Maybor Duvall. They're up for bodyguard duty, and we already have a plan for dealing with the bounties on their heads. It'll mean we're away from you in Jabono for a night, but after that, you'll have all four of us making sure nothing happens to you."

"And you don't mind the shackles?" Javyk asked.

"This is not the first time I've worn them to get paid," Tavyn said. There was no joy in his voice, but there wasn't any resentment either.

"And it's not the first time we've broken prisoners out after getting paid for them." Miranda glanced at Mygal and Tavyn. "I wasn't all that happy about turning them in, but a bounty is a bounty."

Mygal chortled. "*You* weren't pleased?" He got a sour expression on his face. "You also weren't the one getting sent to prison or a chopping block."

"It's a tough business, isn't it," Miranda fired back.

"We're not going to have a problem, are we?" Javyk asked, looking a little concerned.

"Not at all," Mygal said. "I don't have to like the people I'm working with. I should thank you, actually. This gets us off the hook and puts coin in our pockets." He gave Javyk a mischievous smile. "Once this job is done, I'm planning on heading further south with a different name and maybe even a different profession." He glanced at Rellen. "Bounty hunting is hard work with a lot of risk. Being a bodyguard, on the other hand, can sometimes have a lot of creature comforts... especially with the right employer."

"So, everyone is pleased with the arrangement?" Javyk asked.

"We are," Rellen replied. "I'll keep them shackled until Jabono, so nobody in the caravan is any wiser. Miranda and I will turn them in, get paid, and then arrange for them to join us in the caravan a day or three after it leaves. Like Miranda said, it's not the first time we've done this."

"Forgive me," Javyk said, "but I have to ask this question." His eyes flicked to Tavyn and Mygal. "How do you know they won't turn on you?"

"I can answer that," Tavyn said.

"Can you?"

"Yes. The truth is, if our roles had been reversed, it could easily have gone the same way." He looked at Rellen and Miranda. "We've known each other for a while now, and all things being equal, I actually trust those two more than any other bounty hunters I've known." He let out a long breath. "It's all about the coin."

"That's right," Rellen said. "We'll give them half of their bounties, and they both know there's good money to be made on the back side. I know them well enough to know they'd jump at a sack of dakkaris. Frankly, it's why they're wanted in the first place."

"Well," Javyk said, sounding a bit dubious, "if you show up at the caravan, I can assure you there's money to be made. It's vital I get to Yaylo without any further incident."

"We can make sure that happens," Tavyn said. "As long as the coin is genuine, I don't really care who I'm working for."

"Excellent. Seeing as you may be getting into trouble in Jabono, I think it's best that you not spend too much time with us on the road there. If the King's Guard comes asking questions, I don't want the whole caravan pointing them in our direction because of our association."

"That's a good point," Rellen said. "I'll stay close to the carriage the rest of the way. The three of them will hang back just as we've been doing. If you like, I can bed down a little closer to the carriage tonight."

Javyk shook his head. "I don't believe that will be necessary. Your suggestion to camp in the middle of the caravan was a good one, and you're close enough that, if there is any trouble, you can intervene."

"True enough. We'll keep a close eye on things and then join up on the other side of Jabono."

"Then, if you will excuse us, Dancer and I have matters to attend to."

CHAPTER TWENTY-THREE

JABONO

abono lay on the southern side of the Sylverwylde Mountains, situated at the base of the range just as Sylverwynd had been. Jabono had a much more civilized feel to it, however, spreading out further into the countryside, with taller stone structures and fewer wooden ones. The architecture, clearly influenced by the southern cultures, was also dramatically different. The city was a kaleidoscope of bright colors mixed in with pale gray stone and an abundance of straw-colored wooden struts and supports. The air above it was clear, for the inhabitants of Jabono were more interested in textiles and artistry than they were forging steel.

With the sun high in a cloudless sky, the caravan turned off the King's Highway to pass around the outer edge of the city on a swath of cobblestone road only a few decades old. Jabono had become so densely populated it was difficult to get the caravans through the city along the section of the King's Highway that passed through its center. The caravan would set up in an enclave along the river on the far side of Jabono, but

Rellen and the others broke away, assuring Javyk that Rellen and Miranda would rejoin the caravan in a few hours. Later that night, they'd break Mygal and Tavyn out.

When Javyk's carriage was out of sight, the four of them turned their horses and continued into Jabono, riding along the King's Highway. Tavyn and Mygal's shackles came off the moment they entered the city. They were discreet about it, but both of them had been looking forward to the moment they could remove them. They'd gone a few hundred yards along the King's Highway, with homes and shops passing by, when Xilly dropped out of the sky to once again perch on Rellen's shoulder. Rellen greeted her fondly, giving her a scratch beneath her chin as she coiled her tail around his neck.

Missed you, little one, Rellen said.

Missed you too, she replied. *I'll be glad when this is all over.*

Rellen gave her a large chunk of jerky from a pouch at his belt, and she tore into it voraciously.

How are you holding up? With all this flying, you must be getting tired.

Not tired... well, maybe a little, she replied. *It's mostly lots of riding currents. I could do this for weeks.*

Well, hopefully it won't be that long, but Yaylo is a long way from here, Rellen warned.

I'll be fine for as long as it takes.

When this is all over, it's a month of feasts for you, I promise.

Xilly nuzzled his throat. *I'll hold you to that.*

I figured you would, Rellen replied, and gave her another scratch.

"He's not at all what I expected." Miranda's voice broke in on their conversation.

"What?" Rellen replied.

"I said, he's not what I expected."

"Javyk?"

"Exactly."

Rellen got a thoughtful look. "I agree, but he's a Nissran. I have no doubt about that. The Nissran's I encountered in

Calamath mostly seemed like normal folks… until the lights went out, so to speak. Family members, neighbors, people they'd known for years had no idea they'd joined that wretched cult. That's their greatest strength, if you ask me. They're like a slow poison, seeping into a place a little bit at a time. And you don't know they're around until the bodies start stacking up."

"Do you think that's what was going to happen in Sylverwynd?" Mygal asked, massaging his wrists.

The streets were busy and full of music, with merchants and other inhabitants going about their business while bards on every street corner plied the crowds for coin.

"I'd bet my life on it. I can't imagine the six Nissrans who died in that warehouse were all of them. If only we could get that lucky." Rellen shook his head. "The bastards are everywhere now. I think we're going to be fighting them for a while, no matter what happens with Javyk and his employer. My worst fears are slowly coming true. Short of sending in troops and filling the streets with blood, I'm not sure we can stop it."

Mygal got a worried look on his face. "Maybe if we cut off the head?"

"Maybe." Rellen's expression went grim. "Javyk is going to get his. I'm certain of that."

"What if we're wrong about him?" Miranda asked. "What if he's just a courier escorting that artifact from Svennival to Yaylo? Do you know for certain he was involved in the murders?"

"Certain?" Rellen said. "No. I can't say that I am, but that's more a matter of semantics."

"He's just so… normal."

"You didn't see him in that warehouse. There's no doubt in my mind he's a Nissran. As to whether or not he was in the duke's house that night? I may never know with any certainty. That's beside the point. He's a zokurioi, so he *could* have been the one to subdue the duke and his family. Whether he was or not, he has that artifact, he's in charge, and he was ordering the Nissrans around like they were his very own slaves." Rellen let out a long breath. "He's not just a courier, of that I *am* certain. At some point, we're likely to see his true colors, and when he bares those particular teeth, you'll see how terrifying a Nissran can really be."

"Frankly, I hope I never find out."

"So do I. If they come out of the woodwork, blood will run in the streets, and we'll have to kill them all." Rellen intended to recommend a new state policy to his brother. If Nissrans were detected anywhere, the order would be to send a brigade of Corsairs to exterminate them. They'd learned how to detect and cleanse members of the cult in Calamath, and it was high time those methods were utilized in every corner of Pelinon. He just hoped it wasn't already too late.

"This is where we turn off." Miranda nodded toward a four-way intersection up ahead. "The constable I know is stationed up that way, about a quarter way around the city."

"Alright," Rellen said. "I have my own errand to run. Hopefully, I'll be able to learn at least a little about what we've been dealing with."

"Good luck," Miranda said as she turned her horse to the right.

"And be careful," Mygal added, following behind her. "We may have left our troubles behind us with Javyk and the caravan, but then again…"

"We may not," Rellen finished for him. "Don't worry. I'm always careful." He glanced at Tavyn, who seemed to be staring off into space. It struck him as a little odd, but then, they had been on the road for quite a while. Tavyn suddenly blinked several times and then nodded to Rellen, giving him a smile and a halfhearted salute.

CHAPTER TWENTY-FOUR

A SENSE OF URGENCY

T avyn watched the caravan disappear from view as Rellen led them into Jabono. Rellen and Miranda were once again content to chat with each other, and he could count on Mygal to join in. He knew his horse would follow the one in front of it, so it was as good a time as any to check in with his employer. He closed his eyes and focused his will upon the black stone once again. The connection came almost immediately, and with that, he opened his eyes so as not to rouse suspicion.

Milord, he called.

I hear you.

We have reached Jabono without incident and separated from Javyk. The plan is for Rellen and Miranda to meet up with him again tonight, after Miranda arranges for a constable here to legitimize our cover story.

And that is? his employer asked.

Mygal and I will have escaped after being turned in for the bounty. New bounties will be created with bad descriptions and different names. We'll meet up with them in a couple days and travel in the open as additional bodyguards. Rellen fully intends to play this out until he's discovered who is behind it all and why.

I expected nothing less. He was the perfect choice. You have played your part well, and I am more than pleased at how things are evolving. Rest assured, there will be even greater rewards for you once these events have run their course.

Do you know what is going to happen? What that artifact is for? Tavyn asked, hoping to pry at least a little information out of the man.

I do not, but that, after all, is the point of the exercise. Has there been any additional involvement by the Delvers?

No. If they're going to attack, assuming they followed us from Sylverwynd, then it will probably be at some point past Jabono.

Agreed. His employer went quiet for a moment. *It is vital that the Delvers do not take possession of that artifact. Once you learn what it is for, you must find a way to steal it away and bring it to me.*

Rellen isn't going to make that easy, assuming we can get it away from Javyk and whomever he's working for.

I have no doubt. If you can succeed, I shall double what I was going to pay you. With the Delvers involved, Rellen might learn the truth, and if he does, then it is likely that a number of my plans will grow even more complicated, if not completely unravel. Dedicate yourself to this one objective. Discover what Javyk's employer intends to do with that artifact, and then bring it to me. DO YOU UNDERSTAND?

The thought slammed into Tavyn's mind, and his employer's emotions flowed right along with it. They carried a profound urgency, an almost desperate hunger, and underlying it all was something else—something more deeply set in his employer's psyche: a desire to dominate.

I do, Tavyn replied, shaken by what he'd felt. *And I'll do everything in my power to make it happen.*

Excellent.

They're watching! Tavyn blurted. *I have to go.* He broke the connection and met Rellen's gaze, blinking several times. He nodded to Rellen and gave a smile and a halfhearted salute.

CHAPTER TWENTY-FIVE

THE CHANCELLOR'S GUEST

As he rode through the streets of Jabono, Rellen realized he was, for the first time in days, truly alone with his thoughts. He let out a relieved breath and leaned back a little in the saddle.

Are you alright? Xilly's query came gently from where she'd curled up around his saddle horn.

I'm fine, he replied. *It's just quiet.*

We normally travel alone, she observed.

Yes. He rubbed her between her shoulder blades. *I've been doing that a long time.*

To protect yourself, she said gently. *I understand.*

She probably did, Rellen thought.

It wasn't that he didn't like the company of Miranda, Mygal, and Tavyn. Sometimes, he just found it to be... exhausting. The past couple weeks had been especially so, and with Javyk and Dancer added to the noise, it was becoming difficult for him to bear. He was playing a role, and had been, day after day. He had to be careful what he said around Tavyn.

He had to be even more careful about what he said around Javyk and Dancer. He even, to a lesser extent, had to be careful what he said around Miranda and Mygal, although for different reasons.

Mygal...

Rellen shook his head. He'd really taken to the young Guardian—embraced the role as mentor. He hadn't expected it to happen so easily, but the idea of getting close to someone still filled him with... the only word was fear.

Jaquinn El Barad, the Second Guardian of Pelinon, had done something similar for him when he'd first joined the Guardians. Granted, Rellen hadn't been quite as green as Mygal, but there was a lot he'd had to learn, and Jaquinn had been a patient instructor.

He shook his head, pushing thoughts of Jaquinn and Mygal away. He didn't know what he was feeling—or maybe he wouldn't look at the emotions he felt.

He guided Shaddeth to the great, inner wall of Jabono. It was over six hundred years old, maintained obsessively by the duke and his family, and was still as defensible as it had always been. The King's Highway turned east, curving around the city wall. Rellen broke away, following a wide cobblestone of dark gray that led to the massive portcullis of the old city. There were guards on watch atop the wall, but the gate was fully open, and nobody stood in his path.

Navigating his way through the fairly heavy foot traffic, Rellen left the mostly wooden structures of New Jabono behind and entered Old Jabono. The inner portion of the city was more stone than wood and reflected their original Aradinian architecture. The buildings, some three stories high, possessed intricate stone carvings up the corners and along the rooflines. They depicted all manner of demons who, it was said, were the captive souls of Aradinian foes. At the corners of many buildings, just along the roof line, stone demons stood, squatted, or otherwise looked down on the passersby. The statues were frequently part of the gutter system, with rainwater pouring out of their mouths or other orifices. The roofs were very different from Central Pelinon. They curved out from the buildings and then back in, as if giant, squared radishes had been inverted and stuck on top of the buildings.

Rellen finally found himself in the Great Square of Jabono, where a large, three-tiered fountain sprayed water into the air. A ring of demons supported each tier, their grimacing faces showing the strain of their burden. To the right was the baronial seat of Jabono, a tall edifice, covered by demonic statues where the baron governed with—it was said—a magnanimous hand. Across the square from that was the reason Rellen had come. Jabono had the largest magic academy in the southwest regions of Pelinon.

He stabled Shaddeth in an attached livery, securing his gear with the usual protection spells, then walked up the wide, stone steps in the front of the academy. A handful of students, all exuberant and mostly noble youths, moved in and out of the main entrance to the school.

The massive front doors, heavily engraved with a wide assortment of runes, symbols, and sigils and made of thick timbers and steel bands, stood open. The area beyond was thirty feet across and circular. A series of old but colorful banners hung down the high walls, circling the entire chamber. In the center of the room stood an intricate, curving framework of silvery vines four feet high supporting a sphere of blue crystal the size of a human head.

The device was very familiar to him. There was one in the king's palace, as well as in all of the magic academies and most of the ducal palaces. Rellen stepped up to the stone, leaned in and said, "I am Rellen of Corsia. I wish to speak with the chancellor." And then he whispered the phrase only Guardians knew, "Aegon sul vas narivum."

A moment later, a small yellow spark drifted out of the sphere and passed beneath a red banner with a golden phoenix at the center. It passed between the two doors on the right that were now silently opening. Rellen brushed off his armor and strode through the doors to find a wide spiral staircase that went both up and down. The spark drifted upwards, and Rellen followed behind it up four flights of stairs and down a long, glowstone-lit hallway to a pale—almost white—wooden door. Warding runes covered the door.

The spark disappeared through the door, which remained closed, so Rellen stepped up and knocked three times.

Several moments later, it opened silently, exposing a wide room with tall windows that let in a fair amount of daylight. Bookshelves jammed to overflowing lined two inner walls. Off to one side was a long workbench covered with books, scrolls, and all manner of spell components. At the far side of the room was a massive desk made of the same pale wood as the door, and it was covered with more books.

Behind it sat an elderly Kapren female. Her fur was a dark gray with white showing around her eyes and her goat-like muzzle. A white patch of fur flowed from her chin, down her throat, and between her barely covered breasts. Two pairs of curled horns rose from her temples, twisting around each other and rising a foot above her head. They were pale white near her skull, faded into gray, and terminated at gleaming ebony tips. She wore a torc of bright silver, with large rubies set into the ends that almost touched each other beneath her chin. Gossamer robes of violet covered her body, with the front split down to her waist where a silver-chain belt secured it in place. A dark, metallic staff, five feet tall, topped with a large ruby and covered with runes, leaned against the desk. She stared at Rellen as he entered, with curious, yellow eyes that seemed to size him up in an instant. Her irises, flattened and rectangular like the rest of her species, narrowed when she focused on Xilly.

Rellen approached slowly and stopped only a few paces from her desk.

"Good morning, Guardian," the chancellor said. Her voice was soft but with the strange gravelly vibration of her people. "I am Lady Jassym Kag'Atrall. How may I help another servant of the Crown?"

"Good morning, Chancellor," Rellen said, bowing his head slightly. "I have come—" he stopped short. "Did you say another?"

"I did," she replied. "One of your kind was here only a few days ago, seeking answers."

"Was it Jaquinn El Barad?" Rellen asked.

"The very same, Rellen of Corsia." She lifted an eyebrow, and her head tilted to the side. "You look so very much like your father," she said gently. "I was very sorry to hear of his passing, as well as your mother's."

"Thank you, Chancellor," Rellen replied. He searched her eyes to see if there was the same disdain he received from others familiar with the court, and it was noticeably absent. "I appreciate that."

"Before we go too much further, I simply *must* ask." The chancellor fixed her gaze upon Xilly. "Is that an actual dragonette?"

"It is."

"And she's bonded with you?"

"She has." Rellen stroked Xilly's chin, eliciting a soft cooing sound.

"How did you come upon such a creature, let alone bond with it? They're exceptionally rare and, I believe, exceedingly mistrustful of humans."

"It's a long story, but the short answer is that I got her from—I believe—the last Strakhanni. Xilly was originally bonded to him. He perished. She bonded with me."

"A Strakhanni?" Jassym looked stunned. "I thought they were—" She stopped short and shook her head. "Never mind. As much as I would like to hear that story, it's obviously not why you've come."

She opened a drawer and pulled out a small, steel cylinder about two inches long, capped and sealed with wax. A small piece of vellum attached by a string bore his name.

"This arrived yesterday by carrier bird, so I've been expecting you."

"Thank you," Rellen said, taking it. He'd hoped Stevar would be able to provide some sort of reply. He broke the wax seal with a twist, pulled the cap off, and upended the cylinder over his palm. A slim strip of vellum, tightly rolled, fell into his palm. He handed the cylinder to the chancellor so it could be reused and then unrolled the note.

> *I know nothing specific regarding the Delvers in question. Trust them as you trusted Father and as you trust me.*
>
> *~ Stevar.*

It wasn't what he'd hoped for, but it was enough for him to proceed with the plan he had. He uttered a single incantation and the vellum caught fire in his hand, burning up in moments.

"Thank you," he said.

"Good news?" Lady Kag'Atrall asked.

"Useful," Rellen replied.

She nodded, another curious expression on her face. She took a long breath and let it out slowly, focusing her attention once again on him. "So, what is it I can do for you?"

"Before I get into that, can you tell me what Jaquinn came here for?"

"He had questions about possession."

"Let me guess…" Rellen said a bit uneasily. "Nissra's possession of her minions."

"Very good." Jassym looked a bit surprised. "That is precisely so."

"What did you tell him?"

"What I know." Her voice took on that of a scholar giving a lesson. "It is written in the scrolls of Mannesh the Unsleeping. The demon goddess Nissra and her cult employ several types or degrees of possession. Each one is more insidious than the last. The first and most basic is a simple sublimation of a person's higher will, whereby they will act in Nissra's interest and be loyal but would not overtly contradict his or her own personal ethic.

"Those inclined to serve Nissra and her interests would simply be more inclined to do so, with their loyalty running very deep. This can be achieved by the application of either ermajea or, in rare instances, zomajea through a rather lengthy spell that can be cast while the subject is awake or asleep. However, the one casting the spell, in addition to being a kurios, must have been directly influenced by an individual afflicted with the second degree of possession. An individual possessed in this manner is an active and willing participant of Nissra's designs, regardless of what their ethical inclinations might have been previously. They are committed—devoted to the point of taking the lives of others or themselves—in the service of their mistress.

"The third is altogether a different matter. One of Nissra's demons actually possesses the subject, subverting their will completely and assuming total control. Mannesh speculated that the demon within maintained some sort of contact with Nissra herself, but this was never proven or disproven. In the few instances where one was encountered, the subject had to be killed in order to release the demon, which subsequently also perished. This sort of possession is extremely rare, at least according to Mannesh, and involves a particularly complex spell requiring thirteen murders, the participation of twelve separate individuals who may or may not be kurioi, and a single symkurios who requires an entire month to cast the spell. The whole thing culminates on the eve of a new moon nearest a solstice."

With every word, Rellen's heart sank a little further.

"Did Jaquinn say why he was asking about Nissran possession?"

"No," Jassym looked somewhat perplexed. "In fact, he was quite emphatic on not conveying that information." She gazed into his eyes. "Is that why you are here? The Nissrans? I've heard rumors that after centuries, they're beginning to make somewhat of a resurgence."

Rellen hesitated for just a moment. Under normal circumstances, he—like the other Guardians—didn't relate what were considered state secrets involving the security of Pelinon, unless they had no choice. The situation, however, was rapidly growing out of hand. Everywhere he went, it seemed, Nissra and her wretched cultists were cropping up. The whole of Pelinon needed to be warned, as far as he was concerned, although that wasn't up to him. It would be up to his brother.

"All I can tell you is that I came here for a different reason, but it's at least related to the Nissrans. I will also say that you should be on the lookout for any signs of their presence here in Jabono and notify the baron immediately, if you find any. Speak of it to no one else, however. If everyone were to start seeing Nissrans in every alley, it would be that much harder to track them down."

"I understand. That being the case, then my initial question still stands. What can I do for *you*?"

"Do you have vellum and something to write with?" Rellen asked.

"Of course," she replied, making it clear it was a rather foolish question. She opened a drawer to her desk and pulled out a sheet of vellum, a slim blue quill, and an engraved ink and blotting set made of slightly tarnished silver. She placed them on the desk in front of him.

Rellen took the quill, dipped it, and quickly sketched out the artifact. He made it as accurate as possible, getting the symbols around the outer edge as close as he could, but there was no doubt they were, at best, rough approximations. He'd only seen it at night, and at a distance.

As he worked, the chancellor looked increasingly interested.

When Rellen was finished, he turned the sheet of vellum around. "This artifact is about ten inches across, and I'm pretty sure it's made with at least some Mavric iron. The fellow carrying it showed all the signs of Mavric poisoning, including the red skin and blisters."

"Someone is carrying it?" Jassym blurted. "If it's Mavric, it would most certainly kill him."

"I thought it was going to. It's now in a bag lined with, I suspect, lead."

"That would probably be the case," Jassym said, thoughtfully.

"He's with a zokurios who was doing his best to keep him alive. He still seems to be ailing, although it's slowed now that they have it in the lined satchel."

The chancellor opened a desk drawer and pulled out a metal ring. Rellen's eyes went wide. It looked very much like Javyk's artifact, except that it was dark metal and only about six inches across. The cutouts inside the ring were in different positions, and there weren't as many symbols on its surface, but there was no mistaking the similarities.

"What are these things?" Rellen asked

"They're called plunnokoi, or lesser keys," she said simply. "The two I've seen were different sizes, both smaller than the one you've described. They were made from different materials, one plunnokum was of marble, and this one is simple steel. They had different symbols on them, both in the same lost language. They all have the similar grooves and notches along the interior edge, but not in the same positions."

"A key for what?"

"I've been told they're used to secure structures, passages, rooms, even compartments..." She gave Rellen a warning look. "All within *nuraghis.*"

Rellen's eyes went wide.

"An old friend of mine discovered this one recently and let me borrow it for a time to see if I could identify where it came from and where it might be used. He knows much more about plunnokoi than I do."

"I don't suppose you could arrange for me to meet your friend?"

"He'd been away for some time, but you're in luck. He returned to Jabono this morning aboard a dewkalve transport. Thorfyll," she called out, "would you come in here please?"

Dewkalve, Rellen thought. *He must be ridiculously wealthy.*

Heavy, booted feet approached the door, and a moment later, it opened. A short, stocky figure in dark plate mail stepped in. He was less than five feet tall and nearly as wide. His muscular physique seemed to be crammed into the armor. He wore no helm, and his hair was a fiery mix of red, orange, and streaks of gray that spread out from his scalp in a wiry mane. Two thick braids came down from his beard, while the rest stuck out with a life of its own. Etched into the neck ring of his plate was the symbol of the Klymrukaar.

It was the Delver who had saluted Rellen back in Sylverwynd. His fierce, dark eyes met Rellen's, filled with recognition, and narrowed suspiciously.

Rellen grabbed the hilt of a falchion, ready for a fight.

CHAPTER TWENTY-SIX

ANSWERS AND QUESTIONS

"G entlemen!" Jassym shouted as she rose out of her chair. She grabbed her staff. "Aztukahm!" she snapped and pounded the base of the it into the floor. A curtain of pale light sprang up between Rellen and the Delver, shimmering with magical force. "Calm yourselves!" she snapped as she came around the desk. "I'll not have any fighting on academy grounds."

Xilly let out an angry screech, flapping her wings with the commotion.

"You won't need those with me, boy," the Delver said, holding up his hands, a wary look on his face.

Rellen froze, his eyes shifting between the chancellor and the Delver. *What was he doing here?*

"It's alright," the chancellor soothed. "Thorfyll is an old friend of mine, and an ally to the Crown."

"I know he's a Klymrukaar," Rellen said. "I recognized the symbol, but the last time I saw him, he and his friends were trying to kill me."

"Not you, exactly," Thorfyll said, eying Rellen, "So. You know about us, do you? There's not many humans that do. Is that why you pulled that last punch?" Thorfyll took several cautious steps into the room and lowered his hands. "You could have gassed the lot of us, but you didn't on purpose, I think."

"That's right," Rellen said.

"Then you have my thanks," Thorfyll said with a slight bow.

Rellen relaxed and pulled his hand away from his blade.

"So, can I assume you two won't try and kill one another," Jassym asked, eying Rellen suspiciously.

"You have my word," Rellen replied.

"And I wasn't going to," Thorfyll added.

"Very well then." Jassym double-tapped the floor with her staff, and the curtain of light faded from view.

"How is the one I wounded?" Rellen asked.

"Magradol is on the mend," Thorfyll replied, a curious expression on his face. "You have my thanks for that... and my respect. There's not many can get inside Magradol's guard once he has a blade in his hands."

"Perhaps some introductions are in order," the chancellor said, moving back around her desk.

"Agreed," the Delver said heartily. "My name is Thorfyll, Warmaster to the Duke of Draksymsur, and I give you my oath, there is no fight between us, kurios, unless you bring it. In fact, I suspect we have much to discuss, particularly considering the company you keep."

"I'm Rellen of Corsia, and—"

"Are you, now?" Thorfyll said, interrupting him. His expression softened, and a strange look of recognition filled his face, as if he were happy to hear Rellen's name. He cocked his head to the side, examining Rellen's face closely. "You have your father's jaw, lad, and your mother's eyes."

A shock of surprise hit Rellen like a hammer. "You knew my parents?"

"I did. I know you too, although I suspect you were too young to remember me."

"I only remember one Delver ever coming to the palace, and that was Thymvaar Dunkminschakt, the Duke of Draksymsur. I don't remember you."

"I know Thymvaar well. He and I share a father but not a mother." Thorfyll eyed Rellen. "There was a war council. The uprising in Kapren'Maji when the new Kapren duke wanted to break away and join the Freehold of Kapren'Zuur. Your father had asked my brother and I to lend our wits and our blades, as well as guide them under the mountains. You and your brother—you were just boys at the time—came running in, asking to join the fight."

A vague recollection bubbled up in Rellen's memories. The revolt of Kapren'Maji had taken his father away from the palace for several months. The king had returned with a bandaged arm and a victory.

"There were four of you there," Rellen said slowly, "and my father was furious that Stevar and I had interrupted the council. He ordered us to leave, and we ran out." He tried to remember the faces of the Delvers that had been there. One had most certainly been Duke Dunkminschakt. Rellen tried to see his face, and he realized that this Delver did, in fact, look similar to the duke. The memory was distant, fuzzy. He finally shook his head, giving up. It didn't matter. What mattered was Thorfyll had obviously been there with his father and the Duke of Draksymsur. He was also Klymrukaar.

"That's right," Thorfyll said. "So, we can talk, or I can go get my sword and we can step outside?" He gave Rellen an amused smile.

"I think I would much rather *speak* with you," Rellen said.

"I'm glad you feel that way, because there is much we must discuss, considering the circumstances."

"I am obviously missing something," the chancellor said. "Would one of you care to enlighten me?"

"I'm afraid I can't, Jassym," Thorfyll said. "I beg your forgiveness, but I must speak with young Rellen alone. It has

to do with something of vital importance to the Klymrukaar…
and perhaps Pelinon, but the fewer who know about it, the
better."

"As you wish," Jassym said, clearly disappointed. "Feel
free to talk out on the balcony. I have other matters to attend
to in the meantime."

"Thank you, old friend," Thorfyll said.

Rellen was surprised to hear a Delver say something like
that, even to a Kapren.

"Come on, lad," Thorfyll said, turning. "There's juice and
pastries out there, and the sunshine is glorious." Without
another word, Thorfyll turned and walked out the door he'd
entered through.

Rellen followed onto a wide balcony overlooking the city
square. The fountain splashed a short distance away, birds
sang somewhere along the rooftops above, and the sunshine,
was, in fact glorious, casting the entire balcony in bright,
warm, sunlight. Several chairs sat around a table where it
looked as if Thorfyll—and perhaps Jassym—had been having
a light meal before Rellen interrupted them. There were two
decanters of fruit juice, one full and one empty, as well as a
platter of pastries and a large tray of meats and cheeses.

Thorfyll motioned for Rellen to take a seat and then
poured each of them a glass of the amber fruit juice. Thorfyll
took a sip of the juice, eying Rellen carefully. "What brought
you to the academy?"

"I needed answers, and this was the only place between
Sylverwynd and Yaylo where I might get them. Even coming
here was a long shot." Rellen wondered how much he could
or even should tell the Delver.

"And the man you travel with?" Thorfyll asked, raising an
eyebrow. "The pale, thin one in black. How did you come to
be in his company?"

Rellen bit his lips. *Should he tell the Delver everything?* "I'll
answer that question, but first I need to know something."

"Ask."

"Do you know who—I mean *what* I am?"

Thorfyll looked at him, as if he were a scholar gazing upon a portrait he'd studied his entire life. "You are Rellen of Corsia. Born Rellen Falcoria, the eldest son of King Saren II and his first and only wife Lewellyn, may she rest in peace. You abdicated the role of king six years ago—having never placed the crown upon your head—and became a Guardian shortly thereafter at the behest of King Saren III. You are now the ninth of thirteen Guardians, at last count. You are both a warrior and symkurios of respectable ability." Thorfyll leaned back, a thoughtful expression upon his face. "And had I known you were involved before our attack on that wretch Javyk, I would have elicited your help beforehand."

"Help with what?"

"Solving a mystery," Thorfyll said, "a very old one."

"The duke of Svennival was just murdered," Rellen said.

"Not that mystery. While lamentable—Belvenim was a good man—his demise is of no import to us. Dukes come and go."

"Us, who is us?" Rellen felt like the conversation was unraveling. The bloody Delver was only making things worse—stacking mystery on top of mystery.

"The Klymrukaar, of course," Thorfyll said, as if Rellen were a confused child. "I wish there was more I could tell you, but for now, I will tell you what little I can. It will be much more than I should. You see, I believe your presence is fortuitous... perhaps even more than that." He rubbed his chin thoughtfully, as if he were contemplating how far to test a boundary. "There are those," he started slowly, "who would rather all of this get quickly and quietly buried... forgotten in the dust of time, just as we thought it had once been in the dust of Vladysh Belvenim's study."

"The—what did the chancellor call it—the plunnokum?" Rellen asked. "That's what you're after, isn't it?"

"That and the sword, although, for very different reasons." Thorfyll sat forward. "We recovered the sword, and it will soon make its way into the hands of its rightful heir. I and my associates came to Jabono via a dewkalve transport to make another attempt at killing Javyk and taking back the plunnokum. This time, with greater numbers."

"You say that as if you've changed your mind," Rellen said.

"I'm debating that very thing, and to do so would be to disobey an edict set down a thousand years ago." Thorfyll stared deep into Rellen's eyes. "Tell me, what are your intentions? Why is it that a Guardian of Pelinon travels with, nay, *protects* a villain such as Javyk Sukari?"

"Because, before I execute him for the murder of Duke Belvenim, I need to know why he did it. And everything revolves around that damn artifact. He's using a young man from Svennival to deliver it to someone in the south. Above all, I need to know not only who that is, but why they want it."

"Why is that answer so important to you?" Thorfyll asked.

"I believe it has to do with the Nissrans, and it would appear their influence is growing. I'll stop them, even destroy them if I can, and the best place to start is as high up in their ranks as I can reach. Whomever Javyk serves is likely to be high up, indeed."

"Your reasoning is sound," Thorfyll said, "and I'm inclined to let you try, despite the greater risks."

"Risks, what risks?"

"If we—now *you*—fail to stop Javyk and his master..." Thorfyll let out a long, calculating breath. "Well, let's just say the resulting devastation to Pelinon and her allies could be beyond anyone's comprehension."

"What are you talking about?" Rellen said, getting more frustrated with every word the Delver uttered. "Why does my involvement change anything?"

"Because it serves the purposes of the Klymrukaar, and none of us can do what I believe needs doing. Humans breed much faster than Delvers, and we—well, I—believe, despite our best efforts, that a war is coming."

"War?" Rellen asked, a pang of worry coursing through him. "What war? Damn it, what are you talking about?"

Thorfyll shook his head sadly, his face full of regret. "I'm sorry. It is not something I can speak of. At least, not yet. I know this must be maddening, but I'm constrained by an oath that goes back over a millennium. I've already said more than I should, but you must understand, everything I've said is for your benefit and with the best of intentions for all of us. More than anything, I want to at least point you in the right direction. You may be able to expose truths where I would be obligated to bury them."

"You speak in riddles," Rellen blurted. "Can't you just give me one straight answer?"

Thorfyll was thoughtful for a moment and then he slowly nodded his head. "Yes, I believe I can."

"Thank the gods."

"As I said, we traveled by dewkalve to beat Javyk to Jabono and take back the plunnokum. I've concluded that doing so would be more harmful. Your presence opens a number of possibilities, and I believe those possibilities must be permitted to unfold."

"You're doing it again," Rellen warned.

"I haven't finished," Thorfyll said, holding up a hand. "I believe it is now your duty, perhaps your destiny, to unravel the mystery behind the plunnokum. It's a key, a very powerful one."

"A key to what?"

"A door within a nuraghi."

"The chancellor already told me these plunnokoi are keys for locks in a nuraghi," Rellen said. "What—"

"Before you ask," Thorfyll interrupted, holding up a hand, "we do not know which door or what lies behind it. We don't even know where the nuraghi is. However, we are certain Javyk's employer does. They seek what lies beyond, and we believe all their thought is focused upon opening it. Our initial intention was to simply take the key and lock it away in a place no one would ever find. However, I believe your presence has changed all that. With you involved—rather than the

Klymrukaar—the truth may, finally, be known to all. I am inclined to trust to your abilities."

"If this is so important to the Klymrukaar, why trust me?"

"Because, Rellen of Corsia, you have your father's eyes. When I first learned you turned away from the throne and permitted your brother to take your place, I was more than impressed."

"Impressed? Why?"

Thorfyll gave him a thoughtful look. "I've never known a human to turn aside power when it was within such easy reach. You may be just what I've been looking for, and for a very long time."

"I don't understand."

"Unfortunately, I'm not at liberty to explain that either."

Rellen gritted his teeth. He'd had just about enough of the obtuse, little Delver.

"Suffice it to say," Thorfyll continued, "as a Guardian of Pelinon, your duty coincides with our... or rather *my* designs. This has not happened since the war with the Kapren, but I am inclined to trust the portents."

"So, what happens next?" Rellen asked, exasperation filling his voice.

"Continue on your way. Stay with these Nissrans. Follow them to whatever it is they seek. But—and I cannot emphasize this enough—once they use that key, stop them at all costs from going any further. You cannot permit them to reach whatever lies beyond. Stop them. Kill them. At that point, find us, and we will see what we will see."

"How will I know how to reach you?"

"Send word to Jassym. She knows how to reach me."

Rellen let out a long, frustrated breath. "You know, I think this may have been the most exasperating conversation I've ever had... and I'm certain I'm not much better off than when we started."

Thorfyll smiled. "Trust me, you are, you just don't know it yet." He rose to his feet. "I'm afraid I have to get going. This change in plans requires me to attend to a few things before they go into motion. I will, however, leave you with one warning."

"What's that?"

"Whatever you do, do not touch that key directly, and keep any exposure to a minimum. The satchel they procured in Sylverwynd will protect you, but without it, you can expect injury, pain, and a slow death."

"So it *is* Mavric iron?"

"In part… and *much* more." Thorfyll stared at Rellen for several moments. "Farewell, Rellen. Your journey is certain to be perilous. For the sake of us all, we must hope you are up to the task." The Delver turned and strode out through a different door. When it closed, Rellen just sat there, shaking his head.

"Bloody Delvers," he muttered. He looked at Xilly. *Remind me to never trust a Delver to make things better, would you?*

I promise, she said.

● ● ●

Rellen sat astride Shaddeth with Xilly perched upon his shoulder. He was lost in thought as he waited for his companions just outside the southern gate of Jabono. He'd gone over the conversation again and again, looking for some clue, some bit of information that might just make sense of it all. He wondered how the others would take to the idea of entering a nuraghi.

"What's wrong?" Miranda asked as she, Mygal, and Tavyn rode up.

"Hmmm? What?" He said, turning his gaze to her.

"From the looks of it, you didn't get the answer you wanted."

"Oh, I got answers, alright," Rellen snapped.

Several heartbeats ticked by as Rellen continued to fume.

"Well?" Miranda asked, an expectant look on her face.

"That thing Dancer has been carrying? I know what to call it now. It's a plunnokum." He was starting to take a perverse delight in leading her on, the way that damn Delver had led him on.

"A plunnokum." Miranda's expression was blank. She blinked her eyes several times, waiting for him to elaborate. Obviously, she was better at this game than he was.

"It's a *key*. And it opens a door..." He blew out an angry breath.

"That's it?" Miranda asked, cocking her head to the side. "It's a key and it opens a door?"

"That's right," Rellen growled. "I have no idea where the bloody door is, let alone what's on the other side." He slapped his thigh. "Oh! I do know it's in a nuraghi. And we have to go in."

Everyone's eyes went wide, and the driver of a wagon passing by gave Rellen a shocked look before quickly turning away. Nuraghi were things decent people didn't talk about.

"Wait a minute," Mygal said, holding up a finger. "I thought you said going into a nuraghi was bad."

"It is, but it looks like that's where we're headed. To open a door. With a key."

"How'd you learn all this?" Miranda asked.

For a moment, Rellen considered telling them everything, but his good sense got the better of him. Not even Mygal was in a position to be aware of the Klymrukaar. Technically, *he* wasn't supposed to know... only the king. Then there was the matter of Miranda and, *especially*, Tavyn. They certainly couldn't know about the Delver organization. If he told them one of the Delvers he'd fought in Sylverwynd was his source, he'd have to go bounding down that Vuoda hole, and he wasn't prepared to do that.

"I learned it in the magic academy," he finally replied, and let out another frustrated breath. He didn't like keeping them in the dark, but he had no choice. "We were right about one thing. It's made of or at least has Mavric iron in it. Whatever you do, don't touch it."

"Well, that's *something*, at least," Miranda said, giving him a patient smile.

"I suppose," Rellen said grumpily. "I swear, I've never had questions stack up like this. It's maddening."

"You'll figure it out. You always do."

He rolled his eyes and stared off toward the south. Whatever Javyk's employer wanted, it was down there—somewhere.

"Rellen," Miranda said, "there's something you should know." The way she said it made the hairs on Rellen's neck rise.

"What's that?"

"My friend, the constable, told me that three people have gone missing in the past week—people of means, not dregs—and one of them turned up this morning... *butchered*." She leaned over and handed him a piece of vellum. "The man had this carved into his forehead."

Rellen took the vellum, and when he opened it, his blood went cold. He lifted harrowed eyes and peered through the city gates into the bustling city of Jabono.

"Curse them," he growled. "Curse all Nissran swine." He crumpled up the vellum with a creak of straining leather as his gloved hand tightened into a fist. "This just keeps getting better and better."

Miranda nodded slowly.

"What's going on, Rellen?" Mygal asked. "How many cities does that make?"

"They've turned up in at least three that I know of, and I doubt that's all of them at this point."

"So, what do we do now?" Tavyn asked. "Same plan?"

"It has to be." He turned to Miranda. "Did you get everything arranged with the constable?"

She nodded. "He'll make the announcement and post bounties for two escaped prisoners. There will even be sketches of two different people. That *should* keep any bounty hunters from spotting us in the unlikely event they track us to the caravan. I'm not too worried about it."

"Good." Rellen said. He turned to Tavyn. "Miranda and I will go join Javyk and play dumb. You two stay in the city for two nights and then join the caravan as fast as you can."

"It shouldn't be a problem," Tavyn said. "And I'll take the opportunity to collect on what you owe me." He patted the tattoo on his arm beneath his tunic sleeve.

"You do that, just be careful. Use one of the collector's offices on the other side of the city from where you met the constable."

"Good idea," Tavyn said. "We'll find an inn near there as well."

"One other thing," Rellen added, "if you don't have glowstones, get one or two. If we're headed into a nuraghi, then the odds are it'll be dark. The ruins I've been in were generally built deep into the earth, with most of the structure underground. And get extra food."

Mygal said, "I did have one question."

"What?"

"What if those Delvers show up again? You'll be outnumbered pretty badly, even if there's only six of them like last time. They might even come at you with reinforcements."

"We'll have to risk it," Rellen said. "But I'm not too worried. I doubt they'll come this far south to get us. Delvers rarely get too far from the mountains or their duchy." The good news was, that lie was mostly true. "Be on the lookout for them, though."

"I will," Mygal said.

"And from here on out, I want everyone on guard. This thing keeps getting bigger and bigger, and I have no idea where it's going to lead us. Understood?"

They all nodded.

"Then let's get going," he said, looking at Miranda. "I don't want to raise Javyk's suspicions. We've come too far to make a stupid mistake now."

He shook Shaddeth's reins and edged him up to a trot. Miranda fell in beside him, and they left the city gates of

Jabono behind. The enclave was about a half mile away, down a long hill, and set along the bank of the river. It was virtually identical to the one in Sylverwynd, and it looked as if seven large caravans were camped there.

Rellen and Miranda entered the enclave and located Javyk's carriage in short order, again set slightly apart from the others. They rode up to find Mr. Bawth getting a fire started. Javyk seemed to be inspecting Dancer's back again, but he quickly lowered the young man's tunic as Rellen and Miranda drew near. He stepped away from Dancer and waved, giving them an almost friendly smile as they rode up.

"I take it things went well?" Javyk asked.

"They did. We got our bounty—" Rellen patted a saddlebag for emphasis "—and everything is set for tonight. If you hear us getting up in the middle of the night, don't worry. We'll attend to our business and be back in a couple of hours. Nothing is going to happen to you this close to Jabono with all these King's Teamsters around."

"Very good. What happens after your excursion tonight?"

"Our friends will stay here in Jabono an extra day or two in a room under my name. No one will see them enter or leave, and they'll head out the following day. At that point, they're just two travelers hurrying to catch up with a caravan. I still need to arrange for them to join—under different names of course, but that won't be a problem."

"I must say, you are very efficient," Javyk said.

"I'm... *we're*—" he corrected, glancing at Miranda who glared at him with her hands on her hips, "—good at what we do."

"*Hmph!*" she added.

"Now, if you'll excuse me, I have to go pick up some more supplies for tonight's excitement." He looked at Miranda. "My wife will be happy to stay here, won't you, my love?" She glared at him, but she got off her horse and started leading it toward the river. "If you set up the fire," he called out, "I'll be happy to light it when I get back."

She flashed him a very unladylike gesture over her shoulder and kept going.

Rellen looked at Javyk and rolled his eyes. "Isn't love just grand?"

CHAPTER TWENTY-SEVEN
YAYLO AND MILORD

The journey to Yaylo was blessedly uneventful.

When Tavyn and Mygal joined the caravan, they wore a fresh set of clothing and even a few pieces of light armor. Tavyn had reverted to a combination deep blue and indigo garments with a black cloak. Mygal wore green and gray leathers under a hardened, black leather cuirass.

There had been little conversation along the way, as Rellen wanted to make a point that Tavyn and Mygal were working with them but there were still some hard feelings. Xilly kept pace through the forest during the day, and each night, Rellen prepared a new spell or potion, digging deep into his repertoire so he could be as ready as possible.

Each day, Dancer grew weaker and weaker, to the point where Javyk had to help him into and out of the carriage, a thing Rellen was actually surprised to see. It was as if Javyk actually cared for Dancer and his plight. It didn't match up with his notion of a man capable of slaughtering the duke and his family.

Rellen had never seen severe Mavric sickness before, but there was no doubt the plunnokum was slowly killing Dancer. As much as he hated when death took a life, he could find no pity or compassion in his heart for Dancer.

Rolling hills gave way to flat country after the third day and thick forests turned to farmland on the morning of the sixth. The air now smelled of the sea. Gulls danced amidst a spotty, low ceiling of puffy clouds, and there was no sign of rain. Rellen had never been to Yaylo, or even this far south before, so he took in the new sights and sounds with at least a little wonder. He'd grown up in Corsia and spent most of his military career in the Demonspine Mountains or the central valley of Pelinon proper.

In the distance, the high, white walls of Yaylo gleamed in the sun. It, like the king's palace, was nearly a thousand years old, and its architecture was even more markedly different than Jabono's had been. Every tower along the walls and within the city was topped by, what Rellen could only describe as, an inverted turnip, round on the sides and coming to a sharp point at the top. Those along the walls and topping the main fortress within were all a brilliant green, but those around the city had been painted an entire rainbow of hues. Rellen knew little of Yaylo's history, other than that King Jakore IV had conquered the city and created the Duchy of Dharfaal almost three hundred years earlier in a particularly bloody war.

A vast port stretched out to the left and right of the city, with the towering masts of sea-going ships poking up like the spines of some bizarre reptile. Rellen had to admit, Yaylo truly was a beautiful city by the sea, at least at this distance, and he found himself thinking its beauty even rivaled the grandeur of his own home city of Corsia.

A quarter mile from the city, the caravan turned off the King's Highway, headed for an enclave as usual. Javyk's carriage, however, continued on, straight through the main gate, passing beneath the largest iron portcullis Rellen had ever seen.

The city streets were even more busy than Jabono's had been, and the clothing here had a distinct style to it, with splashes of bright color, accentuated by sashes and turbans of metallic silk. Yaylo was a city of wealth, and it showed clearly in the garments and jewelry of the people going about their business.

The carriage had gone several blocks when a small, gray bird fluttered out of the sky and landed on the windowsill of the carriage. Javyk's hands appeared, grasping the bird, and then disappeared from view.

A messenger, Rellen thought. Some zokurios were able to utilize birds and other creatures to deliver messages. Usually, the distances involved were not great, and both the zokurios and the animal had to have encountered either the destination or the person intended. It was one of the skills he wished Miranda possessed. Although she was able to hurt or heal any living thing, such complex manipulation and control of wildlife was beyond her.

Several minutes later, the bird appeared on the windowsill and fluttered out of sight, headed toward the ocean. Javyk leaned out the door and slapped the side of the carriage.

"Mr. Bawth, take us to the Star of the Seven Sisters."

"Yes, milord," the old driver called back. "Straightaway."

Javyk then turned and motioned for Rellen to come closer.

Rellen gave Shaddeth a squeeze and caught up with the carriage. He took a quick glance at Dancer and fought to keep the shock off his face. Only partially hidden by his hood, Dancer was ghostly white and gaunt. Dark circles ringed his sunken eyes, and he seemed to have lost a frightening amount of weight, with his cheekbones and jaw pronounced to the point that Rellen could almost make out the shape of his skull.

The most disturbing part of it was, Dancer had willingly— even enthusiastically endured it. He seemed grateful for the *privilege* of carrying that damn plunnokum. Rellen had seen the fervor—the adoration of Nissrans in Calamath. But this? This was something else altogether, and it sent a shiver down his spine. If all Nissrans were equally willing to endure such torture, then Pelinon was in terrible danger.

He tore his eyes away without giving any reaction and fixed his gaze upon Javyk. He didn't want to ask the obvious question. If Javyk didn't offer, Rellen wouldn't pry.

"I've just received word from my employer."

"I hope this is about our coin."

"Indeed it is. We're headed there now. You will be introduced to my employer—briefly, so he may offer his thanks, pay you in full, and dismiss you. From there, you can go about your business, but I would like to have a means of contacting you in the future. I've been very pleased with your performance."

"We'll be in Yaylo for a while, at least," Rellen replied, keeping the disappointment off his face. "I've never been here before, and one city is as good as the last in my line of work. You should be able to contact us through the local Hunter's Guild, if nothing else." He glanced up to see Xilly circling overhead. If they were dismissed, he'd need her help to follow Javyk and this mysterious employer to wherever it was they were going. It would be harder, riskier, but he'd have no choice. "It'll be some time before we're willing to go back through Jabono, and the only other way north are the long roads east or west along the mountains... either that or a ship around the coast."

"Excellent," Javyk said, and then he disappeared back into the carriage.

For the next thirty minutes, they made their way through the heart of Yaylo, a magnificent, bustling city. The amount of goods being moved around made Corsia look like a village. It wasn't surprising, though. Yaylo was the biggest seaport on the southern half of Pelinon.

The smell of the sea grew even stronger as the carriage rolled. Soon the scents of grain, lumber, and fish most of all, joined it.

They entered a more residential part of the city. Foot traffic turned to carriages. Cotton garments turned to silk.

Shops and warehouses were replaced by large two and three-story manor houses along the cobblestone streets. Most of those had wide gardens, with fountains or statues out front and elaborate carriage houses in the back. These were the homes of the wealthy and influential.

The sound of the ocean and cries of sea birds rose upon the air. They made a last turn toward the water and entered a very different sort of business district. One and two-story shops, clothiers, and eateries lined the streets. In the main part of Yaylo, goods had been moved about on carts and wagons, mixed in with the populace, but not here. There was not a single crate, wagon, or cart along the main street. Whatever goods came in, they came in through the back door, along with the servants, or were stored in the alleys between the buildings.

They were only two blocks from the sea, where a set of long piers stretched away, lined mostly with a variety of smaller sea vessels. These were not the massive cargo ships whose masts Rellen had seen lining the port when they first approached Yaylo. They were the vessels of nobles, with intricate woodwork, colorful sails, and deckhands standing along the docks in bright livery, awaiting their master's beck and call.

At the far end of the pier was a larger passenger transport of some kind, one of fine quality that shouted wealth. Atop its tallest mast was the silver, yellow, and purple pennon of the Duchy of Kaichakahn.

Mr. Bawth drove the carriage down the center of the cobblestone street, drawing the attention of people walking in and out of the shops. Rellen realized it wasn't the carriage they were staring at; it was him and his companions. He straightened his back and put a haughty smile on his face, making a point to nod at the dark-skinned lords and ladies who stared at him with open disdain.

They reached the end of the street, and the carriage pulled up in front of a two-story, white structure that was obviously an inn and tavern for the nobility. The sign hanging over the fine, wooden double doors read, "The Star of the Seven Sisters."

A stiff-looking man in crimson livery stood just outside the doors, and he quickly stepped down and opened the carriage door.

Javyk stepped out, paying the attendant no attention at all, and looked up to the driver. "Take Dancer to the last ship on the right, Mr. Bawth," he said, tossing up a sack of coins, which the old man caught deftly. "The deck hands will see to his needs from there. After that, you are released from my service and free to return to Svennival. I thank you for your diligence."

"Yes, milord," Bawth replied with a curt nod. "And thank you."

Javyk turned to Rellen. "Leave your horses here. We won't be long, and I assure you, no one will meddle with them." He glanced at the attendant. "Will they?"

"No, milord," the attendant said crisply. He glanced at Rellen and the others with just the barest hint of an upturned nose, then barked, "Boys!" At that, four lads, no more than twelve years old, in the same red livery, came dashing out of the inn and stopped in front of the attendant. "Mind these steeds."

The boys nodded crisply and slowly approached the horses, careful not to spook them.

"Please join me inside," Javyk said. "Someone will guide you to us." He then strode up the steps and disappeared through the doors, with the attendant following closely.

As Mr. Bawth guided the carriage away, Rellen and the others dismounted, handing the reins over to the boys.

"Let me do the talking," Rellen said to his comrades. He then stepped up close to Mygal and whispered, "Try and get a read on Javyk's employer, but *be careful*. We don't know what we're dealing with."

Mygal nodded and then closed his eyes. He seemed to mutter something under his breath, and Rellen realized the young Guardians was casting a spell of some sort.

Mygal opened his eyes. "There," he said in a hushed tone, "that should make anything I do relatively undetectable."

Satisfied, Rellen led the four of them up the steps where another lad in the same red livery stood waiting for them. "If you will follow me, please," he said with a bow.

"Lead the way," Rellen replied.

The interior was open, with wide tables throughout and curtained booths along one wall. The tables, covered with white tablecloths, were already set with cloth napkins and silver finery. Everything was done in dark wood and silver.

The attendant led them back and to the right, where another set of doors opened up onto a wide patio full of tables. It looked out onto the docks, and fresh sea air blew through. The patio was empty except for a single table off to the left where Javyk leaned over a slim gentleman in fine clothing, whispering in his ear. A leather sack lay in the middle of the table, and there was a decanter off to the side, half full of wine, and a slim glass of the same in front of the gentleman. An empty plate with traces of a meal sat off to the side.

The man stood up straight as Rellen and the others entered the patio. He was obviously of the nobility, with a black goatee and brown, intelligent eyes. He had the darker skin of the southern peoples and wore crisp, silken robes of deep indigo with bright yellow trim and embroidery. He had a thick, gold ring on each pinky, hoop earrings of gold. He also wore a thin, crimson turban held in place at the front with a large ruby surrounded by diamonds in a silver setting.

The nobleman smiled in a friendly way, motioning for Rellen and the others to join him. His eyes met Rellen's, and a bizarre flash of recognition flared in Rellen's mind. He knew he'd never seen this man before, but there was a strange familiarity about what lay behind those eyes, and it sent a chill up Rellen's spine. In that moment, Rellen knew he'd met the real enemy, but he had no idea why or what this man was really after.

"It is a pleasure to meet you… Rellen, isn't it?" the nobleman said.

"It is," Rellen replied smoothly.

"This must be your lovely wife, Miranda, followed by Tygeth and Maybor, yes?"

They nodded in reply.

"I am Toreth sun'Harrai, and I've heard good things about you from Javyk." He motioned toward the four empty chairs. Please, sit down." Toreth's eyes flicked to Mygal and back to Rellen without any change in his expression. They all took their seats, and as they settled in, Toreth whispered something in Javyk's ear. Javyk nodded.

"Right away, milord," Javyk said and then strode off into the building.

"I was originally going to simply pay you and send you on your way." Toreth pushed the leather sack across the table. "There is what you are owed for your services. I'm a man of my word. However, now that I've laid eyes on you, I'd like to encourage you to stay."

"What is it you require?" Rellen asked, suddenly worried that Javyk might be going to come back with a pack of Nissrans.

Toreth's lips turned up into a slim smile. "Why, you, of course."

Rellen's eyebrow went up. There was something about the way Toreth said it that made his skin crawl.

"I need capable men," he glanced at Miranda, "and women who can help ensure my goals are achieved."

"That's a bit vague," Rellen said, and he was certain Toreth had meant him in particular. *What is it about him?*

"It's as precise as I'm willing to be for the time being," Toreth replied smoothly. "Suffice it to say that I was given the impression all four of you—a most capable group, I might add—were more interested in coin than in the nature of the work, so long as it wasn't an affront to, what I would describe as, your relatively low—but not criminal—ethical standard."

"I've never heard it said better."

"Well, I can assure you that I'll never ask you to do anything you would be unwilling to undertake."

All Rellen could think of was how Dancer was literally giving his life to Toreth's goals and what the chancellor in Jabono had said about the second degree of Nissran possession. He knew Toreth was inviting him into his lair. He didn't know when it would come, or from who, but at some point, Toreth was going to try and possess all four of them.

He stared into the jaws of a dragon and didn't flinch.

"I'll hold you to that," he replied evenly. With that one sentence, the Vuoda hole got that much deeper. As they stared at one another, he thought he saw the corner of Toreth's mouth turn up just a fraction of an inch. "I'd like to talk it over with my associates before we give you our answer, but I'd say the odds are good."

"I would pay you the same as you've earned protecting my people," Toreth assured him. "I have taken care of them, and I would take care of you." He pointed out toward the ocean. "Do you see that ship out there? The big one."

Everyone turned. It was the large transport flying the bright pennon.

"Yes," Rellen said, turning back.

"It sets sail in four hours, bound for its home port of Kaichakahn. Javyk and I will be on it."

A slight commotion rose at the entrance to the patio, drawing everyone's attention. Javyk appeared with a host of waiters in tow.

"Ahh… excellent," Toreth said, sounding quite pleased. "Your timing is perfect, Javyk, as usual. My friends, I have arranged for you to enjoy a meal, with my compliments, as you mull over your decision." He fixed his gaze upon Rellen. "I'm sure you have much to discuss. I've taken the liberty of ordering today's special, a delightfully delicate fish of some kind, although I never caught the name. I'm certain you will enjoy it as much as I did."

With that, Toreth rose from his seat and gave them all a low, almost dramatic bow. "Eat and drink to your heart's content. Consider it a bonus for services rendered. Should any of you decide to join me, then you need only board that ship. Passage will be arranged, comfortable cabins set aside, and your mounts can be stowed below decks along with the other steeds." He stepped around the table, giving Rellen a friendly pat on the shoulder. "I sincerely hope you give my offer very serious consideration."

"Don't worry, we will," Rellen replied, trying not to shy away from Toreth's hand.

"Come, Javyk, let us see to the arrangements," Toreth said, striding away as the waiters started sliding plates in front of everyone.

"Yes, milord," Javyk replied. He stepped in behind Toreth, and they were gone.

"What was that—?" Mygal started.

Rellen locked eyes with him and held up a single finger, cutting Mygal off. Rellen glanced at the waiters and stared at Mygal, who got the message. The waiters served each of them a pleasant-smelling dish and set two more carafes of wine on the table, two pitchers of ale, and all the silverware, glasses, and napkins they would need. Finally, a large basket of fresh bread was set in the center of the table, and the waiters left.

"Don't say anything yet," Rellen said softly. Then he asked, *Xilly, are you near?*

Look up. There was a faint scratching sound on the roof above, and Rellen spotted her small, black head peak over the edge two stories up.

Follow them and tell me if they go any place other than the ship. Stay out of sight though.

I will. What happens if you get on that ship? I can't fly that far over the ocean without eating and sleeping.

The ship leaves around the time it gets dark. I'll open a porthole and you'll stay in my cabin during the journey.

Excellent, she replied, and her thought faded.

He pulled a large patch of cotton from a pouch at his belt. Focusing his majea, he whispered an incantation as he twisted it out into a long strand, coiled it around his finger several times, and then drew a series of small symbols with that finger on the tablecloth. The cotton flared faintly with pale white light and dimmed. Placing the loop of cotton in the middle of the table, he let out a long, relieved breath. "Now the staff can't hear us, but don't raise your voices. First of all, Xilly is going to see where they go."

"So, what was that all about?" Mygal blurted. "I thought they were going to let us go, and he seemed particularly interested in you, Rellen."

"Caught that, did you?" Rellen said.

"He wants you," Miranda said, "and I mean you specifically."

"It was like he couldn't take his eyes off you," Tavyn added.

"Were you able to sense anything?" Rellen asked, turning his eyes to Mygal.

"I didn't push hard. The lightest of touches, just to get a sense of his emotions as we spoke." He shook his head. "It was... *strange*."

"Strange how?"

"It's hard to put into words..." Mygal's brow furrowed as he considered what to say. "Normally, I get fluctuating emotions from people from one moment to the next. Normal stuff as our emotions drive—or are driven by—our thoughts. Javyk is like that, in fact. But Toreth... I didn't really get anything but determination from him. Singular. No sense of whether he was telling the truth or lying. No love, like, or hate. Even when he said he enjoyed his meal, there was nothing except that sense of determination. It was as if he was capable of nothing else."

"Maybe he had some sort of counter-spell up," Rellen offered.

"I suppose," Mygal said. "I have one of my own, although it takes real concentration to maintain it."

"Remember that feeling. It may be a way for us to detect those who have been possessed by Nissra."

"You think he's possessed?" Tavyn asked.

"I don't know." Rellen replied. "If he is, then it means the game has changed somewhat and this Vuoda hole just became a trap. But even if we know who's going to spring it, we don't know when, where, or how. It's vital I see this through to wherever that plunnokum leads. Mygal and I *have* to go. It's our duty." He looked at Miranda and Tavyn. "The two of you don't. I won't lie. Toreth is a Nissran, high up in their ranks, if I'm not mistaken, and if he gains the upper hand..." Rellen shivered. He didn't fear death, but the thought of being butchered alive by a Nissran pleasing his god scared the life out of him. "I've seen what they do, and I can't imagine a worse way to die."

The table went silent for a moment. Miranda met Rellen's eyes, and he knew in an instant what her answer would be. She'd said she was there for the money, but he knew she was there for him—just as he would be if their roles were reversed. He gave her the briefest of nods, an unspoken thank you that could never possibly be put into words. As he did, a wash of dread filled him at the thought of Miranda falling into the hands of the Nissrans. He cast Mygal a sidelong glance and realized he felt something similar for the young Guardian. Mygal was only at the beginning of his journey as a Guardian, and somehow, the young man had gotten past Rellen's defenses. Unlike his old comrade Voren, Rellen feared for Mygal's safety. Maybe it was because he was Mygal's mentor. Maybe it was the conversation he'd had with his brother. A dark, creeping worry seeped into his bones.

"What about you, Tavyn?" he asked. He fully expected Tavyn to flat out refuse. He could see the struggle in Tavyn's face as he mulled over the idea for several heartbeats.

"Alright," he finally said, "I'm in too."

Rellen controlled his surprise. Tavyn's willingness seemed out of place for a coin-driven informant out of Svennival.

There was no reason what-so-ever for him to risk so much for so little reward.

"Are you sure?" Rellen asked. "We may all end up screaming on a slab of granite, gutted under a Nissran blade."

"I've come this far," Tavyn replied, giving Rellen a weak, resigned smile, and then he gave Mygal a strange nod.

It was an almost flippant response—too flippant for Rellen's comfort. The money Rellen and Toreth were paying him didn't even come close to justifying the risk.

This Vuoda hole had more twists than a female Kapren's horn.

CHAPTER TWENTY-EIGHT
THE TASTE OF SACRIFICE

T oreth strode up the long, heavy gangplank of the Kaichakahn transport and nodded to two guards in the king's livery who stood watch at the top. They bowed their heads respectfully and placed their hands over their hearts as he passed by. There were a half dozen more soldiers in the king's livery on watch around the railing of the vessel, as well as several more gathered at the stern, on the quarterdeck.

"Now that we're alone," Toreth said, glancing at Javyk, "I want to thank you, once again, for all you have done." The smile on his face was sublime as they walked across the deck to the bow of the ship. "You continue to surpass every expectation."

"It has always been my greatest desire to serve you, Master," Javyk said. "But these past two months have been a simple matter. Once I knew where the plunnokum was, murdering the duke and returning here was little more than a long carriage ride. I must admit, the trouble in Sylverwynd was disconcerting but not unexpected, thanks to your warning. I *was* surprised that it was Delvers who chose to involve themselves in your affairs. I'd expected the king's troops—even Corsairs—if anyone. Do you know who they were?"

Toreth let out a long, slow breath. "An ancient enemy, but they are of little concern at this point. Merely an obstacle we shall have to deal with once the door is opened and my position and power is more solidified. What matters is that the Delvers failed and you succeeded." Toreth eyed Javyk appreciatively. "And in no small part because of your choice in *protector.*"

"That too, was an easy choice," Javyk replied, "barely more than an accident that I can't take credit for." He looked a bit embarrassed. "Those bounty hunters joined the caravan, so it was mere happenstance. I saw an opportunity and took it. The other two bounty hunters I hired in Sylverwynd were slain, but that fellow Rellen seems quite capable." Javyk hesitated for a moment, as if he were uncertain of something. "I certainly didn't expect you to offer them employment."

Toreth got a pleased look on his face. "Like you, I saw an opportunity and took it."

"I don't understand."

"There's no reason you should. Do you remember me telling you of the failure in Calamath some months ago?"

"I do. The ceremony was interrupted and the host body slain."

Toreth stiffened. His smile faded. "Indeed." There was a trace of simmering anger in his voice. "Rellen was responsible, and Calamath was lost completely to us once the King's Corsairs occupied the city."

Javyk's eyes went wide with surprise. "Rellen?"

"Rellen." Toreth let out a patient, almost relieved breath, gaining control over his frustration and anger. "What's more, he's one of the King's Guardians."

Javyk gasped and dropped to a knee, bowing his head. "Master, I had no idea!" His voice was near panic. "I've brought a Guardian into your midst. I've failed you! I beg forgiveness. I'll accept any punishment."

"Rise, Javyk," Toreth soothed. "Under normal circumstances, I might kill you outright for such a failure, but I told you, I'm grateful. Rellen, it seems, is particularly adept at infiltration and meddling in my affairs." Toreth lifted his eyes and stared out at the Star of the Seven Sisters. "Had I not recognized him from Calamath, even I would have likely accepted him at face value." He turned his gaze to the city and beyond. "Thus far, this contest has been played on *his* turf. When this ship docks again, he will find himself on *mine*, and he'll have no idea what he's walking into."

"So, everything has gone well while I've been away?" Javyk asked tentatively as he rose to his feet.

"Better than I could have hoped," Toreth replied with a grim smile. "And thanks to you, we will be returning home with more than just the plunnokum... *much* more."

"Do you intend to kill him or convert him?" Javyk asked.

"I haven't decided yet. It would seem I now have a choice, where before, I did not."

"I don't understand," Javyk said.

"Again, there's no reason you should." Toreth turned away from the railing. "Come, let us repair to my cabin where we can give young Riven his final reward."

"Of course, Master," Javyk said, falling in step behind Toreth. "It's been some time since I've tasted sacrifice... and his will be freely given."

"That is always the sweetest," Toreth replied, licking his lips. "And it's been days."

"My last was the Duke of Svennival and his wife," Javyk lamented. "There simply wasn't any way to indulge without risking complications."

"You must be hungry indeed."

"Yes, Master."

"Then you shall have the first taste."

"You are truly magnanimous, but I couldn't presume."

"Consider it my gift to you for bringing Rellen to me."

"As you wish."

They crossed the deck, passed through a door set into the front of the quarterdeck, and entered what had once been the captain's cabin before Toreth claimed it as his own. A large, wooden table filled the center of a nicely appointed cabin with a bed, desk, armoire, and several sitting chairs scattered about the room. Upon the table, Dancer lay, asleep and breathing shallowly. He'd been stripped down to his trousers, and his frail-looking, almost skeletal body was surrounded with rolls of cotton sheets that made the table look almost like a shallow bowl.

Javyk closed the cabin door behind them, and they quickly removed their tunics and boots, leaving only their trousers. Bare-chested, they stepped up on either side of the table.

Dancer opened his eyes slowly. He stared up at Toreth. A strange smile filled his face. It was adoration, nothing less—blind and unflinching.

"Are you ready for your reward?" Toreth asked gently.

"I am, my Master," Dancer said.

"Then let us begin," Toreth's eyes began to glow with a strange, green light, as if flames flickered deep within them. He uttered a word in a low, ancient, guttural tongue and placed his hand upon Dancer's forehead. He then carefully drew the tip of his finger down the center of Dancer's chest. A crimson point of light glowed where it touched Dancer's skin, leaving a shallow gash in the flesh. Thin rivulets of blood spread out across pale skin. Dancer tensed but held himself still. He appeared to scream out in something between ecstasy and agony, but no sound came forth.

Toreth nodded to Javyk, who leaned over and ran his tongue over the blood spreading out across Dancer's chest. The sacrifice would occupy the entire journey to Kaichakahn, and they would savor every moment.

CHAPTER TWENTY-NINE

YL JABBATHENE

R ellen set his empty wine glass on the table beside his empty plate. He had to admit, the fish, whatever it had been, was exceptional. He wondered how much of that had to do with two weeks eating trail rations and teamster prepared meals. He let out a long, weary breath and looked at his comrades. It was time to dive back down the Vuoda hole, and he honestly didn't know if any of them would be coming back out again.

"Let's get moving," he finally said. "That ship is waiting."

They all rose from their seats, and Rellen glanced at Tavyn. The man's willingness to join them still bothered him. "You're sure you want to come along?"

"When I said before that it was for the money, that was only part of it." He looked to Mygal. "He's told me what they did to Belvenim and his family in pretty gruesome detail." He shrugged. "I can't get those images out of my head, and I figure if I can help you somehow put an end to it... the better off we'll all be."

Rellen nodded, and his suspicions eased, at least a little. It was an answer he could live with.

They shuffled off, perhaps a little slower than they'd walked in, but it had been a good meal with excellent drink. They crossed through the interior of the tavern and out onto the front steps where the four attendants still stood holding the reins of the horses. They looked bored but apparently hadn't moved.

Rellen lifted his eyes to the sky.

Xilly, where are you?

On the roof, she replied.

Did they go anywhere else?

No. They went straight to the ship, had a conversation at the front of it for a while, and then disappeared inside.

Good, then—

But there's something else, she said, cutting him off. *Someone has been watching the horses. He's in the alley to your right, hidden in the shadows. He's been there since shortly after you started lunch.*

What's he look like?

Large. Local clothing mostly in red and yellow. He has a big scimitar across his back.

"Damn it," Rellen whispered.

"What is it?" Miranda said, turning back as Mygal and Tavyn moved down toward their mounts.

"Oh, I just left something inside." Using the military sign language, he said, *Being watched. Don't react. To your right.* "Go on and head for the ship. I'll catch up."

"You got it." Miranda replied. *Understood. Be careful.*

Rellen gave her an imperceptible nod, turned, and walked back into the Star of the Seven Sisters. He quickly moved out onto the patio, where one of the waiters who was clearing their plates gave him a curious look.

Rellen put his finger to his lips and pressed a dakkari into the waiter's hand. The waiter's eyes went wide with happy surprise as Rellen stepped past him, hopped over the railing of the patio, and dropped down to the alley behind the establishment.

Pulling two different spell components from pouches on his belt, he cast his magic shield and then the spell that would create a silencing bubble around him. The sounds of the world around him dimmed, but he could still hear. Pulling the long knife from the back of his belt, he hurried down the alley, pausing at the corner of the building. He peered around the corner just enough to see a figure behind some crates at the far corner of the building. The man was just as Xilly had described, and there was no doubt he was doing his best to watch the others without being seen himself.

Rellen drew in a deep breath and let it out slowly. He turned the corner and moved quickly up, relying upon his spell to suppress the sound of his approach. When he was within five feet, he paused and prepared himself. He leapt, grabbed the man's shoulder tightly, and set the point of his dagger in the small of the man's back.

"Don't make a sound, or I'll kill you right here."

The man stiffened, raised his hands, and slowly looked over his shoulder. His skin was ebony, and when he saw Rellen, there was a moment of recognition.

"Aegon sul vas narivum," the man said in a deep voice.

"Jaquinn?" Rellen said, stunned. "What in blazes are you doing here?"

The Second Guardian turned part way around. "Waiting for you." His eyes flicked toward the knife at his back. "Do you mind?"

"Oh!" Rellen said. He slid the knife into its sheath and stepped back a pace while keeping Jaquinn inside the silencing bubble.

Rellen's old mentor lowered his hands and turned fully around. "How did you know I was here?"

"The dragonette," Rellen replied. He glanced up and saw her peeking over the edge of the roof, looking down on them.

Jaquinn lifted his eyes and spotted her. A slow and exceedingly rare smile crossed his lips. "That must give you a nice edge."

"She does," Rellen replied. "I didn't expect to find you here."

"I didn't expect to *still* be here. When I discovered two days ago that Duke kyp'Tukeem's grand vizier was here, I decided to stay and watch him."

"That sounds very interesting, but that doesn't explain why you were waiting for me here in this alley."

Jaquinn's eyes narrowed slightly. He cocked his head to the side and got a concerned look on his face. "Because you met with Toreth sun'Harrai, the grand vizier for the Duchy of Nikostohr, and he bought you and your companions lunch before getting aboard the *Yl Jabbathene*."

Rellen's jaw dropped.

"What are you into, Rellen?" Jaquinn asked.

"There's a lot I could explain, but I have to get aboard that ship. The short answer is that Toreth's... aide? ... Lackey?... Javyk Sukari—do you know him?"

"Of him, but he's not been seen in Kaichakahn in months."

"Well, Toreth sent Javyk to Svennival. *He's* the one who murdered the duke, and all to acquire some ancient key."

"A key?" Jaquinn asked. "A key to what?"

"All I know is that it opens a door in a nuraghi somewhere, probably near Kaichakahn."

"Stukelladios?" Jaquinn asked.

"What?" Rellen had never heard the word before.

"Nuraghi Stukelladios," Jaquinn said. "It's a legend really, one not many people know about. My father told me stories when I was a boy. He said that there was supposed to be a hidden nuraghi in the jungles near Kaichakahn somewhere."

"I'm betting that's it." Rellen thought furiously. "Why were you following the vizier?"

"Because I think he's at the heart of sedition brewing in Kaichakahn. Many people in the south still resent being a part of Pelinon."

"But they were brought into the fold more than a hundred years ago."

"These people have a long memory when it comes to what they think is treachery."

"There's something you should know," Rellen said. The pieces were starting to fall into place. "Toreth is a Nissran, and I think he may be possessed."

Jaquinn's jaw muscles tightened. "I'd suspected as much, but I couldn't prove it."

"Why'd you suspect the Nissrans?"

"Some months ago, there was a series of murders in Kaichakahn—all gutter trash. No bodies were found, and the investigation was quietly buried. The duke had no knowledge it was even happening, and the soldiers involved in the cover-up have all since turned up dead of one cause or another. I'd narrowed it down to three people who could manipulate things so thoroughly and keep them from the duke. Toreth was one of them. Nothing made sense until the king sent out a message to watch for Nissrans."

"Calamath," Rellen said.

Jaquinn nodded. "And I doubt that was the only one, and certainly not the last." He met Rellen's gaze with worry in his eyes. "What we don't know gives me grave concerns."

Rellen nodded. The implications were clear. There could be any number of Pelinese cities similarly under siege.

"If the grand vizier is a possessed Nissran, then he'd be in a perfect position to either kill or control the duke, assuming the duke hadn't already been subverted by the Nissrans. With a resentful populace—which much of it is—it wouldn't be hard to manipulate them into a revolt against the king." He locked angry, burning eyes with Rellen. "We should go take him right now."

"We can't," Rellen said, a twinge of worry coursing through him. He was about to go against a senior Guardian.

"It is my call, and you know it, *Nine*." There was no missing the warning tone in the Second Guardian's voice. "No matter who your brother is."

Rellen swallowed. "I know that, but there's more going on here than either of us fully comprehends." Rellen drew in a deep breath and let it out slowly. He was about to betray a confidence—two of them actually. But he didn't have a choice. He couldn't trust even Miranda with what he was about to say, but this was the *Second Guardian of Pelinon.* "Have you heard of the Klymrukaar?"

Jaquinn's eyes narrowed, and he stiffened. "I know something of them from conversations I overheard between both kings and Saleeria, although I also know I'm not supposed to. Why?"

"Because they're involved too."

"What?" Jaquinn blurted, his face a mask of confusion.

"A group of them tried to take that artifact—that key— from Javyk back in Sylverwynd. I'd been hired as a bodyguard, and we fought. When I recognized the emblem on their armor, I managed to get away without killing any of them. And then, in Jabono, I encountered the Delver leader again, this time in Chancellor Kag'Atrall's study. That's when I learned about the plunnokum and that the Delver wants that door opened so they can find out what's on the other side. He also said I needed to stop Javyk—and Toreth—from going through. I was going to kill them there and take the key back to Saleeria so she can figure out what the blazes is going on."

"Which means we can't take them now," Jaquinn said, frustration filling his voice.

Rellen nodded slowly. "I could use your help, but there's no way I'd be able to convince them that I just happened to run into another bounty hunter looking for work."

"It's not a problem. I've already booked passage on that ship under an assumed name. From here on out, we'll avoid each other, but I'll follow you when you go to the nuraghi. They won't see me until it's too late."

Rellen let out a sigh of relief. "I'm not embarrassed to tell you, that makes me feel better about this whole thing. Miranda I trust, and she's deadly in a fight, but we have no idea what we're getting into. Mygal is a good erkurios and talented with that sword of his, but I have no idea what he's capable of when things get really rough."

"Don't worry," Jaquinn said. "I'll be there no matter what. Now, catch up with your comrades before you are missed. I'll board shortly."

Rellen placed his hand on Jaquinn's shoulder and met his gaze. "For the Honor of Pelinon," he said.

"For the Honor of Pelinon. And be *careful*. You know better than most that the Nissrans are not to be taken lightly."

"I'm always careful," Rellen replied as he stepped out from behind the crates and paused to make sure there wasn't anyone nearby.

"That's not what your brother told me…"

Rellen shot Jaquinn a rude gesture over his shoulder, prompting the big man to chuckle, and stepped out into the street. He walked over to the young attendant, took Shaddeth's reigns from the lad, and mounted up. He spotted Miranda and the others at the far end of the pier. He hastened Shaddeth into a trot, the horse's massive hooves clomping heavily across the weathered planks.

When he reached the wide, heavy gangplank for livestock, he dismounted, pulled off his saddlebags and the stack of spell books he always carried with him. He'd trust the handlers with his bedroll and saddle, but nothing else.

A crewman stepped up away from the gangplank and held out his hand for Shaddeth's reins.

Rellen held them out and then pulled back slightly.

"You'd be well advised to treat this one with care and respect, or he'll stomp your brains in."

"Yes, sir," the crewman said.

Rellen locked eyes with the crewman. "And if I find a mark on him when we disembark, *I'll* stomp your brains in. Understood?"

"Perfectly sir," the crewman said with a good deal of respect. "I'll treat him like he was my own."

"You do that," Rellen said. He then hefted his gear over a shoulder and patted Shaddeth's shoulder. "Don't give them any trouble unless they ask for it."

Shaddeth snorted and seemed to stare intently at the crewman, almost as if he were daring the man to mistreat him.

The crewman's eyes shifted between Shaddeth and Rellen several times, and then he swallowed hard. "Like he was my own, sir."

Rellen walked away chuckling. He made his way down to the passenger gangplank and strode up it, eyeing the soldiers at the top. They both wore the king's livery, which made him feel a bit better. Looking from stem to stern, he spotted a number of the king's men on watch. Despite being on a ship with two murdering Nissrans, he might just be able to relax a bit on the journey to Kaichakahn.

He topped the gangplank and spotted Miranda, Mygal, and Tavyn aft, just in front of steps leading down into the ship. They all had their gear over their shoulders and were speaking to a man in the king's livery who, Rellen assumed, was a steward for the voyage.

Miranda looked at Rellen expectantly.

Rellen nodded, it was all he could do, for now, but it let her know there hadn't been a problem.

"Good evening, sir," the steward said. "As I was just saying, your cabins have been prepared. You and your wife are on the first deck below us, last door on the port side. Your associates here will be sharing a cabin one deck below, first cabin on the starboard side, just at the bottom of the stairs. Privies are fore and aft on all decks." He handed a key to Miranda and one to Mygal. "We'll be departing just after the sun sets. The galley is generally open, so you may eat when you like. We'll reach Kaichakahn in three days." He bowed once. "If there is anything else you need, please find me or one of the other stewards. It is our pleasure to serve."

"Thank you…" Rellen started.

"Jakeen," the man said.

"Thank you, Jakeen." Rellen pulled out three sepiks and handed them over.

"Thank you, sir," the steward said, and then he hurried off toward an older, affluent couple coming up the gangplank.

"Let's get a look at our cabins," Rellen said.

They made their way below. Mygal and Tavyn continued down the next flight of stairs. Rellen and Miranda moved forward to the last cabin on the port side and entered a nicely appointed cabin with a writing desk on one side and a large feather bed in the center. Both were bolted to the floor, and the desk sat below a large, circular porthole with a heavy latch. Rellen set his gear on the floor just inside the door and went over to the window. He twisted the latch and pushed the porthole open without any difficulty. Once the sun went down, Xilly would have no problem coming in, and she could curl up beneath his saddle should anyone need to come into the room.

"So?" Miranda asked, closing the door. "Are you going to tell me what happened?"

Rellen hesitated for a few heartbeats, worry battering against his thoughts like a besieging army.

Turning around, he told her nearly everything, and with each word, her dismay grew. He left out only two details. He didn't mention the Klymrukaar at all, and he left out the fact that Jaquinn was a Guardian, calling him just an old contact that happened to spot Rellen riding through town. Those were secrets he wasn't prepared to share with her just yet. He hated it, but it was necessary.

Rellen and Miranda stood upon the forecastle of *Yl Jabbathene* beneath a starry, cloudless sky as tropical winds tussled their hair. The rush of the ocean flowing past the hull beneath their feet filled the air. They'd eaten a good meal with Mygal and Tavyn, although the conversation had been—by way of necessity—banal.

As the meal had progressed, however, something started to bother Rellen. He'd seen no sign of Toreth, Javyk, Dancer, or even Jaquinn since they'd come aboard. As a result, he felt both relief and worry.

After dinner, he'd brought back a napkin full of roast meat for Xilly, who had come in through the portal without any incident. She'd immediately crawled under his saddle and gone to sleep. He knew she'd gobble up what he'd brought her the moment she woke up. With his companion taken care of, he and Miranda had gone up to the main deck to enjoy the breeze and talk quietly.

As the waves surged against the bow, the sails filled by a wind controlled by a gekurios at the stern, Rellen worried over their situation like a dog with a bone. The more he thought about it, the more he leaned toward relief that he hadn't seen the others. Seeing them would mean conversation, and any conversation at this point held the greatest risk. If he could get three quiet days before he had to deal with whatever Toreth had in store for them, he'd feel much better about everything.

Footsteps creaked on the stairs leading to the forecastle. Rellen and Miranda both instinctively placed their hands on their weapons.

"It's just me," Mygal's voice floated out of the darkness as he reached the top and stepped up beside them.

"Where's Tygeth?" Rellen asked.

"In his bunk," Mygal replied. "He said that meal put him to sleep."

"He certainly ate enough," Miranda observed.

Rellen turned to Mygal and locked eyes with him. "What do you think of him?"

Mygal looked around. They were alone on the forecastle. "Against my better judgment," Mygal started slowly, "I've come to like him. He's good company, and, impossibly, I'm starting to trust him."

Rellen thought about that. "But not a hundred percent."

"Certainly not," Mygal said. He looked to Miranda. "No offense, but Rellen is the only one I trust completely."

"None taken," Miranda assured him. "Nature of the business."

Rellen drew in a deep breath and let it out slowly. "Has he done anything at all that gives you pause?"

Mygal seemed to mull the question over. "I don't know... maybe there is one thing... but it may just be paranoia."

"Don't worry," Rellen said. "I've been fighting with my own paranoia for a couple weeks now."

"Have you ever liked someone too much? Liked them when your better judgment told you to keep your distance, but you ignored it?"

Rellen tried not to smile. He'd been having the same problem with Mygal. He didn't want to like the young Guardian, but that hadn't worked out at all like he'd intended.

"Yes," he said flatly. "I've experienced that."

"That's what it's like with Tavyn. I know he's just an informant from a city on my patrol route. We needed him to get us this far, and it should have ended there. I'll be honest, I was surprised when he agreed to set foot on this ship. I would have bet a sack of gold dakkaris he'd go home the moment things turned out like they did."

"I thought the same thing," Rellen said. "It's the main reason I asked you the question. Could a really good erkurios have held you at bay all this time?"

"The short answer is yes. A really good one could have pulled that off." Mygal stared off into the distance, his eyes shifting as he thought about the question. "I've delved into his feelings more than once since we left Svennival, and there's been nothing that gave me cause for alarm. I have to say, though, that I didn't dig deep. Going that deep would alert even someone without majea. I didn't want him to take offense, because we needed him." He blew out a frustrated breath. "It's always a balancing act."

"Are you worried he's working for the enemy?" Miranda asked.

"If he is, then it means we've all been led here from the very beginning," Rellen said. "And I find that hard to believe. I know someone who could have pulled something like that off. She's a truly gifted clikurios, but if it were someone like her, then it would have had to start even before I arrived in

Svennival." Rellen's mind raced down that Vuoda hole. "Bah!" he blurted, slamming his fist down on the railing. "Short of tying Tavyn down and reaming out his brains, there's no way to know for certain."

"Here's the thing," Mygal said thoughtfully, "if he was or is working for someone, would it change what we're doing right now?"

"No," Rellen said immediately. "We'd still be standing right here, with or without him."

"And since I have a good feeling about him and don't plan on turning my back on him, we have a pretty good chance of seeing something coming, if it even exists, correct?"

"Correct," Rellen said, nodding his head slowly. He had to admit, Mygal had a sharp mind.

"Then I'll see if I can't dig a little deeper into his emotions as all this unfolds. If he's really gifted, I won't find out anything until he makes a move. If he's not, and there is something odd, then I have at least a slim chance of finding out. The odds are I won't be able to do better than I've done, short of, like you said, pinning him down and digging into his head. I don't see us doing that here."

"That's right," Rellen said, letting out a weary breath. "Right back where we started."

"It does mean one thing though," Miranda offered in a lighter tone.

"What's that?" Rellen turned suspicious eyes toward her.

"It means that, barring getting attacked, we get to just relax for the next few days." She stared out over the ocean, drawing a deep breath of air and letting it out slowly. "I, for one, intend to enjoy it." She glanced at Rellen. "I mean, it's not like Toreth can do anything with all of these guards and passengers around, can he? And if we do eventually end up on a slab, then these next few will be the best we've had in quite a while."

"That," Rellen said, relaxing his shoulders a bit, "is pure genius."

CHAPTER THIRTY

SHIFTING WEBS

Tavyn waited for Mygal to shut the door and walk up the stairs before he closed his eyes. He focused his will upon the black stone, reaching out for the connection, which came almost immediately.

Milord, he called.

I hear you.

We've been retained. We're aboard a sailing ship, headed for Kaichakahn.

Then it is Stukelladios they're after.

Stukelladios? Tavyn had never heard the word before.

It doesn't matter, his employer said dismissively, but Tavyn felt a swell of excitement bloom in the man's emotions. There was something about that one word, something ominous that was of tremendous importance. *When last we spoke,* his employer continued, *you said Rellen expected you all would have to follow them surreptitiously. What has changed?*

We met Javyk's employer, or whatever he is. Rellen believes he's high up in the Nissran organization. He told us that he'd initially intended to pay us and send us on our way, but when he saw Rellen—Rellen specifically—he became keenly interested. That's when he offered to have us join them on the next leg of their journey and left it open that there might be more work down the road.

Did this superior give his name?

Toreth sun'Harrai, Tavyn replied. *He struck me as nobility, but I've never heard of him before.*

Grand Vizier Toreth sun'Harrai?

Tavyn felt his employer's excitement shift to concern... even worry. In fact, the name had elicited something close to dread.

He never said.

Tell me, what did he look like?

About five-foot-ten, maybe one-sixty. Black hair, brown eyes. He had a black goatee and darker skin like most of the people this far south. Dark blue silken robes with bright yellow trim. Gold rings, hoop earrings, and red turban secured with a large ruby surrounded by diamonds.

That certainly does sound like him.

Tavyn could feel his employer's anxiety growing.

What is it? Tavyn asked. *What's wrong?*

There was a long pause.

It's nothing you can do anything about right now, but you must be even more cautious from here on out. If it is who I think it is, then he will have tremendous resources and power. If he discovers who any of you are, the consequences will be more than severe.

Rellen said the same thing, Tavyn replied. *He asked me if I was certain I wanted to go along with them. I only did so because of our arrangement, but I must tell you, I'm not certain our original bargain covers what this is turning into.*

It certainly doesn't, his employer replied quickly. *I'll add another five hundred dakkaris worth of gems, but you must see this through and bring me back the artifact once you've discovered what it does.*

I'll see to it. Mygal trusts me. He's good, but not as good as I am. If Rellen is successful, then I should be able to find an opportunity to take it from him. If Rellen fails, then we all do, as near as I can tell. And we both know what that means.

You understand perfectly, his employer replied.

Everything is going as you'd hoped, Tavyn said. *Better even.*

I don't hope, I weave, but you're right, it is turning out better than I'd anticipated, despite the surprises.

Weave? Tavyn asked.

You wouldn't understand. Was there anything else?

No, sir, Tavyn said. *We arrive in two or three days, and I expect we'll go straight from the docks to wherever it is Toreth has in mind.*

Then I haven't long to wait. Notify me once it's done.

I will.

Oh, and one last thing, his employer said *If you get the opportunity, kill Mygal.*

Mygal? Why?

It would make a different plan of mine go a little easier. And yes, it will warrant more coin.

His employer broke the connection.

Tavyn opened his eyes and started doing some addition in his head. By the time everything was over, he'd have earned a tidy sum. He'd feel bad about killing Mygal. He liked the fellow, but business was business, after all.

CHAPTER THIRTY-ONE

THE WARNING

 aleeria…

Her mentor's voice slipped into her thoughts as she strolled through the Royal Gardens.

I hear you, she replied. *Give me a moment.* She had not expected him to contact her for several days, although such contact wasn't completely out of the ordinary.

She'd just come from a meeting with the king. They'd gone over the latest reports from the four Guardians on special assignment. Kell Duranti had uncovered a large nest of Nissrans in Saritu'e'Mere. He'd killed one of the leaders, but two had gotten away. The king was sending Corsairs to help root out the infestation. Grall Akkrond had almost been killed and was recuperating in Caspari. Apparently, the vellish he'd run into were incredibly large and—it seemed—possessed of an intelligence heretofore unknown. Faleesh Namarre had, in fact, rooted out a plot to murder the duke in the Duchy of Mallorand. Three nobles as well as members of their family had been executed for their treason, but both Faleesh and the king worried she hadn't gotten all the traitors. Rellen was neck deep in Nissrans and might be in over his head.

She turned down a narrow path between several tall, flowering shrubs and took up a seat on a stone bench. *What is it you require, milord?*

Kaichakahn and possibly the entire Duchy of Nikostohr may be in jeopardy.

Impossible! Saleeria blurted. *Duke kyp'Tukeem is loyal to the king, and our forces there were hand-picked to cull out the old grievances.*

The Nissrans are there. I believe the grand vizier has been subverted... perhaps possessed. He may even be at the heart of the Nissrans.

Toreth sun'Harrai?

Did you not say yourself that the Second Guardian had concerns about him?

Yes, but possession? It seems hard to believe. How? When? The ceremony involved requires thirteen murders, and Jaquinn had only uncovered a few in Kaichakahn.

It would seem the vizier gets around, and what better way to surreptitiously manipulate a duchy than by doing so from the shadows, only a step or two from the duke? The irony was not lost on either of them.

So, what do we do? she asked, although she suspected there really was only one answer.

How long would it take to march a brigade of Corsairs from the capital to Kaichakahn?

More than a month. Perhaps more than two, and we'd have to shift troops around in order to do so. At least some of those the king just sent to secure our northern border with the Soo Kari'Ma would have to be recalled. A fair portion of our reserves were sent to Calamath and now Svennival. I just learned that there are Nissrans in Saritu'e'Mere and that the sedition in Mallorand was real. Troops will need to go there as well. Our forces are being spread out very thin.

I don't believe we have months, her mentor said. *And there is more at stake in Nikostohr than just the duchy.*

What else?

Stukelladios.

No one has ever found it, Saleeria said.

I believe someone has, and where else could a plunnokum be used? The other nuraghi on that peninsula are in ruins. I know Rellen has been hired by Toreth, and Toreth now has the plunnokum. You should receive word of this in a day or so, once Rellen's avatar arrives.

How can you know this?

That is my secret to keep, pupil, he said. *There are many reasons I am the Vice Master of the Readers, and you are my student. That is but one of them. Knowledge is strength.*

Knowledge is strength, she replied.

You should suggest to the king that he secure enough dewkalves to transport a brigade of Corsairs down to Nikostohr as quickly as possible. It would still take weeks, but I fear every second counts at this point.

It would cost a fortune and every last favor the king might have with the Transport Guild. Pelinon hasn't used the Guild for that in a hundred years, and with good reason.

Not doing so could cost us an entire duchy and perhaps more than any of us realizes. Whatever Toreth is after must be of incredible value and likely a threat to the whole kingdom. A single weed in an untended garden can quickly multiply and choke everything else out. It would seem Kaichakahn has been untended for far too long.

Saleeria let out a long, resigned breath. *I will speak with the king.*

CHAPTER THIRTY-TWO
FOR THE HONOR OF PELINON

Are you sure you're ready for this?" Rellen asked Miranda, setting his saddlebags and spell books over a shoulder. "It's not too late to back out, and things are likely to get considerably more dangerous from here on out. I have no idea what we're heading into."

The ship had reached the port of Kaichakahn an hour earlier, sounding out a horn to announce their arrival. They'd heard the crew dropping the sails. A large school of Bhirtas'Vuoda had towed the ship in to where they secured *Yl Jabbathene* against a dock. Neither Rellen nor Miranda had seen Kaichakahn before, so they'd waited before going up. They wanted to share the experience. It was an old tradition whenever the two of them came to a new city together.

"Risk was always part of the deal," Miranda replied. "And how is this any different from the battles we fought when we were in uniform?" She gave him a smile and opened the portal above the desk in their cabin. It faced out toward the bay. "Besides, we got three days of rest beforehand. A soft bed, no rain, hot meals… I don't remember the last time I had it this easy."

Rellen let out a long breath. "It has been relaxing, hasn't it?" He'd slept better the past three nights than he had in months. He'd had his side of the bed, she'd had hers. They were comrades, nothing less or more.

She stepped away from the desk and grabbed her own saddlebags.

Rellen scratched Xilly's neck gently where she sat on the bed, wondering if he should encourage her to leave too. *Once we get above decks, I'll let you know when there isn't anyone watching,* Rellen said to the dragonette. *You can fly out then.*

I can't wait to spread my wings. She yawned and stretched her wings out slightly in anticipation.

It won't be much longer.

"You know," Miranda started, "it's not like I missed those bastards, but I do think it's more than peculiar we never saw Toreth or Javyk."

"Or Dancer, for that matter," Rellen added. "I wonder if he's recovered. Not seeing them has bothered me too. I can't imagine what they've been doing, although Toreth is a noble-man and nobility can often be a bit eccentric. I've seen odder behaviors, and far too many of them don't like to commingle with the commoners." On the second night, at least, he had seen Jaquinn in the dining room, off in a corner, eating by himself. They'd barely exchanged glances, and that was it.

"I'm glad you're not like that," Miranda said, giving him a gentle shove.

"So am I," Rellen replied. "Let's get going. I really am excited to see the city. I've heard it's spectacular, even more so than Yaylo." The populace of Nikostohr, despite being a Duchy of Pelinon, was renowned for maintaining the ancient traditions of the peoples who had lived there for over a thousand years.

"Be ready for my signal, Xilly," Rellen said, picking up his saddle and hefting it over his other shoulder.

She nodded her tiny head, hopped off the bed, and crawled beneath it, in case someone came into the room. Rellen opened the door and let Miranda step past him. They walked down the corridor and spotted two of the ship's guards in king's livery standing outside the open door of a cabin a few doors down from the stairs.

"We hope you enjoyed the voyage," one of them called out with a wave and a friendly smile.

"We did," Miranda replied. "Thank you." She and Rellen continued down the hallway and stopped at the top of the stairs. "Tygeth, Maybor," she called down. "It's time to go!"

"I believe your companions went above deck some time ago," the guard replied. "The two gentlemen, right? You'll probably find them up there."

"Thanks," Rellen replied.

The guard nodded.

"I'm looking forward to getting some solid footing beneath me," Miranda said.

"If all goes well, we'll be heading back north soon enough," Rellen said. "I guess that's both good and bad news, isn't it?" He motioned toward the stairs. "After you."

She turned and moved up the stairs, with Rellen close behind.

"I wonder if we'll have time to—" Miranda's voice caught in her throat, and she stood frozen in the stairwell, two-thirds the way up. Her body stiffened.

"Miranda?"

Without a word, Miranda continued up the stairs. His view was blocked, but he thought he saw lots of people on deck, which didn't surprise him. Most of the passengers probably wanted to get a view of Kaichakahn as they came into port.

Miranda topped the stairs, took two steps forward, and then stepped aside, still without saying a word. As she did, Rellen's eyes went wide. His heart sank, his mind racing.

At least fifteen guards stood a short distance from the top of the stairs, all aiming crossbows at the two of them. The one with a captain's insignia on his collar placed a finger to his lips and motioned for Rellen to keep coming up. He stepped aside, and Rellen gasped. Fear, pain, and guilt clutched at his insides like a predator clawing at raw meat.

Stripped to the waist, his cardinal tattoo exposed, Mygal stood chained to the main mast. His face was a mask of blood, and bruises covered his arms and torso, as if he'd been beaten with a club. His head sagged to the side, and blood dripped from his ruined face down onto the deck. Javyk stood a short distance behind him to the right, a maddeningly pleased look upon his face.

Up against the port railing, a guard held a knife to Jaquinn's throat. Two more guards stood a few paces behind them, crossbows aimed. The dark-skinned Guardian had also been beaten bloody and was wrapped with heavy chains secured by a padlock. One of Jaquinn's eyes was swollen shut, his nose was a ruin, and his torn, saffron-colored garments were covered with his own blood. When Rellen met Jaquinn's gaze, there was only rage in his mentor's eyes.

On the other side of the deck, Tavyn stood in front of a line of guards, a defeated and fearful look upon his battered face. "They came for us early this morning," he said weakly. "We never heard them."

Rellen's worst fears had been realized in an instant. He tensed as the emotional storm in his breast turned to rage.

"Ah-ah," Javyk said, holding up a warning finger. "I wouldn't try anything. The only thing keeping them alive right now is your cooperation."

Mygal lifted his head. His eyes met Rellen's. There was no fear, only resolve. The young Guardian drew in a slow, long breath. "For the Honor of Pelinon," he whispered weakly.

Pain and impotent rage tore through Rellen's heart.

"Keep moving," a harsh voice barked from behind him.

Rellen glanced over his shoulder.

Four more guards had appeared at the bottom of the stairs, including the one who had greeted them from down the corridor. They held crossbows aimed straight up at Rellen.

"Come on all the way out of there, Rellen," Javyk called out. "We've been waiting for you, and you wouldn't want so much Guardian's blood on your hands, would you?"

Rellen's blood turned cold. *They know.*

He stepped forward a couple paces, his eyes slipping across the guards and fixing upon Javyk. He was looking for some sort of opening, any chance at all where he could drop his gear and do—*something.*

Javyk cocked his head to the side. "Think carefully," he said, that same maddening smile on his face. "You could try to do something, I suppose, *Guardian,* and you might just get me or the captain, but not before the rest of them filled her with crossbow bolts, and this Guardian's windpipe was opened to the sun." He motioned towards Jaquinn. "You would hear their screams and watch them die… and it would have no bearing whatsoever on your own fate." He glanced at Mygal. "Or *his.*" He stepped forward. "I must admit, you had me fooled. I salute you for that. There aren't many who could, but my master saw right through you. Now, both of you, stand over there with Tygeth."

Rellen let out a long breath. There was no way out of this that he could see. For a moment, he thought about going down fighting, but the longer the four of them were alive, the longer they'd have for an opportunity to present itself.

He met Miranda's eyes and nodded slightly. "Do as they say." He followed her over, and they took up a position beside Tavyn, their gear over their shoulders.

"Please," Javyk said agreeably, "feel free to put your things down. Just don't try anything or… it will go badly."

They set their gear on the deck. Rellen glanced up to the top of the quarterdeck where six more guards with loaded handheld crossbows stood.

Javyk turned to the two guards beside him. "You two, put those down and come with me." He strode calmly to the door beside the top of the stairs. Turning back to the captain, he said, "If any of them moves, kill everyone except that one," he pointed at Rellen. "Shoot him in the groin. Twice. Our master will be able to deal with that."

Javyk then opened the door and strode in, with the two guards following close behind.

"It's time, milord." Javyk's voice came faintly from within the room a few moments later. "You two, pick that up and throw it over the port side. Try not to leave a mess."

Moments later, the two guards came out carrying a naked body between them. Miranda gasped in horror.

"Gods have mercy," Tavyn whispered. He dry-heaved once and turned away.

Rellen could only stare. He knew all too well what Nissran torture looked like, although this was beyond his worst nightmare.

It was Dancer... at least, what was left of him. His body had been thin and sickly before. He was bald now, not a single hair left on his entire body. His chest had been carefully flayed, the blood-red musculature exposed. The rest of his flesh was a latticework of bleeding wounds and, pink, freshly healed scars. It looked like someone had cut on him over and over again, as if they'd cut and healed and cut again. Rellen couldn't comprehend how anyone could live long enough to endure such savagery.

The guards carried Dancer's ravaged body to the port railing and tossed him over the side, leaving a trail of crimson droplets along the deck. Whey they turned away from the railing, they both licked their hands clean of blood. The look in their eyes made the hair on the back of Rellen's neck stand up.

A moment later, Javyk stepped through the doorway with the satchel Dancer had been carrying slung over his shoulder. He walked back to his earlier position near Mygal. Toreth sun'Harrai followed him. Toreth's head was bare, and he now wore the traditional blue and black robes of Nikostohr nobility. Toreth took several steps closer to Rellen, an almost apologetic look on his face.

"Please forgive the theater," he said, "but Javyk seems to have an appetite for such things, and I felt like indulging him.

He wanted some recompense for your deceit. I suspect the look on your face was worth all this trouble." He glanced at Javyk. "Did it meet your expectations?"

"It was delicious," Javyk purred. "Almost as delicious as Dancer."

Toreth turned back to Rellen. "As I said in Yaylo, I do like to spoil those who give me their complete devotion." His head canted to the side with an almost expectant look upon his face. "You don't recognize me... although there's no reason you should." He leaned forward slightly, peering deep into Rellen's eyes, as if he were looking for something. "I, however, remember you. From *Calamath*."

"What are you talking about?" Rellen snapped, a confused look on his face. They'd gotten every last Nissran. He was sure of it. And the demon that tried to enter the baron's son had been sent back to wherever it came from. Even the demon possessing the leader of the Nissran cult had been destroyed. Rellen watched it happen.

Toreth smiled. "You really have no idea what you're dealing with, which will make this all the sweeter when you do." He drew in a breath and let it out with sublime satisfaction. "You'll see things from this side of the mirror soon enough, but not before we indulge ourselves in a bit of suffering first. It's such a lovely morning, after all."

"What? Are you going to kill them right here? What about the dock workers? The other passengers?"

"Kill them?" Toreth stared at Rellen like he was a foolish child. "What I do to them is the least of your worries. Look around you, Guardian." He motioned toward the guards. "They are mine." He glanced out at the docks. "The docks are mine. At this point, most of the city is mine, and many came along *willingly*. Even Duke kyp'Tukeem and his family are mine. As for the passengers, their life force—their very lives— allowed me to keep Dancer alive for three days. The best part is that *his* agony was freely given. It was as sweet as anything I've tasted in a very, *very* long time." He nodded toward

Jaquinn. "He had no idea what was going on, and it happened right under his nose. I had originally planned on perverting him to my purposes, but now I have *you*." Toreth's eyes flared green. "The arrogance of humans, even after all this time, still astounds me."

A look of realization filled Rellen's features. "So, you *are* one of them," he growled. "Another one of that bitch-goddess's vile, stinking demons." He spat on the deck.

Toreth chuckled. "Only a human could be so completely wrong on all counts." He looked over his shoulder and stared at Mygal for a moment. "Here, let me show you something." He strode over and stood beside the young Guardian, whose face filled with fear. Mygal strained against the chains. When Toreth turned back to Rellen, his eyes flared with green flames, and the malevolent smile on his face sent a shock of terror along Rellen's spine. He lifted his right index finger, where a bright, ruby, pinpoint of light glowed. Holding Mygal's head in an iron grip, he traced a line straight down Mygal's cheek. Blood flowed. Mygal's scream pierced the air, echoing along the docks. He jerked and twisted against the chains, but he couldn't escape Toreth's torture.

Rellen surged, but the guards behind him clamped their hands around his arms and held him in place.

Toreth laughed as he turned Mygal's head. Mygal strained against it, but to no avail. Toreth ran another bloody line down Mygal's other cheek. Again, Mygal let out an agonized scream. The guards all started laughing, delighting in the young Guardian's pain.

"Enough!" Jaquinn surged within his chains and bashed his forehead into the face of the guard who held the dagger at his throat. The guard staggered back as Jaquinn tipped backwards. He gave Rellen one last look, his eyes still full of fury, and then toppled over the railing.

Everyone turned.

"Jaquinn!" Rellen screamed as the big man disappeared over the railing. A short length of chain dangling from his feet clattered against the railing as Jaquinn fell. It slapped once against the wood and followed the Guardian over. There was a mighty splash.

Blind rage and anguish surged through Rellen's breast.

Toreth glanced at the spot where Jaquinn had disappeared. "That is a pity." He let out a long, disappointed breath and strode across the deck, stopping only a few feet away from Rellen. "Javyk and I were looking forward to savoring every last drop of him."

"I'll kill you!" Rellen shouted. Fueled by hatred, he broke free from the guards, surged forward, and wrapped his hands around Toreth's throat.

Toreth never moved, and a reptilian smile crimped his lips.

The thrum of four small crossbows filled the air. Rellen felt a sharp pain in his arm.

His vision blurred. His hands went numb. His fingers loosened around Toreth's throat and slipped free to dangle at the ends of limp arms.

"Good night, Guardian. It took a month for Javyk and one of my cabals to open the way for me. You *know* what I'm talking about." As Rellen's vision darkened and his knees wobbled, Toreth leaned in. "What took them a month to do to this body, I'm going to do to yours in a day."

Rellen! Xilly's panicked thought hammered through the fog that surrounded Rellen's consciousness. Rellen could only manage one thought.

Save Jaquinn... save your...self...

The darkness swallowed him like he was a stone tossed into the sea.

CHAPTER THIRTY-THREE
PRISONERS

A cacophony of bird calls filtered into Rellen's slowly returning consciousness. A dozen other animal sounds—*monkeys?*—added themselves to the chorus. The air was hot... humid... even more so than it had been aboard the ship. He wasn't on the ship anymore. He knew that. There was no rocking, no motion, and the shriek of gulls was noticeably absent.

His thoughts were fuzzy, unfocused. He struggled to think clearly. Bit by bit, enough clarity came for him to realize his shoulders hurt. And his arms. His chest felt tight, as if some heavy weight was pressing into it.

A single, low, thrumming voice—in a strange, guttural language Rellen didn't recognize—filtered into his awareness. Like nothing else in his experience, he could sense the power of majea flowing with it. The language seemed strangely familiar, as if he'd heard it before, but he couldn't place where. The words crescendoed and cut off. In that moment, two things happened, and one of them Rellen wouldn't have thought was possible. Deep in his mind, he sensed a distant buzzing, as if there were an insect locked away inside his skull somewhere. But there was something else. He tried to wrap his mind around what he was feeling. Something was very wrong. Then it occurred to him that the problem lay in what he *wasn't* feeling. Something that had been with him since he was a teen had disappeared.

He reached within himself, tried to tap into the majea that had been with him for almost as long as he could remember, and... nothing. It wasn't there. It had been cut off. He knew—he'd been taught—that such a thing wasn't possible. He reached for his majea once again, straining against the emptiness like a man in utter darkness straining to see, but there was nothing.

He opened his eyes to find a slim man in black and blue robes walking away from him, moving toward a large campfire with a circle of stumps set around it. Bright, tropical sunshine filled a wide clearing within what had to be an immense jungle. Tall trees rose above them, and there were several fresh stumps just at the edge of the clearing, with the felled trees laying on their sides. It looked like the shrubs and vines in the clearing had also been recently cleared away.

Toreth! Rellen blinked his eyes several times to try and clear the haze. It *was* Toreth sun'Harrai, and he held the plunnokum in his hand. Rellen feared they stood upon the precipice of whatever lay at the center of Toreth's designs, and there was nothing he could do about it. He reached vainly for his majea once again, fighting against the fog that filled his thoughts, but he found nothing to grab onto. Desperation filled him.

Xilly? he called out. *Are you there?*

There was no reply.

He tried to move and realized he couldn't. He glanced to his right to find his arm outstretched and secured to a wagon with stout chain at wrist and elbow. He still wore his leather armor, but the chain was also wrapped around his torso, secured with a padlock that dangled over his breast. The chains around that arm also secured Miranda's arm, with Mygal and Tavyn similarly secured and unconscious on the other side of her. Their bodies sagged against their bonds. All of their weapons were gone, and his bandoleer and belt were also missing.

On the ground, laid out in the shape of a box surrounding Rellen and the others, were four dark stones that glowed with an ethereal, emerald light. They were just beyond the reach of his legs, and beams of flowing majea connected them. He could feel the power emanating from them, like heat pouring off of a red-hot brand. The stones must be what had cut off his majea, but such a thing wasn't supposed to be possible. This was a magic he'd never even heard of.

He glared at Toreth. "What have you done?" The words came out slurred. His tongue felt like it was wrapped in wool.

Toreth turned at the sound. A slim smile spread across his face. He cocked his head to the side and peered at Rellen, as if he were inspecting an animal before deciding if he should stable or slaughter it.

Rellen struggled to get his feet beneath him. His knees wobbled. He sagged again, marshaling what little strength he had. He steadied himself and stood up, as much as the chains allowed. Voices on the other side of the wagon caught his ear.

"It seems I finished my work just in time," Toreth said, stepping away from the campfire. "I must admit, it wasn't easy." He held up the plunnokum. "This helped." He drew in a deep breath and let it out slowly, as if he'd undertaken something strenuous. "I am glad you're awake." He shifted his focus to the right of the wagon. "Javyk, come here, and bring the others," he called out. "It is time."

"I asked you a question," Rellen snapped. The fog in his head was clearing quickly. He felt a bit more like himself—except for his majea.

Miranda groaned, and then Mygal.

"Not that I'm inclined to answer any of your questions, *human*," Toreth said, "but I'll grant you this one. Still, I would have thought the answer was obvious, even to you. And here I thought Guardians were supposed to be intelligent." He chuckled lightly. "The answer is that I've denied you access to your majea."

"That's not possible," Rellen whispered.

"For humans," Toreth said. "Perhaps I gave you too much credit." He rolled his eyes. "Your race can be so very obtuse. Putting it simply, I've prevented your puny mind from accessing a power you never should have had to begin with. It took me a very long time to come up with something like this, but it will be most useful in the future. Today, it is merely a convenience."

"When was Toreth possessed by you, demon?"

"Demon...?" Toreth mused. "I suppose that word is as good as any." Again, he seemed to be talking to himself. He finally locked eyes with Rellen. "But you're less than half-right."

Javyk, in his black robes, came around the side of the wagon, with ten guards in the king's livery behind him. Rellen didn't recognized any from the ship. He had to wonder how many in Kaichakahn willingly served Toreth and how many had been converted to his will. Did he now control the entire city? The duchy?

"You called for us, Master," Javyk said with a slight bow.

"They're waking... and my efforts," he motioned toward the glowing lines of light at Rellen's feet, "have been successful."

"Was there ever any doubt?" Javyk replied.

"No," Toreth replied. "I've prepared for so long. My toehold in this place is about to become an entrenchment." Toreth glanced at the jungle behind him, as if there were something there. "It's time for me to undo that thrice-cursed lock." There was pure venom in his voice. He turned back to Javyk. "The prisoners should give you no trouble at all, and that spell should last long enough to give me ample time to do what I must and return. Make sure they don't escape those chains and that none of them dies."

"It will be as you wish, Master." Javyk hesitated for just a moment. He licked his lips, as if he were starving but feared of asking for a crust of bread.

"What is it, pet?" Toreth said, and there was a strange affection in his voice.

"Forgive me, but I had hoped you might grant me the gift of at least one of them to entertain myself and feed while you went below. May I... may I have just one of them, my lord?" Javyk looked first at Rellen and then the others.

"I think not. I'll need Rellen and his companions for the next phase of my plans. They should make perfect instruments for my designs."

"*Please*... just one." The sound of it filled Rellen with disgust and dread.

Toreth let out a long breath, his face a mask of deep thought. "Very well," he finally said. "Take that one... on the end." He pointed at Mygal. "You can finish what I started. Of the two, his gifts are the weakest."

The statement confused Rellen. Mygal might be the weakest, but, including Miranda and himself, there were three kurioi.

Mygal's blackened eyes, still somewhat dazed by whatever poison they'd used, suddenly went wide with fear.

"Perfect!" Javyk said with a good deal of enthusiasm. "We'll have no difficulty at all with him."

"Then let it be done," Toreth replied with a dismissive hand. With the plunnokum in hand, he turned and strode past the campfire. A dozen paces later, he vanished before their eyes, as if he'd walked through a curtain.

"What the—?" Rellen blurted.

"Where did he go?" Miranda blinked several times at the spot where Toreth had disappeared.

"Welcome to Stukelladios," Javyk said with a good deal of enthusiasm. He turned to the two largest guards and pointed at Mygal. "Release that one. Be sure not to disturb the stones."

"Yes, sir," they said in unison.

The captain handed one of them a ring of keys.

"You may have to incapacitate him first," Javyk offered with a good deal of enthusiasm. "I suspect he'll fight vigorously the moment those chains are released. I know I would."

The guards crossed over to Mygal, who again struggled fiercely, but the chains held him tight.

"You bastards!" he screamed. "I'll kill you both! I'll kill all of you!"

"Wretch," Rellen growled, glaring at Javyk. "If I get out of these chains, I'm going to cut your heart out."

Javyk smiled. "Now you sound like a servant of my master. Don't worry, you'll be cutting hearts out soon enough. They just won't be mine."

The guards stepped up in front of Mygal, careful to avoid even getting near the stones. Mygal stopped struggling and went limp.

That's it. Suck them in. Look for an opening. Fight, Rellen thought. He hoped the young informant planned on kicking the nearest stone. If Toreth's magic was broken, they might have a chance. Mygal could influence them. Miranda might be able to wound them. Rellen… well… he wasn't sure what he'd do. Much of his magic was stored up in the objects in his bandoleer and pouches. He only had a few useful spells that he could cast without a material component.

One of the guards reared back an arm and swung hard. His fist struck Mygal's jaw with a wet, meaty *thwack*. Mygal's head snapped around and came back with a spray of blood. His eyes rolled. His tongue lolled. The guard hit him again. And again.

Mygal sagged in the chains, unconscious. Blood spilled from his mouth and nose.

"You miserable bastards!" Rellen screamed.

Javyk laughed.

The other guard used a key to open the lock dangling in front of Mygal's chest. When he was free, they took a firm grip on his arms and carefully dragged his body toward the campfire.

"You two," Javyk pointed at two more guards. "Help carry him. I want him tied down before he regains consciousness. The rest of you can relax around the fire, if you like, but stay here and keep an eye on them. If they try to escape, feel free to beat them. Just don't kill them. If any of them dies, you'll all answer to the master."

"Yes sir," they replied.

The guard with the key ring tossed them back to the captain, who caught them and slipped them into his belt.

The other two guards moved over and picked up Mygal's legs. Javyk led them past the campfire, and moments later, they too disappeared. Rellen's eyes shifted back and forth, trying to find something—anything that would create such an illusion. There was nothing. The jungle seemed undisturbed, extending out into green shadows and shafts of light for as far as he could see.

"What can we do?" Miranda hissed at Rellen, panic filling her eyes.

"We've got to do something," Tavyn said quietly.

The same old fear clutched at Rellen's heart—of losing someone he was responsible for. Mygal was about to be butchered, and he had no way to stop it. He thought furiously, trying to come up with some idea of how they might escape, but nothing came.

CHAPTER THIRTY-FOUR

REVELATION

R ellen dug deep, drawing strength from his desperation. He strained against the chains... shifted, twisted, jerked against them. He struggled to get free with everything he had, screaming out his anger, frustration, and fear. He finally sagged back into the chains, gasping.

The guards sitting casually around the campfire laughed.

"Save your strength, Guardian," the captain called out. "You're going to need it once Master Toreth gets back."

"Traitor," Rellen barked.

"Traitor?" The captain gave Rellen a disgusted look. "I serve my people. Look at my hair, my skin." He had black hair and dark skin of Nikostohr. "The king of Pelinon conquered my people... consumed them. I serve Toreth because he wants us to be free of the Pelinese yoke."

"That was over a hundred years ago, and Pelinon didn't start that war, Nikostohr did when they invaded Aradeen and tried to sack Jabono. Nikostohr started a fight it couldn't finish, and all because their king was a fool."

"You can—" the captain started.

"*What?*" Javyk's angry shout rose from up beyond the illusory curtain. His voice was distant and muffled, as if it had come from inside a building. Several moments passed. "Go get more rope, you imbecile!"

One of the guards seemed to appear out of thin air and entered the clearing. He headed straight for the back of the wagon, and as he did, a small, dark shadow passed over the thick grass covering the ground only a few feet behind the guards.

Rellen looked up.

Xilly! he cried as she passed overhead.

There was no answer as she circled back and looked straight down at him.

You can't help us. Get out of here! There was nothing she could do, and then she'd die too. *Save yourself, little one…*

Still, she said nothing. Had she heard him? Maybe Toreth's magic prevented that as well. The buzzing in his mind was still present. He shook his head, trying to break free of it, but it remained, a sliver in his mind that wouldn't come loose. Not since that first nuraghi had Rellen felt so completely defeated…

Xilly disappeared from sight, passing over the wagon and, presumably, into the trees.

Please don't try anything, Rellen thought.

The guard Javyk sent out moved around to the back of the wagon. He rummaged through whatever lay inside for a few moments and then stopped abruptly.

"Hey!" His surprised shout made everyone turn their heads.

The sickly wet sound of steel cleaving meat and bone filled the air. The guard's head tumbled out into view, rolling a short distance toward the campfire. There was no mistaking the sound of a crumpling body against soft earth. Twin gouts of blood spurted out from behind the wagon, spraying onto the surprised look filling the face of the severed head.

Everyone—guards and prisoners alike—stood frozen in shock, stupefied by what had just happened.

Xilly? Rellen thought. It couldn't be.

A tall figure in tattered, saffron-colored silks stepped out from behind the wagon. He held a large, gleaming scimitar in one hand and a crossbow in the other. He raised the crossbow and fired at the nearest guard. The bolt chunked into the guard's leather cuirass, staggering him back. The guard fell onto his back, clutching at the shaft sticking out the center of his chest. He gave one, bloody, gurgling grunt and went still.

"Jaquinn!" Rellen shouted. He couldn't believe his eyes.

"Kill him!" one of the guards shouted, pointing at Jaquinn.

The six remaining guards scrambled to their feet as Xilly flew over the campsite again.

Three of the guards reached for the crossbows they'd laid on the grass. The rest drew their blades.

In the distance, Mygal shrieked in pain. It cut off. A moment later, Javyk screamed in terror. As his voice faded, the ring of steel clashing on steel rose upon the air.

Several of the guards hesitated, turning toward the new conflict with confusion on their faces.

As three of the guards charged Jaquinn, he raised his hand and seemed to freeze, his face a mask of concentration. The other guards raised their crossbows. An instant later, the crossbow strings snapped in their faces, but not before one bolt shot out, swerving wildly to the right.

The bolt struck Tavyn in the shoulder and pinned him to the wagon. He yowled in pain.

Jaquinn came to life, raising his blade to parry a slash from the closest guard.

"The stones!" Rellen screamed at Xilly. Jaquinn was about to be outnumbered six to one. "Move the stones!"

Xilly folded her wings and dove.

The other guards drew their swords as the first three engaged Jaquinn. They slashed and thrust. Jaquinn parried and dodged, stepped back, gave ground to keep them from surrounding him. He'd been badly beaten, but his scimitar was a blur as he kept the first three at bay.

Xilly hit the ground at Rellen's feet, just outside the glowing lines of energy. She charged the nearest stone and slammed her body into it, shoving with her front legs. The stone rolled over. The energy surged, flaring bright—and detonated with a release of light and sound that hammered into Rellen's body.

Stunned, Rellen shook his head to clear the ringing in his ears. His entire body tingled with the jolt of energy that had passed through him. Blinking, he regained his senses, and the scene came into focus.

The three closest guards had staggered sideways. They shook their heads, dazed.

Jaquinn now faced two opponents. The third lay on the ground groaning with a deep belly wound from which a river of blood poured out onto the grass.

Xilly lay on the ground just past the campfire, motionless, with her neck, legs, and wings akimbo. Thin tendrils of smoke rose from her body.

"Xilly!" Rellen screamed, despair and rage filling his heart.

"Rellen!" Miranda barked urgently. "We're *free…*"

He met her gaze. The buzzing in his mind was gone. He reached out and could feel his majea once again stirring within his breast. Xilly had done it—but at a terrible cost.

Miranda turned her eyes to the nearest guard, and her face twisted into rage. *"Pain,"* she growled in a voice guttural and primitive.

The guard shrieked in agony. He crumpled to the ground, writhing, and his screams went on, sounding as if he'd been set on fire.

Tavyn lifted his head and seemed to focus on the captain. His forehead was beaded with sweat, and he looked pale. His face compressed into one of intense concentration. "Free your friends." His pained voice rose above the screams and the clashing battle Jaquinn still fought. He locked eyes with the captain. "We're in trouble. We need your help."

A shock of realization slammed into Rellen. Tavyn was an erkurioi. He'd lied the entire time. With that, everything fell into place. *He* had attacked Mygal in Svennival. Rage and betrayal surged through Rellen. He wanted to kill Tavyn right then and there, but he couldn't. He needed him—for now.

The captain regained his senses, and an almost friendly smile crossed his face. He stared back at Tavyn, his head cocked to the side.

"That's it," Tavyn said through clenched teeth. "Help your friends..." He groaned with the strain... "Stop... fighting me... you bastard... *Now.*"

The captain swayed slightly, and then he straightened up.

"Captain?" the guard beside him said.

The captain glanced at his subordinate, a strange look on his face. Anger blossomed there. In a fluid motion, he placed his hand on the guard's shoulder and drove his sword up with a quick thrust. The blade entered beneath the guard's chin and sprang out the top of his head, covered in blood.

The guard jerked once.

The captain released the blade, letting the guard crumple to the ground. He turned back to Tavyn, a strangely satisfied look on his face.

"Free me first," Rellen ordered, looking to Tavyn, whose face was still contorted with concentration. "We'll settle up once all of this is over. *Trust me.* I can get us out of here."

Tavyn gave him a sidelong glance, a worried expression on his face. He nodded and turned back to the captain. "You heard my friend."

The captain strode straight toward Rellen.

Rellen closed his eyes and tapped deeply into his majea. He'd used this spell to release leather bonds and entangle the garments of his opponents. What he had in mind would take a good deal more energy, but fueled by his rage and hate, he had plenty to spare. He focused his will and shaped small, potent symbols in the air with his hands. As he completed the spell, his majea coursed through his limbs and spread out across his bonds. An instant later, the chains rattled, quivering and shifting as they strained against the padlock that secured them.

The captain grasped the padlock, inserted the key, and twisted. The hasp clicked and came free.

Rellen's smile was predatory. He poured all his rage for Xilly's loss, his hatred of the Nissrans, and the betrayal of the traitorous guards *and* Tavyn into the magic that pulsed within the chains. He wrapped his mind around them. In a flash, the length of chain erupted in a blur of motion. It uncoiled itself from around Rellen's arms, slipped through the posts and boards of the wagon, and slithered from around his torso like an angry snake.

"Hold him, Tavyn," Rellen commanded grimly.

"You better hurry," Tavyn said through gritted teeth.

The chains became a living thing, coiling, writhing, and clinking at Rellen's feet. He stepped away from the wagon and turned to help Jaquinn, who barely kept ahead of the guard's blades as they rained blows down, pushing him up to the edge of the trees.

"Enough!" Rellen shouted. He looked down at the long length of chain, and like some mad serpent, it slithered and streaked through the grass. Rellen willed one end of the chain to coil up a guard's leg. The other end wrapped around the other guard's leg. Loop after loop spiraled up and around their legs, torsos, and finally necks.

They screamed out their shock and fear.

Jaquinn staggered back, leaning against a tree as he sucked in air. He was covered with small cuts.

Rellen closed his fist, tightening the loops around their necks.

Both guards dropped their swords, clutching at the chains that choked the life out of them. Rellen squeezed harder... and harder. The guards gurgled, gagged. Their breaths came out in raspy bursts until, finally, the sound was cut off completely. They stiffened, their faces crimson and eyes bulging as they clawed at the chains. First one fell over, and then the other. Rellen waited for their legs to stop kicking. He waited a little longer, his knuckles white as everyone watched the guards die.

Finally, Rellen relaxed his fist. His grip on the spell slipped away. The chains went slack around the two dead guards. Rellen sagged, blowing out an exhausted breath. Sucking in hard, he lifted his eyes and saw Xilly still lying on the grass. Anger surged once again.

"I can't hold—" Tavyn said, his voice fading.

Rellen turned, grabbed the captain by the shoulder, and spun him around.

The man stood before him, a friendly smile on his face that started to fade, replaced by a look of confusion.

Rellen plucked the keyring from the captain's hand and a dagger from his belt. He didn't know if the captain had willingly followed Toreth or if he'd been possessed. He knew he didn't care. "Say hello to Nissra for me," he said quietly and drove the blade into the captain's throat, twisting it viciously.

The captain gurgled, a horrified look on his face.

Rellen yanked on his shoulder again and stepped out of the way. The captain staggered and fell forward onto his face. Rellen glanced at where Javyk and the others had disappeared, wondering why they hadn't joined the fight. Something was very wrong. He bent over to pick up a sword.

"Let's get those two out of there," he said. "But keep an eye out. Javyk and three other guards went through that barrier with Mygal. I don't know what happened, but they might just come after us now."

"Did they have crossbows?" Jaquinn asked as he waked over, still sucking in heavy breaths.

"No," Rellen replied. "You alright?" he asked, realizing how slow Jaquinn was moving.

"I'll manage," Jaquinn replied. "You better hurry though," he added, his eyes flicking to the locks that secured Miranda and Tavyn.

Rellen leaned the sword against his leg and turned a key in one padlock, then the other. The hasps came free, and he started undoing Miranda's chains as Jaquinn worked on freeing Tavyn.

"We saw you go over the side," Rellen said as he worked. "How?"

Tavyn hissed in pain as Jaquinn jostled him. Rellen's eyes met Tavyn's for just a moment, but in that flicker of time, the rage in Rellen's eyes burned through Tavyn's pain and turned it to fear.

"The Bhirtas'Vuoda," Jaquinn explained. "The tribe that docks the ships in Kaichakahn Bay? Their shaman and I have been—well, you couldn't call it friends. We've been *allies* for a very long time. His people grabbed me as I sank, and you saw what I did to those bowstrings... Chain takes longer, more majea, but it's possible."

"But the water," Rellen said, tearing his gaze away from Tavyn as he pulled another loop free. "You should have drowned."

"Water is just two elements, Rellen, one of which is the air we breathe," Jaquinn replied. "Separating them is one of the first advanced lessons they teach gekurioi at the academy. It takes even more energy, but it's possible for a talented Land Magician."

"You must be exhausted," Rellen said, pulling the last loop from around Miranda's chest. She stepped away and stretched her arms and neck.

"Well, I won't be *bending* any steel for a while," Jaquinn said, blowing out a weary breath as he freed one of Mygal's arms, "but I can still swing it, as you saw." He glanced at Rellen. "My mind is spent. My body is not."

"One last question."

Jaquinn smiled knowingly. "The dragonette led me here. I believe she followed your scent."

Rellen shook his head. "I never dreamed—"

"Kaichakahn is about five or six miles that way." Jaquinn pointed almost due east past the other side of the wagon, "and the King's Highway is a few hundred yards down a path that cuts through the forest." He hesitated for a moment, glancing towards where Xilly lay, then said gently, "She, I hope, *is* an amazing little creature."

Pain tore at Rellen's heart. "Thank you." He wanted to go to her, but they had to free themselves first, in case Javyk and the soldiers came back.

"I'll go see about her," Miranda said, placing a hand on Rellen's arm.

Rellen nodded as Jaquinn pulled the last of the chains from around Tavyn's chest. Tavyn hissed in pain again, which gave Rellen a certain sense of satisfaction. The informant was still pinned to the wagon by the crossbow bolt, and they would have to find a way to cut the bolt or slide him off of it.

Rellen picked up the sword and looked at the barrier again. He couldn't imagine why Javyk and the others hadn't attacked. And what happened to Mygal? *Is he dead?* A pang of fear washed through him.

"There are saws and axes in the back of the wagon," Jaquinn said, "along with your weapons and bandoleer."

"That's something, at least," Rellen said with a relieved breath. "Toreth said he intended to stuff one of Nissra's demons inside me." He shook his head at the thought of it. "That would have put two of those things in the world, and one of them a Guardian."

"Two that we know of," Jaquinn corrected. "You heard the reports at the Conclave. I think this is happening all over, and whatever Toreth is doing inside Stukelladios is just a part of a larger strategy." He looked around. "That's where we are, isn't it?"

Rellen nodded. "There's some sort of barrier over there... we can't see what's past it, but Toreth, Javyk, and those guards walked right through it."

"That would explain why nobody ever found the place," Jaquinn said.

"She's alive, Rellen," Miranda called out from where she leaned over Xilly.

Rellen spun, hope blossoming in his heart.

Miranda carefully picked up Xilly's limp body and cradled the dragonette in her arms.

"Bring her to the back of the wagon," Rellen called out. He looked at Tavyn and narrowed his eyes. "We'll have you off of there momentarily." He placed the tip of the sword in the notch beneath Tavyn's throat. "The question you should ask yourself is what happens after that."

"Rellen?" Jaquinn blurted. "What are you doing?"

Rellen locked eyes with the Second Guardian. "The attack on Thirteen that brought me to Svennival?"

"Yes…"

"He's the one who did it."

Jaquinn's eyes went wide, and then he glared at Tavyn. He placed a hand on the grip of his scimitar, and his knuckles went pale.

"Not yet," Rellen said, placing a hand on Jaquinn's arm. "I have questions that need answering." He turned to Tavyn. "If he does exactly what I tell him, I might just commute the death sentence hanging over his head."

Tavyn gulped. "Whatever you need."

"Tell me why you're here," Rellen growled.

"To get that artifact." There was no hesitation in Tavyn's voice, and fear filled his eyes.

"For who?"

"I don't know his name. He wants it, he didn't tell me why, and he pays well…" Tavyn paused for a moment. "It's only business," he said, as if that excused everything.

Rellen's knuckles went white.

Miranda stepped up to the back of the wagon. "Rellen, can you come back here?"

"Keep an eye on that barrier or whatever it is," Rellen said as he passed by Jaquinn. "I'll find a saw."

Jaquinn nodded.

Rellen joined Miranda as she gently laid Xilly's limp body on a folded-up section of canvass. The fabric was pulled partially back, and beneath lay the coil of rope the guard was after. Rellen pulled it all the way out and let it fall to the ground. He spotted their weapons further in and quickly grabbed his belt, strapping it on quickly. The weight of his falchions felt good on his hips. He pulled several large tree saws out of the way, moved a couple large axes, and found a small hand saw.

"You're going to let Tavyn live?" Miranda eyes held barely contained rage.

"For now, at least. He has information I need. He's working for someone. I'm sure of it. He wouldn't have gone to all this trouble, risked his neck, unless there was a good reason for it. Maybe it's just coin, but I have to know who put him on us and why he drew a second Guardian into Svennival."

"How do you know he did that?" Miranda looked dubious.

"It's the only thing that makes sense."

"You wretched swine!" Javyk's enraged voice filled the air.

In a flash, Rellen dropped the saw and bolted out from behind the wagon just as Jaquinn spun toward Javyk's voice.

The Nissran stood there, his face contorted in a mask of rage. His robes had been cut along his right forearm and belly. Blood had spread out over his dark robes.

Javyk swung his arm. A ruby scythe of light lanced out, aimed straight at Tavyn, who was still pinned to the wagon. Jaquinn stepped in front, shielding Tavyn's body with his own. The scythe of light struck Jaquinn in the center of his chest. Blood splashed out from a gaping wound. He staggered back, slammed against the wagon, and dropped to the ground.

"Pin him down!" Rellen shouted at Miranda, as he dashed to his left and jerked a falchion free.

Javyk slashed again with his hand. A ruby scythe sailed straight at Rellen as he raced across the grass. He hoped Miranda was fast enough… and still strong enough.

Miranda slashed with her own arm. The ruby scythe splintered and faded from view only a foot from Rellen's body. She lifted her other hand and focused on Javyk. *"Pain,"* she roared.

Just as Javyk was about to slash again, he cried out in pain and locked eyes with Miranda. He closed his mouth. His body went rigid. He shook as he fought to counter Miranda's majea with his own.

Rellen charged forward, making sure he didn't get between the two of them.

A low, primeval growl rose from Javyk's lips as he strained against Miranda's assault. Her angry roar turned to a scream of pain. She shook with agony, but her outstretched hand never wavered.

Rellen pounded toward Javyk, whose eyes had rolled back into his head. His screams were horrifying, full of lunatic rage, like some unnatural beast that had crept out of an unholy darkness.

Rellen closed with Javyk, raised his falchion, and swung with all of his strength. The heavy blade came down onto Javyk's shoulder at a steep angle, cleaving through flesh and bone as it sank all the way to his sternum. Javyk's terrible howl cut off as his eyes went wide and blood sprayed.

Rellen jerked the falchion free, twisting Javyk's body around. He leaned in. "I told you I'd cut your heart out." He drove his falchion into the center of Javyk's back. The point sprang out through his chest as blood spurted along the bright steel. Rellen twisted the blade as hard as he could and jerked it free.

Javyk shuddered and coughed with a sickly wet sound as blood sprayed out onto the grass.

Rellen wound up one last time and cleaved Javyk's head from his shoulders.

Javyk's knees folded beneath him, and his lifeless body dropped, toppling sideways. His head tumbled across the grass to roll up against a tree.

Rellen spat once on the ground and turned back. Jaquinn lay on the ground, motionless. His chest had been split from shoulder to groin. The Second Guardian of Pelinon was dead. Pain and regret filled Rellen's heart. Off to the side, Miranda had fallen to her hands and knees, her head sagging toward the ground.

"Miranda!" He raced to her side.

She lifted her head, breathing heavily. Her forehead was bathed in sweat, and her eyes were bloodshot, her skin flushed.

"I'm alright," she said, gasping. She met his gaze. "But you got him just in time." Rellen helped her to her feet. "That nasty bastard was *strong*."

"Not anymore," he said grimly.

Miranda turned to where Xilly's limp form still lay.

"See to her," Rellen sheathed his falchion. "I'm going to cut Tavyn free."

"Do you see my saddlebags?" she asked.

Rellen peered inside the wagon. "Yes."

"Then open the right one and pull out a kara root."

Rellen obliged and set the tuber on the back of the wagon within Miranda's reach. He then grabbed the saw.

"What about those other guards, the ones that went in with Javyk?" She gently placed her hand on Xilly's chest. "And what happened in there?"

"He wouldn't have come out alone. Maybe Mygal got them before they got him?"

"He was in pretty bad shape." She looked dubious. "Him against Javyk *and* three guards? And did you notice Javyk had been bloodied?"

"Yes, badly," Rellen said. "But he fought like a vellish. I don't get it."

"Do you think Mygal's dead?"

Rellen fought off a wave of guilt. It had happened again. He was supposed to mentor Mygal, not get him killed. "I guess we'll find out soon enough."

"So, we're going in," Miranda said. She closed her eyes and focused her mind on Xilly.

"We have to." He pulled out his bandoleer and slipped it over his head. He drew forth a small crystal, gestured, and muttered the incantation. A soft white glow flashed over his body, and the subsequent tingle quickly subsided.

He let out a resigned breath and stepped out to eye Tavyn. "That includes you." He stepped up, carefully moving over Jaquinn's body, and stared into Tavyn's pained, fearful eyes.

The informant's face was pale, his hair damp with sweat.

"You're going to help us get Toreth. When he's dead, you're going to answer every question I ask you. If I like what I hear, you might—*might*—just have a way out of this. I've sentenced you to death. Only I can commute it, and only if you do exactly as I say. That's the bargain. Take it, or die here, and if you so much as touch me with your magic, I'll spill your guts around your boots. Understood?"

"I don't know how much good I'll be to you in a fight," Tavyn said weakly.

"I guess you'll just have to dig deep, then, won't you?" He held up the saw and drew one of his falchions. "Which is it going to be?"

Tavyn nodded towards the saw, his mouth pressed into a thin line.

"This is going to hurt." Rellen sheathed his blade. "And I'm going to enjoy every moment of it."

"Just do it," Tavyn clenched his teeth.

Rellen placed the saw as close to Tavyn's body as he could and started cutting. The informant flinched with every stroke. It didn't take long before the shaft came free. Tavyn stood up straight and tried to lift his arm. He yelped in pain again and looked at Rellen.

"Don't worry. We'll take care of that."

"Miranda," Rellen called out, "how is Xilly?"

"She's unconscious and breathing shallowly. I couldn't sense any damage inside her, but I have no idea how long it will be before she wakes up, assuming she even does. I don't even know what kind of magic did this."

Rellen's guts churned. "I need you to tend Tavyn's wound. There's still a hell of a fight ahead of us, and he's coming with."

She leaned out, a stern expression on her face. "You sure about that?"

"No choice," Rellen replied. "And hurry."

"I can at least stop the bleeding and give him some mobility in that arm."

"It's the erkurios in him that I want."

"If you say so." She didn't look convinced as Rellen helped his prisoner around to the back of the wagon. "Let's get that bolt out, and then I'll see what I can do."

Rellen met Tavyn's gaze. "Slow or fast?"

"Yank it."

Rellen looked at Miranda. "You ready?" He wrapped his fingers around the bolt.

Holding a kara root tightly, she closed her eyes, drew in a long breath, and let it out slowly. When she opened her eyes again, she raised her hand to hover near Tavyn's shoulder, and then nodded.

Rellen jerked the bolt out with a spatter of blood.

Tavyn screamed as Miranda placed her hand on the wound and closed her eyes.

They waited for a dozen heartbeats as Miranda concentrated on the wound. Finally, she opened her eyes and pulled her hand back. The kara root was now shriveled, desiccated, as if it had been set under the sun in a desert.

Tavyn breathed a sigh of relief. "That's a little better." He lifted his arm, wincing with pain.

"Like I said, dig deep." Rellen pulled the canvas back a bit more, pulled out their gear, and handed Miranda's to her. Locking eyes with Tavyn, he said, "Do I need to warn you again?"

"No," came the immediate reply. "Helping you is the only way out for me. I get it."

"Good." Rellen handed Tavyn his weapons, and they all secured their belongings. "Now help me lift Jaquinn into the wagon. If anything comes sniffing around, I don't want anything feeding on him."

Tavyn nodded.

With a good deal of effort, and a few pained groans from Tavyn, they managed to lift Jaquinn's heavy, bloodied body into the wagon, laying him out along the side.

"For the Honor of Pelinon," Rellen whispered, and then he peered through whatever barrier hid Stukelladios from view.

CHAPTER THIRTY-FIVE

STUKELLADIOS

Rellen didn't feel a thing as he passed through the invisible barrier.

One moment, he was striding toward a long stretch of dense jungle. The next, the scene changed to something very different. He froze in his tracks as a gasp escaped his lips. A shiver ran down his spine. Miranda and Tavyn had halted beside him, their eyes wide.

A large, circular dome of gray stone, a hundred yards across and twenty high, rose before them a stone's throw away. It was windowless, with a single, arched doorway twenty feet high and at least ten wide. It looked like the top of the structure had been cleaved off and open to the sky. Sunlight shined down into the interior, and Rellen could see several bodies lying around a large, stone platform. Mygal's bare-chested body lay upon it, off to one side, and it looked like something was sticking out of his belly.

Rellen wanted to rush forward, but he restrained himself. They were hunting Toreth, and anything could be a trap.

Two horrifying statues supported an intricately carved keystone at the top of the portal. They were monstrous, demonic, with deeply honed muscles, fierce faces, and twisting horns sprouting from their foreheads and jaws. Extremely weathered, the statues and the dome looked like they'd been there for millennia, yet everything was devoid of vines or moss.

Thick jungle lay in every direction, but the edge of the vegetation maintained that same stones-throw distance from the entire structure. Only grass grew in the space between, and it looked as if it had been trimmed or made to grow only a couple inches to a perfectly uniform height. Beyond the dome was a truly massive keep of the same, gray stone.

The architecture was similar to the other nuraghi Rellen had seen, but there were differences in the details. The towers and walls of the keep were decorated with a wide variety of strange symbols, some large, some small, and all of them in a language he had only seen once before... on the plunnokum.

"Stukelladios," Rellen said, almost to himself. "I really didn't want to have to go into a nuraghi again." He turned to Miranda. "Stay behind me and to the left." She nodded. They'd done this many times before. He led, she followed, and they ran interference for each. He eyed Tavyn. "You stay ahead of me and to the right."

"I go first?"

"You go first."

Tavyn sighed with resignation but said nothing as he drew his blade and strode forward.

Rellen drew a falchion, pulled one of the poison vials from his bandoleer, and followed. The group fell into an easy, automatic cadence.

They approached the towering demonic statues, and a strange sense of familiarity struck him. The recollection smacked into him. *Jabono.* They resembled the stone demons that filled the city. It seemed an impossible coincidence. There was some sort of connection between Jabono and this place.

It didn't make any sense, but he was staring straight at it. He vowed to return to the city and speak with Chancellor Jassym.

He paused at the threshold of the dome, searching the interior for any sign of danger. The chamber was empty except for the bodies and the platform. On the far side, a section of the curved wall, twenty feet wide and high, had opened up, exposing a dark, gigantic hallway beyond. Torches set along the wall burned with bright green flame, spaced every thirty feet or so on both sides.

A large, scorched patch of black earth lay between him and the platform. The ground throughout was covered with footprints, and as his eyes passed over the area, he spotted animal tracks mixed in with the boot prints. A variety of creatures had passed through, but none of the tracks looked recent.

The platform reminded him of a stone pillar that had been cut cleanly about three or four feet off the ground. It was ten feet across, with the severed sections of rope lying on top, not far from where Mygal lay.

Hope suddenly blossomed in Rellen's heart. Mygal's chest rose and fell, just barely, in a slow, steady rhythm, despite a slim dagger sticking out of his belly, just below the ribs. Two guards lay off to the side of the pillar, their swords driven into each other's bodies. The third body, laying at Mygal's feet, was completely desiccated, as if he'd been mummified.

"He's alive," Miranda blurted, looking to Rellen. "How?"

"Let's see if we can find out. Tavyn, move up, but stay away from Mygal and keep an eye on that hallway." They moved forward, Tavyn giving Mygal a wide berth as Rellen and Miranda stopped near the young Guardian. Mygal's face was one big, purple bruise. The gashes on his face were crusty with dried blood, and his body was a latticework of bruises. "See what you can do for him."

As she worked, Rellen inspected the scene, amazed that Mygal was alive and Javyk had left him that way. The rope that bound one of Mygal's wrists had been cut. Rellen played back those moments in his head. Mygal had screamed—maybe at the first touch of Javyk's magic. Then Javyk had screamed in terror. *Why?* Maybe the young Guardian had used the shock to send a bolt of terror into Javyk. Rage can increase a kurioi's potency, even range, at least briefly. Perhaps Mygal turned one of the guards as they walked in, maybe even two if he was capable of it. It was a lot of maybes.

Rellen glanced at the two guards clutching each other in a death embrace.

Once Mygal had driven Javyk off, the fight ensued, and he got free—with the help of the third guard. *That's* why it took Javyk so long to come after us and why he came alone. He'd been wounded in the fight and had to drain the last guard to heal himself. *But why not drain Mygal?*

There was only one answer Rellen could think of. Mygal had already been stabbed as the last guard tried to kill Javyk. Or maybe Javyk stabbed Mygal but didn't want to kill him—wanted to savor his pain later on. And by that time, Jaquinn had engaged the guards out front. If Mygal was out of the fight with a blade in his belly, Javyk had to choose between cutting Mygal's life short and stopping the rest of us from escaping.

Rellen had to admit, it was pretty thin, but it made sense.

Mygal's groan filled the dome.

Rellen turned to see Miranda drop the dagger onto the stone platform beside Mygal.

"Don't move," she said gently. "You're in bad shape."

"You're telling me?" He opened his eyes. "I guess I can assume I'm not dead."

"Thankfully, no," Rellen said. "And I intend to keep it that way."

Mygal shifted and cried out in pain. "Gods, that hurts!"

"I told you not to move," Miranda scolded.

"You're not laying on cold stone."

"Point taken." Miranda turned to Rellen. "I don't want to move him."

Rellen hesitated, struggling against what he knew he had to do. His heart—the pain of old memories tearing at him—told him to help Mygal, but the Guardian in him said otherwise. "We have to leave him here."

"Toreth?" Mygal asked weakly.

Rellen nodded.

"Go get him... and don't worry about me." He met Rellen's eyes. "For the Honor of Pelinon."

"For the Honor of Pelinon," Rellen said, placing his hand gently on Mygal's leg. "Just stay alive." His eyes flicked to Tavyn and back. "I have much to tell you." He pulled off his cloak, draped it over Mygal and turned away from him. "Get going, Tavyn." Without another word, the three of them marched straight toward the opening on the far side of the dome.

The passage they entered was enormous, with the torches set eight or nine feet off the ground. As Rellen moved forward, he once again got a strange sense of scale, like he was a toddler walking through someone else's home. The other three nuraghi he'd been in seemed to have been built on a grand scale, but those had been mostly ruins—tumbled stone and broken rubble. Things seemed larger, but he hadn't truly gotten a sense that the ruins were anything other than ancient keeps lost to the mysteries of time.

This felt very different. There was the sense of an immeasurable passage of time, and yet, this fortress still stood tall. Like the invisible curtain that hid it, tremendous magics must have also held it together. Either that, or someone still lived here and maintained it... but he didn't get that sense either. There was a profound emptiness to the place, as if it had lain dormant for millennia, and now, with the help of Toreth, it was being brought back to life.

They'd gone about twenty feet in when he knelt to examine the floor. The soil in the dome and along the hallway had slowly diminished, until he realized he was walking on closely cut stone covered by a thick layer of dust. In the dust, he'd thought he would find only Toreth's tracks.

He did find signs of the man's passage. However, there was much more than that. He found the tracks of quite a few different creatures, and they were all heading *out*. That didn't make any sense. As he moved, he identified vellish tracks, koodoo buck or some other cloven-hoofed creature, a large slithering beast with a tail that cut a swath in the dust behind it.

"Why would there be animal tracks coming out of this place, but none going in?" Miranda asked, perplexed.

"I don't know." Rellen's voice carried a good deal of concern, and then he stopped. Mixed in with the other tracks was a set of prints that had to come from one of the largest vellish in history. "Look at this."

The paws were massive, as large as a bear's, but there was no mistaking what they came from. And then he remembered the vellish pack that had attacked them. He couldn't be sure, but the tracks looked identical. *Could it be?* The odds that the same vellish that walked out of this nuraghi had attacked them along the King's Highway north of Sylverwynd was beyond reason. Rellen shook his head.

"I've never seen one that big," Miranda said, awed.

"Yes, you have." Rellen met her gaze. "These look an awful lot like that big vellish that attacked us."

"Impossible."

"I'm not sure that word applies anymore," Rellen said. "Come on, let's keep going."

About a hundred feet in, spaced between the torches, they started to see pairs of identical bas relief sculptures on each side of the hallway. The images depicted the same demonic figure. It was clearly a female, if demons had such things, with all the appropriate bumps and curves. In the first one, the demon wore strange armor of some kind, with flanges and spikes. A pair of spiraling horns rose up from her temples, not unlike a Kapren or Kapron, save that these were thicker and spread out a little wider before smoothing out and coming back into sharp, dagger-like points. She stood atop a bastion, pointing out and away from a keep of some kind. Rellen suspected it was Nuraghi Stukelladios, but he couldn't be certain.

The next image showed the same demon standing near a beachhead, watching the construction of a fortress. The laborers were *human*. The humans looked like they only came up to the demon's thighs, as if she were twelve or fifteen feet tall.

There were plenty of legends and childhood stories about an ancient race of Giants that once ruled the world, but they were just tales—told to frighten children and inspire bards. Giants were a myth, like the mystical lands across the oceans where ancient heroes once fought. *They weren't true... were they?*

They continued down the long passage. Each new sculpture showed the same demon doing something different. In some, humans were present and always working on some great structure. In others, the demon stood alone. There didn't seem to be any story being told, and the more Rellen saw, the more he got a sense that the sculptures were more about a noble's ego than anything else. He'd seen the same thing in a few ducal palaces, where the duke—or duchess—chose to have images of themselves in as many places as they could.

The far end of the passage opened up into a cavernous room that reminded Rellen of the palatial grand entryways he'd walked through. Only the front half seemed to be illuminated by the green torchlight. The back side was darker, mostly lost in flickering shadows. From what he could see, there was a large open space in the middle of the floor that might be a ramp going down. A pair of massive, curving staircases flowed up on either side.

As they stepped in, they gasped in unison at the sheer scale of it all.

"It's like a colosseum," Miranda whispered.

Rellen didn't reply.

It was a grand foyer of some kind, with massive iron doors to the left and right. Between the passage opening and those doors were eight titanic, demonic statues along the wall. They served as pillars, sculpted to look like they were straining to hold up the ceiling, sixty or seventy feet above them. These sculptures were also reminiscent of the ones he'd seen in Jabono.

The stairs curving up to the left and right had been made for something with a tremendous stride. Each step was roughly twice the size of a normal one. That wasn't the only thing that convinced Rellen the place had been built for a much larger race of beings. Enormous swords hung on the walls, set between the demonic pillars. In crossed pairs, the weapons were at least eight feet long, with long grips, intricately carved guards and pommels, and curving blades similar to the saber Miranda carried. The dimensions reminded Rellen of a two-handed weapon, but even at that scale, the grip was almost two feet long.

"Rellen..." Miranda said, "*everything* is..."

"Giant," Rellen finished for her. "Yes."

"How can this be?" Tavyn asked.

"Maybe all those children's stories aren't just stories..." he replied softly, as if he were trying to convince himself. "It doesn't matter right now." He pointed to where Toreth's tracks continued down a ramp as wide as the passage they'd come through. It went down for at least a hundred feet, with more green torches lining the walls. Toreth's tracks went down into the gloom—and all of the animal tracks came out. "We have to keep going."

He strode forward and began the long descent beneath the fortress. The walls were devoid of bas reliefs, but burning green torches illuminated the path as far as he could see. The passage was another hundred feet long with iron doors along the way, each pair facing each other and spaced thirty or forty feet apart. They kept following the tracks, and at the end of the passage, it opened up into another large and fairly long room. The sides of that chamber were also lined with demonic statues, but rather than holding up the ceiling, these held large torches that all burned with green flame.

On the far side, they could just make out a human figure in blue and black robes.

Toreth...

His body was silhouetted by a pattern of blue lines and lights set into a stone wall that rose to a high, pointed arch of carved stone. Large, glowing sigils of some kind ran up and down the archway. Toreth moved his arms around in what Rellen believed had to be the somatic part of a spell.

As they drew nearer, they heard his voice echoing down the chamber, low and guttural, speaking in that same, bizarre language.

Miranda caught up with Rellen, pulled up on his arm and hissed at Tavyn to get him to stop.

Sneak up on him? Miranda asked using their sign language. *Kill him outright while he casts that spell?*

Rellen shook his head. *Wait until he's finished,* he signed. *Must see what's on other side of wall. I think it's a door. The artifact is the key. We attack with everything once he's done.*

Why?

Explain later. I promise.

She gave him a dubious look, let out a worried breath, and then nodded. She motioned for him to lead on. Rellen gripped his falchion more tightly, and as he moved forward as silently as possible, he swapped out the poison vial for something with more punch. If he was lucky, the timing would work out.

They reached the end of the passage. Toreth's voice grew louder with every step. They entered another high hallway that rose above them to a pointed ceiling high above. Sixteen demonic statues lined the walls, their monstrous, horned heads bowed and eyes closed. They held the torches before them almost reverently. Toreth was still focused on his spell, and now that Rellen was closer, he could see that the man stood in front of a door covered by interlocking rings etched into the stone, which also glowed a brilliant blue. They pulsed with a strange inner power, in cadence with Toreth's spell. It was as if, with each word, Toreth was battering against the light, trying to force it back into darkness.

Tavyn halted and looked back, a questioning expression on his face.

Rellen signaled for Tavyn to move over to the right side and creep up on the other side of the pillars. He signaled for Miranda to approach the same way from the left side. He would take the middle, out in the open, and they would attack.

It was a calculated risk, but he didn't see how they had much choice. He motioned for them to get moving as he crept forward, one silent step after another. He'd closed to within about twenty feet when Toreth's voice grew to a crescendo.

Toreth, practically shouting out the words of the spell, raised his arms above his head, the plunnokum held high. It flared with an inner light and ignited with bright, green flames. As it did, the glowing blue lines upon the door flared and went dark.

Toreth went silent. He sagged, letting out a weary breath.

Rellen tapped into his majea, preparing for their attack.

Toreth stepped up to the doors. It looked like he set the plunnokum into the center of them, but Rellen couldn't be sure. He seemed to twist something, and then a flash of blue light surged along the seam of the door, followed by a loud, metallic *CLUNK*.

Toreth stepped back, the burning plunnokum in his hand, as the doors swung open with a harsh grinding of metal and stone.

Rellen tightened his grip on the vial and started his spell.

"At last, I can escape my prison," Toreth said, his voice thick with satisfaction.

The doors had opened almost fully, revealing a room beyond, where the far wall, at least twenty feet tall, glowed with an impossible, luminescent swirl of light.

Rellen glanced at Miranda and nodded. He uttered the last word of his spell and threw the vial in *front* of Toreth. It landed with a clatter and flared bright white with a hiss of smoke and heat.

Toreth screamed, turning his head away. He spun around and roared out his fury. "Impudent wretches," he screamed. His wide, unseeing eyes passed right over Rellen and Miranda. "I don't need to see you to kill you!"

Rellen yanked a poison vial from his bandoleer as Miranda slashed with her arm.

The ruby scythe struck Toreth in the chest. He growled out his pain, but there was no blood.

Rellen had hoped for blood, preferably gushing, but there was nothing at all, and then he hesitated, not believing what he saw. Toreth's body was changing... morphing somehow. His skin darkened—turned blue. The whites of his eyes shifted to red. Thick, dark horns sprouted from his temples. He grew taller, more curvaceous.

The demon is coming out! Rellen came to his senses, finished his incantation, and threw the vial just as Toreth uttered a spell of his own. The green flames around the plunnokum flared as Toreth swept his other hand forward. The vial shattered at his feet. A cloud of poison gas erupted around him—*it*—as a massive wall of green flame sprang into existence, racing toward Rellen.

Rellen dove to the side and dodged it by mere inches. A wash of searing heat slammed against him as the wall rolled past and exploded against one of the stone pillars.

The demon swept its hands downward, and the billowing clouds of poison blew away, dissipating in a tornado of wind.

It can use Land Magic too? Rellen thought in a panic. *It's not possible!*

"Get out of my mind, you miserable bug!" the demon howled, turning to Rellen's right.

Tavyn had engaged it somehow.

The demon gestured and another wall of flame sprang into existence, raced along the floor, and slammed against a nearby pillar, engulfing it completely in green flame.

Tavyn screamed in pain. Rellen couldn't see how badly he'd been burned.

A ruby scythe sailed in from the left and struck the demon. It shrieked in rage and pain, and this time a thin line of blood appeared on its face, running from its cheek down its neck.

What had once been Toreth now stood seven feet tall, with blue skin, a shapely woman's body, and thick dark horns that spread out from her temples in tight curves to end in sharp, dagger-like points. Recognition slammed into Rellen. The demon was the spitting image of the creature carved into the bas relief sculptures they'd found in the first hallway.

She turned and slashed her hand towards Miranda. A ruby scythe sailed out.

Miranda slashed back and their scythes met in mid-air. The edges of the demon's scythe shattered, but some of it kept going and slammed into Miranda. A gash opened up on her face, running down her neck beneath her armor.

Rellen jerked a different vial from his bandoleer, uttered a single incantation and threw it. The vial streaked towards the demon and exploded. The demon howled in rage and pain, staggering back.

The demon's head snapped toward him. She slashed at him, and a ruby scythe filled the air in front of him.

Miranda countered with one of her own, shattering some of the demon's spell, but what remained struck Rellen. The magic shield around him flashed. A deep, burning pain coursed along his body, and he cried out in pain.

He couldn't take much more of that. He traced a quick symbol in the air before him, the tip of his blade glowing, and uttered a familiar incantation, just as the demon sent another scythe streaking toward him. Miranda countered again.

Again, shards of the demon's scythe got through, staggering him. He felt a gash open up across his leg and belly but managed to finish his spell. The demon's clothing came alive around her body. Her robes slithered up and wrapped around her head, blinding her.

Rellen drew his other falchion. "For the Honor of Pelinon!" he shouted and charged, hoping Miranda would still be able to protect him—at least a little.

The demon shrieked out her frustration, yanking at her robes as Rellen closed the distance.

She touched the flaming plunnokum to her robes, and they ignited, burning away in a flash. She fixed flaming eyes upon Rellen and slashed again. Miranda countered. What remained slammed into Rellen's body. His protection spell flashed white as pain flared over his body. He felt another gash open up across his chest. His protection spell had been consumed. He closed with the demon and swung his blade.

She slapped the weapon aside with the plunnokum. Rellen thrust as one of Miranda's scythes flew in and struck the demon's arm. The demon roared as she grabbed Rellen's arm, wrapping clawed fingers around his bracer. She twisted, using Rellen as a shield, and uttered a spell in her strange, guttural language. Rellen gasped, tried to draw in a breath, but the air felt like poison burning in his lungs.

She raised the plunnokum and swung. Rellen parried with another ring of steel. A sharp pain ran up his arm with the impact, he'd stopped the plunnokum only inches from his head. He tried to draw another breath but was met with only fire. His vision blurred.

Searing pain flared along his arm where the demon clutched it. The bracer caught fire, burning with green flame. Rellen tried to scream out his agony but managed only a hissing croak. He saw spots. The world spun. He dropped the falchion from the hand caught in her grasp.

The demon raised the plunnokum again, ready to bash Rellen's head in as his armor burned.

A dagger sailed out of the darkness and struck the demon in the shoulder. Her arm dropped almost instantly. Her magic failed. The fire burning around Rellen's arm went out, and he sucked in a single breath of cool air as the plunnokum fell from her limp fingers, struck the floor, and rolled away to his right.

"Filthy poison!" she screamed, releasing Rellen as she jerked the dagger from her shoulder.

It was all the opening Rellen needed.

He stepped in, drove his falchion into the center of her chest, and staggered back.

A massive ruby scythe sailed in from his left and struck the demon in the center of her body. A deep gash appeared, running from her forehead all the way down her face and neck. Black blood poured forth. Another dagger flew in and sank to the hilt in her throat.

The demon's eyes rolled back in her head. Her mouth yawned open, and a soul-ripping wail lifted out of her body and filled the room. The flame in her eyes spread out, and she started to topple forward. Rellen turned, and as he did, a burning emerald light shone forth from where his falchion had impaled her. The light flared and spread, pouring out from each of her wounds.

It expanded out. Rellen felt the magic building up to a crescendo.

"Run!" he said, turning toward Miranda… it was too late.

He took three running steps when the detonation enveloped him, hammered his senses, filled the chamber with bright, green light. The force of the blast sent him sailing straight toward Miranda.

He blacked out before he hit the ground.

CHAPTER THIRTY-SIX

AFTERMATH

R ellen?" Miranda's voice came from far away, drawing him out of darkness.

He opened his eyes to find her staring down at him, a slim gash running down her face, a worried expression in her eyes. The green torches were no longer lit, but he recognized the light of a glowstone. He turned his head, wincing with pain, to see one laying on the floor beside him.

He drew in a deep breath. That hurt. He tried to move his arms. That hurt too. He shifted his legs slightly. They hurt. He quickly came to the conclusion that everything hurt. The soldier inside, however, reminded him, pain was a good thing.

It proves I'm still alive.

"Toreth, or whatever that was?" Rellen asked, looking up at her.

"Gone," she replied. "Consumed by whatever magics held the wretched thing inside him, I suspect."

"I'm not so sure."

"What do you mean?" she said, confused. "That thing is definitely dead."

"It knew me… from Calamath. I thought it was destroyed then, too." *Could it be the same one?* He thought about it, but the timing seemed off. It would all depend upon when Toreth had been possessed. How could they exist simultaneously? He shook his head, afraid he might have to face the same terrible monstrosity over and over again. Either way, he knew there was lots of fighting ahead of him… fighting demons. "My falchion?" he asked, wondering if the demon exploding had taken his falchion with her.

Miranda reached out, grabbed something, and then held the blade before him.

"That's something, at least," he said. "Tavyn?"

"Gone by the time I came to," Miranda replied ominously. "He took that key with him."

Rellen closed his eyes, a sense of dread filling him. *So that's what he was after.*

He opened his eyes again, drew in a long breath in preparation for what he was about to do, and let it out slowly.

"How long were we out?"

"A while, I think," Miranda said weakly.

"He must be long gone by now, and Mygal was in no position to stop him from running out on us." He let out a pained groan. "Help me up, would you?"

With a little straining and a lot of groaning from both of them, Rellen managed to get his feet under him. He could feel blood beneath his armor where the demon's scythes had bit into him. His left forearm was a seared wreck. Just moving it sent waves of pain up his entire arm. He knew the flesh below had been burned, and probably quite badly.

When he finally stood up straight, his eyes fixed upon the glowing wall that lay a short distance past the now open doors. He took a moment to return both falchions to his sheathes. Picking up the glowstone, he slowly made his way across the chamber and through the open doors. As he passed them by, he noticed that the pattern of circles, now mere stone, had also been etched onto the interior surface of the doors. There was a deep groove set into the edge of each door that obviously would fit the plunnokum if the doors were closed. *It locks on both sides?* he thought. *That doesn't make any sense.*

Supporting each other, they limped into the next chamber and approached the glowing wall. A pattern on the floor caught his eye. Holding the glowstone out, he gasped. He'd seen the pattern before, although in a very different way. Carved into the dark stone was the shape of a horned, demonic skull. Four small horns rose from its crown, and two larger, curving ones came up from its temples. A pair of downward curving horns came out from its jawline on each side, and there were three, bony horns descending from below its mouth.

It was the skull he'd seen on the neck rings of the Klymrukaar, without the sword going up through it. Rellen's insides churned. Why would the symbol be in both places? It didn't make sense. He shook his head, weary of mysteries. He turned his focus to the faintly glowing wall.

Although, now that he was standing in front of it, the thing didn't seem like a wall so much as a mirror or maybe a portal of some kind, although he'd never even heard of such magic. A stone framework surrounded it, carved deeply with circles and lines in a style he'd never seen before. Patterns of color, light and darkness—a mix of every color of the rainbow—slowly swirled along its surface. He couldn't tell if it was solid or some sort of magical manifestation, but he dared not touch it. Who knew what the damn thing was or what it did? As he stared into it, the words Toreth had spoken when the demon had opened the doors floated up out of Rellen's memory.

"At last, I can escape my prison."

Rellen looked back at the stone doors, a deeply troubled look on his face. They hadn't been meant to keep something out... they'd kept something *in*, and now the way was clear.

What have I done?

"Damn it," he growled. More than anything, he wanted to confront that little bastard Thorfyll.

"What's wrong?" Miranda asked.

"We have to get out of here," he said, stepping away from the portal. "Something may be coming through that thing," he added with a growing sense of panic. "We have to notify the king immediately." He tugged on her arm and started walking away. *"Hurry…"*

The two of them limped and staggered—as quickly as they were able—through the long, dark hallway, helping each other along. They finally reached the dome where Mygal lay.

"Mygal," Rellen called out as they stepped into the dome. "We're back."

There was no reply.

"Mygal?" Rellen called out again, fear clutching at his insides. He scanned the interior of the dome as he drew a falchion, although he wasn't in much shape to get into another fight. He quickened his pace and gasped when his eyes focused on Mygal's body.

"Gods, no…" Rellen's heart broke.

Mygal lay there, his sightless eyes staring up at the open sky, with the dagger they'd pulled out of his side now sticking up from the center of his chest.

Rellen ground his teeth. His knuckles went white. A spark of impotent rage ignited in his breast, fueled by the terrible sadness that clawed at his emotions. He'd lost so much today, and once again proven he couldn't be responsible for others. He would kill Tavyn—butcher him—when they finally crossed paths. And he would draw it out for as long and painfully as he could. He'd make Tavyn wish the Nissran's had gotten hold of him.

"The bastard just murdered him," Miranda said, her voice full of fury.

A shock of fear slammed into Rellen.

"Xilly!" he cried out, dreading he'd lost her too. Ignoring the pain, he limped as fast as he could out of the dome and through the barrier that hid Stukelladios. Miranda followed, keeping pace, as he rushed to the back of the wagon.

Everything looked just as it had when they'd left it. He slowly pulled the canvass back, dreading what he'd find. He exposed her dark body, curled up into a ball.

Rellen? The weak thought slipped into his mind, and she lifted her head slowly.

"You're alive," Rellen whispered, running a hand gently across her body. *I thought I'd lost you too.*

Too?

Mygal is dead… so is Jaquinn.

I'm sorry, Xilly said. It carried with it sadness, but also confusion.

And Tavyn is the one who killed Mygal.

What?

I'll explain everything later.

Rellen looked around the far side of the wagon. Shaddeth, as well as Miranda and Mygal's mounts were still tied up with the others.

"Tavyn's mount is gone," he said, turning to Miranda.

"So, what do we do now? Chase him?"

That was exactly what Rellen wanted to do, but Tavyn couldn't be his priority—*yet.*

"First, I notify the king of everything that's happened," Rellen said. "Then, we bury our dead. We're beat to the breaking point. The king has lost *two* Guardians this day. And we're in no shape to track Tavyn down." He locked eyes with her. "The whole of Pelinon may be on the verge of coming apart, and whatever that thing down there is for—whatever might come through it—can't be good."

"So, back to Kaichakahn?" she asked, pulling several kara roots out of her saddlebags.

"I'm debating that." He remembered what Toreth had said aboard the ship: *Even Duke kyp'Tukeem and his family are mine.* Rellen knew they had to get out of Kaichakahn… out of the Duchy of Nikostohr—and as quickly as possible. Either they took the King's Highway up through the Duchy of Nikostohr, or they tried to book passage on the next ship bound for

Yaylo. If they moved quickly and kept themselves hidden, it might be possible.

"Kaichakahn," he said firmly. "We disguise ourselves and get on a ship."

He looked to the east where the port lay, and then an idea slid into his thoughts. They'd lost two Guardians today. He glanced at Miranda, a thoughtful look on his face. He wouldn't have to be responsible for her, because she was as capable as he was—maybe even more so. Working together, they might just have a chance.

"What?" she asked.

He had an offer to make her... he just hoped his brother would go for it.

Epilogue

THE SPIDER'S WEB

A bissar guided his grypharri, Glimmerwing, out of a clear night sky. The limitless black cradled a quarter moon set amidst a wash of stars that filled the heavens to overflowing. Abissar had an appointment to keep.

He let out a deeply satisfied sigh and patted her neck. In his estimation, Glimmerwing had made him the most influential clikurioi in the history of the Readers. The animal was his one conceit to station, influence, and affluence. The Corsairs had several flights of the beasts. The king, of course, had six in his own stable, and there were several nobles with the means and mettle to be grypharri riders. None of them, not even the king, used theirs to such profound effect.

Capable of carrying a fully armed and armored warrior, the feathered, four-legged creatures had massive wingspans; large, bird-like heads; and long plumage running back from their necks. They ate whatever they could get down their throats, although they preferred fresh meat. Their limbs were rough and scaly like a large bird of prey, but thick like a lion's, ending in long, sharp talons. They also had long, sinuous tails covered with rigid feathers that they used as both rudders and for forward momentum once they were aloft.

He'd ridden her to nearly every corner of Pelinon and beyond for twenty years, in pursuit of his weavings, and until only recently, she'd been his greatest asset.

Patting her once more with affection, he aimed for the bright bonfire set to guide him in. The lights of Svennival spread out a mile to the south and several hundred feet below him. The dark mass of the lake filled the horizon, and he could just make out the lights of several ships cutting their way across the water.

The air had been frigid on the journey south from Daemonostra Keep, but his fur-lined flying suit and rider's helm had made the long journey bearable, if not comfortable. And he did so enjoy the stars as seen from Glimmerwing's saddle, a thousand feet above the ground. That perspective had always been a perfect reflection of his own designs… with the world flowing under his watchful eye and deliberate control.

Glimmerwing descended swiftly and with exhilarating speed. At the last moment, she spread her mighty wings and braked hard with a fierce flapping. She came down onto a rut-filled, dirt road at a gallop. Abissar reflexively shifted back and forth in the saddle, absorbing the impact with the skill of a Corsair. He tugged lightly on the bridle and guided her down an overgrown cart path toward a bonfire next to an old, abandoned farmhouse.

Releasing the straps that secured him to the saddle, Abissar urged Glimmerwing through an old gate that had fallen to ruin. He pulled up a short distance from the bonfire where Tavyn, the young informant that had played such a pivotal role in Abissar's primary weaving, stood waiting.

Unbidden, the gossamer threads of Fate drifted before Abissar's eyes. Some were almost too pale to see, while others were as bright as the glowing moon above. Young Tavyn had been a nexus for Abissar's designs for months now, and as a result, dozens of threads, almost like strands of a spider's web, intersected with Tavyn's heart.

Abissar focused on them for just a moment. Each one was unique, and he'd learned to differentiate those imperceptible variations from an early age. One of them connected Tavyn to Rellen. Another connected him to Miranda, and another, the most obvious, connected Tavyn to the Black Wyrm Clan and Rickavyn Dennilish. The brightest thread of them all, of course, connected the informant to the heart of the bonfire.

Since Abissar could remember, he'd seen the threads of his mistress, Fate. She'd chosen him from the cradle. Unlike most people, whose majea manifested with puberty, his had manifested when he was barely out of the womb, and he could see the threads of Fate like none other. He'd studied the histories of every great Reader over their fifteen-hundred-year history, and none of them could see what he could—what he always had been able to see. For Abissar, the threads of Fate were the master weaving of the world, and he could pluck on those threads like a spider in its web. They were always there for him, everywhere, and he'd learned from childhood how to pull and push and weave them into his own designs... He could even create them. And now, staring down at Tavyn Daggerayne, it was time to pull on another strand.

"I've never seen a grypharri up close before," Tavyn said as he took several tentative steps closer to the grypharri. The young man seemed cautious but unafraid of a beast that could rend him apart in an instant, if Abissar willed it.

"Magnificent creatures, aren't they?" Abissar asked in a friendly tone as he climbed out of the saddle. He grabbed a heavy leather sack that clicked and jingled. It was Tavyn's payment for a job well done.

"Truly," Tavyn replied, taking several steps closer.

The young man was much the same as when Abissar had engaged his services: slender and twenty-ish, although his blond hair was now cut short, and his trim goatee had become a full but closely cut beard. He still had keen eyes that missed little... but just enough.

"Have you brought what I asked for?" Abissar's eyes flicked to the leather satchel over Tavyn's shoulder, with whatever lay within pulling down hard, as if it were made of stone or metal.

"I have," Tavyn replied. "Is that my payment?" His eyes shifted to the heavy sack in Abissar's hand. A hungry smile spread across his face.

Abissar held it out without answering.

"I meant to ask you, why did you have me kill Mygal? I rather liked him." Tavyn pulled the satchel off his shoulder, and they quickly exchanged their hard-earned prizes.

"Because I am in a position to influence the selection of his replacement, and I now find it advantageous to do so." Abissar gave him a slim smile. "I believe that concludes our arrangement, yes?"

Tavyn shrugged amicably. "It's been a pleasure doing business with you." He opened the sack and peered inside. It was full of golden dakkaris and an assortment of glittering gemstones. He nodded, satisfied with his payment, and met Abissar's gaze. "Let me know when you need me again," Tavyn offered before turning toward his horse. He held up his wrist exposing the slim band of dark metal. The leafy vine pattern glittered in the firelight, and the simple onyx stone flashed brightly. "You know how to reach me."

Abissar took a moment to open the satchel. Within lay the plunnokum, and now that he'd laid eyes upon it, countless gossamer threads of potential appeared, all of them coalescing at the center of that potent green circle of metal. It was *real*. He'd worried Tavyn might have the temerity to present a fake, but the young informant had been true to his word.

He let out an almost disappointed sigh. "I'm afraid that won't be possible."

Tavyn turned, a confused look upon his face as Abissar's eyes followed a gossamer thread running from Tavyn to the back corner of the farmhouse.

Abissar felt Tavyn's ermajea slide over his mind and then slip into it. Abissar didn't even try to hide his thoughts.

Tavyn's eyes went wide in surprised anger, but it was too late.

Abissar raised a hand and casually pointed at Tavyn as the young man reached for his blade.

"Why—" Tavyn started, anger filling his voice.

A crossbow bolt shot out of the darkness and transected Tavyn's neck.

The young informant staggered, gurgling as he clutched at the bolt. Blood poured from his neck.

Abissar stepped forward slowly, dispassionately. He drew a slim dagger.

Tavyn clumsily clutched at the hilt of his rapier, panic and pain filling his face, but Abissar lunged and drove his dagger up to the hilt into the center of Tavyn's chest, piercing his heart.

Tavyn coughed up a splash of blood, shook his head weakly in disbelief, and crumpled to the ground.

A burly figure with no neck to speak of stepped out from behind the empty farmhouse as Abissar bent over and rolled up Tavyn's sleeve. He carefully removed the dark bracelet he'd given Tavyn and peered at the onyx stone gleaming in the firelight. He made the bracelet disappear into his robes. He would keep this useful little seed of his will until he found new soil in which to plant it.

He leaned over even further, peering down into Tavyn's lifeless eyes, still frozen in terror. "I'm afraid you knew too much," he whispered, patting the satchel, "and there are countless more just like you who don't."

As he rose, he slipped the satchel over his shoulder, making sure the heavy flap was closed. He turned toward the neckless man walking slowly toward him. Rickavyn Dennilish held the heavy crossbow that had ended Tavyn's journey.

"Place the body in the fire," Abissar said. "That sack on the ground should more than cover your fee."

Rickavyn picked up the sack, peered inside, and his eyebrows raised.

"Think I may just celebrate tonight," he replied, cinching it up and tying it off.

Abissar strode to Glimmerwing and climbed deftly into the saddle. Out of habit, he peered closely at the many threads that flowed into Rickavyn's heart. Not unexpectedly, most were completely unknown to him, and the one connecting him to Tavyn was fading quickly.

"I still don't know your name," Rickavyn said, dragging Tavyn's body toward the fire.

"And you never will," Abissar replied. "But you may yet *see* me again." He traced through the gossamer threads, and as he examined them, he froze. He focused on one that was more than familiar to him. It connected Rickavyn to Talliah Essoch, of all people. The line was faint, barely noticeable, but Abissar was more familiar with her thread than any other. "In fact," he added, giving Rickavyn a most friendly smile, "I'm certain of it. A man of your talents is certain to be of assistance to me soon. Very soon."

"You know how to find me," Rickavyn said, hefting Tavyn's body unceremoniously into the bonfire.

"Indeed, I do," Abissar said as he pulled on Glimmerwing's reins and guided her back out onto the rough road. He ran a finger over the bracelet hidden in his robes. It was one of thirty pieces of jewelry he'd had commissioned by a master jeweler in Corsia. Each stone set into a bracelet, necklace, pendant, or ring had a matching one safely locked away in his study. He'd come to call them his Seeds of Dominion, and through them, his grand design might come to fruition far sooner than he could have ever imagined, just as Fate willed.

He'd planted this particular seed in the fertile soil of Tavyn Daggerayne's avarice, and as a result, he'd been able to harvest nothing less than a plunnokum of the Giants. It wasn't a plunnoi, to be sure, but this ancient relic might just lead him to one. And a plunnoi would be the key to his greatest weaving yet. A Reader who held a plunnoi, and knew how to use it, would hold the reins of an entire world in the palm of his hand... *Abissar's* hand.

The threads were coming together exactly as planned.

As Glimmerwing lifted him off the ground, he couldn't help but reflect on the one, pivotal event that had set everything in motion, and he thanked Fate for that fool Darjhen, whose panic had made it all possible.

INTERLUDE

Five months earlier...

Fools," Abissar growled, his mind still tingling from the summons of the Aurora. "All of them... dotards and fools." A glowstone illuminated his descent deeper into the bowels of Daemonostra Keep... and further from the Fakimiar Stones. His irritation grew with each step. Locked securely away in his study, thirty matched pairs of ancient, profoundly magical gems beckoned. They were the key to achieving all his designs. Through them, what would have taken him decades would only take years, but he needed to bond with them, first.

Wyrd curse that wretched Aurora! It had taken him away from his studies... from the stones. He cursed the inconvenience. He cursed the Hand of Fate Conclave. He cursed whichever one of its thrice-cursed, mewling Readers had invoked the Aurora.

Had it been any other summons, he would have ignored it and made an excuse later—even to High Master Talliah.

However, there was no turning away from this particular summons without suffering consequences. Once invoked, the Aurora—a magical pulse that spanned all five continents— resonated in the minds of all ten members of the Hand of Fate Conclave, no matter where they were. Under normal circumstances, the council met only once on the cusp of each New Year, but the Aurora brought them running like a fire brigade and generally carried with it a promise of revelation or disaster for the Conclave and beyond.

All he wanted to do was return to his study, to the stones, and to the destiny that Wyrd—the goddess of Fate—had seen fit to bestow upon him. The stones had come into his hands alone, and if ever there was a better signal that Wyrd desired Abissar to one day rule the Hand of Fate, he couldn't conceive of it. He soothed his irritation with thoughts of Fakimiar. He sent up quiet thanks and a hint of regret for the erstwhile adventurer and archaeologist who had given his life—albeit unwillingly—so Abissar would be the only soul alive who knew of the stones' existence.

Once again, the stones filled his thoughts.

He blew out a frustrated breath and shook his head, trying to clear his mind of everything but the task before him. He was about to face the most potent clikurioi in all the world— and the greatest threat to his designs. In order to continue manipulating them, there was no room for mistakes. As always, his performance needed to be perfection.

He reached the bottom of the stone steps, worn by fifteen hundred years of Reader sandals, and moved down a short passage with equally ancient wooden doors on either side. They—like everything else in Daemonostra—were meticulously maintained. The dark iron bands didn't have a spot of rust, and the reddish grain of the stakka wood had a polished sheet that reflected the light of his glowstone. He opened the last one on the left with only the faintest groan of well-oiled hinges and entered what every Reader in the keep— save two—believed was merely another storeroom. Dust lay upon crates and barrels stacked in the corners. The floor, however, was clean, swept by Reader acolytes tasked with the daily duty of ensuring it stayed that way.

He crossed the room and uttered an ancient incantation known by only by the High Master and himself. The wall before him swung away with a faint grating of stone and squeal of metal, exposing a long, dark hallway of immense proportions. The ceiling rose above him nearly eighteen feet, and the hallway was twelve feet wide.

Muttering an expletive, he stepped into the darkened passage and spoke the incantation again. As the door closed behind him, he strode forward, his footsteps echoing off stonework far older than the keep he'd left behind. A pale, luminescent glow filled the far end of the passage a hundred yards distant, terminating in a wall that swirled and glowed with patterns of light and color.

The thuros, he thought. *That too will one day be mine.*

He kept his pace brisk but didn't hurry. Hurrying was beneath him, even if it was Talliah Essoch and the entire Hand of Fate who waited.

He passed several massive intersections along the hallway, each one leading into musty, dark regions of an ancient, underground fortress that he'd never taken time to explore. There hadn't been cause. Such knowledge had no place in his designs… yet. Soon though—sooner, perhaps, then he'd ever thought possible—that would change.

At the far end of the passage, the pale glow of the thuros filled a large, stone chamber where a lone figure stood in the dark green robes of Daemanon's wing of the Reader Order— Talliah Essoch.

Abissar swore again, silently this time, and made his way to where she waited, standing off to the side before the ancient glowing surface of the thuros. He felt her cool, hard eyes upon him. She might say something about his tardiness, she might not. It was always difficult to tell with the High Master, for her eyes were always cold and calculating. He often wondered if she'd been born with those eyes, and one day he hoped Wyrd would permit him the privilege of gouging them out.

Talliah Essoch, at over a century old, had led Daemanon's Reader order for more than sixty years. She was the epitome of strength and vitality, seemingly eternal. Short, alabaster hair rose above her head like a crown of flame. Her body, neither thick nor thin, could have been sculpted by a master, with every muscle and curve distinct beneath her robes. She towered over most, with a propensity for looking down her sharp, angular nose at them. There was a natural haughtiness to the woman, wrapped in a cold demeanor that Abissar surmised was born of noble breeding, although he'd never been able to prove it.

He hated her most of all.

She carried herself with resilient strength, every move and gesture as deliberate and precise as clockwork. Such precision was reflected in her words as well. She wasted nothing, with an obsession for logic above all things—even in others. Passionless, she viewed everything within her purview as little more than a knot to be untied, a puzzle solved. And she condemned any who injected emotion into any conundrum before her, large or small.

To Abissar, she was… a fool. The entire council was made of fools, but he did not let this assessment show—they would never know until it was precisely too late. For now, he would play the part, be the subservient pupil to Talliah's grand, stoic, ego.

As he neared the High Master, the kairoi—the gossamer threads of Fate—drifted unbidden before his eyes, with Talliah as their nexus. They were as pale as spiderweb in moonlight, and he recognized dozens of the kairoi that were connected to specific people. He quickly identified that of young King Saren III and Abissar's own prize pupil, Saleeria Beskovar. He picked out several members of the Order and even the king's older brother, the wastrel Rellen. There were others, but those glowed the brightest.

He closed his eyes and pushed his majea away. There was no place for such things with Talliah or the Hand of Fate. They would sense any sort of manipulation, and as much as he wanted to pluck those threads, weave them further into his designs, the danger was far too high...

As Abissar approached, he drew in a deep breath, let it out, and straightened his robes. He would play his role... and continue using his words, rather than his majea, to shape her perception.

"High Master," he said, bowing his head slightly. "Do you know why the Aurora has been invoked?"

"No," Talliah replied, the tips of her white hair seemingly ablaze in the pale glow of the thuros. She looked down upon him, her face devoid of emotion. "I expected you to be here sooner, Vice Master."

"My apologies," he replied, abasing himself. He forced himself not to clench his teeth. "I was engrossed in research when the call came." It had the merit of being the truth. If she asked him what that research was, however, he would lie. "You know how it can be, High Master."

"Have you uncovered anything noteworthy?" Her eyebrow lifted a fraction of an inch.

"Not yet," he said, which was only partly truth. "I've only just begun. It might be nothing at all. Rest assured, should I feel it worth your attention, you will most certainly be made aware."

"Very well." She turned away from him. "Let us find out why we have been summoned, yes?"

"Yes, High Master," Abissar said, turning his eyes to the pale, luminescent swirl of color before them. The thuros— nearly the same dimensions as the passage behind him—was an ancient portal, a remnant of millenniums-old magic left over from a time before humanity and the other races made the world their own.

Talliah reached into the folds of her robe and extracted a large, black coin of sorts, with a singular engraving upon both sides. It was a plunnos, one of five keys in existence that allowed passage through a thuros. Each High Master possessed one, and each plunnos was different.

In all the world, mere dozens knew there were other continents, and of those, nearly all were Readers. It was the Order's second most closely guarded secret, behind the truth that the Giants of myth had been real, and that they had once ruled all five continents.

She touched plunnos to thuros. There was no visible reaction, but Abissar knew from experience the way had been opened.

"Come," Talliah said, and she stepped forward. The surface didn't ripple. The shifting patterns of color and light didn't change their course. Her form simply passed through its surface, as if she'd stepped through a mirror and disappeared.

Abissar stepped forward. After more than fifteen years of passing through, he still marveled at the experience. The surface of the thuros gave way, slipping around him, soaking through him. There was no sensation, more a palpable absence of it, and yet, when he completed that step, he found himself in a very different place, one where the air was thick with moisture and heavy with the scent of the sea.

The room, built on the same scale as the thuros, was pentagonal, with a thuros set in the middle of each ancient, stone wall. Above each door was a dark, metal emblem several feet across, and each one bore the same motif as on the plunnos that opened the thuros beneath it: an open scroll for Lathranon, Drakanon's golden dragon, the burning keep of Pyranon, Noksonon's sun and consuming shadow, and Daemanon's horned demon skull. Massive stone doors filled the corners, although what lay beyond was a mystery to Abissar. Only the High Masters were permitted access. Was it one of the five continents that lay beyond? For all Abissar knew, an island or entirely new continent lay beyond those doors.

One day, I will solve that mystery too, he thought.

Six robed figures stood around a large stone table with three concentric circles carved in its center. They clustered in pairs, with each pair wearing the color designated for their continent: blue for Lathranon, gold for Drakanon, and red for Pyranon. Talliah and Abissar wore their own, deep green.

"Did one of you invoke the Aurora?" Talliah asked as she took her position at the table. Abissar took his position on her right, and half a step behind.

"If not you," Ulient of Haapavesa said quietly, "then it must have been Lengstrom." The short, portly man was the High Master of Lathranon. Calm, quiet, and reserved, he spoke only when it was necessary. His eyes were intelligent, his demeanor almost as stoic as Talliah's. He was also, arguably, one of the most dangerous Readers to Abissar's designs. Ever did Abissar feel Ulient's eyes upon him, evaluating, calculating. Ulient watched, and that was the one thing Abissar didn't want.

"Lengstrom, then," Talliah replied. "So we wait."

Several heads around the table nodded. Although the silence was deafening—there were no comrades at this table—they didn't have to endure it for very long.

A dozen heartbeats later, two figures in the black robes of Noksonon stepped through their thuros, hoods pulled over their heads. Abissar recognized the woman's form immediately: Vice Master Elegathe Ventine—the newest addition to the Hand of Fate. Even fully cloaked and cowled, he recognized the sway of her walk. She'd stood beside High Master Lengstrom at the Conclave only once before, at the annual gathering.

He turned his eyes to High Master Lengstrom—and froze. He fought to keep his face emotionless. The man hidden beneath that hood wasn't Lengstrom. The High Master that Abissar knew, was slightly taller, his frame smoother and less angular. This fellow stood strong and tall, but there was a sense of age about him that didn't quite fit.

What's going on here? Abissar thought. The newcomer seemed oddly familiar, but he couldn't figure out why.

"Lengstrom," Jekka, the High Master of Pyranon said, focusing her attention on the cloaked Elegathe. "Why have you called us?"

Abissar's eyes flicked to the striking woman in red robes. At a glance, she was a lovely young thing, with piercing eyes that bored into wherever she fixed her gaze... a predator's eyes. Although she appeared to be no more than nineteen or twenty, she had been on the council longer than any of them. She was ancient... and insane. She was also one of Abissar's favorites. While it was difficult to control madness, once set in motion, insanity could be counted upon to inflict mayhem. One day, Abissar fully intended to set the crazed Reader in motion as part of his grand design. He looked forward to it, in fact, for Jekka was a formidable creature, and would serve his purposes well.

"Not Lengstrom," Elegathe said. Abissar turned curious eyes to her as she flipped her cowl back, exposing long, dark hair framing a face no more than thirty-five years old. "I summoned you."

Abissar raised an eyebrow.

Several others around the table looked surprised. She had spoken out of turn. There were several exchanged glances, and then everyone focused their attention on the lovely, dark-haired, young woman. She wore a perfect mask of confidence, her chin raised and jaw tight. Abissar knew masks better than anyone and suspected hers hid something very different underneath—youth and inexperience. He had to wonder why this mere youth was speaking for the High Master.

"And who are you, a lowly apprentice, to summon us?" Talliah asked with steely disapproval in her voice. She firmly placed her fingertips upon the table and stared down at Elegathe as a noblewoman might examine a dirty peasant.

Abissar again dropped his gaze from Elegathe's face to the curve of her breasts and hips. Her robes had been cut to accentuate her ample cleavage and shapely curves. He kept his face placid and let his eyes flick over the pale décolletage

Elegathe presented. As on their first meeting, he would play along with her game and find ways to use it to his advantage later, reinforcing her perception of him as a lascivious cad. He raised an eyebrow ever so slightly, to ensure she took notice.

"Lengstrom..." Te'zla, the High Master of Drakanon blurted. "Why did you allow your apprentice to break protocol?" The man seemed shocked and appalled all at once. "She summoned us? Only a High Master can activate the Aurora."

Abissar kept the smile off his face.

Te'zla was a curiosity, with all the subtlety of a yapping hound. He reacted before he spoke—prone to outbursts and a propensity for jumping to conclusions. Te'zla's appearance fit the man, with wild gray hair sticking out every which way and gold robes that looked unkempt and ill-fitting. Abissar and Te'zla had joined the Hand of Fate at nearly the same time, and for whatever reason, the wild-looking Reader of Drakanon seemed to trust Abissar more than the others. He too would have his place in Abissar's grand designs... as a pet, perhaps.

"Lengstrom is dead," Elegathe said. "*I* am High Master of Noksonon now."

"What?" Abissar blurted.

Of all the things the young woman could have said, that surprised him. The revelation forced him to elevate his respect for her. Everyone knew she'd killed her old mentor Darjhen Torai—the High Master of Noksonon at the time—ten years earlier for using his magical power and Reader resources for his own designs. Everyone on the Conclave had approved. Rogue Readers could not be tolerated; it was a capital offense throughout the Order. At the time, Abissar had been relieved, for Darjhen was an enigma he'd not yet been able to fit into his designs.

Because of her history, Elegathe's sudden statement begged the question: had she murdered Lengstrom as well? Deliberately taken his place as High Master? For that matter, had she done the same to Darjhen and lied about him going rogue? The thought had never occurred to Abissar until now.

If she had killed them both and orchestrated her new position, she would have to be a truly remarkable young woman indeed. His respect for her grew even more. Such ruthlessness... It made him reevaluate what her future use to him might be. The faintest of smiles crept onto his face.

Talliah reached back and, without looking, placed a quieting hand on Abissar's arm. His smile instantly disappeared. He kept the disgust off his face as his gaze flicked to her hand. He decided right then that he would cut off that hand when he gouged out her eyes. For now, though, he acknowledged her with a slight bow of his head.

"It is as I feared," Ulient, the blue-robed High Master of Lathranon, said softly. Abissar dared not look at the man for fear Ulient might see through Abissar's seemingly calm façade.

"I told you!" Te'zla waved his arms almost frantically, looking like a frightened child as his wild, white mane quivered and shook. "The Giants killed him."

"Calm yourself," Talliah commanded, as if she were speaking to a sob-wracked wet-nurse. She stared at Te'zla, and contempt filled her eyes. "It's far too soon to draw conclusions." She turned all of her attention back to Elegathe... as did Jekka.

Jekka, her eyes narrowed to menacing, angry slits, jabbed two long-nailed fingers at the still hooded figure as if they were a weapon as deadly as her daggers. "This is your new apprentice?" she asked Elegathe.

Abissar watched Elegathe take a breath, as if she were preparing to say something. Instead, she stepped back, and the hooded figure beside her stepped forward. As he did, a distant recollection came into focus in Abissar's mind. Could it be? The figure beneath the cowl—the shape of his body, the width of his shoulders, how he carried himself. A suspicion grew deep within Abissar's heart. Darjhen Torai... If it was the supposedly dead High Master, it would mean Elegathe had lied—perhaps about everything—that Darjhen was playing a very different and dangerous game, and that the conversation was about to become very lively indeed.

"In a manner of speaking," Darjhen said and threw back his cowl, revealing his bare scalp and piercing blue gaze.

Abissar let a subtle, impressed smile cross his face. This new truth could change everything. Darjhen was alive, after ten years in the grave, and Abissar had no doubt that it was all by Darjhen's design. He'd fooled them all—including Abissar—and that made him dangerous. But had he fooled Elegathe, or was she complicit?

Jekka hissed like an angry animal. Most of the others jerked in surprise—including Talliah—all save Ulient, who hadn't reacted at all.

"What is *that* doing here?" Talliah pointed, her voice icy, threatening, like a monarch about to hand down a death warrant. Young Elegathe flinched. "*That* was supposed to be dead. And if it is not dead, it should be executed immediately."

Jekka drew a long dagger from her belt and held it at the ready, a vicious gleam in her eyes. "I can make that happen."

Ulient held up a hand. "Wait. Let's hear what the oathbreaker says first."

"No!" Anya Scany shouted. The young woman was Te'zla's Vice Master and normally soft-spoken, prone to deferring to her High Master in all things. She was a stern, plain-looking creature, with her straight, brown hair pulled back impossibly tight and accentuating her sharp features. To date, Abissar had found little use for her, but perhaps that was about to change. She shot a brief, accusatory glare at Elegathe, then focused her ire upon Darjhen fully. "He has forfeited the right to live much less speak."

"He is an oathbreaker," Bakhar, Ulient's Vice Master, said with iron, "but Wyrd demands that we follow Her, not our own passions."

"We must hear his warning," Te'zla pronounced like a zealot from his pulpit.

Abissar knew Talliah enough to know what she would suggest. Darjhen was a rogue Reader. He had broken the oath they all swore to uphold on pain of death. For her, there was only one answer: kill him. But Abissar sensed whatever was about to happen would hold tremendous sway over their collective futures. His mind raced, coursing over permutations of the future as he factored in this new piece of information.

The Fakimiar Stones had just come into his possession—a pivotal moment in his designs—but he had not yet decided how best to employ them. Now, Darjhen stood before him— a second pivotal moment in as many weeks. What if Wyrd had placed both momentous events directly in Abissar's path? Talliah could ruin all that. The very world was about to change, he could feel it, and until he knew what that meant, he was unwilling to make an irrevocable decision.

No, Abissar thought. *Darjhen must live… at least for now.*

"Forgive me, High Master," Abissar said gently but loud enough to draw everyone's attention. He caught Elegathe narrowing her eyes at him. "Perhaps we should hear him out and then kill him." He put as much calming reason as he could into his tone, knowing Talliah would respond well to it. "Knowledge, after all, is the root of our power."

Talliah pondered his words for several heartbeats and then nodded once. "Very well. If it is the will of the Hand of Fate, I shall listen to his lies." She turned cool eyes to Jekka. "I trust your blade is sharp."

Jekka's hungry stare never left Darjhen. She said nothing, as if she were frozen in that singular moment before a predator leaps upon its prey.

Jekka's Vice Master, Traemic, placed a hand on her arm. "Hold," he said… and to Abissar's surprise, she did. Abissar would have expected Jekka to leap across the table with murder in her eyes, but she didn't. Her response seemed… off.

Abissar took a good, long look at Traemic. He'd never really considered the young man before and, come to think of it, that was odd in itself. Traemic was handsome, young, and quiet. The more Abissar thought about it, the more he realized Traemic intentionally stayed in the background… just like Abissar.

In an instant, Traemic transformed from inconsequential apprentice to a person of interest. Abissar vowed to pay more attention to him in the future.

Traemic faced Darjhen. "Speak your truth and know it may not be Fate's." His voice was soothing, almost commanding, and even Abissar found himself swayed by the young man's words. *Strange.*

Darjhen gave a single nod, yet his lip curled almost imperceptibly, as if the mere mention of truth... or was it Fate... had been distasteful to him.

"My truth. Fate's truth. Soon enough, nothing we think or want will matter anymore. Not unless we do something right now."

Darjhen reached into his robes and pulled out a large, heavy metal disk. He flipped it onto the table with a hearty *THUNK.* For several moments, it spun on its edge, the dark object rotating too quickly to see what was engraved into it. It slowed and then tipped over, gyrating loudly on its edge as it sunk down onto the table. It flattened with a final ring that echoed in the silence. It was a coin, at least twice the size of the plunnos Talliah used to open the thuros, and where hers held the image of Daemanon's horned demon, this one held them all.

Yet it was a plunnos. It had to be. And if Talliah's key opened the door between Daemanon and this place, it stood to reason that this larger, Giant-sized key opened them all... and perhaps more.

"It holds all of our symbols, not just our own," Ulient noted.

The rest of the council seemed to draw in breath at the same time. Abissar felt the power of the huge coin, but he didn't know what it meant. The others apparently did.

"The Giants have returned," Darjhen said.

"It was a mistake to let him live," Talliah said as they walked down the long passage beneath Daemonostra Keep. "That makes us all a party to his treason."

"The Hand of Fate voted differently, High Master. I'm sorry," Abissar said. He'd supported Talliah publicly, but he was delighted. Wyrd was presenting him with one boon after another. The Fakimiar Stones, the pot-stirring troublemaker Darjhen, and the revelation of more and more powerful plunnoi.

"They let their emotions take hold, and over little more than childish fears stoked by a traitor." She shook her head, as if she might dislodge that fact by motion alone. "The very idea of the Giants returning is laughable. That plunnos should be buried and forgotten."

"I agree, of course," Abissar said. He didn't know what to make of Darjhen's notion that the Giants were coming back. For Abissar, that circumstance—be it eventuality or mere hysteria—meant nothing. Either they were coming back, or they weren't. What mattered was that his designs continued to unfold, continued to lead him inexorably toward ruling the Hand of Fate and the continents that lay beyond each High Master. If there were more plunnoi, that meant there were other thuroi. Who knew how many? He had every intention of finding out. Once he did, he would do everything in his power to control them, just as he would the Fakimiar Stones.

The whole world was about to open up, and those who controlled the portals would control the world.

The End

of

Seeds of Dominion
Legacy of Deceit

ABOUT THE AUTHOR

National Bestselling Author Quincy J. Allen is a cross-genre author with a wide assortment of publications under his belt. His media tie-in novel *Colt the Outlander: Shadow of Ruin* was a Scribe Award finalist in 2019, and his noir sci-fi novel *Chemical Burn* was a Colorado Gold Award finalist in 2010.

He's actively working on his fantasy steampunk series the Blood War Chronicles, and he just wrapped up book three in the fantasy series The Way of Legend with Marc Alan Edelheit. He and Kevin Ikenberry are working on *Scourge*, the sequel to *Enforcer*, and he's also working on *Cradle and All*, a novel in Jamie Ibson's Myrmidon's universe. Most importantly, he is a founding member of the Eldros Legacy, and his debut novel *Seeds of Dominion* kicks off a ten-book series entitled the Legacy of Deceit.

In short, he's going in eight directions at once and is loving every minute of it. He works out of his home in Charlotte, North Carolina, and hopes to one day be a *New York Times* bestselling author.

For more information about his ongoing efforts, check him out at:

QuincyAllen.com

EldrosLegacy.com/the-founders/Quincy-J-Allen

IF YOU LIKED...

If you enjoyed this novel and the world it's set in, then the creators of the Eldros Legacy would like to encourage you to don thy traveling pack and journey deeper into the mysteries of the world Eldros and all the myriad adventures set therein.

The mortal world of Eldros is coming apart. The Giants, who once ruled its five continents with draconian malice have set their mighty designs on a return to power. Mortals across the globe must be victorious against insurmountable odds or die.

Come join us as the Eldros Legacy unfolds in a growing library of novels and short stories.

You can find all the novels at:

www.EldrosLegacy.com/books

Our website is, of course:

EldrosLegacy.com

The Books by Series

Legacy of Shadows
by Todd Fahnestock

Khyven the Unkillable

Lorelle of the Dark

Rhenn the Traveler

Legacy of Deceit
by Quincy J. Allen

Seeds of Dominion

Demons of Veynkal

Legacy of Dragons
by Mark Stallings

The Forgotten King

Knights of Drakanon (Forthcoming)

Sword of Binding (Forthcoming)

Return of the Lightbringer (Forthcoming)

Legacy of Queens
by Marie Whittaker

Embers & Ash

Cinder & Stone (Forthcoming)

The Dog Soldier's War
by Jamie Ibson

A Murder of Wolves

Valleys of Death (Forthcoming)

Other Eldros Legacy Novels

Deadly Fortune by Aaron Rosenberg

The Pain Bearer by Kendra Merritt

Short Stories

Here There Be Giants by The Founders (FREE!)

The Darkest Door by Todd Fahnestock

Fistful of Silver by Quincy J. Allen

Electrum by Marie Whittaker

Dawn of the Lightbringer by Mark Stallings

What the Eye Sees by Quincy J. Allen

Trust Not the Trickster by Jamie Ibson

A Rhakha for the Tokonn by Quincy J. Allen

Ingram Content Group UK Ltd.
Milton Keynes UK
UKHW010721190423
420414UK00002B/268

9 781959 994145